Seduction

Praise for the Legacy series

LEGACY:

"Will satisfy readers hungry for a little paranormal excitement and romance in a post-*Twilight* world . . . A quick, entertaining read."

—*Kirkus Reviews*

"An exciting and well-written tale of contemporary witchcraft and romance. . . . Should please the legions of paranormal fans looking for a sophisticated supernatural thriller." —*Publishers Weekly*

"The unsettling and unique plot details and well-drawn secondary characters make this novel stand out from others in the genre."

—*School Library Journal*

POISON:

"The introduction of Arthurian legend is intriguing, and the last few chapters are real nail-biters." —*Kirkus Reviews*

SEDUCTION:

"An exciting, sexy and sometimes heartbreaking ride. . . . This is a layered and well-told story with an unlikely and endearing heroine." —*Kirkus Reviews*

Also by Molly Cochran

Legacy

Poison

Wishes

Seduction

MOLLY COCHRAN

A PAULA WISEMAN BOOK
SIMON & SCHUSTER BFYR
NEW YORK LONDON TORONTO SYDNEY NEW DELHI

An imprint of Simon & Schuster Children's Publishing Division
1230 Avenue of the Americas, New York, New York 10020

Also available in a SIMON & SCHUSTER BFYR hardcover edition
Book design by Krista Vossen
The text for this book is set in Bodoni.
Manufactured in the United States of America
First SIMON & SCHUSTER BFYR paperback edition December 2015
2 4 6 8 10 9 7 5 3 1
The Library of Congress has cataloged the hardcover edition as follows:
Cochran, Molly.
Seduction / Molly Cochran.
pages cm
"A Paula Wiseman book."
Summary: Distressed that her boyfriend has changed so much since his wealthy uncle took him under his wing, Katy flies to Paris to attend cooking school and discovers a mysterious mansion, which seems to be occupied by only beautiful, shallow people who never age.
ISBN 978-1-4814-0023-7 (hc)
[1. Good and evil—Fiction. 2. Supernatural—Fiction. 3. Witches—Fiction. 4. Love—Fiction. 5. Paris (France) —Fiction. 6. France—Fiction.] I. Title.
PZ7.C6394Se 2014
[Fic]—dc23
2013025929
ISBN 978-1-4814-0024-4 (pbk)
ISBN 978-1-4814-0025-1 (eBook)

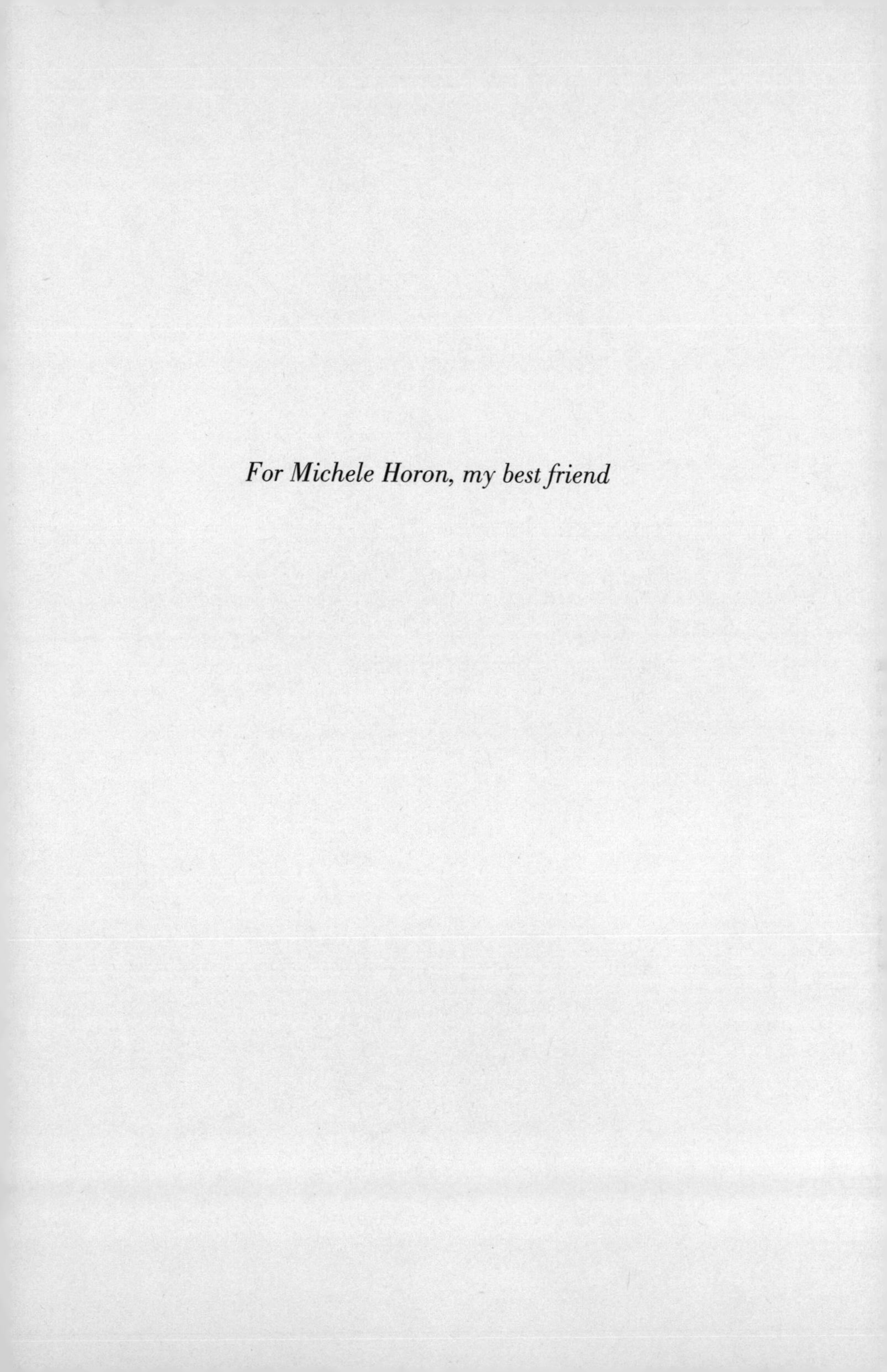

For Michele Horon, my best friend

Acknowledgments

Although most of *Seduction* was researched through public sources or based on my own experiences while living in Paris, there are a number of people who profoundly influenced the final version of this book: my marvelous literary agent, Lucienne Diver, who never allows me to submit anything that isn't ready; my publisher son, Devin Murphy, who tries (with limited success) to curb my more reckless half-baked creative impulses; and my pre-readers, Pam Williamson and Lynne Carrera, who read *all* my dreadful first drafts without gagging in my presence.

Mostly, though, I need to thank two people at Simon & Schuster. First, I am indebted to my new editor, Sylvie Frank, who forced me to think clearly and steered me through the many arcane passageways of this unusual novel. Together we rethought, rewrote, and reworked the manuscript until we got the book you're reading now. I believe the love shows. The second debt is to publisher Paula Wiseman, who not only brought this novel under her aegis at a time when it had no editor at all, but who has also maintained an unreasonable faith in me from the beginning of my YA journey. To her, and to all those working under her imprint, I owe my unflagging gratitude.

People and Places

Whitfield

Katy Ainsworth	A sixteen-year-old student at Ainsworth School
Peter Shaw	Katy's boyfriend, a disinherited member of the wealthy Shaw family; an orphan
Jeremiah Shaw	Peter's great-uncle
Hattie Scott	Peter's guardian; a cook and owner of Hattie's Kitchen, where Katy and Peter both work after school
Elizabeth Ainsworth	a.k.a. Gram; Katy's great-grandmother
Agnes Ainsworth	Katy's aunt
Harrison Jessevar	Katy's father; a professor of medieval studies at Columbia University
Fabienne de la Soubise	a.k.a. Fabby; a French student temporarily studying at Ainsworth School

Paris, the Present

The Abbey of Lost Souls	a.k.a. L'Abbaye des Âmes Perdues, an ancient mansion
Marie-Therèse LePetit, Sophie de la Soubise, Joelle, Annabelle	Residents of the Abbey of Lost Souls
Belmondo	Hereditary owner of the Abbey of Lost Souls; Fabienne's favorite "uncle"
Azrael	An old man who lives in the *carrières* beneath the city
the Poplars	A retirement home

Paris, the Past

Jean-Loup de Villeneuve	An alchemist
Veronique de Theuderic	Charlemagne's eleventh wife
Avremarus	
Sister Béatrice	Veronique's devotee and successor as abbess at the Abbey of Lost Souls
Sister Clément	Sister Béatrice's successor as abbess
Drago	Jean-Loup and Veronique's son, their only child
Toujours	Jean-Loup and Veronique's home
Henry Shaw	Jean-Loup's apprentice and assistant
Zenobia	Henry Shaw's wife in America
Ola'ea Olokun	A West African shaman who settled in Whitfield and aided Henry Shaw during his stay there
The Darkness	Immortal evil that can take any form

PROLOGUE

Dear Peter,

Wow, here I am in Paris! I can hardly believe it! Everything is SO beautiful! I've already gotten to know some of my neighbors here in Le Marais. It's the oldest section of the city, with narrow cobblestone streets and buildings that lean in toward each other. Every block looks like an illustration from a book of fairy tales. All sorts of famous people used to live here, such as Victor Hugo and Robespierre and Napoleon . . . and now ME!!

Hope things are going great for you in Whitfield. Say hi to everyone for me, if you get the chance.

~~Love~~
~~Your friend~~
~~All the best~~
~~Sincerely~~
~~Very truly yours~~
Katy

I put a skull and crossbones sticker over all the closings. I didn't know if Peter was a "Love" kind of guy anymore. He was probably more than a "Very truly yours," but you never knew.

"What difference does it make, anyway," I muttered as I crumpled the letter into a ball and threw it away. I didn't know what to say to Peter. Or to any of the people back in Whitfield. At least not anything that was true.

The fact was, I was living in a squalid room in a ramshackle building with mold, holes, nearly nonexistent plumbing, and vermin of various descriptions, all disgusting. Two weeks after I'd moved in, I got robbed. Whoever it was took my laptop, my iPod, my alarm clock, and my two extra pairs of jeans, which amounted to just about everything I owned, except for my cell phone. Then the next day a pickpocket relieved me of that, too.

My apartment—well, one room with a hotplate and a bathroom in the hallway that I shared with everyone else on the floor—was in Le Marais, this grand old historical district full of antique charm, but my particular dwelling was a lot more antique than charming, and the only historical thing about it was the arthritic old drag queen who lived next door, next to the five rowdy Nordic brothers who took turns leering at me and murmuring insults with umlauts in them as I passed them on the stairs. Incidentally, the light in the stairway lit up for only thirty seconds after you turned a knob at the doorway. If I didn't make it up the four flights of urine-scented wooden steps by then, I had to feel my way past my neighbors in the dark.

To add to the international flavor of my building, the entire floor below was populated by a large Chinese family who constantly seemed to be cooking. I wished they'd invite me in for a snack sometime, since my diet consisted mainly of croissants and coffee, which I was hoping I'd learn to like. I only drank it because it made me feel French.

I wore a beret for the same reason.

Mostly, I wished I'd never left Whitfield.

Let me back up. Before I came to Paris, I led a normal life. Well, as normal as can be expected in Whitfield, Massachusetts, which is a very strange place. I'll get to that later. Anyway, I was happy there. I was a boarding student at a school I liked. I worked part-time in a restaurant called Hattie's Kitchen, and my boss, Hattie Scott, taught me to love cooking. My dad lived in New York City, but my aunt and great-grandmother lived in Whitfield, and took me in whenever I needed some extra TLC. I had some friends, too, even though I'd only lived there for a couple of years. And I had a boyfriend, Peter Shaw, who meant more to me than anything on earth.

That's how all the trouble began, with Peter, on the last day of our junior year.

CHAPTER • ONE

You and a guest are cordially invited

to an end-of-term party for

Peter Henry Shaw

Saturday, June fifteenth

Eight o'clock p.m.

2409 Belmont Boulevard

Whitfield, Massachusetts

R.S.V.P. *Black Tie*

Graduation was still a year away, but Peter's great-uncle Jeremiah gave him a couple of presents anyway: a red Lexus SC10 convertible and a party that would make *My Super Sweet 16* look like an afternoon at Chuck E. Cheese's.

Don't get me wrong. This is not sour grapes talking. In fact, if any seventeen-year-old could be said to be deserving of a new Lexus, it would be Peter Shaw. He is humble and hardworking and respectful of his elders and conscientious about the environment. Also generous, modest, levelheaded, kind, sensitive, spiritual, and deep, not to mention extremely good-looking. He smells good too.

So no, it's not that he's a wiener with a car. It's just that it all came as such a shock. Peter's great-uncle, Jeremiah Shaw, had never spoken to him before last year. Nor had any of his other relatives. A birthday card from the old man would have been a surprise, let alone a Lexus. Or this amazing party at the biggest house in town.

The Shaw mansion had fifty rooms on four floors, plus five or six outbuildings, an Olympic-size pool, tennis court, and a number of gardens, including one with a waterfall. Double stairways led to a huge balcony at the front entrance to the house, and there were several patios and balconies in the back, where gigantic party tents outlined in lights had been erected.

On the lawn, an army of waiters carried trays of canapés and soft drinks in crystal champagne glasses. SOMA, a nine-piece band that won a bunch of Grammy awards last year, was playing in a specially built amphitheater.

The guests were sharply divided by dress. The townies—meaning my friends—wore the same clothes they'd worn to junior prom or Winter Frolic. But the Muffies—that was my term for the rich girls who boarded at my school—all seemed to be in new gowns.

Actually, I got a new dress too, but it wasn't my idea. As Peter's "official" girlfriend, I guess I was expected to look as if I lived up to the Shaw standard. So one of Jeremiah's assistants brought over a Vera Wang dress the color of glacial ice that must have cost a fortune, plus a lot of blue jewelry that I thought were rhinestones but that turned out to be sapphires rented from Tiffany in New York.

I looked good, I admit, but I felt ridiculous. For one thing, it must have seemed as if I was trying to show off, which offended my friends while at the same time eliciting the contempt of the Muffies, who thought I was trying to be one of them. For another—and this was much worse—some guy was assigned to follow me wherever I went to make sure I didn't lose or steal any of the jewelry.

"Well, so what?" Peter said when I complained about the security guy. "It's not like you have to talk to him or anything."

"That's not the point," I insisted as I wobbled on my Jimmy Choo sandals with five-inch heels. "I feel like I'm being stalked."

"Don't be ridiculous," Peter said. "You're practically the guest of honor."

"No, Peter," I answered hotly. "*You're* the guest of honor. I'm just one of the locals that thug over there's been asked to keep an eye on in case I walk out with the family silver."

That was the extent of our conversation, because a second later Peter was pulled away by someone wearing a Rolex and a toupee.

I turned around to face the lurking security guy and gave him the stink eye. His face never changed expression.

I sighed. He had already creeped out everyone I knew there. Whenever I tried to make conversation with the few people I'd made friends with since I came to Ainsworth in my sophomore year, they fled as soon as the beefy guy with the earpiece lumbered into view. I couldn't blame them. This was supposed to be Peter's party, but none of us saw much of Peter. Well, we *saw* him, looking like a movie star in an Armani tuxedo, but he spent almost every minute with Jeremiah and the old people.

Oh, and yes, also a cluster of fashion model types who seemed to be there for the sole purpose of having their pictures taken with Peter. They spoke only French. That is to say, they *were* French. And did I say gorgeous? Grr.

The only one I knew was a girl named Fabienne de la Soubise. Yes, that was really her name. She'd spent her freshman year at Ainsworth School, where Peter and I both had scholarships. I hadn't seen much of her since Winter Frolic, which she'd attended as Peter's date. That hadn't been her idea—or Peter's—so I'd let it go, but I hadn't been really chummy with her afterward. Not that she needed any attention from me. Everyone noticed Fabienne.

She was beautiful. I mean really, deeply beautiful. Pale, blond, willowy, and tall—all the things I'd always wished I was, instead of being short, dark-haired, and with green eyes that most people described as "strange" or "supernatural." Whatever. I don't remember ever seeing Fabienne when she wasn't surrounded by guys. She never went out with them, though. At least that was the gossip circulating: The fabulously attractive Miss de la Soubise wouldn't even think of dating anyone from Ainsworth, *merci beaucoup*.

The Muffies had taken her under their wing at first, but I guess she was too good-looking even for them. So most of the time it was just Fabienne in the middle of a bunch of drooling guys. Served her right, I thought. Outdo the Muffies and you walk alone.

So anyway, here was this huge party filled with beautiful people in gorgeous clothes, with great music and terrific food, so you'd think everyone would be having a great time.

Everyone except me.

It wasn't just that Peter wasn't paying any attention to me. I didn't love that, but I'm not really so insecure that not spending every minute in Peter's arms was going to ruin the party for me. I knew that Jeremiah Shaw's influence was going to make a big difference in Peter's life.

I just didn't understand why the old man had chosen Peter in the first place. The Shaws were one of the oldest families in Whitfield. There were hundreds of them who lived right in town, and most of them worked for Jeremiah. So if he was looking for an heir or whatever, it seemed weird that he would seek out someone he'd ignored for the past eleven years. That, incidentally, had been when Jeremiah Shaw disinherited Peter as payback for his father's unpardonable offense: The man had appointed Hattie Scott, a restaurant cook, as Peter's guardian in the event of his death, instead of Jeremiah. And then he had died.

So Peter had grown up totally outside the patrician family he'd been born into. That had been fine with him, though. Peter didn't need a pedigree to prove his value, and Hattie had been a better mother to him than anyone else on earth could have been. But then one day last fall Jeremiah—who is *the* Shaw, by the way, the big Kahuna of Shaw Enterprises—phoned Hattie's Kitchen and said he wanted to get to know Peter better.

At first neither of us took the invitation very seriously. It wasn't much of an invitation in the first place, and this codger who'd hardly made an appearance in Peter's life until that day wasn't exactly on either of our buddy lists.

Except that he'd been serious. He started sending limos to the dorm to pick Peter up on Saturday mornings, and they didn't bring him back until after nightfall.

"What'd he want?" I asked after one of Peter's all-day sessions with his great-uncle.

Peter shook his head slowly, incredulously. "He wants to teach me the family business."

"Which is what?"

He shrugged. "Shipping. Import-export. International labor. It's *Shaw Enterprises*, Katy. You know what Shaw does."

I blinked. "I guess," I said.

Shaw Enterprises was a vast multinational conglomerate, the umbrella for a host of businesses from parking garages to African banks. "It's just strange that he'd suddenly want you in his life, that's all."

"Maybe," he said. That was the sort of noncommittal answer Peter liked and that drove me crazy. "Just trust me, okay?" He spoke close to my face. I could feel the stubble of his beard against my cheek. His hair, silky waves of it, fell over my eyes. "It's going to be okay, Katy," he whispered, and kissed me, making me shudder all over. "Better than okay. He's going to send me to college. Maybe I could even go to Harvard, like you."

"I don't know if I'll go to Harvard," I said, although that prospect had pretty much been a given, at least as far as my dad was concerned.

"Of course you will. And now I will too. I'll be able to make a life for us."

"We have a life," I said. "Two lives."

"Not like what Shaw Enterprises can give us."

I backed away. I wasn't part of this deal. "Don't say *us*."

He looked annoyed. "All right. Me. I'm getting a big break, bigger than I can even explain to you right now. You just have to trust me."

"You already said that," I said.

But I did. I would trust Peter with my life. I *have* trusted him with my life, more than once. Peter wasn't the problem.

Jeremiah Shaw was.

Everything changed after that. A tailor came up from Boston to make clothes for Peter, and just about every day some fabulous electronic gizmo would show up in the mail. One of Jeremiah's assistants took Peter into New York every two weeks just to get his hair cut. He had a standing meeting with Aldritch, the Shaw butler, who gave him etiquette lessons. For a while, he even moved into the Shaw mansion.

It was all pretty disgusting, and didn't accomplish much except to estrange Peter from the townies. The Muffies, of course, loved it. They judged everyone on things like clothes and hair and which generation smartphone they owned.

But then, they'd liked Peter even before his two-hundred-dollar haircuts and True Religion jeans. And who wouldn't? He was six feet tall, with honey-blond hair and gray eyes, and long legs and a thin but muscular body, and soft lips and skin that blushed easily, and big hands and a kind of sexy-without-meaning-to-be walk, and a soft voice, and thick dark eyelashes. Did I mention that he always smelled good? Really, really good.

And, hard as it was for me to believe, he loved me.

To give him credit, Peter had used the technology available to him through the Shaw laboratories to do a lot of good in our community. There were quite a few people in Whitfield who owed Peter their lives after he'd quelled the kind of crisis that could only happen in a town like Whitfield—but more about that later.

Back at Peter's megabuck non-graduation party, the grounds were lit by thousands of twinkling lights. At around ten, the band changed and the music turned into old people's dance tunes. That was when most of my friends left—I guess they were afraid the musicians were going to swing into a rendition of the Hokey Pokey—and the waiters brought out the hard liquor. I wandered over to where Peter had spent most of the evening, to see if he would dance with me. The French girls, I noticed, were clustered around him.

"Where is everyone?" he asked as we walked toward the dance floor.

"I think they went for pizza," I said.

"Chicken hearts," Peter said as he twirled me decisively. Jeremiah had made him take dancing lessons in preparation for the party, along with the tutoring in etiquette.

I guessed Peter could be a wiener after all.

"We'd have had a lot more fun at Hattie's Kitchen," I said. He only smiled. I tried to make the best of things. "At least we didn't have to work tonight." As after-school employees, Peter and I had to serve and clean up at every party at Hattie's. At least this one was labor-free.

"My uncle wanted to introduce me to the people he works with," he said.

"Who work for him, you mean."

"Yeah. I guess."

"So you're like the son Jeremiah never had?"

He shrugged.

I couldn't hold it in any longer. "But *why*?" I demanded, as if it were the first time I'd asked him that question. "Why you? Why now?"

Peter looked uncomfortable. "Maybe he just likes me."

I stared at him. He didn't meet my eyes. "Right," I said coldly. If he thought I was that dumb, I wasn't even going to argue about it. "That must be it."

"Try not to be cynical, Katy," he said quietly. Then he smiled. "You look beautiful."

I looked away.

"Like always," he said.

God. No wonder I love him.

"I think I'll be able to get away before too long," he whispered in my ear. "Maybe we could go—"

"Excuse me," someone said as an ancient hand separated us. It was Jeremiah Shaw. Of course.

"Pardon me for interrupting, Peter." He stared at me. "Ummm . . ."

"Katy," I reminded him.

"Yes," Jeremiah said, his momentary notice of me already a distant memory. "Peter, I want you to meet someone . . ." He led Peter away, leaving me behind without a backward glance.

CHAPTER • TWO

I tried not to feel resentful that I hadn't been introduced (or even acknowledged, aside from Jeremiah's distracted *ummm*). But there I stood, alone in the middle of the dance floor, wishing I could disappear in a puff of smoke. Everyone had seen Peter walk away from me. The Muffies were giggling. The French girls were talking behind their hands. I swallowed, held up my head in a meaningless show of bravado, and headed for the parking lot. I'd had enough of this funfest.

A dainty hand touched my elbow. "'Allo, Katy," Fabienne said, smiling behind a cloud of pink tulle. She pronounced my name as if it consisted of two letters, *K* and *T*, with the accent on the *T*. "Are you having the good time?"

Before I could lie, she smiled and said, "No, I think perhaps not so good." She looked over at Peter and his corporate cohorts. "The men are boring, no?"

I shrugged, not trusting my voice. Not trusting anything. If Fabienne had come to hit me with a Mean Girl zinger, she'd picked the right time. I looked over at the French girls.

"Oh, they are boring too," she said, laughing. "Come with me." She hooked her arm through mine. "We go to the powder room, hokay? We look for something more interesting."

I didn't know what to say, but at least it was a less humiliating way to leave the dance floor than Plan A.

We had to go into the house for the restrooms. The nearest one was off the billiards room. When I came out, Fabienne had racked up a set of balls.

"You will play?" she asked, chalking a stick.

"Why not," I muttered. I wasn't a very good pool player, but sometimes my friends and I—and Peter, before he became the darling of Shaw Enterprises—would hang out at Buzzy's Billiards for pizza and a few racks.

She broke surprisingly well. "Impressive," I said.

"Pool is very popular in Los Angeles now."

"When were you in L.A.?"

"I go to school there before," she answered offhandedly. "Six months, two year ago. Before that I am in Rome. Tokyo, too." She pocketed three striped balls. "Now here. But I finish now. No more school."

"What? You're dropping out of high school?"

She missed the fourth pocket by a hair. "The education, it is not important," she said breezily, adjusting her tulle.

"What planet are you from?" I blurted. But then I regretted it because she blushed and ducked her head slightly, and I knew that she was feeling ashamed.

"In my family, the women do not study beyond fifteen years," she said quietly, her eyes not meeting mine. "Too much reading ruins the eyes."

I blinked. "But . . . what will you do, then? With the rest of your life?"

She made a Gallic gesture. "Oh, I visit, I travel. Perhaps I will fall in love, when I am of age. Who knows?" Her lips formed a glistening pout. "And you? You will continue to study, yes?"

If there was anything in my life that had never been open to discussion, it was whether I would go to college. My father, who is a professor of medieval literature at Columbia University, began planning my academic career at approximately the moment of my conception. I was to go to Harvard, of course, where I would begin a broad overview of English and other languages during my freshman year, with a focus on post–World War I poetry, and proceed from there through my first doctorate. So that was pretty much a done deal. One of the reasons I'd been sent to Ainsworth in the first place was that 95 percent of its graduates went on to college. I presume the remaining 5 percent died or lapsed into comas, since no mention is ever made of them. I couldn't imagine what the school officials would have to say about Fabienne's ambitions, or lack of them.

"Uh . . . yeah," I said. "At least eight years after high school." That was, if one Ph.D. would be enough to please Dad.

"Eight years! To study cooking?"

"Cooking?"

"But you are a cook, *non*?"

"Well, I've been working at a restaurant after school for a couple of years—"

"*Oui*, at Hattie's Kitchen. But you are *merveilleuse*! Everyone talks about how you are the great chef already."

"I wouldn't say that," I said, although her words made me feel like bursting with pride. I loved cooking. It was artistic and harrowing and endlessly complex. It was about beauty and intellect and wild physical activity and huge stress, but also love. For me, it was mostly about love.

"You should study at Le Clef d'Or in Paris," Fabienne said. "This is the best cooking school in the world. Very close to my mother's house."

"Paris," I mused. "I'd love that."

"Then go. Maybe I am there myself when you arrive. Then I show you *le vrai Paris*."

I dreamed on for another second or two, but then reality set in. "That's never going to happen," I said, shaking my head as if it had suddenly been filled with Styrofoam peanuts. "My dad would literally have a heart attack if I didn't go to college."

She shrugged. "But of course you can go. Cooking is not a long study, one year, perhaps. You can even go for the summer only."

I laughed. Partly it was because she kept saying "kook-ing," but also, I was nervous and just sort of tittering stupidly because I didn't know what else to do. I'd never before allowed myself to think about cooking seriously.

Fabienne gave me one of those French gestures with her chin to let me know it was my turn to shoot.

I chalked up my stick, but the idea she had stuck in my head wasn't easy to ignore. "It's not just the time involved," I said. "The Clef d'Or would cost a lot of money. Maybe all my savings."

"Money?" She looked amazed, as if the word "money" were an alien sound communicated through tap-dancing frogs. "You are worried about money? You?"

I blinked. "Yes, me," I answered. "The kitchen wench, remember?"

"But Peter . . ." Her voice died away.

"What about him?" I prodded.

"Peter is your *amant*, no?"

Although my grasp of French was limited, I knew that *amant* meant *lover*. "Er . . . well, not exactly," I waffled. First base, maybe, but definitely no home run. "Just my boyfriend."

"*Eh bien*," Fabienne said. "Still, he will give you the money, surely."

"What?" Then I got it. She must have thought that a) Peter was rich, and b) I would accept money from him if he were. "That's not going to fly," I said tersely, leaning over the pool table.

"But he gives it to me."

My stick skimmed wildly off the top of the ball. I closed my eyes, counted to ten, and straightened up. "He gives you money?" I seethed.

"You do not know this?" She opened her sparkly evening bag and dumped a bunch of coins onto the green baize of the pool table.

I stared at the pile for a moment. They were coins, all right, but none of them were engraved in any way. They were just plain disks of gleaming, bright gold.

"What are these?" I asked, picking one up and dropping it again.

"Gold, *bien sur*. From Peter and Monsieur Shaw. But surely you know what they do."

I looked over at her, my eyes narrowed. "Besides give you money?"

"Not just me. All of us."

"Meaning exactly . . . ?"

"My friends. *Les Françaises.*"

"Er . . . why?"

She shrugged. "Ask Peter," she said.

"Well, uh . . . uh. . . ." Peter squirmed in our booth at Pizza World the next day.

"Look, this isn't *Jeopardy*. I just want to know why—and how—you're giving Fabienne money."

"Fabienne?" He looked puzzled.

I sighed. "The French girl?" I prodded. "The one you took to Winter Frolic?"

"Oh, yeah. She was a freshman," he added unnecessarily.

"A very rich one, apparently. So are her friends, who also have you to thank for their newfound wealth."

"Uh," he said, running his hand through his hair. "That is, I'm not exactly sure. I mean, I don't know the rest of them personally."

"I see. You're just kind of tossing gold coins their way."

"No, it's not like that. It's . . ." The waitress came to take our order. We got our pizza date after all, the day after the party. Only it wasn't turning out to be as much fun as I'd thought it would be. "I wish you wouldn't do this, Katy."

I wished I wouldn't either. I didn't like giving Peter the third degree. It was demeaning, to Peter and to me both. "Oh, forget it," I said. "Keep your stupid secrets."

"Katy, please. Wait." He took my arm. "I hate keeping things from you." He pulled me close to him over the table in our booth, and he spoke in a whisper. "It's Jeremiah. He's taught me . . . some things."

"Yeah," I said with as much sarcasm as I could muster. "Like turning lead into gold, I suppose."

He gazed at me levelly.

I felt my throat close. "Oh, my God," I finally managed. My blood felt cold in my veins. "That's it, isn't it?"

He swallowed.

"How . . . how long?"

Peter understood exactly what I was asking. "Since Jeremiah showed me," he said quietly.

"He showed you how to make gold?"

"Shh." He looked over his shoulder to make sure no one was listening to us. "Not exactly. That is, not everyone can do it. But he recognized the . . . the gift I had, and he's been teaching me how to develop it. That's what's been taking up so much of my time."

I sat back, stunned.

"So?" he asked. "What are you thinking?"

"I'm speechless," I said.

He grinned. "Well, I guess there's a first time for everything."

CHAPTER • THREE

Now, the fact that Peter could do magic was not, in itself, really extraordinary. Not for Whitfield, Massachusetts.

I've mentioned that it's a strange place. Most of the families in town have lived here since before the American Revolution. It's a nice town, after all is said and done, where there isn't much crime except for the occasional demonic possession. Well, there was the incident a couple of years ago when someone was nearly burned at the stake as a witch.

That was me.

The only thing that was really weird about that was that not only am I a witch, but so is almost everyone else who lives in Whitfield. Everybody has some kind of talent—that is, we can all do things that most (read *normal*) people would consider impossible. Like reading minds, or healing by touch, or being able to disappear at will. I myself am a telekinetic, which means I can move objects with my mind. It's not a great talent or a rare one, but it comes in handy from time to time.

We're all different, but we all fit together in Whitfield. It's a perfect town for someone like me. Well, usually. We're more troubled than most about something we call the Darkness, but we try not to think about that. At least I do. I've had a couple of run-ins with It—call It the Devil, or the Dark Passenger, or just plain evil—and I hope never to encounter It again.

The burning-at-the-stake incident had been an accident, not the work of the Darkness. Still, as you might guess, even minor misunderstandings among witches can have disastrous consequences, the most serious of which is *publicity*.

Publicity is something witches don't like. Not even a little bit. There are no famous witches who are really witches. That is because if cowen—that is, ordinary people—knew about us, it would only be a matter of time before the burnings would be held in earnest.

It's understandable. People don't generally like what's different. We've got people in Whitfield who can travel without their bodies. Who can shape-shift. One of us, known as a djinn, can actually command a whole group of people to do her bidding. Can you imagine what cowen would do if they got hold of her?

Or someone who can create gold? It made me shiver just to think about it.

The funny thing is, until this revelation, nobody thought Peter had much magical talent at all. Don't get me wrong, he was a valuable member of the community. It was his genius with computers that had saved the lives of a whole village whose water supply had been poisoned (again by accident, and alas, again by me). But as far as magic went, Peter had never been considered much of a force to be reckoned with.

The fact that he had any magic at all was surprising, given that he was a Shaw.

You see, the Shaws were notoriously cowen—or at least they seemed to be, before Peter dropped the bombshell about Jeremiah on me. The Shaw family had been the bane of the Whitfield witches ever since the first American Shaw (Henry, 1646–?) turned his own wife over to the righteously murderous Puritans on suspicion of witchcraft.

Why he had done that if he had been a witch himself was a mystery that hadn't yet been solved, but there were a lot of mysteries in Whitfield, so I wasn't about to lose any sleep over Henry Shaw.

But Peter . . . holy cats, I just couldn't believe it.

"Katy?" Peter asked anxiously. I guess he wasn't used to my silence. "Are you all right?"

I cleared my throat. "You never told me," I said. "About being . . . being . . ."

"Don't say it out loud," he warned. "I wanted to tell you. Really, I did."

I could feel my bottom lip quivering. "Didn't you trust me?"

"Of course I did. It's just that . . . well, sometimes you talk . . . a little . . . not much, but . . ." He wiped his forehead with a handkerchief.

"You thought I would blab?"

Peter swallowed. "No," he answered, too quickly. "Besides, I . . . I wasn't even sure myself, until Jeremiah taught me how to do it."

"Okay, okay," I said. "Whatever. I get it."

"You do?" He sounded relieved.

"I do," I said resignedly. I had to admit I didn't have a great track record in the secret-keeping department.

At least I knew now. I finally understood why the old man had shown up when he did, after having nothing to do with Peter for most of his life. And why he had chosen Peter to be his heir.

Jeremiah Shaw was an alchemist. And so was his great-nephew.

"So?" I said, regaining some of my composure. "Show me."

"Show you what?"

"You know." I rubbed my fingers together in the universal symbol for money.

Peter shook his head. "C'mon, Katy."

"I need to see it with my own eyes."

"Quit it."

"I thought you trusted me," I said.

We stared at each other for a long moment. Finally he sighed. "Okay, fine," he said unenthusiastically. "I'll need something made of base metal."

"Like lead?" I asked. He nodded. "But what's made of lead? Bullets?"

"It can be any metal," Peter said. He tapped on my necklace. "How about that?"

I put my hand protectively over the pendant around my neck. It was a heart with "Katy" inscribed on it. "You gave this to me, remember? On Valentine's Day."

"Of course I remember," he said softly. "I'd have turned it to gold then, if I'd known how."

"I thought you did know how."

"Not really. Not well, anyway, until—"

"Right. Jeremiah Midas."

He blew air out of his nose. "So do you want me to do it, or what?"

Reluctantly, I undid the clasp. I'd never taken the necklace off since he'd first put it around my neck, but now it slid down the length of its chain until it lay in the palm of Peter's hand. I almost snatched it back, but he curled his fingers around it.

"Ouch. The edges are sharp," he said. "Guess that's what happens when you buy jewelry at Fred's Bargain Mart."

"It doesn't matter where it came from," I said. "I've always loved it."

"Well, you're going to love it more after I'm done. Trust me."

There was something in the way he said that—his confidence, I guess, or something else—that made me feel as if I were seeing a new side to Peter, a facet of his personality that I hadn't known existed.

I wasn't sure if I liked it either, but I let it go, the way I let my father's remarks go when he got obnoxious. It made life less complicated.

He held the metal heart between his fingers, concentrating in a way I'd never seen in him before. Concentration and focus were the real secrets to magic of any kind. That's what Hattie meant when she said, as she often did, that magic had to be believed to be seen. First, you had to picture what was going to happen—what you were going to *make* happen. That was the key to everything, even something as outlandish as making gold.

Actually, changing lesser metals into gold was one of the rarest magical gifts there was. Magicians have been trying to do it for millennia, mostly without success. Some of them—the most famous failures—concluded that it was possible only with the aid of what they called a "philosopher's stone," which not only produced gold, but also gave its owner immortality.

"Do you have a philosopher's stone?" I asked.

"No. Shh."

That was what I thought. A crock. But then, if anyone had asked me an hour before what I'd thought of alchemy, I'd have said it was bogus too.

"The moon's full, isn't it?" he asked.

I had to think. The phases of the moon was something every witch learned along with her ABCs, but sometimes I lost track. "I think so," I said.

"Good." He closed his eyes, and then he hummed or something. He made this low sound as he rubbed my tin Bargain Mart heart between his fingers, and I could almost see the magic crackling in the air between his lips and the object in his fingers.

Then he stopped. For a moment, time itself seemed to stand still. Peter's face was as distant as the image in a painting, as if he weren't on the same plane with me at all. "Peter?" I whispered.

"Huh?"

The moment was gone. He smiled. In his hand was a heart that glinted with pure, glowing gold.

"Katy," the waitress said, cocking her head to the side as she read the inscription on the golden heart. She was carrying a pizza on her shoulder. "That you, hon?"

I choked. When I was done coughing, I downed half my soda.

"Hey, you okay?"

I nodded, afraid to speak.

"That's real cute," the waitress said, gesturing toward the heart in Peter's hand as she set down the pizza. "Can I get you guys anything else?"

We both shook our heads, and she winked at us before leaving.

"Oh, my God," I said. It was more like a breath than any type of speech.

"I know. Amazing, isn't it?" He picked up the chain, which had been pooled on the table beside the napkin dispenser, and looped it through the brilliant heart. Then he stood up and fastened it around my neck.

I could immediately feel the difference in its weight. In its quality.

"That's more like it," he said proudly.

I looked into his eyes. "It's a big gift, Peter."

I had meant the alchemy, but he must have misunderstood, because he touched the heart on my chest with his finger and smiled. "It's what you deserve," he said. Then he leaned over and kissed me.

Now, I love kissing Peter. It's probably my favorite thing in life. But I've got to say, my heart wasn't really in it this time. I just couldn't shake the feeling that Peter's "gift" was going to have strings attached. Long strings.

"Peter . . ."

He sighed. "I thought we were done talking," he said.

Well, we're not, I thought. "What exactly does your uncle want you to do with this . . . this talent of yours?"

He frowned. "I don't know," he said. "He's not the sort of person I feel comfortable grilling with a lot of questions."

"But . . ." I was thinking hard. "If you can make gold, why do you need to work for Jeremiah? You could send yourself to college. That's what you want, isn't it?"

He looked annoyed. "Well, yes," he admitted. "But that would be pretty ungrateful of me, wouldn't it? I mean, after he *taught* me? After he's told me he's going to take me into the business?"

"Okay, okay," I said placatingly. I should have known Peter would feel obligated. That's how he is. Fair to a fault.

"It would be like slapping him in the face," he went on. "My only relative."

"I said okay, okay? Sorry I brought it up, Peter."

This time I tried to kiss him. "Don't be mad at me," I said.

"I can't be mad at you." He smiled and kissed me back.

But I still had that feeling. The feeling that there were strings all around us, and that sooner or later we'd both end up dangling from them like puppets.

CHAPTER • FOUR

"One thing . . ."

Peter pulled away from me. I could still feel his kiss on my mouth. "I need for you to keep this to yourself."

I sat up, rigid with indignation. "Well, *duh*."

"I'm serious," he said. "If anyone finds out, even the witches—"

"What will happen?" I taunted. "Is Jeremiah afraid that one of us will try to take some of his money?"

"Yes!" he said, bulging his eyes at me. "Someone will. Count on it. Maybe not you or your relatives, but it's inevitable that somewhere along the line—"

"Excuse mc?" I put my hands on my hips. "Am I mistaken, or are you putting Jeremiah Shaw ahead of the people you grew up with?"

"That's the point, Katy. They're *people*. It's human nature."

"What's human nature? Greed?"

"That's exactly what I mean."

I rummaged in my purse, trying not to look at him. "You sound more like your uncle every minute," I said.

He sighed. "And how would you know that? Have you ever even had a conversation with him?"

"Well—" I was going to say *but everybody knows what he's like*.

"Or are you just going to follow the Whitfield party line that all the Shaws are evil?"

"No," I said, relenting. I had been pretty unreasonable, I knew. I held his hand. "They're not all evil, because *you're* a Shaw and you're not evil. But aren't you going to tell anyone? Not even Hattie?"

"No one," he said.

"Up to you," I said, trying to sound casual. "But I think it's going to be tough to mass-produce gold coins while you're slinging hash at Hattie's this summer."

Suddenly his cheeks turned flamingo pink.

"What's with you?" I asked.

"I'm not going to be at Hattie's." It sounded like a confession.

I blinked. "But . . ." That had been the plan. We were both going to work full-time at the restaurant all summer. We were going to start a vegetable garden and grow herbs on the patio. We were going to save up all our money so that this time next year we'd be checking out dorm rooms at Harvard. "Where are you going to be?" My voice sounded like a squeak.

He cleared his throat. "With Jeremiah," he said.

"Where?"

He shrugged. "Wherever. New York, maybe. I don't really know."

"But you're going to go there. Wherever he says."

He sighed. "It's not like he's going to hurt me or anything. He's my uncle. I just have to trust him."

"Do you?" I asked belligerently. "You didn't trust me enough to tell me you had magic, but you'll follow this guy—this uncle who disinherited you and didn't talk to you for eleven years—to the ends of the earth, is that right?"

"Oh, think whatever you want," Peter said.

I felt as if I'd been kicked in the stomach.

I busied myself with the pizza, which served as a substitute for talking since we really had nothing more to say to each other at that point. I tried to eat, but the conversation had made me so nauseated that I threw my piece back onto my plate.

"Look," Peter said, a little louder than he had to be. "I'm going to make something of myself, whatever it takes, okay? So stop lecturing me."

"I'm not lecturing." I bristled. "I'm just surprised."

"At what? That anyone would think I was worth anything?"

"Quit it. You know as well as I do that Jeremiah Shaw is going to use you."

"And how do you know that?"

"Because he uses everyone!" I almost shouted.

"So what?" People were staring now. He looked around and lowered his voice. "That's what all business comes down to. I do something for you, and you do something for me. It doesn't make anybody good or bad."

I was so mad by now, it was all I could do to keep from screaming. "Look, Peter, all I'm saying is that changing all your plans to do something that you can't tell anyone about, even me or Hattie, doesn't seem like the best way to go."

"Yeah, well, maybe you're not my mom," he said, his gray eyes blazing. "You're just acting like it."

That did it. I walked out of there like my feet were on fire, and I didn't look back.

His *mom*! That was a low blow, as well as stupid, since neither of us even had mothers. They'd both died when Peter and I were children. Peter had been an orphan most of his life. I at least still had my dad, though I hadn't seen much of him since I went to boarding school.

Before then, though, for about ten years, I pretty much took care of things around the house. My father was never much for cooking or cleaning. Maybe that's how I got to be the way I am.

Sensible. Reliable. Mom-like.

Arggh. How long had he thought of me like that?

The worst of it was, I don't think Peter was just being malicious. It's not his nature. So somewhere in the back of his mind—or maybe in the front of it—he'd been thinking mom thoughts about me before now. Which meant that in some way, some subtle permutation of the truth, I really was mom-like.

Oh, God, I thought. *Let me die.*

But then, while rolling in my quilt like a shrieking, weeping cigar that night, I had a thought. It was such a strange thought that I even forgot to cry for a second or two. It was this:

Why?

That was all, just that one question. Why did I always have to do the right thing, follow the right path, counsel good advice? I mean, I could be as self-centered and foolish as the next guy, couldn't I? I could blow off my responsibilities like every other kid. I could do what I wanted for once, instead of what was expected of me.

I didn't have to spend my summer making gumbo and canning tomatoes while Peter went off to New York or wherever with Jeremiah Shaw. He was probably going to break up with me, anyway.

For being like somebody's mom.

There are some things you just have to accept when they're handed to you and then move on from there. If that was the way Peter felt about me, then he might not ever change his mind, no matter what I did.

Unless I did something really radical.

Maybe it was time for me to break away. From Whitfield, from Peter, from my own sorry self. There were wonderful places to see. Legendary places like Venice or Vienna or Hong Kong or New Delhi.

Or Paris.

The word caught in my throat. Paris.

Yes. *Paris.*

So that's how I came to be in the dump where I lived in the middle of what everyone told me was the most fabulous city in the world.

As it turned out, my dad didn't mind my leaving after all, so long as I paid for the trip out of my savings from my job at Hattie's. Hattie herself was a little put out—she thought she'd already taught me everything I needed to know about cooking—but ended up giving me her blessing.

"Maybe you'll be able to teach me a thing or two from

that fancy school," she'd said. Well, maybe I would.

My aunt and great-grandmother were entirely on board too. At least they pretended to be. I knew they were trying not to smother me.

"This will broaden your horizons," Aunt Agnes said with a brittle sort of cheer.

"And if you need anything, just whistle," Gram added. Gram is an empath, meaning she's a healer and also a bit of a telepath. She was saying that if I ever needed help, I could reach her just by thinking. That's easier said than done, though. Agnes and Gram communicate telepathically with each other all the time, but I don't exactly have the hang of it yet. But we could still write letters and e-mails.

The hardest good-bye was Peter. That is, I didn't say good-bye to him at all. We hadn't spoken since that terrible lunch at Pizza World, and . . . well, I was afraid he'd blow me off if I tried to see him, and that would ruin my whole summer in Paris.

So I didn't say anything. He was working on the day I left.

Anyway, I made it to Paris, and was enrolled at the Clef d'Or.

"Kooking school," as Fabienne called it.

I'd done it. Found the razor's edge. Took a walk on the wild side. Said good-bye to my inner mom.

He probably doesn't even miss me, I thought.

CHAPTER • FIVE

Dear Gram,

Well, the Clef d'Or surely lives up to its reputation as the greatest cooking school in the world! We are learning time-honored methods of preparing traditional French food, with no shortcuts. There are about thirty students in my class (Soups and Appetizers for the next two weeks). Most of them are French. Some are Japanese. There is one other English speaker, a Canadian named Margot. I'm sure we'll get to be good friends.

Love,
Katy

Never mind that Margot was a fifty-two-year-old travel writer for the Toronto *Sun*, and was in Paris to cover a story about her close friend Chef Durant, the head chef of the school. Chef Durant does not speak to students, and neither does Margot, except in the capacity of interviewer. The one time I tried to talk to her, she asked me if I missed McDonald's, which was pretty dumb, since there are McDonald's all over Paris. Fortunately, she's only staying around for Soups and Appetizers.

Today we made *coquelets sur canapés*, which translates roughly to "disgusting critters on toast." The class began with the chef's assistant handing out little dead birds. I didn't know what kind of birds they were, although he told us—one of the many mysteries of French cooking is the French language—but they were pitiful, scrawny little things, with their limp little necks and pathetic, blank eyes. We were told to plunge them into boiling water and then pluck the feathers off them, cut off their heads and feet, and remove their organs (the liver, mixed with raw pork fat, is a big part of the dish) before roasting them.

The whole process was hideous. When I was working in Hattie's Kitchen, I never had to chop anything's head off, although I suppose someone did. I never had to sauté animal glands or skin eels (I won't even begin to tell you how that's done). Hattie didn't even serve lobster, because she didn't like the idea of taking an eight-year-old sea being and boiling it alive.

"Deserves a sweet old age, if you ask me," she'd say.

At Hattie's, I'd learned to cook with love. That is, love was my specialty. Hattie's Kitchen was a magical restaurant. It was said that everybody got what they needed at Hattie's, and when what they needed was love, my job was to stir a dose of it into their food.

But I wouldn't be using any magic at the Clef d'Or. I was going to learn the right way to cook, even if it was repulsive and took forever. And no shortcuts.

That was another thing about Hattie's Kitchen: We hadn't been that fussy about making everything from scratch. Hattie's grilled cheese sandwiches were made from processed American cheese. The chefs at the Clef would probably faint at the thought of that, but to tell the truth, those sandwiches tasted really good. When you're sick, there's nothing like grilled cheese on white bread with a bowl of canned tomato soup.

We made real tomato soup at school. First we roasted the tomatoes, then put them through a Folcy mill, cooked a lot of vegetables for stock, sautéed shallots and garlic, and then sprinkled in dill, which we'd grown in pots. If I'd been sick, I think I'd rather have stayed hungry than go through all that.

Anyway, speaking of hungry, I was. Usually at the end of class we got to eat whatever we'd made that day, but after all the horrible things I'd done to my poor bird, all I wanted to do was give it a decent burial. My stomach started growling on my way home.

Except for my morning croissant and coffee, consumed standing up at the zinc bar near the school, I hadn't eaten anything all day. I hadn't sat down all day either. So, throwing my dirty chef's coat over my shoulder, I took a stroll down the treelined avenues of the sixth arrondisement, where the school and some of the more comfortable Parisians could be found, to look for a café where I could buy myself a special dinner.

Ernest Hemingway, F. Scott Fitzgerald, Gertrude Stein,

James Baldwin, Mary Cassatt, Ben Franklin, and Thomas Jefferson had all walked these elegantly cobbled streets before me. They had looked up at the tall windows showing glimpses of gilt-paneled rooms and chic salons. They, too, had followed their rumbling stomachs to the finest food the world had to offer, available on every street corner.

Unfortunately, my meandering route took me past no restaurants that weren't American burger joints. I was about to give up and order a Blimpie's special when I spotted a street sign reading *Rue des Âmes Perdues*.

It rang a bell. Fabienne had said her mother lived near the school, and that she herself would be in Paris before long. She'd even given me her address on a card I'd stashed somewhere in the backpack I used instead of a purse.

On impulse, I scrambled through my things until I found it. There it was: 24 Rue des Âmes Perdues. I checked the house numbers around me. It wouldn't be far, I realized, five or six blocks.

It occurred to me that I really *wanted* to see Fabienne. I'd been in Paris for weeks, but I hadn't made any friends at all. I certainly couldn't count Margot the snooty middle-aged Canadian. The other students in my cooking class seemed all right—some of them were actually my age—but, being French speakers, they understandably preferred to be around people they could talk to. My grasp of the language was still limited to statements like, "We get bird chop head?"

I hadn't spoken a word of English, except in my dreams, when someone promised to love me for a year and a day . . .

Witches called it *handfasting*. That was when two people promised to stay together faithfully for a year and a day. It wasn't marriage, but it was more than dating. Handfasting meant you loved someone, and wanted to look after them and would never hurt them.

Peter and I were handfasted, although I didn't know if that meant much to him anymore.

I walked more quickly, trying not to remember. The sun was beginning to set, a wash of pink and blue over the stately grays of the city.

Then I saw the house, if you could call it that. Number twenty-four was a magnificent three-story mansion shaped like a gigantic horseshoe behind a tall iron gate. There was a courtyard in front with green grass and a lot of pretty flowers, entrances at both ends of the horseshoe—one for people and one for cars—and a grand entrance in the middle, above a long flight of marble stairs and between imposing columns.

"Wow," I said out loud as I double-checked the address. Fabienne hadn't told me that her family abode was a palace the size of most big-city museums. Even the gate intimidated me, with its wrought-iron fleur-de-lis design nestled between its forbidding bars. There was a button of some kind tucked near the upper left hinge. I pressed it, not really expecting anything to happen, but after a few seconds a buzzer sounded and the gate clicked open.

I walked inside, marveling at the gorgeousness of the tall windows and decorative stonework. Most of the buildings in Paris, I'd read, were either seventeenth or eighteenth century. But this place didn't look like anything I'd seen in the guidebooks I'd amassed for my journey here. There was something timeless and ancient about the place, as if it held the secrets of the whole city.

As I walked toward the main door, I occasionally saw a face gazing down at me from behind the draperies in one or another of the windows on the upper floor, and felt my heart beating faster as I approached two enormous stone lions on either side of the broad stairs leading to the colonnaded entrance.

Sweaty and out of breath, I finally made it to the top, looking up at a huge brass knocker in the shape of a stylized wolf's head. I lifted it and let it fall with a thud. No one answered. I tried again. The third time, the heavy door swung open.

I'd been hoping Fabienne herself would answer the door, so I wouldn't have to deal with parents or housekeepers, but that was not to be. The person who stood in front of me was a guy, a tall, handsome guy with honey-blond hair and gray eyes and a mouth that dropped open in surprise when he recognized me.

"Peter?" I croaked.

CHAPTER • SIX

I don't know if it was because I hadn't eaten enough, or because I just wanted to die then and there, but before I could make my escape, my legs gave out from beneath me and I felt myself spiraling toward the marble landing.

No! I kept shouting to myself as Peter swooped me into his arms. I didn't want him to rescue me! Not after what he'd said to me at Pizza World! I didn't want my ex-boyfriend who no longer cared about me to be smelling the odor of sautéed pork fat in my hair, to see dried bird blood on my clothes.

"Please," I grunted as he set me down on an uncomfortable chair upholstered in white damask. "I'll be all right."

"Just take it easy," he said, unbuttoning my collar. I pushed his hand away. Then I blacked out.

Suddenly there seemed to be a whole lot of people in the room, all gathered around me. Most of them were women. They were of vastly different ages, but all of them were dressed beautifully, their hair saucy, their makeup flawless as they all talked at once in rapid-fire French. I caught a few words—"homeless" seemed to have been repeated more than once—but after a few seconds, I gave up on trying to follow anything they were saying. I just wanted to get out of there.

"*Zut-zut-zut!*" an elegant elderly woman said, cutting through the throng with a wave of her perfectly manicured hand. To my surprise, she knelt down, offering me tea in a delicate porcelain cup and saucer.

She smiled at me. Her teeth were perfect, but it was her eyes, crinkling kindly at the corners, that were smiling. For the first time since my arrival, I felt that I could breathe.

"Marie-Therèse," she said, indicating herself. She pronounced it *Ter-EZZ*. "Drink this." She said it in French, but slowly enough so that I could understand her.

The tea she gave me was hot and sweet, and honestly did make me feel better. I looked around, first at my legs that were sprawled on the floor. My dirty chef's jacket was bunched up in a ball over my stomach. I tried to arrange myself more attractively, but there's only so much dignity you can muster after collapsing in the middle of a house full of beautiful European strangers. Peter was wearing a black band-collar silk shirt and slim jeans over a pair of expensive-looking loafers. He didn't look even slightly American.

"What are you doing here?" he asked.

"Me?" I shrieked. "You were supposed to be in New York. Or something . . ." I squeezed my eyes shut so I wouldn't pass out again. Peter was the reason I'd left Whitfield in the first place. Now here he was, dressed in black silk and surrounded by beautiful women.

"Katy—"

"I'll let myself out," I said, staggering to my feet.

He caught my arm. "Why are you acting like this?"

Suddenly I was blinded by tears that welled up, unbidden and embarrassing. "Forget it," I said. I projected myself toward the front door. "*Merci*," I said to the woman who'd offered me a cup of tea. Then I tripped over the threshold and hurled myself down the marble steps.

"Don't go," Peter called after me. With his long legs, he caught up with me before I reached the street. "How'd you know I'd be here?"

"I didn't come to see you," I said, feeling the corners of my mouth trembling. "And you didn't come to see me. So we're even."

"I just got here myself. I was going to look for you, I swear."

"Oh, go away." I ran down the street, my vision blurry with tears. I would have collided with a lamppost, but Peter caught my arm. "Please, Katy," he said. "Just talk to me." Then he wrapped his arms around me.

I covered my face with my hands, willing myself not to feel anything. But I did. I felt as if I was where I'd always belonged.

"You didn't answer your cell phone," he said.

"It got stolen."

"You called your Aunt Agnes. She told me."

"That was from the post office. I didn't want them to know I'd been robbed."

"Did you get my e-mails?"

I shook my head. "My laptop got stolen too," I said into his chest. "I send them e-mails from an Internet café so they won't know."

He stroked my hair. "I couldn't believe you left without saying good-bye."

I looked up at him. "You said I acted like a mom," I whispered.

"What? That was what you were so mad about?"

I pulled away from him. "I need to get home," I said.

"I'll go with you." He pulled a piece of paper out of his pocket. "Seventeen Rue Cujas, right? Agnes gave it to me."

I kept walking, although I didn't really know where I was, and in the dusky light, I couldn't read the street signs.

"You could have written to me," Peter said.

I had. I'd written to him every day. I just hadn't sent the letters. "I didn't think you'd be interested in hearing from me."

"That's insane," he said.

That wasn't worth answering. We walked on in silence for a while. I saw a couple of things I recognized, like the Pompidou Center and the Rue des Rosiers, where all the Jewish bakeries are.

"Are you still mad at me?" he asked softly. "For the mom thing?"

I shrugged.

"I was hoping that maybe you'd be glad to see me. At least a little."

At that point, I didn't know what I was thinking anymore. Of course I was glad to see him. I'd been hungry and lonely and tired and disappointed since I'd arrived, and seeing Peter was like going to heaven.

It just hadn't happened the way I'd wanted.

"I wish we hadn't fought," he said.

"Me too," I squeaked. Somehow, what had been so important to me back then suddenly seemed pointless. "Okay," I said, pulling myself together. "So what *are* you doing here?" I ventured. "In Fabienne's house?"

"Fabienne's?"

"The French girl from school," I said for what must have been the tenth time.

"I know who she is. That's her house?"

"It's the address she gave me."

"I really don't know who lives there," Peter said. "A bunch of people, from what I can see. Jeremiah stays there when he's in Paris."

"And who else? Are all those people related to him or something?"

He shrugged. "Don't know. Those are his friends, I guess. His driver picked us up at the airport and dropped me off about an hour ago. Nobody in the place even seemed to know I was coming. A maid took me to my room." He grinned and shook his head. "It was all like a movie."

We were back in my neighborhood. "This is where I live," I said.

Peter looked up at the dingy, narrow building that leaned toward the street like a nosy old woman. "Here?" he asked as if he couldn't believe anyone would actually set foot inside.

I nodded. The place looked even worse than I'd remembered. "Want to come in?"

He seemed dubious about entering, but finally stepped into the dark entryway with me.

"Run," I said, turning on the *minutière* and heading full speed up the stairs. Peter sprinted behind me, nearly colliding with one of the Norwegians coming out of the (ugh) communal toilet (the shower was separate, and two euros extra) and eliciting an appreciative murmur from Hernan the transvestite, who had come out to spy so quickly that he forgot his wig.

"Hey," Peter called when the lights went out. There was never enough time to make it up to my door.

"Follow my voice," I said.

Inside, the place smelled like three hundred years of dirty feet. Plus it was July and sickeningly hot, with no hope of anything resembling air conditioning. I turned on my lamp with its twenty-watt bulb to show off my two decorations, a wall calendar from the meat market displaying a color photograph of a raw rack of lamb, and a wallet-size junior class picture of Peter, put up with a thumbtack. Quickly I took his picture off the wall.

Peter stood in the doorway for a time. I suppose he was trying to get used to the ugliness of the place. "That a friend of yours?" he asked, looking over his shoulder at Hernan. "The bald guy in the dress?"

I ignored him, and turned on the hotplate. It sparked. The smell of electricity filled the room. "Tea?" I asked.

"No, thanks." He looked around incredulously. "What are you doing here?" He sounded genuinely astonished.

"I live here," I answered truculently.

"Good God."

"That bad?"

"Excuse me for a moment," he said, and walked outside. In a few minutes he was back. "I'd like you to move into the place where I'm staying," he said.

I blinked. "What?"

"I asked Jeremiah. We can go back to the house now. I'll help you pack."

"Wait a minute," I objected. "You can't just order me out of my home like some kind of *policeman*."

"For crying out loud, Katy."

"Not everybody has a rich uncle!"

"But I do," Peter said. "And he says it's okay if you move in."

"Well, maybe I don't want to," I shrilled. "Why would I want to move in with you, anyway?"

He sighed. "It wouldn't be *with* me," he said. "There are more than a dozen bedrooms at the house. People move in and out all the time. Jeremiah says it's like a hotel. In fact, I think it's called a hotel."

"That's a French thing," I said. "A lot of big old houses are called hotels. It doesn't mean they rent rooms or—"

"No, not a hotel. An *abbey*, that was it. L'Abbaye des Âmes Perdues." Peter smiled. "Did I totally fracture that?"

"Totally," I said. "Not that I could do much better."

"What does it mean?"

I picked apart the words. "The Abbey of Lost Souls, I think. Strange name for a house. Or the street it's on, for that matter."

"Jeremiah said that some of these places are hundreds of years old. Who knows who named it, or why?" He touched my hair.

"Don't butter me up," I said, pushing his hand away.

He spread his hands by his sides. "Okay, Katy. Be as stubborn as you want. But you've got to admit, Jeremiah's house—or Fabienne's, or whoever owns that place—is going to be a lot less dangerous and more comfortable than this dump."

I was about to object, but really, I couldn't. It *was* a dump. I'd called it that many times myself. He looked out the window. "Don't do it for me," he said. "Do it for your Gram. She'd want you to be safe."

Of course she would. And Peter was right. I just hated to admit it. "I'll be okay," I whispered, wondering how true that was. "I'll stay here."

He slid down to the floor. "Then I will too," he said.

"What are you talking about?"

He nestled his head on my lap. "Well, if you won't come with me, I've got no choice but to stay here in Hotel Cucaracha with you."

"Why?" I asked defensively.

"Because I need to know you're not being murdered in an alley someplace." He was struggling to keep his eyes open. "And because I love you," he added softly.

"You . . . you love me?"

"Of course I do," he said, frowning and making smacking sounds with his lips. "I always love you. No matter how cranky you get."

Within a few minutes he was asleep. I guess he'd had a busy day too. When he started to snore, I took the sheet off my bed and draped it over him. Then, after thinking about it for a second or two, I crawled under it with him.

He shifted toward me. Then, with a soft sleep-noise that sounded like a kitten's meow, he put his arm around me.

"Okay," I whispered. "I'll move in. For a while. I mean, I

can think of worse things than living in a mansion with the person I love most in the world, even if we do argue a lot."

He twitched and snorted a little in response.

I lay my head on his shoulder. It was a perfect fit.

CHAPTER • SEVEN

So here I was, hobnobbing with the Haughty Queens of Evil.

Oh, did I mention that my half-dozen new roommates were obnoxious, rude, arrogant, and horrible? *Tzchtzchtzch.* That is the sound of my teeth grinding at the mere thought of my fellow residents at the Abbey of Lost Souls.

To begin with, Fabienne wasn't even there. She was in Italy somewhere buying shoes. Her mother, Sophie, was, though.

Let me tell you about Sophie. First, picture the most beautiful face you can think of, and then multiply that beauty by ten. Or twenty. With thick, wavy, blond hair pulled into a casual chignon and a Barbie-doll figure. Blinding white teeth. Four-inch heels, at home. Couturier clothes. And the disposition of a Tasmanian devil.

The first thing she did when Peter and I walked into the house's main sitting room was look me up and down with her hands on her hips, blabbing something in French that the other people in the room seemed to find *très amusant*. I was already beginning to think moving in with these people might be a bad idea, but the older woman who'd given me a cup of tea earlier approached me. She shook her finger at Sophie, who turned away with a sneer.

"Marie-Therèse?"

She seemed pleased that I'd remembered her name. "*Oui*," she trilled. "And you are?"

"Katy Ainsworth," Peter said. "My uncle Jeremiah—Jeremiah Shaw—said she could stay here."

"*Mais oui*," Marie-Therèse said. "That will be no problem at all." She motioned for a servant in livery to take my "luggage," which consisted of one suitcase and a plastic bag filled with dirty clothes, upstairs. "And Mademoiselle Katy will be staying with you, Peter?"

I noticed at least six pairs of eyes narrow into slits as they regarded me.

"Er . . . no," Peter said. "That is . . ."

"I'll need my own room," I said, figuring if there was a problem with that, I'd just leave. I was awfully tired, but I'd be able to make one more trip back to the Black Lagoon if I had to.

"Of course, of course," Marie-Therèse said. "Such a young girl. And an Américaine. There is a lovely room for you, ma chère." Then she put her arm around my shoulder and, gesturing for Peter to follow, led me up a curving flight of stairs covered with carpet so thick I would have been happy to sleep right there. At the top, she opened the door to the most luxurious room I'd ever seen.

It was white. Blizzard white—white carpet, white sheer draperies that billowed in the breeze from the tall casement windows, a white canopy over the enormous bed—accented with touches of gold here and there. I don't know much about furniture, but it looked really delicate, really old, really valuable.

"Would you like something to eat or drink? Some *chocolat*, perhaps?" Marie-Therèse asked.

"Oh, no," I said, instantly regretting my refusal. "I'm fine. Thanks."

"*Eh, bien*," she said with a warm smile. "*Bon nuit*."

Peter and I looked at each other. The catnap we'd taken in my former digs hadn't been enough of a rest for either of us. Peter's eyes were rimmed with dark circles, and I was pretty sure mine were a match.

"I'm just down the hall," he said. "Second door on the right."

"Okay," I said. Then he kissed me goodnight, as if we'd gone on a date. I waited until he'd walked into his own room before I closed the door and leaned against it.

I was starving. I was exhausted. The blinding white canopy bed with its gold tassels was calling to me. But I still had to wash out my chef's coat and take a shower.

Downstairs, it sounded like a party was going on. In time, I would learn that parties were a daily event at the house, but on that night it still seemed like a novelty. Tinkling women's voices rose in hilarity. Someone played the piano. I could already recognize Sophie's laughter.

As I drifted off to sleep, I wondered if the women downstairs were the same ones who'd come to Peter's party back in Whitfield. I hadn't paid much attention to them then, but now they seemed . . . well, *odd*. The whole situation was odd. For one thing, why was old man Shaw's continental *pied à terre* filled with gorgeous women? For another, what was Peter supposed to do with them? Why would Shaw Enterprises need even one alchemist, let alone two? And how was I supposed to fit in with this crew of party-hearty beauties?

Once again, I was filled with questions. And once again, I felt the way I had when Peter had first told me about his newly developed talent for creating gold:

This gift comes with strings attached.

Strings that reached all the way to Paris.

After school the next day, I walked to my old apartment on the Rue Cujas. The Abbaye des Âmes Perdues was a lot—and I mean a *whole* lot—nicer, but I hadn't really felt comfortable there. Even with Peter just down the hall, I'd hardly slept. So I returned to my old building to decide whether or not I wanted to move back. I'd paid the rent till the end of the month, so it wasn't as if I had nowhere other than the Barbie Mansion to live. Still, the place was pretty grim.

Hernan, my neighbor, leaned against the building's entryway. He was wearing short shorts and a halter top, smoking a cigarette and coughing.

"Don't bother," he said. Or I thought he said. My schoolgirl French didn't sound much like the way French people really talked. Mostly the language sounded to me like horns honking. Hernan went on for a while. What he said sounded like "*honk honk honk* bucket *honk cough* one thousand sequins *shoo* (sucking on cigarette) *honk pa!* (expelling smoke) *cough* landlord is a piece of *merde*."

I understood the last part, and I didn't think it boded well.

Nevertheless, I climbed up the four flights of stairs—the Chinese family was cooking roast pork with ginger, if my nose served me—to my apartment. I was going to unlock the door, but as it turned out, that wasn't necessary since it was already open. The door was off its hinges, and the framework above it was broken. Inside, the ceiling had collapsed onto the middle of the floor in a pile of broken slate, along with a soggy bird's nest, a broken weather vane, and quite a bit of mud. A drop of water hit me between my eyebrows. I looked up to see a threatening sky peeking through the foot-wide hole.

"So much for this place," I muttered as I clattered down the stairs. Hernan blew me a kiss on a plume of cigarette smoke.

I doubted if I'd be able to find another apartment as cheap as this one, and I'd already lost a month's rent on it. So it looked like I would be calling the Abbey of Lost Souls home, for a while, at least, whether I liked it or not.

CHAPTER • EIGHT

One good thing about the abbey was that it was walking distance to the school, so I didn't have to bother with the Metro or a bus anymore.

What was less great was that there always seemed to be a party going on there.

I got back from my foray to my former dwelling on the Rue Cujas just in time for the first party of the evening. This one was in honor of Fabienne's return to France from the wilds of Milan, Italy. When I walked through the door of the main parlor, she was showing off her new purchases to a rapt audience of women who all appeared to be very excited by a pair of shoes that were painted to look like bananas.

"Katy!" she called, running over to me despite my grungy appearance and wrapping me in a bear hug—that is, as far as a five-foot-ten-inch, hundred-fifteen-pound girl can resemble a bear.

To be honest, it was great to see her. "You are kooking,

yes?" she asked, fingering the chef's jacket in my hands. At least I'd had the foresight to take it off before coming into the house.

"Uh, yes. *Oui*. I'm taking a summer session at Le Clef d'Or," I said. "At your suggestion."

"Oh, I am so happy for you. Now you must cook for us, okay?"

"Now?" I asked.

"No, I do not mean right now, *toute de suite*!" She laughed, and I remembered why I liked her. She was open and kind and sweet-natured, unlike her snooty mother. "Perhaps if we speak French, it will be easier for you to understand me," she said.

I told her that would be fine, since I needed the practice. I also didn't intend to stay at this paean to shopping longer than another three seconds, but I didn't tell her that.

"I know we'll have a wonderful time together this summer," she trilled. "There are so many people I'd like you to . . . Oh, here's one of them now. Belmondo!" She waved eagerly at a man who was leaning against the doorway, his jacket slung over his shoulder. "My favorite uncle," she confided. "And also the most handsome man in Paris."

She wasn't kidding. As he made his way toward us, I felt as if I'd swallowed my tongue. I couldn't understand a word he was saying, but I don't think that had anything to do with the quality of his French.

For one thing, he didn't look like anyone's uncle. He was in his early twenties, I think, with dark, straight hair that he wore almost to his shoulders, which were broad and muscular in a Skinny Buff Guy kind of way under a tight black T-shirt.

He had a strong chin and really white teeth, and a long, Gallic nose that looked like he'd come from an ancient line of aristocrats. But the most interesting thing about him was his eyes. They were blue in the same way mine were green—that is, they seemed to change from turquoise to cobalt to sky to navy. They were changing color now, as he hugged Fabienne and exchanged a greeting with her.

And then he looked at me.

My breath caught. Time seemed to stand still. It was as if he knew everything about me, and liked it all.

Honkhonkhonkhonk.

"Huh?" I mumbled weakly.

He laughed. At the moment, his eyes were the color of bluebirds. "Forgive me," he said. "We'll speak English. Fabienne tells me that you're a student at the Clef d'Or?"

OMG. The perfect accent. Slightly French—French enough to make the hairs on my arms stand on end—but grammatically perfect. "Er . . ." I got lost in his eyes again. "What did you say?"

He smiled. "May I get you something to drink? Champagne?"

"Oh, no," I said breathlessly, backing away. I looked around for Peter. "Um, thank you, but I've got to . . . to . . ." Then I turned and ran up the stairs to my room.

Why did I do that?

I lay on my bed and furiously kicked my feet, feeling like the biggest doofus on the face of the earth. It's not like gorgeous guys—*adult* guys—offer me champagne every day.

I took a deep breath. *Don't be stupid,* I told myself. That guy—what was his name, Mondo?—was just being polite. Which was more than I could say for myself.

And what did it matter, anyway, I thought as I stripped down for my shower. I belonged with that group downstairs about as much as a daisy at an orchid show.

After showering, I put on a clean T-shirt and crawled into bed with a secondhand Agatha Christie that had cost me nearly twenty dollars at the English bookstore. I'd nearly finished the chapter I was reading when someone knocked on my door. "Peter?" I called out hopefully.

It was Fabienne. "Why did you leave?" she asked. She seemed to be sincerely bewildered. "Belmondo liked you."

I shrugged. "I didn't belong down there, Fabienne," I said honestly. "I don't belong here in general."

"But you do!" she insisted. "Peter wants you to live here, and so you shall. The opinions of others are of no importance."

I frowned. "Why is Peter so important?" I asked.

Fabienne rubbed her fingers together. "Money is always important," she said sagely. "For them, *bien sur*"—she gestured with her chin toward the festivities below—"it is most important. They will do nothing to lose Peter."

"But Jeremiah . . ." I was going to say that Jeremiah could also make gold, but I stopped myself. I didn't know how much Fabienne knew about the alchemy, and I'd practically given Peter a solemn oath not to blab about it.

"But it is not Peter who worries you," she said. "It is the others, yes?"

It was embarrassing to be so transparent, but she'd managed to go right to the heart of my discomfort, just as she had back in Whitfield. "I guess," I said. "They don't seem to like me much."

She laughed. "You're talking about my mother." She rolled her eyes. "Sophie doesn't like anyone much. Not even me. Not that I care. *Je m'en fiche.* I've hardly seen her, after all."

"You mean today? Since you've been home?"

She shook her head. "I mean ever." She took a deep breath. "I was raised by nannies in Switzerland until I was eight. Then I was sent away to boarding school. I only saw Sophie twice before I was twelve years old."

"What happened then?"

"Then I was transferred to a school in Tokyo, then Los Angeles, and then Ainsworth. I think she didn't want me to become attached to any one place, so that I would think of this place as home. During vacations I came back here."

"So at least you got to be with your mom then," I said.

"Not so much. She was rarely present. Sophie doesn't like children." She flipped her hair. "That is her way. The women in her circle believe children should remain in their own milieu until they are old enough to enter the adult world. That is why I have come now. I shall be one of them. An adult."

"At fifteen?" I asked, dismayed. "Isn't that kind of young?"

"It is our way," she said.

"And who are the women, anyway? The women who live here?"

"Friends," she said. "Or what passes for friends. With Sophie, one never knows." She smiled.

I couldn't believe how okay she was about her mom. I mean, I also grew up without a mother, but that was because she died. Apparently, Fabienne's just didn't want her around.

"Where's your dad?" I blurted.

"I don't know," she said. "I don't know who he is. None of us do."

I pictured my great-grandmother fainting dead away at that. "Er . . . none?"

"We do not marry," she said.

This time, I was the one who almost fainted. "Never?"

She shrugged. "*Non.* For us, marriage is not so important. But I never needed a father, because there was always Belmondo."

"Oh, right. Your uncle."

"Well, not really my uncle. Just our friend. And also our landlord. He owns this building."

"Does he work for Jeremiah?"

"Belmondo?" She laughed. "I don't believe he works at all, except for playing the guitar from time to time. He's quite good at that."

"Er . . . great," I said.

"'Belmondo' means 'beautiful world.' He is beautiful, *non*?"

He was beautiful, *oui*, but I wasn't about to turn into an idiot over him. "Has Peter come in?" I asked.

"*Alors*, he has not." She must have seen the disappointment on my face, because she took my hand and squeezed it. "You love him, yes?"

Reluctantly, I nodded. "Sometimes I wish I didn't," I said.

"You don't mean that," she said. "Because if you have not fallen in love with Belmondo, then you must love Peter very much."

We both laughed. "Oh, Fabienne," I said. "You're so right."

"Please call me Fabby. And so, without Peter, I think maybe you want to be alone now?" It was a simple question without any emotional overtones, as direct and honest as she was. I felt that I'd finally found someone I could tell the truth to.

"Thanks, Fabby. I would."

She gave me a kiss on my cheek before she left.

CHAPTER • NINE

Aside from Fabienne and the elderly Marie-Therèse, my fellow roomies on the Street of Lost Souls made little effort to speak to me. I did get to know a couple of them in passing, though. There was Joelle—early twenties, I guessed, with dark hair cut into a severe bob, dramatic makeup, and partial to geometrically structured, space-agey-type outfits; and Annabelle, who was blond, Asian, and six feet tall. A professional model, Annabelle seemed to be one of the few women in the house who worked. She also had a steady boyfriend who came around almost every day. Presiding over them all, of course, was the insufferable Sophie and her coterie of gentleman callers.

Everyone there seemed to love Peter, though. Especially Sophie, who was constantly nuzzling up to him and touching him, whispering in his ear and showing off. What was that about? She looked good, but she had to be at least thirty-something to be Fabienne's mother. Weren't these women embarrassed about *anything*?

Fortunately, I couldn't spend that much time with them, since I had to be at school at eight in the morning. No one in the house was even awake then, except occasionally for Marie-Therèse, who would sometimes be having coffee on the balcony while I was scrambling to leave.

"Will you join me?" she asked one day.

I checked my watch. It was barely seven. I hadn't wanted to be a bother to anyone in the house, so I still took my morning coffee at the stand-up coffee bar down the street from the school, but it was kind of her to offer. "Okay," I said.

She called for one of the servants to bring another cup. When it came, it was gigantic, the size of a soup bowl. On the tray beside it was a pot of steaming milk and a big butter croissant. Much better than at the zinc bar.

She touched my hand. "My dear," she said, her blue eyes crinkling. "Please don't be offended by our ways. We are not accustomed to outsiders."

"I could tell," I said, sipping my *café au lait*.

"You must find us very odd indeed."

Ya think? "Er . . . maybe it's a cultural difference," I said.

"Ah. Very diplomatic, Katy." She set down her cup with a tiny tap. "I do apologize for the way you've been ignored by the others. They just don't know what to do with you, I suppose."

"Do with me?"

She sighed. "Don't you see, it's all about Peter, dear," she said. "You're the one person who could take him away."

"But . . ." My mind was racing. "You mean from here?" How long did they think he was going to stay, anyway?

"Oh, don't listen to me," she said, shaking her head

dismissively. "Such a foolish old woman." The gesture made her look almost like a girl. It was obvious that she had once been very beautiful. She still looked good, despite her age. Her white hair was perfectly coiffed into lush waves that framed her face, with its perfect cheekbones and lovely teeth. She wore a silk robe and high-heeled slippers, and her nails were manicured and painted a delicate shade of pink.

She was so different from Gram, who dressed in long skirts and shawls and wore her hair in a bun with a doily on top of her head. But then, the witches of Whitfield were different from most people in a whole lot of ways, and beauty was probably the least of them. But fundamentally, she was like Gram. She was kind. She was gentle. She had a sense of humor. And she was willing to be nice to me when almost no one else was.

"Perhaps you would like a party?" Marie-Therèse suggested.

I groaned. Didn't these people think about anything else? "Er . . . thanks, but parties aren't exactly my thing."

"Ah. For me as well. But I am old. The other women—the younger ones—adore them. They live for parties."

Why didn't that surprise me, I thought.

"But soon my birthday will arrive—my eightieth—and there will be a party for me that I must attend."

"Oh, of course," I said. "That's different. I'll certainly come to your birthday party."

She smiled a little, although I couldn't read the emotion in that smile. She didn't look at me.

I should mention that I have a talent besides telekinesis. I'm also an *object empath*, which means I can "read" objects. I can tell a lot about where things have been just by touching them, if I concentrate. And it's not just objects that I can read. I can learn a lot about people, too—sometimes more than I want to—by touching them. That doesn't happen, though, unless I concentrate on it. Otherwise, I'd go crazy feeling other people's feelings all the time. It also doesn't seem fair, peeking into people's secret selves. I mean, if someone wants you to know something about them, they'll tell you, right? It's an invasion of privacy.

But there was something about the old woman's smile that touched my heart. Was she sad about growing older? Was she afraid that no one would come to her party? I thought maybe if I knew her story, I could help in some way.

So I touched her hand. Gently. Deliberately. *Let me in.*

Her feelings were like a car crash happening. Screeching metal, blurry images, unnamed, unspeakable horror. She was terrified down to the marrow of her bones.

I pulled away, gasping involuntarily at the shock, my own heart racing. "I need to go," I said.

Marie-Therèse looked at me strangely, as if she knew what I'd done and was ashamed of what I'd found inside her mind.

"Er . . . can't be late for class," I mumbled as I picked up my knife carrier and edged out the door.

She nodded slightly, graciously. But I saw her hands. They were trembling.

CHAPTER • TEN

To: Ainsworth.A@Stanford.edu
From: KTA@gmail.com
Subject: Hi

Hi, Aunt Agnes—

Well, we're nearly done with Soups and Appetizers! Today we made things stuffed in pastry—baked brie en croute with a bunch of different coulis, or fruit sauces, mini Wellingtons, spinach pie in phyllo, apple strudel, and some other things. Margot the Canadian overcooked her Wellingtons and Chef Durant called her a barbarian. Then she called him a lot of things I didn't think middle-aged women ever even thought, let alone said, and threw her name tag at Chef before stomping out. Chef picked it up between his thumb and index finger like it was a rat, and then dropped it in the twenty-gallon garbage can.

Hope you and Gram are enjoying the summer. I miss you both. ☺

—Katy

I hit send from a computer at the nearest Internet café, then headed back to the Rue des Âmes Perdues. Back at the house, Sophie asked me—all smiles and dimples, of course—to cook dinner for twenty this weekend, as a formal welcome for Fabienne. Frankly, I wouldn't cook a turd sandwich for Sophie, but I liked Fabby, so I agreed to do it.

"Your friend Peter—he is very busy, I think," Sophie said, primping her hair in the ornate living room mirror.

"Uh . . . I guess." I didn't want her to know how much it bothered me that Peter's schedule and mine were so different.

"And so Fabienne's dinner will be good for you."

"Oh?"

"But of course. Peter should see your talent, your skill."

What he would see, most likely, would be my food-encrusted clothes and sweaty face, but I understood her point. Peter hadn't tried my cooking since I'd started at the Clef d'Or, and I was kind of excited that he would be at my big meal.

"It is important to use the assets one has."

Oh. Meaning that I couldn't rely on my *beauty* the way she could, because, according to her, I didn't have any. What a piece of work. "Okay, I'll do it," I said. "I'll give you my grocery list as soon as I've worked it out."

She waved me away. "Give it to the cook."

I decided on a menu of clear soup with chanterelle

mushrooms, beet salad with Roquefort cheese and pears, *turbot en papillot* with remoulade sauce, potatoes Lyonnaise, asparagus in browned butter, candied tomatoes, and little cheesy pastry balls called *gougères*, followed by an eight-layer, mousse-filled chocolate cake covered in chocolate buttercream and a parti-colored bow made of rolled fondant. It was a pretty ambitious menu, especially since I hadn't gone past Roasts and Braises at school, but I'd learned to cook most of the other things from Hattie, although she hadn't used the French names for them. At Hattie's Kitchen, we used terms like "fish cooked in paper" and "baked fried potatoes with onions." We'd made the cake together for Peter's brother Eric's eleventh birthday.

Maybe I wasn't learning that much new stuff at the Clef d'Or, after all.

The mansion's cook, whose name was Mathilde, was fine about my making dinner and even offered to help me, except that Sophie gave her the night off. Actually—surprise!—all of the servants had been given the night off.

So I found out on the day of the dinner that I'd be preparing meals for twenty people absolutely by myself. I was so nervous, I thought about asking the general populace of the house if anyone felt like helping me, but I could guess what the response to that would be. Not that they'd have been much help, anyway; most of these women couldn't tell the difference between a kitchen and a library, since they never set foot in either.

I was putting the finishing touches on the cake—had to make that first—when a miracle happened. Fabienne tiptoed downstairs into the kitchen with her finger over her mouth.

"Shh," she whispered. "I'm here to help you."

I looked around. "Is this a secret?"

"Yes," she whispered.

"Well, okay, thanks," I whispered back. "Er . . . can you tell me why we're whispering?"

"My mother," Fabby said. "She has forbidden me to come into the kitchen. She says it's a dangerous place."

Normally I wouldn't give any credence to any thoughts Sophie had about food preparation, but in this case she was right. A kitchen *was* a dangerous place, especially if you didn't know what you were doing. Even professional cooks got hurt all the time. So I asked Fabby if she was afraid, and she said no, although I knew she was lying. That's something only a friend would do, lie so they could help you.

"You'll be fine," I reassured her, "as long as you do exactly what I say, okay?"

She nodded, swallowing.

"It won't be that hard, I promise. Just a little hectic. And I really, really appreciate your help, Fab—"

I blinked. She was gone. *WTH*?

"Fab—" I gasped. She was back. Or something.

"*Zut alors*," she said groggily.

"Where'd you go?"

"I . . . I don't know. I was just so . . . nervous about cooking, that I . . ." She blinked. "It felt like Hawaii."

"What?"

"I thought I was in Hawaii."

I looked at the tomatoes in my hands. However weird Fabby's behavior was, the dinner party would take place in five hours, and there wasn't any time to waste.

"Well, you're here now," I said. Whatever had happened, we'd have to figure it out later. "Cut these in half and then take out the seeds with a spoon," I said, handing her the tomatoes. "Go as fast as you can. We've got a lot to do."

An hour later, we were doing pretty well, considering there were only two of us. Fabby set the table in the dining room upstairs and got out ingredients for me while I tried to keep everything moving on schedule. She was pulling bones out of the turbot when we heard Sophie shriek outside the kitchen.

"Fabienne! Are you in there?" she shouted as I heard her high heels *clack-clack* in the hallway. "How dare you—" Sophie appeared in the doorway like Darth Vader in a black pleather dress. "Where is she?" she demanded, stomping around the kitchen. "Where is my daughter?"

I was ready to protect Fabby by saying I'd forced her into K.P. duty, but then I noticed she wasn't there at all. "Nobody here but us turbots," I said, but Sophie didn't hear me because she was busy slipping on a fallen beet skin and hollering like a banshee.

"The *Américaine* is trying to kill me!" Sophie screamed as she ran out, limping on a broken stiletto heel.

"Sheesh," I muttered as I picked up the offending beet. She hadn't even hit the floor. "Come out, come out, wherever you are," I sing-songed. "Fabby?"

With an almost indiscernible *ping*, someone appeared on my prep counter. But it wasn't Fabby.

"Aunt Agnes?" I asked, astonished.

Agnes is an astral traveler. She works in California, at Stanford University, and commutes there via magic.

"Grandmother felt you were in some kind of difficulty," she said. "She sent me to you."

"I'm just kind of busy," I said as I ran my fingers along the turbot checking for pin bones. "But I'm glad you came."

Agnes frowned, annoyed. "I knew she was overreacting," she snapped, looking at her watch. "Well, I'm here now. May I help?"

I didn't recall ever having seen Agnes in a kitchen except to pour coffee or make toast. Still, I'd lost the only helper I'd had, so I was grateful for the offer. "Could you cut some onions?"

"Certainly," she said. "One? Two?"

"How about sixteen," I said, tossing them over to her. "Slice them a quarter inch thick." I gave her an apron, which made her look even more like Mary Poppins than she already did, with her long skirt and her hair in a prim bun.

While I made the soup and the batter for the *gougères*, I heard Agnes's determined chopping: *Thunk. Thunk. Thunk.* At about the speed you'd use to chop down a tree. I looked at the kitchen clock.

I was running out of time. Sweat was running down my face. Before I knew it, Sophie was shouting, "Hurry up! The guests have all arrived!"

"Oh, no," I moaned. This was more than I could handle.

Thunk. Thunk. Thunk.

I must have been staring, because Agnes looked up at me. "What is it, Katy?" she asked, as if she were inquiring about my day at school.

"We're not going to be done on time," I said, hearing my voice tremble.

"Of course we will. What do you need?"

I shook my head. "Hattie," I whispered. I hated to admit it, but this was all too much for me. "I need Hattie."

"Very well," Agnes said. And disappeared.

"No!" I shouted. "Don't go!"

But she'd gone. What had I done? I should never have said I wanted Hattie to help me when Agnes was *actually* helping. I'd just spoken without thinking. As usual.

I started on the potatoes, knowing that they weren't going to be cooked through by dinnertime. They had to be sautéed and then baked. Everything else could be done in a hurry, but the potatoes . . .

Ping. Agnes was back. And Hattie Scott was with her.

"Hattie!" I said, wanting to kneel at her feet and kiss her hand.

"Hmmph," Hattie grumbled. "Guess your fancy school didn't teach you everything."

"Agnes brought you?" I turned to Agnes. "I didn't know you could—"

"Less talk," Hattie said. A small smile crept across her face. "More . . . *magic!*"

With that, seventeen potatoes sailed across the room. I could feel the breeze as they passed.

I gasped. "Magic?" I whispered.

"Why are you so surprised?" Hattie asked crankily.

"It's just that . . . you never use magic at the restaurant."

"Of course I do. How do you think everybody gets what they need in Hattie's Kitchen? I just don't usually waste magic on things like chopping." Her eyes slid toward Aunt Agnes, who was still hacking onions at an elephantine pace. "But I can see that desperate times call for desperate measures."

"You're right," I said, closing my eyes in gratitude.

"Move out of the way," Hattie commanded as all the knives on the magnetic rack snicked free and fell upon the potatoes in midair, raining a pile of perfect dice into three huge skillets, which appeared out of nowhere.

"Now, where are those onions?" The onions flew off Aunt Agnes's cutting board.

"Excuse me," Agnes said with her hands on her hips. "I was cutting those."

Hattie narrowed her eyes at the uneven onion slices floating before her eyes. "Pitiful," she said. With a jerk of her chin, the knives cut the onions into thin, even slivers.

"Arrange the salads," she commanded as twenty turbot fillets wrapped themselves in parchment. With a laugh that made me feel good all over, I sent a knife flying toward the beets, carving them into rosettes nestled atop a bed of paper-thin pear slices dotted with dollops of blue-veined cheese shaped like tiny bees.

"Not bad," Hattie said as she batted a dozen airborne eggs into a bowl. I tossed over the flour and other dry ingredients while Hattie sent a big metal whisk into the mix. Then we both flicked five fingers at the dough, and an army of two-inch balls rolled through the air onto some baking sheets.

"I still need to trim the—"

Ping.

"Asparagus," I finished.

"Who's that?" Hattie demanded.

It was Fabienne.

"Where'd you go?" I shrieked.

"I . . . I don't know. The last thing I remember is my mother complaining. . . . Oh, *mon Dieu.*" She took in the sight of all the vegetables flying around us.

"I'll explain later, Fabby," I said.

"Get the potatoes and onions into the oven," Hattie commanded.

Tossing the asparagus into the air, where a peeler spinning like a Dervish trimmed off all the tough ends, I ran to the stove. Fabienne's problems would have to be sorted out later.

"Come here, dear," Aunt Agnes said, putting her arm around Fabby.

"She can serve!" Hattie shouted across the room.

"No, she can't!" I shouted back. "She's the guest of honor!" I sent Fabienne out to join the other diners.

"Then you do it, Agnes," Hattie amended.

"She can't either," I said, knowing that Sophie would raise a stink if I brought in outside help. "I'll do it. Just give me a clear path."

"And a clean apron," Hattie said, producing a black bistro apron like the ones we used in Hattie's Kitchen when we had to serve.

"Thanks, Hattie," I said. "The dining room's upstairs."

She sent six platters holding bowls of consommé shooting past me. "They'll be waiting for you at the top," she said as I climbed the steep flight of steps.

Everyone was served on time, and every course went without a hitch. By the time dessert was finished, all the entrée and appetizer dishes had washed themselves. Fabienne tiptoed into the kitchen just as the last platter slid into the cabinet.

"Oh, but you are so marvelous!" she said, hugging me.

"Thank you for such a wonderful dinner, Katy. I wish you had joined us."

"I couldn't. There was too much to do here," I said.

"And thank you, Madame Hattie."

"My pleasure," Hattie said. "Hope you enjoyed your dinner party."

"It was perfect," Fabby said. She turned to Agnes. "And thank you, too," she said shyly. "So much."

Agnes took her in her arms and patted her shoulder. Then Fabby left the kitchen, looking as if there were tears in her eyes.

"What was that about?" I asked.

Agnes smiled. "We were in Hawaii," she said softly. "I met her there. I'll bet you didn't even notice I was gone."

"Well . . ." It was true. In the rush of magical food preparation, I hadn't paid any attention to Aunt Agnes.

"Fabienne is a teleporter," she went on, "an astral traveler, like me. She just didn't know it until tonight. Every time she feels stressed, she winks out, but she can't control it."

I was stunned. "Winks out?"

"Travels."

"You mean she's a witch?"

"Of course she's a witch. Cowen can't do what she does."

"But . . . the others . . ."

"She may be the only one in her family," Agnes said sympathetically. "Perhaps after your experience here in France is done, you'll bring her back to Whitfield. I'll teach her how to use her gift to best advantage." She washed her hands. "Well, Hattie and I must be off."

Hattie grinned. "We're leaving the glasses and dessert dishes for you."

"That's okay. I appreciate your help."

"Don't expect it every day," Hattie grumbled.

"Actually," Agnes said, "we probably won't be able to come back at all, unless it's an emergency. Gram and I are going to Hakone, Japan. The hot springs will be good for her bones."

"Oh," I said. "Japan sounds wonderful."

"But you have Paris, dear."

Hattie snorted. "And your French cooking school."

I felt abashed. I hadn't served one dish that Hattie couldn't make in her sleep. And without her magic, not even one dish would have been served on time.

She lifted my chin with her strong brown hand. "Still, you did well tonight," she said. "And you've got a job waiting for you back home, whenever you're ready."

I closed my eyes. *Back home.* Yes. "Thanks, Hattie," I said. "Thanks for—"

But just then Agnes gave a curt nod of her head, and the two of them winked out.

CHAPTER • ELEVEN

Even though most of the dishes had already been washed and put away, there were still a lot of glasses, coffee cups, and dessert dishes on the table. By the time I got around to clearing everything away, the diners had all gone into one of the sitting rooms.

I don't know what I'd expected—maybe that I'd be called out to take a bow. I mean, even if they didn't like the food, the meal had been an awful lot of work. I thought at least Peter would have said something, maybe sent word back with Fabby. Something.

But I didn't remember seeing Peter when I'd served the dinner. True, I'd had a lot on my mind just then, but I would have noticed him. After all, I'd really cooked the whole meal for him.

I peered into the library. Fabby spotted me and came over to help me clear away the dishes.

"Better not," I said. "Your mom—"

But she just shook her head and kept working. I guessed Sophie had already gotten to her.

"Er . . . have you seen Peter?" I asked when we were back in the kitchen. "I don't remember seeing him at the dinner."

She blushed a deep red.

"What's the matter?"

Fabby took a deep breath. "I am sorry, Katy," she said. "Peter did not attend."

I looked away. That hurt more than anything anyone could have said about my cooking.

"Everyone loved the food," she said as we brought the dessert dishes into the kitchen.

"That's nice." I could hear the vinegar in my voice.

"No one has said anything to you because my mother did not mention that you made the meal."

I looked up, squinting. I could hardly believe it. "But it was her idea! She said . . ."

"I know. When I tried to tell them, she interrupted me. And when I tried again, she sent me from the table."

"I thought the dinner was in your honor."

"That was her excuse. She does not care anything for me. I only came down from my room now to talk with her. To tell her that you should have been invited to eat with us. To say—"

"Don't bother," I said. "I was stupid to listen to her in the first place."

"But—"

"Do me a favor, Fabby. Just pretend nothing's wrong, okay? There isn't anything I can do now anyway. Just . . . leave me to myself."

She looked tragic. "You do not want me to help with the dishwashing?"

"No. I'm fine," I said. "Really."

She nodded in understanding and touched my shoulder. "I'm sorry," she whispered.

I shrugged and put on some rubber gloves. At this point, I was too demoralized to conjure up any magic. All I wanted was to get this day over with.

After Fabby left, I let the noise of the running water cover up my self-pitying sobs as I washed an endless stream of stemware.

Okay, so I was being a drama queen, but it wasn't as if anyone was there to see me. I just felt bad. And it wasn't that no one had complimented me, or even that Sophie hadn't mentioned me. It was that Peter hadn't shown up. If he had, he would have been with me now, washing up together like old times.

But the old times were gone, I guessed. Old times, old friends, old promises . . .

"Everything sucks!" I yelled in a welter of soapsuds.

"I beg your pardon?"

Oh, *merde*, it was Belmondo. "Nothing," I said quickly, wiping my hand over my eyes.

He grinned. "Is this a disguise?" he asked, touching my face and coming away with a handful of bubbles.

Great, I thought. As if having the worst life on the planet weren't bad enough, I also happened to look like a Kentucky colonel.

"Your meal was delicious," he said.

"Did Fabienne—"

"No," he said. "I have dined here many times. Mathilde is a terrible cook." He laughed and shook his head. "But seriously, tonight the food was prepared with care, with passion. I thank you for sharing your passion with me."

I didn't know what to say. "Uh, no problem," was the best I could do.

And then, before I could stop him, Mr. Beautiful World stuck his hands into the dishwater and started singing "Edge of Glory" in French. He sounded good, too.

I laughed. "Where did you learn to do that?"

He shrugged. "I do it every weekend," he said. "At a club in the Latin Quartcr."

"You're a singer?"

"Guitarist, mostly. The club is called Mozambique. We can go there, if you like. A friend is subbing for me tonight."

That took me by surprise. "Oh," I said. "Okay. I'll go sometime."

"Not sometime. Now."

"Right," I said, laughing. "Just let me get my evening bag."

"You can change clothes," he said.

I stood there for a few seconds, blinking. He couldn't be serious.

"Go ahead. I'll finish here."

"Now? Are you kidding me?"

"No," he said, as if he were suggesting a cup of coffee at the kitchen table. "Hurry up. We can still catch the second set." He grinned. "Of my band, Eterna."

"No," I protested. "I can't."

"Yes, you can." He pinched my nose. It was the strangest gesture. I couldn't help but laugh. He did too.

And then I thought of Peter. I'd never gone out with anyone else. What would he say?

Oh, you mean what would he say after he comes back from wherever he's been during the dinner you spent all day cooking?

"No!" I looked up. Belmondo was staring at me. "I mean . . ."

"You mean yes," he said.

I looked back at him for a long moment. "I mean yes," I said quietly, and went upstairs.

What are you doing? I asked myself as I was looking through my nearly empty closet. I didn't even know how old Belmondo was. Out of school, for sure. Maybe even out of college. Fabby had said he was the landlord of the building where we lived.

Well, so what? That didn't make any difference. It's not like I was dating him or anything.

Oh, no? What do you call going to a club with a guy at eleven o'clock at night? Non-*dating?*

"Just hanging out," I said out loud as I got into my only good pair of jeans. I pulled a tank top over my head. Not very stylish for Paris, but still better than an apron and rubber clogs. I'd brought a pair of strappy heels with me that I hadn't worn since I got to France, and I put them on too. Then I brushed my hair and applied some red lipstick that a friend had forced on me before I left Whitfield.

When I checked myself out in the mirror, I was pretty surprised. I looked *good.* At least, I thought so, although I was sure Belmondo (Was that his first name, or his last?) was used to being with girls who were lots cuter. Still, I didn't usually look like this at all. The heels, the lipstick, a smear of charcoal eyeshadow, my hair hanging down almost to my waist . . .

What would Peter say?

Maybe that he's sorry. Maybe that he's missed me. Or maybe that he just didn't think anyone else would want to go out with me.

I saw myself blushing in the mirror. Peter obviously didn't care what I did.

So maybe I didn't either.

CHAPTER • TWELVE

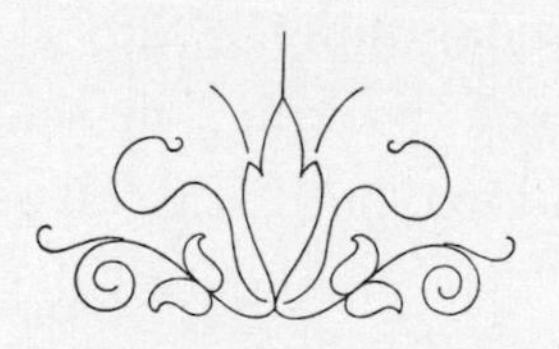

Mozambique was, without doubt, the coolest place I'd ever been. There was a long line outside, but we went right to the front of it, and the guard or whoever—he looked like Channing Tatum, with muscles popping out all over the place—just smiled at Belmondo and nodded at me, and we breezed in like celebrities.

Belmondo *was* kind of like a celebrity there. I guessed it was because he was a musician in the house band. Girls kept trying to come over to talk to him all night, but every time they got near our table, some serious-looking guy would intercept them and shoo the girls away.

"Did you ask those guys to do that?" I asked. "You know, the . . ."

He looked over his shoulder, where a gorgeous blond was waving frantically at him. He turned back to me without acknowledging her. "I want to spend my time here with you," he said. "Not with her. Not with any of them." I felt as if my heart had dropped into my stomach.

"But . . . why?" I really wanted to know, although I spoke so quietly that I didn't think he'd even hear me in that noisy place.

He shook his head with this kind of half smile. "You don't even know, do you," he said.

Well, that was true. I didn't.

"It's because of your cooking," he said, smiling.

I knew he was joking, but I still felt as if I would die from joy. "Champagne?" He pronounced it with three syllables, with a little "nyuh" at the end.

"Um . . . I don't think so," I said, even though I knew how lame I sounded. Oh, God, it was my Mom Mentality again, that cautious, unattractive characteristic that had made Peter lose interest in me. Why couldn't I drink one damn glass, I berated myself. Then I'd know. Maybe it would be fun. It probably would be fun. And Belmondo was probably a good person. There'd be nothing to worry about, and no one would ever have to know. Yes? Yes, yes, yes . . .

"Are you sure?" he asked.

I took a deep breath. "I'm sure," I said. "No champagne for me." Gaa. What a toad.

He sent away the server and then stood up. *Here's where you find your own taxi,* I told myself, but he didn't leave. Instead, he leaned down close to my ear and said, "Very well. If you will not drink, then you must dance."

I could feel my heart pounding in my chest as Belmondo led me onto the dance floor. The band had switched from funky blues to a beautiful ballad. I was nervous, so I tried to pretend I was just having fun, but at one point I let my head touch his shoulder and I closed my eyes. At that moment, I felt like nothing bad would ever happen to me again as long as I stayed inside the circle of his arms.

"I don't think you know how beautiful you are," he said softly.

I felt myself blushing from the top of my head down to my toes. I smiled at him, and he smiled back, and I felt my stomach drop out of my body again.

And then something weird happened. A butterfly flew between us. Right between our faces.

"What . . . ," I started, but Belmondo only laughed and pointed to the section where the tables were.

"It's Joelle," he said.

Sure enough, there was my housemate, her face framed by a chic brunette bob with long bangs and a pair of dangly diamond earrings. She was holding a cigarette in a long gold holder while a male model type looked at her adoringly.

I was trying to process what it all meant when Belmondo blew Joelle a kiss and a frog appeared on the table in front of her. With a disdainful expression, she tapped it with her cigarette holder and it disappeared.

"You . . . ," I whispered breathlessly. "You're all . . ." I lowered my voice until it was barely audible. ". . . *witches*," I finished.

"*Mais oui!*" he said, beaming. "Although, I admit, not very good ones." He rolled his eyes. "That butterfly was the extent of Joelle's magic. She's not like you."

"Me?"

He laughed. "Are you going to pretend with me?"

Our eyes met. *Belmondo's one of them, too. Like me.*

"No," I whispered in his ear while we danced. "I am too."

"I know," he said, holding me close to him. "I can almost taste it in the air around you." He breathed in deeply. "Everything about you is magic." His breath tickled my ear. "You are made of it, Katy. Powerful, pure . . . so beautiful."

Suddenly I felt as if I were watching myself. And there I was, dancing with this beautiful man who thought *I* was beautiful.

Magic, he'd called me. As far as I was concerned, everything about this night was magical. While we danced, I flicked five fingers at the ceiling, and a thousand stars appeared. It was nothing special, just elementary magic that even children in Whitfield can do, but the crowd sighed in appreciation. I knew I probably shouldn't have been showboating, even though I didn't think any cowen would believe it had been anything but a staged effect.

Belmondo loved it. "You make me happy to be alive," he said. Then we stopped dancing. He pulled me closer to him, and I knew he was going to kiss me. Part of me really wanted to—well, at least 90 percent of me wanted to—but the other 10 percent won out. I backed away.

It wasn't that I was afraid, or even that I was a prude, although a lot of people would have thought so. It was Peter. Peter was the only guy I'd ever kissed, the only guy I'd ever loved. If I was going to get involved with someone else, I wanted to be sure I didn't love Peter anymore.

And I wasn't sure. No matter what had happened between us, I knew I still loved him. Kissing anyone else would feel like betrayal.

"Are you all right?" Belmondo held me at arm's length and studied my face. "I'm fine," I said. "Really . . ." But I had to stop talking, because my eyes were welling with tears.

"*Pardon*," Belmondo said softly. "How crude I am."

"No, it's not . . . you . . ."

"Shh." He held both my hands. "We'll sit down, okay?"

I nodded.

"With Joelle and her friend?" he suggested.

Oh. Joelle had never been particularly nice to me. Well, not nice at all, really. Whenever we were in the same room together, I'd see her looking at me and talking to someone—usually Sophie—behind her hand. The two of them seemed to make a point of sneering at my clothes or wrinkling their noses when I'd come back after cooking school, as if I smelled bad. "Sure," I said brightly. I didn't want him to think of me as a total baby.

"*Chèri*," Joelle said, clearly talking to Belmondo. Then she went on in French, which sounded liquid and beautiful the way she spoke it, and gestured with her cigarette in its long holder. An ash flew off and landed on my tank top. Joelle ignored it, but Belmondo blasted her with his own rapid-fire French.

He sounded really angry. Joelle blanched for a moment, but then recovered faster than I ever would have, and turned to me. "Darling, forgive me," she said in English. "I forget you are a foreigner."

Just then the cocktail waitress came back and whispered something in Belmondo's ear. He looked over at the stage, where the band was playing. The lead singer motioned broadly and spoke into the mike. I knew enough French to understand that he was inviting Belmondo to come up and play with them.

A cheer rang out from the crowd.

"Oh, no," Belmondo said, resting his head in his hands.

"Go ahead, darling," Joelle said, touching his neck tenderly. "Everyone is calling for you."

Oh God, no, I thought. *Don't leave me here with Joelle. Don't . . .*

But he did. I guess he had to, with everybody shouting and stomping and clapping. He shrugged apologetically and stood up. "I won't be long," he said before leaving.

Which left me with Joelle, who managed to tear her eyes away from Belmondo long enough to glance at me as if she were observing a hair on her ice cream. I tried to smile. She introduced me to her date, Jacques, who thrust out his chin disdainfully, lit a cigarette of his own, and blew the smoke in my face. Charming.

"So," Joelle said, drumming her fingers on the table. "You are Belmondo's new *amant*?" she asked.

"What? Er, no," I said.

"But then how have you . . ." She stubbed out her cigarette. "Never mind. *Je m'en fou.* So," she continued, admiring her manicure, "how is it you come to this place with . . ." She nodded toward Belmondo, who was tuning a guitar onstage.

"Well . . . ," I waffled. Part of me wanted to slap her and stomp off, but I didn't want to get all heated over what was probably Joelle's naturally obnoxious personality. Besides, I understood that she might have felt trumped when I'd shown up her paltry butterfly magic with my canopy of stars. "Not really," I explained. "I was washing up after dinner, and—"

"Ah, the dinner. Yes. Very nice." As an afterthought, she flashed me a big smile. "Sophie told me that you cooked."

"Then you were the only one she told," I said.

She waved me away. "In France, we do not ask who cooks. That is unimportant."

"Then why did she tell you?"

Joelle blinked a few times, as if she were unable to compute what I was saying. Then she turned to Jacques, who had obviously been waiting for her to pay attention to him because he responded by grabbing her in a passionate embrace. She practically had to knock him out with her purse to make him stop. Meanwhile, onstage Belmondo had begun playing the guitar that one of the musicians had offered him.

He was wailing. I was shocked at how good he was. His sound was like a cross between Dan Auerbach of the Black Keys and Jimi Hendrix—dark, bluesy, *American*. "Wow," I said.

"He is very fine, *non*?" Joelle asked. "All the women love him. And he loves them." She laughed, high, tinkly, and refined.

"Oh," I said. I didn't want to talk during Belmondo's performance.

"He and I are very close," she said, looking smug. Then, as if a thought had accidentally wandered into her brain, she blinked twice and her face brightened. "I know!" she exclaimed.

Jacques, who apparently spoke no English, must have misunderstood her enthusiasm, because he grabbed her again, lips thrust forward. I tried not to watch, but I think Joelle elbowed him in the neck.

She cleared her throat and turned back to me. "I know!" she repeated with the exact same inflection as before.

I turned to her wearily. I didn't want to talk. I wanted to listen to Belmondo, not Joelle.

"We shall all go out together!" She clapped her hands together in a parody of sincerity. "Tomorrow. Yes?"

All? Who did she mean by *all*? My eyes slid toward Jacques, who was groping his way toward Joelle's face again.

"We shall show you the sights of Paris!" she exclaimed. "You can see Belmondo again, yes?"

"Belmondo's going to come?"

"Of course!" she chirped. "Belmondo, others . . ." She looked over her shoulder at Jacques. "You will make many friends, okay? I will arrange everything."

"Uh, okay," I said just as Belmondo finished playing. So I'd missed the end of his gig.

It was all downhill after that. Jacques kept groping Joelle, Joelle flirted with Belmondo, and I was getting really tired. When I checked the time, it was nearly two in the morning, and I was tired from cooking all day.

"I think I'd better take you home," Belmondo said. I nodded. Joelle wanted to come with us, but he put her off.

"You were really good," I told him in the car, which was, by the way, a sea-green Jaguar.

He smiled like it didn't matter that he was a brilliant guitarist and a world-class singer.

"How long have you been playing?"

"A long time," he said.

"Belmondo?"

"Yes, *Katarine*?"

I liked how that sounded. "Are you . . . are you our landlord?"

He laughed out loud. "I suppose," he said, pulling up on the street in front of the house. "My family has owned this building for the past several hundred years."

"Several *hundred*?"

He shrugged. "Europe is ancient," he said, his voice drawing me closer. "Our culture is ancient. Our souls are ancient."

"Er . . . okay." I cleared my throat. It was very hard to be so close to him. "But there was one other thing—" I began.

"Yes," he said, taking my hand. "Always for you, my answer is yes."

I was going to ask him what his first (or last) name was, but at that moment I saw Peter climbing the front steps to the house. "I'd better go," I said, suddenly nervous. Belmondo and I weren't doing anything wrong, but I still felt as if I were betraying Peter.

"I'll drive you to the door," he said.

"No!" I looked back at Peter. "That is, I'll walk."

Belmondo knew what was going on. He sighed. "Do you love him?"

I swallowed. "Yes," I said hoarsely. "I'm sorry. I wish I didn't." He started to get out of the car, but I stopped him. "Just let me go," I said.

He nodded reluctantly as I sprang open the door and ran after Peter. Halfway across the courtyard, though, I turned around and looked back at Belmondo. He was standing outside the car, his head bowed.

I forced myself to turn away. *Tonight didn't mean anything,* I told myself.

Over and over.

CHAPTER • THIRTEEN

"Peter!" I shouted as I sprinted up the marble steps. "Wait up!"

He turned around in time to see Belmondo's Jag speed down the street. "Who's that?"

I ignored him. "Where've you been?" I demanded.

He smiled crookedly. "Brussels," he said. "Can you believe it?" He stuck his key in the door. "There's a trucking company—"

"Why didn't you come to my dinner?"

"What? What dinner?"

"Sophie said you'd be there," I said as he pushed the heavy door open. Brazilian samba music was playing, nearly drowned out by the voices of people who'd had too much to drink.

Peter closed the door again so the two of us were alone outside. "She didn't tell me anything," he said. "Not that I could have come anyway."

"Right," I said abstractedly. I tried to remember exactly what Sophie had said. *Peter should see your talent.* Yes, that was it. She hadn't said he'd attend the dinner; only that he *should*. Very clever.

He put his hands on my shoulders. "Did you cook?"

I nodded, trying not to show how humiliated I felt.

"Was it good?" he asked softly.

I nodded again.

He pulled me close to him and held me. At first I just stood there with my hands hanging at my sides, but after a couple of minutes I put my arms around him, too.

"I'm sorry," he whispered.

"Not your fault."

The moon was young and thin as a fingernail paring. I could feel Peter's heart beating.

"We're good, then?"

"Yes," I breathed.

"Who was that guy?"

I felt as if a jolt of electricity shot through me. My throat suddenly went so dry that I couldn't speak, so I just shrugged.

"What's that supposed to mean?" Peter asked. There was an edge to his voice.

I pushed open the door again and went inside, my heart thumping with guilt.

Jeremiah and Sophie and some others were standing in the foyer. "Peter, darling!" Sophie called, brushing past me to kiss Peter on both cheeks.

He was blushing fiercely. I didn't know if that was because of Sophie's attentions or his anger with me.

"I'm glad the two of you were able to get together," she

said, smiling at me. "Jeremiah told me that he and Peter would be out of town until late tonight, but I forgot all about it, silly goose that I am."

I narrowed my eyes at her. "You did it on purpose," I seethed between clenched teeth.

Sophie batted her eyelashes at me. "I'm sure I don't know what you mean," she said sweetly. "You certainly didn't seem very distressed when you left with Belmondo."

I felt Peter's gaze locking onto me, but I couldn't meet his eyes.

"Are you feeling well, dear?" Sophie asked, digging her barb in even deeper. "Perhaps it's past your bedtime."

Without another word, I pushed past her and headed toward the stairs leading to my bedroom.

"Oh, Katy!" Joelle had just come in. "Don't forget about tomorrow!" she called after me.

CHAPTER • FOURTEEN

"Shall we go?" Joelle asked the next afternoon. The others she'd invited on our outing murmured and rose. Annabelle, dressed in a sky-blue silk blouse and red polka-dot shorts, stretched languorously, unfolding her lanky frame from the antique chair where she was sitting. Her boyfriend, Rémy, and Jacques, hovering protectively over Joelle, headed for the door. "Well, come on." She was talking to me.

"No, it's okay," I said. Talk about awkward. After the confusing events of yesterday, the last thing I felt like doing was trolling around the streets of Paris with Joelle and her friends. Belmondo hadn't even shown up, which I supposed was a good thing, after the uncomfortable rift his presence had caused between Peter and me. I didn't know why I'd agreed to this sightseeing tour in the first place. Now here I was, tagging along with two couples I barely knew and didn't much like. "I think I'll just—"

"Of course you'll come," she said, showing me feral

teeth. "We're doing this for you, *Katarine*," she said, using Belmondo's name for me.

The four of them practically dragged me to Joelle's Peugeot, which she drove as if it were a ride in an amusement park. "You must see our beautiful city!" she shouted as the Peugeot screeched around a corner on two wheels. "At least the most interesting part."

"Which . . ." I swallowed. "Which part is that?" I asked, hoping with all my heart that her answer would be *here*.

To my amazement, it was. In another second, she pulled the car over near one of the ancient bridges that cross the Seine, and everyone climbed out.

"Why, the sewers, of course."

I stopped in my tracks. "You're going to . . . the *sewers*?"

"Yes!" Annabelle shouted as she ran toward the street. "Come on, it's wonderful fun!"

I'd read about the tour through the Paris sewers and, frankly, it didn't seem that fascinating to me, especially since the guide books all warned about the long lines to get in. I looked around. There was no one. "Are you sure this is the place?" I asked.

"The tourist entrance is in the fourteenth arrondisement," Joelle said knowledgeably. "But we're going another way. It'll be fun."

The four of them ran giggling like schoolchildren through the streets until they came to an old bridge. Beside it were steps leading down to a wide sidewalk running parallel to the river.

"Hurry up!" Joelle called, waving us forward like a general commanding her troops. She leaped over the guardrail, high heels and all, and raced down the embankment into some dusty weeds. Whooping and shouting, the others followed her as she ran toward the underside of the bridge and, presumably, the secret entrance to the sought-after sewers.

I had my doubts—walking though the bowels of a thousand-year-old city hadn't exactly been on my bucket list—but if Jacques wasn't worried about his eight-hundred-dollar loafers, I guessed my Converse high tops were safe.

Once we were under the bridge, Joelle looked around furtively before summoning the rest of us to the far corner where, after our eyes got used to the darkness, we were able to see a door of sorts. That is, it was a slab of stone covered in vines that resembled a door, except there was no knob or knocker.

"Well, go on, move it!" Joelle hissed. The two men jumped to comply, grunting as they slowly slid the slab of ancient stone far enough to reveal an opening.

"How do you know about this place?" Annabelle asked, waving her long fingernails in front of her in case of spiderwebs.

"Belmondo showed me." Joelle turned toward me. "He's full of surprises." She batted her eyelashes.

I was glad it was dark in there, so she didn't see me blushing. To tell the truth, though, I wasn't thinking about Belmondo at all at that point. I just had a creepy feeling about this place, and couldn't wait for Joelle and her friends to get their fill of it.

"The sewers are that way," she whispered in my ear. I nearly jumped out of my skin. Twenty feet in, it was impossible to see anything. I wished I had someone to hold on to, but I wasn't about to show these people how afraid I was.

"I think we turn right here." Her voice was farther away now.

"Where?" I asked, nearly shouting.

"Right about where you are," Joelle said helpfully. "Put your hand on the wall and follow it."

That was the last thing I wanted to do, but I guessed she had a point. My hand might encounter something disgusting, but at least I wouldn't get lost.

Or I thought I wouldn't, until I reached a crease in the wall. It wasn't an angle, exactly, but a turn of some kind. I followed it for a time before realizing that I wasn't hearing the others any longer.

"Joelle?" I called experimentally. "Joelle? Hello, anyone?"

There was no answer.

Breathing hard, trying not to panic, I reached into the pocket of my jeans and pulled out the house key Marie-Therèse had given me the day after I'd moved in. Attached to it was a little rubber pig I'd bought at a junk store on the way home from school. On top of the pig's head was a metal button that turned on a light when pressed. Unfortunately, it also made a loud oinking sound, which filled the cavernous stone tunnel where I was walking.

The thin beam of light didn't show me much—only that I was standing in a virtual spiderweb of intersecting passageways. God only knew how many times I'd turned without knowing it. And where I'd become separated from the others.

"Joelle?" I called again, hearing the note of fear in my voice. There was no response. "If this is some kind of joke, please stop," I pleaded.

But I had to face it. They'd left me. I was all alone.

"Okay," I breathed, trying to pull myself together. "You got here by following the right wall, so you can get back by following the left wall, right?" I aimed my beam at the other side of the walkway. It oinked as I crossed a swampy, wet stream to make my way there. Despite the silly noise, I kept the beam trained ahead of me as the tunnel bent and twisted and then headed downhill. Before I knew it, I'd wandered into a section where there was no light at all except for the feeble glow of my pig light with its accompanying grunting.

"Oh, man," I moaned. None of this looked familiar. Granted, there hadn't been enough light to really look at the tunnel since I'd entered it, but I knew it never went in the strange directions I was headed now. Still, I didn't know what else to do, so I kept walking, allowing the oinking of the rubber pig to soothe me into a state of optimistic denial.

And then three things happened. One was that it occurred to me—duh—that I should have followed the *right* wall back, since that was the wall that had led me into the sewers. Instead, I'd stupidly crossed to the other side and gone down a whole series of new passageways. I couldn't have found my way back now if I'd had a map.

Oink, oink, oink. The second thing was that the light from my keychain was getting dimmer by the second. I guess the flashlight built into a two-inch rubber pig hadn't been meant for long-term use. Dimmer . . . dim . . . out.

Oink.

And then the third thing: Just before the faint light oinked out into total blackness, I saw a gaping hole in the ground right in front of my feet. A second later, I was falling into it, screaming.

• • •

I landed hard on my rear, but, aside from having the breath knocked out of me, I didn't seem any the worse for wear. The problem was the darkness. If I'd thought it had been dark before, this was a whole new dimension of darkness. I tried holding my hand in front of my face. I couldn't see it.

"Oh, boy," I said out loud.

I didn't know how far I'd fallen, but I knew I was at a whole different level from where I'd been before. And where had that been? The sewer? Could I somehow have fallen into a place *beneath* the sewer?

Keep it together, I told myself. It wasn't all bad. I was still in one piece.

That was the only thing that wasn't bad. I'd lost my keys, along with the pig flashlight.

But you're a telekinetic, I told myself. Yes. Yes. I could summon my keys back to me.

"Pig!" I shouted, and I heard a whizzing sound and a single loud *oink!* as the light illuminated the keys that had struck the sound button as they flew. I reached up and grabbed them before they sailed past. There are relatively few times in life when my particular talent comes in handy, but this was one of them.

I pressed the button on the pig's head. Nothing happened. I'd been lucky. Without the tiny amount of reserve power in the pig, the keys would have zinged past me in the dark and been lost forever.

On all fours, I swept the ground around me. Since I had no idea which direction I should go, I just started crawling, hoping that sooner or later I'd run into a wall that I could follow.

I'd traveled about four feet when I encountered something

that felt like sticks. One dug painfully into the heel of my hand; another was under my knee. They were suddenly everywhere, as if I'd crawled into some underground forest. I explored one of the sticks with my fingers: it was smooth and dry, with knobs on both ends. Another was flat and curved; yet another was spiny. Finally I picked up one that wasn't a stick at all, but sort of globe-shaped, and I started to get nervous. Flicking obsessively at the light on my keychain, I finally elicited a faint sound from the pig that sounded more like a moan than an oink, accompanied by a very brief beam of light, which I aimed at the object in my hand.

It was a skull. And the sticks all around me were bones. Human bones.

With a shriek, I dropped it and scrambled away. That is, I thought I was moving away until I crashed into a mountain of bones that cascaded over my body until I was buried neck-deep in them.

I'd read about—and even seen photographs of—the catacombs, the big underground ossuary on the outskirts of the city that had been a tourist attraction since the late 1800s, but that was more or less an art exhibit, well lit, organized, and overseen by a staff of docents and historians. It wasn't anything like this random pile of decomposed dead people.

Whimpering, I waded through them, squeezing my pig light for all I was worth, hoping it had one or two more seconds of battery life left. Occasionally it emitted a tiny grunt and an increasingly feeble light showed me that I was slowly moving away from the weird repository of bones, until finally I had to admit defeat. The light was gone for good. And I was in the middle of a pitch-black tunnel somewhere in the bowels of Paris, with no idea how to get out.

Sitting down, I picked a bone out of my hair and sobbed, even though a part of my brain was rolling its brain-eyes and telling me to grow up. *Enjoying our tantrum, are we?* Katy Brain asked.

"Well, what am I supposed to do?" I yelled.

How about . . . anything, suggested Katy Brain with her usual sarcasm. *Like maybe try to find your way out of here, if I may be so bold.*

"Easy for you to say," I muttered.

Actually, you could follow that light.

"Light?" I craned my neck in all directions. "I don't see . . ." But wait, I *did* see. When I moved my head to the extreme left and squinted, the darkness wasn't quite as dark. Carefully, I began to move toward that place, wherever it was, more on instinct than vision, feeling the air around me lighten.

And I was right. After a few minutes I could actually see something like a curving wall overhead. I was in a tunnel, a second tunnel below the tunnel of the sewers. My ears popped. I was heading down still farther. And yet the tunnel continued to get infinitesimally brighter.

I stood up to my full height and saw my breath steaming in the cold air. I felt the skin of my legs stand up in gooseflesh. The tunnel veered off to the right, and the walls grew brighter. Light. There was definitely light ahead. I began to run.

And then I stopped in my tracks, feeling my heart jump into my throat.

There was something in the light. Something that stood on two feet like a man, but was bent over and covered with hair and making sounds like a wild beast.

A monster.

I turned around and doubled back to where the tunnel had branched, and plastered myself against the mold-covered wall. It was much darker here. My eyes had gotten used to a small amount of light. Now I was again as blind as I'd been when I first fell through the hole into this place.

In the silence, I heard the creature loping toward me, invisible in the darkness.

CHAPTER • FIFTEEN

It was close enough that I could hear it breathing.

Oh, God, I thought. *Oh God oh God oh God* . . . I didn't know anything about fighting—especially fighting something big and hairy and grunting louder than my pig ever did.

The pig! Except for a few euro notes in my pocket, it was all I had in my possession. Pressing myself against the stone wall, I ran my fingers up the little chain that connected the pig to my house key. I supposed I could stab the monster—or whatever the thing was—in the eye. That is, if I had any idea where its eye was. Meanwhile, I mentally scrolled through my inventory of magic to see if I knew anything that would give me an advantage in this situation.

I did know how to call objects to me, and if I yelled "stick!" or "rock!", I was sure those items would come flying in my direction. But I'd learned my lesson from calling for the pig: Rocks didn't come with penlights, and I couldn't see well enough in this darkness to be able to catch them once I called them to me. They could easily smack me on the side of my head or break my legs. No, I supposed the key would have to do.

I closed my eyes. I could always think better with my eyes closed, and in this situation, sight wasn't much of an option, anyway. Then I deliberately slowed my breathing, willing myself into the wall behind me, convincing myself that I was invisible.

This wasn't magic. It was something I'd done since I was little, trying to keep my dad from noticing me so I wouldn't have to spend my evenings or weekends taking sample SAT tests or listening to CDs like *Great Thinkers of the Eighteenth Century* or *Learn Romanian Now!* Sometimes it even worked.

So I was hoping and praying it would work now, as I disappeared into the wall.

The monster was coming toward me, questing. He moved slowly, his feet shuffling, turning from side to side in the darkness. Then he sniffed deeply, and I knew he was trying to smell me.

There wasn't any more time. I jumped out with my key poised like a knife inside my fist. With a scream, I attacked, feeling the key strike flesh.

The creature shrieked, and I attacked again, but this time I didn't make contact. Instead, I felt him rolling at my feet, sobbing and whimpering in terror.

"Hey," I said, but he just kept crying pitifully.

I knew it was my chance—probably my only chance—to get away, but I just couldn't leave him suffering like that.

"Gosh, I'm sorry," I said, leaning over him. "*Pardonnez-moi.*" As if apologizing in his language would make up for stabbing him. Still, I didn't have much experience with subterranean monsters. I didn't know what language he spoke, or what I could do to make things better. I didn't even know where I'd stabbed him. In the eye? God, I hoped not. In the darkness I felt for the wound inside his matted fur. He didn't object.

As it turned out, he wasn't exactly covered with hair. It was really long, but actually, it just grew from his head the way it did with everybody. A stream of blood, from what I could tell by touch, seemed to be coming from his neck. Judging from the amount of it, he needed a bandage. I knew money wasn't very sanitary, but that was all I had on me, so I slapped a euro note around the spot where it felt like the wound was bleeding the worst, and then I tore the bottom of my T-shirt to wrap it around his neck. I only hoped I got the right spot.

"We need light," I said. Then, translating in the hope that he might understand me: "*lumière.*"

"Ah," he said. At least that's what I thought he said. I jumped backward into a crouch, key at the ready. He shuffled around some more, and I realized how stupid I was acting. I doubted very much that I'd have to fight him again, since I hadn't *fought* him in the first place. I'd *attacked* him, plain and simple. He'd never done a thing except scare the bejezus out of me. For all I knew, he was just another lost soul wandering through the sewers, hoping to find a way out, just like me.

The question was, how long had he been wandering? Maybe he'd been searching for an exit for fifty years. Maybe living in the dark had made him hairy. Maybe that was my fate too.

Oh God.

Just then, he lit a match, illuminating a small circle for

a moment that showed his trembling hand trying to light a candle, which he held aloft. He was shaking so hard that I thought the match would go out before he finished the job, so I reached out to steady his hand. As the candlewick caught, I finally saw his face.

The first thing I noticed about him, aside from the fact that he was human—and that was a big relief, let me tell you—was that he was old. Really old, maybe older than anyone I'd ever seen. His eyes were filmy with cataracts, and his skin was as spotted as a fawn's. The white hair on top of his head was nearly gone, even though what grew on the sides hung down almost to his waist. Ditto his ears and nose. Well, those hairs weren't down to his waist, but they were long, and there were a lot of them. In the tricky light of the candle, he might have passed for a yeti, or some fairy-tale ogre.

But really, he was just an old man. He fumbled with the candle, then raised his hand with its swollen, arthritic fingers to touch the makeshift bandage I'd put on his neck.

"Let me help you," I said, tucking myself under his arm to help hold him up. "Where do you want to go? *Ou voulez vous aller?*"

He gestured with the candle. With every step, I became more aware of his frailty, and of the seriousness of his wound. "I think we ought to go to the hospital," I said in French, but he only smiled and shook his head.

"My home is not far," he said. "Thank you."

That made me feel like a total creep. I'd stabbed the poor old soul with a dirty key, and then staunched the wound with the equivalent of a dollar bill—possibly the filthiest thing on earth—and he was *thanking* me.

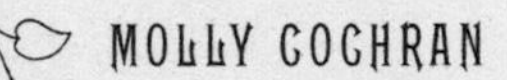

"I'm really sorry," I whispered. "I can't tell you how—"

"No, no. I surprised you."

Some excuse.

"How far . . . ," I began, but then I saw a glowing light off to the right. "Is that it?"

Here? I wondered. Was this old man saying he lived beneath the sewer?

He nodded.

CHAPTER • SIXTEEN

He lived in an alcove in the massive underground tunnel system. At one time, I guessed, it might have been a storage space for machinery or tools, although I couldn't imagine what sort of construction went on before the sewers were built. As we followed the glowing light of the candle, I watched the centuries-old stone change color from black to sandstone beige. It had been scrubbed, I realized, probably by the old man himself.

A few feet later, we walked through a short passageway into his living quarters. I was stunned.

It was a huge space, illuminated by a hundred candles perched on rough stones that jutted out from the walls, lending a golden glow to the area. It was filled with beautiful furniture. There were chairs with carved wooden arms and a fainting couch upholstered in thick green silk, a velvet ottoman with tassels, and a small rosewood writing desk. There were also gorgeous vases made of porcelain so fine you could see light through them, an ornate gold clock, and a variety of boxes made of wood, crystal, silver, and stained glass. On the far wall hung a large portrait of a beautiful woman dressed in the style of the Renaissance.

"This is . . . fantastic," I whispered, looking around. There was a huge cherrywood case filled with leather-bound books, some decorated with gold leaf. On the writing desk was a pen made from an actual feather, sticking out of a faceted crystal inkpot.

"I have lived here a long time," the old man said, peeling off the euro note on his neck and looking at it.

I ran over to him. "I'm sorry," I said again. How could I have been so carried away with the man's house—well, cave—that I'd forgotten he was injured? "Please let me help you." I looked around for a sink, but there was none. The closest thing I could find was a gilt-edged porcelain basin filled with clean water. "Can I use this?"

He held up a hand to stop me, but then relented with a sigh and sat down. There was a folded linen cloth near the basin, and I used that, dipped in the water, to clean his wound.

It wasn't that bad. I'd missed all the big blood vessels, apparently, because it had already stopped bleeding, but there was still dried blood all over him, not to mention the disgusting euro note and its cooties. "Do you have anything like . . ." I had to think. With Gram as a healer, I didn't have much need of medicines. ". . . iodine?"

He nodded and gestured toward an ornate gilded cabinet. From the looks of the rest of the room, I'd have thought the old guy's medical supplies might have stopped at eye of newt, but to my surprise he was well stocked with first aid necessities, ointments, bandages, and tape, and even a bottle of wound wash. I guessed he must bang himself up against those exposed stones fairly often.

He sat quietly as I applied the wound wash and then some Neosporin under a gauze bandage. "There," I said, admiring my work. He smiled and patted my hand. It was such a kind, forgiving thing to do, considering what a jerk I'd been. I kneeled in front of his chair so I wouldn't be looking down at him, and held his hand in both of my own.

"I know it doesn't do any good for me to keep apologizing, but . . . well, I'll never forgive myself for hurting you like that—"

"Nonsense," he said. "You were frightened. It was natural. You thought I was a monster."

I swallowed. That was exactly what I'd thought. "No," I lied. "You're nothing like—"

He laughed. "Of course I am. Who else would live underground, in a forgotten section of the *carrières*?"

"The whats?"

"Old limestone quarries, from the time of the Romans," he said. "These tunnels were here long before the sewers were built. No one even knew they existed until 1774, when a cave-in swallowed up a number of houses in the middle of the city."

"Were there . . . er, a lot of people in those houses?" I asked.

"I beg your pardon?" He frowned, his brows knitted.

I told him about the bones I'd crashed into.

"Oh, those!" He laughed, wheezing. "Yes, I'll bet you were scared silly! Still, they're less horrifying than when they were first placed there."

It seems that during the reign of Louis the Sixteenth, the city's cemeteries had grown so populous that the ground, overloaded with corpses, had begun to fester and stink. In the interests of hygiene, the remains of the cemeteries' residents were dug up under cover of night and "relocated"—that is, dumped—into one of a handful of street-level sewer openings.

"It was used during the Revolution, too," he said. "So many headless bodies, you know." He drew a finger along his neck. "Guillotined."

I swallowed, remembering the skull I'd held in my hand.

He laughed. "They're quite sanitary now, I believe," he said reassuringly. "Someone even organized a few thousand of them. Stacked them neatly and called them 'catacombs' for tourists to visit."

Ewww, I thought. I'd read about the catacombs, but I'd never thought of that ossuary as being filled with actual people. Dead people.

"But that area is fairly distant. Where you were, one finds only random bones, the undignified remains of the dead who cannot complain of their ill treatment."

"Er . . . right," I said. I cleared my throat. "So this place is beneath the sewers?"

"Far beneath," he said. "Although there are passageways into the sewers, and passageways to the street as well. One just has to know where to turn."

No kidding. "Do a lot of people come down here?"

"Alas, the *carrières* have become popular with some of the youth. They come down here to be daring, to have parties. Fortunately, none has ventured as far as here." He lowered his head and looked at me. "Unless you plan to tell them."

"Who, me?" That was a laugh. "I'd never have come down here in the first place if I hadn't been tricked into it."

"Oh?"

"Someone in the house where I live said she was taking me to see the sights of Paris, and then dumped me here. Oh. Excuse me. I didn't mean—"

"It's all right. I know this may not seem like an ideal habitation to many," he said, gesturing around the beautiful room. "Please, go on with your story."

I told him all about being double-crossed by Joelle and her stupid friends, hardly realizing that we'd been speaking French the whole time. There was just something about the old man—his easy acceptance of me, maybe, or the slowness of his speech, as if he had all the time in the world to listen to my tale of woe—that made me want to talk to him.

"So," he said, when I'd finished griping about Joelle. "What do you do in Paris, aside from wandering through the sewers?"

I blushed. "I'm taking a summer course at the Clef d'Or," I said.

"The cooking school? *Formidable!* And how did you come to be interested in *haute cuisine*?"

I told him about Hattie's Kitchen and Whitfield—minus the magic, of course—and Gram and Agnes and my friends at school. And Peter. "He's one of the main reasons I came here," I confessed. "He said I was acting like his mother."

"Is that so bad?"

"Well . . . *yes*," I said, and he laughed. I told him more about myself, about my dad and Chef Durant at the school, and about the strange people I'd ended up living with.

"They're all beautiful," I said.

He shrugged. "They are *Parisiennes*."

"Maybe, but I think it's more than that. That is, looking good seems to be the only thing they're interested in." I told him how Sophie had made her daughter Fabienne drop out of school at fifteen. "They're like some club or something," I went on. "They don't seem to do very much, but they're mysterious. Even the servants don't know anything about them, since they hire new staff every six months. It's hard to figure them out."

"A puzzle indeed," he said, hoisting himself out of his chair with difficulty. "May I offer you a cup of tea?"

"Oh. Sure," I said, catching up with him as he walked a few steps to a charcoal brazier that had coals burning in it. Even though it was June, it was cool in this place. He put a teakettle on top of the grate and, with great effort, shook out some loose tea into a pretty teapot. "Is this the only heat you have here?" I asked baldly.

"Unfortunately, yes," he said.

"But what about winter?"

He smiled. "I manage," he said.

He seemed to be busy concentrating on making the tea, so I wandered around the room, taking in the titles of the beautiful books that filled a wooden case.

"Jules Verne," I said.

"A first edition. Oh, dear, we need lemons. Pardon." He left the cave.

One of the books looked particularly interesting. It was bound in pebbled leather, with a design of leaves in gold along the spine. I took it out and opened it to the first page. There was no title, no author, and no publishing information. It wasn't even printed, but was handwritten in a beautiful script.

He was born Jean-Loup de Villeneuve, third son of the Duc du Capet, in the year 1155 under the rule of Louis VII, it began in French.

A handwritten novel? But who wrote it, the old man himself? Wouldn't that be—

Just then the binding of the book snapped in my hands. *Oh. My. God,* I thought as the book slipped from my fingers onto the floor, its pages fluttering like leaves around my feet.

"No," I moaned, picking up the pages as fast as I could. "Oh, nonononono . . ." I looked around wildly. I couldn't give it back to the old man in this condition. I knew I could fix it—somehow—but I'd need a little time. Just a day or two, just—

I heard his footfalls. I didn't know what to do. *What to do, what to do . . .*

Taking a deep breath, I stashed the book inside the back of my jeans and covered it with my T-shirt.

"Here we go. Lemons," he said, holding up two yellow fruits. "I keep perishable foods in a separate cave. You see, I have all the room in the world!" He laughed. I laughed harder. I laughed like a hyena, trying to cover up my shame and discomfort.

With palsied hands he passed me an exquisite porcelain cup filled with hot, clear tea. "Forgive me. I have no sugar or cream to offer you."

"No problem," I said, laughing some more. God, what a geek.

We strolled slowly back to his favorite chair and placed our teacups on a tiny table of filigreed wood inlaid with mother-of-pearl doves. I pulled up the ottoman beside him and swigged down my tea in one gulp.

"My, you must have been thirsty," he said. "Would you care for another?"

"Oh, no," I said, waving away the possibility of staying any longer than I had to. I'd loved being here before I'd ruined the old man's book, but now I just wanted to get away before I got caught.

"Er . . . how's the family?" I asked breezily.

"Long dead," he said.

Definitely the wrong question. "Sorry."

"No need. I enjoy my own company, my books."

I felt my stomach churn.

"I write, on occasion, the foolish thoughts of an old man."

He patted the arm of his chair. "I have the gift of time. That is something the young of the world do not understand. They want always to *do*, to act, to connect. But the old . . . we are content just to be. In that way we are like dogs, I suppose, living for the moment, salivating over an old bone that has no interest for anyone else." He smiled sweetly.

"I need to go," I said, standing up abruptly.

"Of course. You've taken too much time with me already."

"No, it's not that. It's . . ."

"Please. Don't explain. I've enjoyed our chat."

"I'll come back, I promise."

"Please do not," he said, gesturing for me to go through the arched entrance to his cave.

I didn't think I'd heard him correctly. "Do not come back?"

Holding a candle aloft, he led me back into the tunnels. "Do not come. Do not speak of me. Forget about this day. Please," he said.

"But why?" I was hurt. "Is it because I'm leaving? Am I rude?"

"No, no." He shook his shaggy head, smiling.

"Don't you like me?"

He clasped his hands together. "I like you very much, little one. But without doubt you will tell your friends about the charming old man who lives in the *carrières* surrounded by lovely antiques, and one day an enterprising young fellow will pay me a visit and kill me for my old clock. Do you understand?"

"I do." I bristled. "But I'm not like that. I can keep a secret." Hattie would have had a good laugh over that, since in Whitfield I was famous for being a class A blabbermouth. But this was different. His life depended on my silence. "I promise you, I'll never tell."

He looked skeptical. "Perhaps so, perhaps not," he said philosophically. "Either way, I have enjoyed your company."

"Please," I pleaded. "Don't say I can't come back. I have no other friends here. Even my boyfriend, Peter . . . well, he's too busy to spend much time with me. And I've hardly said two words to those awful women in the house, except for Marie-Therèse, who's really old. . . . Oh." I put my hand over my lips.

"And I am not?" he asked jocularly.

"Just let me come back." *Because I have to get this book back to you before you realize I've taken it.*

"Perhaps," he said. "I will let you know."

"How? I mean, okay. That is, I won't forget about you."

"Excellent," he said. "To be remembered kindly is the greatest sort of immortality." He pointed to a crack of light ahead. "Go through there."

It was then that I realized we hadn't been walking the way I'd come. He'd taken me in a whole different direction, and the distance from his cave to this exit had been much shorter than the other way.

"Wait," I said, stopping suddenly. "My name is Katy," I said. "Katy Ainsworth."

"Ah. I shall remember. Katy Ainsworth, student chef at the Clef d'Or, *amant* of the woefully insensitive Peter, enemy of the evil Joelle, and sometime confidante of Madame Marie-Therèse, despite the lady's advanced years. Have I got it right?"

I blushed. "Peter isn't really that insensitive," I said.

"I am happy to hear it. As for me, the name I was given at birth is no longer of any importance. You may call me by my chosen name, Azrael."

"Azrael?"

"An ancient name which is translated as 'whom God helps.' He bowed in a courtly manner. "At your service, mademoiselle."

CHAPTER
SEVENTEEN

Azrael . . . What a strange name.

His route out of the *carrières* led me to the ruins of an ancient stone building on the outskirts of a pocket park near the Rue des Âmes Perdues. Ecstatic that my walk home was miles shorter than the trek leading from the river, I entered the house in a great mood.

Which was immediately soured by the sight of Joelle, Annabelle, and Sophie in the main salon room. They were sitting on one of the long couches with their feet tucked beneath them, giggling and whispering as they watched me.

"You ran away from us!" Joelle called out with mock concern.

Marie-Therèse was also there, or else I would have ignored them and gone immediately upstairs to my room. But the old lady held her arms out to me, so I had to enter the salon and go to her, out of politeness. "My dear, are you all right?" she asked, giving Joelle a dirty look.

"Yes, poor thing," Joelle said. "All alone in the sewers!"

"Ick," Sophie said.

"*Mon Dieu*, the smell!" Annabelle stage-whispered, and the three of them laughed like that was the funniest thing they'd ever heard.

It took all the self-control I could muster not to run up and punch them both in their overly made-up faces, but I forced myself to smile and tell Marie-Therèse that I felt great. And then I turned to Joelle and said, "Sorry, I guess I got lost for a minute, but I found my way out again. No problem."

"How resourceful you are," Joelle said, barely concealing her glee. "But it was such a long way away. You must be exhausted."

Marie-Therèse made an exasperated sound. "I'll bring a cup of tea up to your room," she said, and left, staring daggers at the gorgons on the sofa.

So they don't know about the other exit, I realized. And they didn't know about Azrael.

Good.

I nodded to them by way of farewell. They didn't speak. Sophie wrinkled her nose so I'd get the message that I smelled like a sewer.

Yeah, and you smell like a rat, I thought, heading upstairs.

The first thing I did when I got to my room was to take Azrael's dismembered book from the waistband of my pants and lay the pages on my bed. A couple of them were creased, but at least none were torn. The problem was that the pages weren't numbered. Plus the text was in Old French, which meant I had to read each page carefully to figure out which came next.

I remembered the beginning: the guy's name and when he was born, or something. I shuffled through the pages until I found the opening passage beneath the heading

Paris, A.D. 1172
The Gift

He was born Jean-Loup de Villeneuve, third son of the Duc du Capet, in the year 1155 under the rule of Louis VII.

If he had been the firstborn son, Jean-Loup would have inherited his family's vast estate. His mother had been born a Capet, first cousin to King Louis the Seventh, and had been raised within the fortifications of the royal chatelet. But it was his brother, a brainless bully, who was slotted to become the next duke.

The second son, a pious coward, had been groomed for the clergy from childhood. The Church had received a fortune from the de Villeneuve family to ensure that the boy would be elected archbishop before his twentieth birthday.

That left Jean-Loup, the third son of the de Villeneuves, with two choices: He could become a soldier, or he could enter the University of Paris for a six- to twelve-year stint at the School of Arts before committing to further study in medicine, law, or theology.

The choice was easy. Jean-Loup had always loved reading, and the prospect of a life of learning filled him with joy, despite the hardships of student life. Most of the classrooms at the acclaimed University of Paris—one of the first in all Europe—were no more than stone chambers with a single chair for the professor's use. Students sat for hours on piles of hay, with only their own body heat for warmth. Meals and lodgings were not provided, and many a student spent his nights wandering the streets searching for garbage to eat and a place out of the elements to sleep.

Nevertheless, in his first year, when Jean-Loup was seventeen, he proved himself a worthy scholar in all the required fields: grammar, arithmetic, geometry, and music. In his second year, he studied rhetoric, dialectics, astronomy, and alchemy, the theory behind turning base metal into gold.

This class seemed like a puzzling choice to be included in the university's illustrious roster because no one at the school actually made *gold, or was even expected to. Instead, the alchemy classes were devoted to studying fourth- or fifth-hand translated accounts of the efforts of alchemists in ancient Egypt, China, and India, which had also failed to produce gold. Although the class was wildly popular among students, Jean-Loup concluded that the course was more in the area of philosophy than science, with a dollop of wishful thinking thrown in. It also attracted more than one charlatan who tried to impress the professors by producing gold through sleight of hand. These students were summarily dismissed as pranksters who had shown disrespect for the somber tone of the university.*

Alas, this was how Jean-Loup de Villeneuve came to discover the great rare gift that had begun mankind's pursuit of alchemy in the first place.

"An ancient text from Egypt, translated into Greek as The Unknowableness of Magic*, states that alchemy, like all other*

forms of magic, cannot be achieved unless the practitioner is himself a magician with a proclivity for making gold." The professor, the venerable Anselm of Paris, smiled to show his polite disdain for the misguided views of the barbarian Egyptians as he set down the worthless book. His students followed suit, smirking in imitation of men of the world.

"However, as we of modern sensibilities are aware," he went on urbanely, "alchemy does not fall under the realm of magic. Magicians are sorcerers, evil beings who are put on earth to do the bidding of Satan, and can be defeated only by death or the pious works of the true Church. Alchemy is *science.*" He raised his index finger in the air for emphasis. "Therefore, those who study and practice alchemy are not *magicians*"—he crossed himself at the utterance—"but rather, men of intellect."

"Too bad," whispered Jean-Loup's seatmate, Alphonse Patou. He was twirling a *dénier,* a silver coin worth one-twelfth of a *sou,* in his fingers. "I was hoping to turn this into next month's rent."

"Do I detect *levity* in my classroom?" Professor Anselm hissed. Alphonse froze.

"Monsieur Patou?"

"N-no," Alphonse replied. "No levity." He was in the process of pocketing the coin when Anselm held out his palm impatiently. With a sigh, the student placed the *dénier*—his last—in the professor's hand.

"Good heavens, I don't believe your coin even has the worth of a common silver *dénier,*" the professor said. There were many counterfeit coins circulating in Paris. "My guess is zinc."

"Figures," Alphonse said. "I have the luck of a convict."

"You would do well to take it to the authorities."

"Yes, Professor," Alphonse said with a sigh.

"But your wretched coin will serve my purpose," Anselm said. "Now, according to our Egyptian friend," the professor went on, nodding at the discarded book, "one ought to be able to produce gold just by thinking about it. Allow me to demonstrate." He closed his hand around the coin, then shut his eyes tightly. "I am at this moment concentrating very diligently on turning Monsieur Patou's dénier into a gleaming golden nugget, and I would appreciate it if you would all do the same."

The students laughed. They all loved Professor Anselm for his humor and egalitarian ways, but they knew not to go too far. He was, after all, a professor and, as such, in the employ of the Church.

He made a show of grunting and pretending to wipe sweat off his brow. "Oh, how I have concentrated!" he exclaimed to the guffaws of his students. "Have you? Go on now, focus!"

Dutifully, the students closed their eyes and murmured exhortations that the coin be turned into gold. Like Alphonse and most of the other students at the university, Jean-Loup de Villeneuve was virtually penniless, despite the exalted position of his family. A university education was costly—perhaps too costly, many parents felt, to waste on a younger son. And so, while listening to his stomach rumbling against the drone of the class's efforts to concentrate, he began to fantasize about the optimistic Egyptian writer and his preposterous assertion that one could turn lead—or a zinc dénier—into gold just by willing it.

It's gold, it's gold, it's gold, Jean-Loup sang inwardly.

What the hell, it was worth a try. The coin in the professor's hand is gold. Whatever I touch is gold. I am King Midas!

His eyelids drooped, and his breathing became even and deep. Before me, all base metals will be elevated, just as base personalities are elevated in the presence of holiness. I am the pope of déniers! All I need do—

"Are you with us, Monsieur de Villeneuve?"

Jean-Loup startled awake with a snort. The other students laughed. "Uh . . ."

"Pay attention!" Professor Anselm admonished exasperatedly. "For the benefit of any other scholars who may have preferred sleeping to heeding our experiment, we are attempting to transform a humble dénier into pure gold through magic." He opened his hand. "But alack, it is still only a dénier." The corners of his mouth turned down comically. "And why, might I ask, has this humble dénier behaved so disappointingly toward a don of our great university?"

"Because we have no philosopher's stone!" someone shouted from the back row.

Anselm pointed at the student. "Exactly!" He held up the coin. "In order to turn this into gold, a catalyst must be used. In this case, that catalyst, the philosopher's stone, has been lost to mankind for a thousand years. Until it is found, or until a substitute can be invented, we can only theorize about the elements that transform metals. Those theories are what constitute the science of alchemy."

Dramatically, he tossed the coin high in the air toward its original owner. Alphonse grabbed at it and missed, but Jean-Loup caught it just as it entered the bed of straw he was sitting on.

"Ah," said Anselm, "I see that Mr. de Villeneuve has managed to stay awake long enough to retrieve our counterfeit dénier. Perhaps Mr. Patou will allow him to keep the treasure as reward."

Alphonse bowed toward his friend. "By all means," he said. "Be my guest, Jean-Loup." The students applauded.

"I thank you." Jean-Loup bowed in return. On his way back up, he stuck the coin between his teeth and wiggled his eyebrows, expecting a laugh. But all he got was a shocked look from Alphonse and a few nervous titters from the students around them.

"What?" Jean-Loup quickly spat out the coin. "Is there something . . ." But the words dried up in his throat as he gazed at the coin. "Oh, my Lord," he whispered.

The dénier had turned to gold.

"How dare you insult me in this way," Professor Anselm hissed as he walked slowly over to him.

"No! I didn't . . . I mean, it wasn't . . ."

"Get out of my classroom at once," the professor said.

"But—"

"Charlatan! Fraud!" The professor was shaking so violently that his robe trembled. "Your name will be stricken from the university's records. You will never be permitted to return."

"Professor, I swear . . ."

"Go play your tricks at the fair. You might make a good living duping innocent working people there. But not here, at the greatest seat of knowledge in the world."

"Please—"

"Goat! Scoundrel!" Anselm picked up his walking stick

and brandished it overhead as he strode toward Jean-Loup. "Get out, I say! Get out!"

Jean-Loup rose from his place in the straw and headed for the door.

"I do not know why I bother to attempt instruction to such cretins," Professor Anselm decreed as the young student exited. With a sigh, he went on. "Now, what is the result of melting copper with zinc?"

"Brass," Jean-Loup said softly from the other side of the classroom door—a door he would never again be permitted to enter. Because of this, he thought, holding the golden coin up to the light.

Thus began Jean-Loup de Villeneuve's long, long journey toward discovering the truth about magic and the unfortunate creatures who are blessed with it.

CHAPTER • EIGHTEEN

KT—

Can you meet me after work today? The Dome Café, 5 PM. Please! I miss you.

Peter

Madame Rossine, Chef Durant's secretary, handed me the note with an air of barely restrained rage. "This came via messenger," she said huffily. "We do not appreciate personal messages here, mademoiselle."

"Er . . . okay."

"I brought it to you only because the person who delivered it said that it was an emergency." She waited while I read the sealed card. "Is there a response?"

I tried to conceal the joy I felt. "Please tell . . . er, the messenger . . . that I'll take care of it."

She nodded crisply and walked away.

Peter! He wanted to see me! We hadn't really spoken since the night I'd been with Belmondo. Maybe he'd forgotten about that. Maybe everything could go back to the way things used to be before the dinner party.

I attacked my *coquilles Saint Jacques* with so much gusto that Chef Durant actually complimented me on how neatly I cleaned my scallops. *Score!* I checked my watch. 3:27. I cleaned my station, packed up my scallops, took off my apron, and said good-bye to the chef. I could barely keep from running out the door.

I was early, but that was okay. Spending an hour at an outdoor café in Paris on a beautiful July day was no hardship. Besides, I'd brought along chapter two. The book had been slowgoing at first, but I was gradually getting better at reading Old French. Also, it was beyond weird that Jean-Loup had been an alchemist. I mean, I'd never given alchemy a moment's thought until I'd found out about Peter. I hadn't been sure it even existed. And now here was a whole book about someone just like my boyfriend, except that he'd lived almost nine hundred years ago.

Sometimes life is just too strange, *non*?

1181

The Goldsmith

With his expulsion from the university, Jean-Loup was disinherited by his family, who considered his "prank" to be a gross show of disrespect.

For a time he wandered, getting work wherever he could—as a private tutor for the children of the nobility, or as a scribe, writing letters and drawing up legal documents for the illiterate. He did not exercise the strange ability that he had discovered in Professor Anselm's classroom. If that talent were discovered, he knew, he would be executed as a sorcerer.

But times were lean, and when there was no money for food and no work available, he quietly took a handful of nails or some foreign coins and guiltily turned these objects into gold, traveling widely to spend them. For this reason, Jean-Loup had no permanent home, living in rented rooms in the city when he did not have to travel, and in flea-infested inns when he did.

He was nearing his twenty-sixth birthday when he was robbed and beaten in one of these inns by a band of thieves. When he came to, bruised and bleeding, he knew he could not continue to live this way, ignoring his inborn power and living like an animal when he could possess the luxuries of a king.

He decided to become a goldsmith. Normally, mastery of this craft took many years of study and apprenticeship, but that was partly because gold was such a precious commodity that beginners had to practice with other metals. Jean-Loup did not have this problem. He sought out an aged, retired goldsmith whose eyes were no longer keen enough for the delicate work required, and paid him a fortune.

"Teach me your craft using the gold I give you," he told the old smith. "Spend what you like, and when my apprenticeship is done, keep the rest."

The smith blinked wordlessly in astonishment.

"All I ask is that you tell no one about the gold or where it came from."

"Rest easy, my lord," the old man said, chuckling. "I would not like to end my days at the end of a cutthroat's knife. I will say nothing."

Jean-Loup learned quickly. He had always had leanings toward making art. From an early age he had been able to capture a person's likeness with no more than a piece of charcoal, but his family had considered art to be an unworthy pursuit for a member of the nobility. Now that he was no longer restrained by the class he had been born into, he was able to let his imagination fly.

He began by learning to file, solder, polish, saw, forge, and cast the beautiful metal. From there he learned how to produce plates, spoons, and goblets.

"Even a king could not eat his meals on something so fine," the old smith said as he examined one of Jean-Loup's bowls. "I think I should make it known to the guild that I have an apprentice."

The guilds were strict about their rules for membership, and the goldsmiths' guild was one of the most particular. "Tell them I've been here for years, working as your servant," Jean-Loup said. Because he was older than most apprentices, he anticipated problems in joining the guild when the time came, but he needn't have worried. Once he was permitted to make jewelry, Jean-Loup's artistic genius flowered. By the time he applied to the guild for membership, noblewomen from as far away as England were already sending emissaries begging to purchase his magnificent *pieces. And although he gave all the credit for his work to the old smith who had trained him, the shop he bought on the Pont au Change, the bridge where all the city's goldsmiths kept their businesses, was bustling with activity as soon as it opened.*

Thus did Jean-Loup de Villeneuve, former aristocrat, become a tradesman and a new addition to Paris's growing middle class. He lived in rooms above the shop on the busy bridge, ate well, enjoyed the company of his fellow guild members, and employed several assistants, although he took on no apprentices for fear that one of them would discover his secret.

Indeed, he almost never had to make gold anymore. He was successful as a merchant and an artist. But sometimes when business was slow, he would rub his thumb along a lead slug and watch it come to life as it transformed into a gleaming, glowing nugget of gold. This is what he was doing when the bell above the door to his shop opened and the most beautiful woman he had ever seen walked in.

Her eyes were violet. She was tall and slender, with a smattering of black curls peeking from beneath the hood of her cloak. The cloak itself was of plain undyed wool, but its coarseness could not disguise the nobility of her bearing or the stunning vibrancy of those extraordinary eyes.

"Are you the goldsmith?" she asked.

He stood mutely, all thought having flown out of his head the moment he'd set eyes on her.

"Sir?"

"What? Oh." Jean-Loup felt himself blush. "Yes. May I help you?" The words dropped out of his mouth mechanically, while his mind only registered that something very unusual

was behind her exotic gaze—a wisdom, perhaps, or a sadness so deep that he could not even imagine its depths.

"I brought something for you to appraise," she said as she drew a silk-wrapped parcel out of her sleeve and laid it on the counter between them. Jean-Loup could barely bring himself to tear his gaze away from her, but he reminded himself that he was a master craftsman with obligations to his profession.

The object on the silk cloth was a long necklace of heavy gold links that held a pendant that bore a crude likeness of a man's face. Studded around the edges of the pendant were eighteen uncut diamonds. Jean-Loup gaped at the necklace in astonishment. He had seen drawings of Carolingian goldwork forged from the time of the early Franks, hundreds of years earlier, but he had never seen any actual examples. Until now.

"May I?" he asked diffidently before lifting it. The piece was enormously heavy. He examined the portrait on the pendant with a magnifying glass.

"It's Charlemagne," the woman said.

Jean-Loup's head snapped up.

"It belonged to him." She swallowed nervously and looked down at her hands. "He gave it to his last wife before he died."

"How do you know?" he asked stupidly. She didn't answer. <u>*But of course she doesn't know,*</u> *he thought. She was just telling him a story in an attempt to increase its value.*

As it turned out, the story wasn't necessary. Even if it were a forgery, the sheer weight of the gold in the necklace was staggering. And if it really did belong to Charlemagne, well, then the piece would be beyond price.

"How did you acquire this?" he asked.

The woman ignored him. "I'd like you to melt it down and

cast it into pennyweights. As payment, you may keep one of the stones."

"Ah. A forgery, then."

"No. It is genuine."

"Then why would you have me melt it down?"

The woman sighed. "We need the money," she said, her eyes downcast.

"Perhaps you could sell it—"

"No one could pay what it is worth, and a pawnbroker would only cheat me. I came to you because of your reputation for honesty." She picked up the necklace and handed it to him. "Please weigh it," she said.

He did. "Three pounds, eight and three-quarter ounces."

"It must weigh at least three and a half pounds when I pick up the gold," she said. "And you must return seventeen of the stones to me."

He bristled. She had expected him to cheat her! "If I were to melt down the gold, I would return three pounds, eight and three-quarter ounces to you," he said with dignity. "And eighteen stones. The payment for my work would be twenty francs."

"I apologize," the woman said. "I was only trying to control how badly I would be mistreated."

Jean-Loup inhaled sharply. He was aware of the ways merchants took advantage of women. "At any rate, however, I cannot do as you ask."

She looked up, alarmed.

"If this piece is genuine—as I suspect it may be—I also cannot pay you what it is worth. But neither can I destroy it. Instead, I will give you an equal measure of gold for it, and polished diamonds that you will be able to sell."

Confused, the woman nodded her agreement. Jean-Loup went to the back of the store and returned with the exact measure of gold and a handful of good, if small, diamonds. The woman accepted them with thanks, and he wrote her a receipt. "Your name?" he asked, feeling his heart pounding as he dipped the quill into the ink.

"Veronique de Caroligne," she said.

A drop of ink fell onto the receipt. "Caroligne? From the House of Charlemagne?"

"Yes," she said, collecting her things. But before she reached the shop door, she turned around to face Jean-Loup again. "Forgive me, but what will you do with the necklace?"

Jean-Loup smiled shyly. "I don't know," he said. "Look at it, I suppose."

She smiled. As she left, Jean-Loup's chief assistant, Thibault, entered the shop, his mouth agape as he watched the beautiful woman walk away.

"Well, we're surely the top shop in the guild now," Thibault said.

"Oh?"

Thibault jerked his head toward the north end of the bridge. "That was the abbess, wasn't it?"

"Abbess?" His heart sank. "She's a nun?"

"I think so. You know the Abbey of Lost Souls?"

Jean-Loup nodded glumly. Everyone knew the place. It had been in existence since before Paris had been chartered.

"Well, that lady's the head of it," Thibault explained, glancing over at the necklace. "Looks like the sisters are doing pretty well."

CHAPTER
•
NINETEEN

Peter arrived a few minutes before five. As soon as I saw him, I ran into his arms and he twirled me around and kissed me so hard it took my breath away. Some of the people at the other tables applauded, but I didn't care. I was just happy to see him.

"How long has it been?" he whispered.

"You know the answer," I whispered back. For a moment, I could only stand there and look at him, at his honey-blond hair, his gray eyes, the soft lips that were red from pressing against mine. "Too long," I breathed into his ear.

And then he kissed me again, and it was as if nothing in the world existed except the two of us. That is, until we were interrupted by a waiter clearing his throat.

"*Vous voulez?*" he inquired, smoothing the white cloth draped over his arm.

Once we'd gotten over our initial flush of passion and managed to stop staring into each other's eyes, we sat down and ordered two *limonades*, otherwise known as lemon sodas.

It was funny, but after such a prolonged PDA, neither of us seemed to know what to say. I think that even though we both wanted to forget about the other night, it was hard to pretend it never happened, although we were both giving it our best effort.

"So we're all good now?" I asked in a small voice.

He looked at me for a moment. "Yeah," he said finally. "You thought I'd stood you up, so you—"

"I didn't do anything," I said quickly.

"Okay. I was just jealous."

"There was no reason for that."

He looked away, his jaw clenched.

"Maybe you could have told me you were going to Brussels," I said.

"Look, I . . ." He closed his eyes, which had practically been flashing sparks, and took a deep breath. "You're right. I will next time."

Then all was quiet. We were all right. I could feel the muscles in my neck loosening with relief. "So what are you doing for Jeremiah these days?" I asked, eager to bring the conversation back to neutral ground.

"All kinds of strange things." He sighed. "Right now I've got to arrange for a truck to come pick up an old lady's belongings. You know her, Marie something."

"Marie-Therèse? What do you mean, pick up her belongings?"

"On her birthday, she's going to leave the house. I'm supposed to help her move out."

"What?" *Maybe that's why she felt so scared when I touched her hand,* I thought. "She never mentioned leaving."

"No? That's weird."

"She's being kicked out on her birthday?"

"I guess. There's a country house or something, staffed with servants. Jeremiah says it's kind of a reward."

"So why is it so secret, then?"

"I don't know. These people have a lot of secrets." He paid the bill. "They call themselves 'the Enclave.'"

"Enclave?" My mind was racing. "That's like a special group or something, right?"

"Right. I think they're witches."

I clucked. Sometimes Peter was just dense. "Of course they are. That's not what they're trying to hide. It's something else."

"What else?"

"I don't know. They don't confide in me." Understatement of the year.

"Yeah, I heard about the thing with Joelle and the sewer. You could have been lost down there forever."

"That's what I mean. It makes no sense that they hate me so much. I'm no threat to them. Plus, I'm in school all day and have to study recipes at night." *And read a handwritten book in antique French,* I might have added.

"Maybe they just don't like Americans," Peter said.

"They like you," I countered. "A lot. Especially Sophie."

Peter smiled. "Who's acting jealous now?"

I swallowed. That hit close to home. "I'm not jealous," I lied. "She's way too old for you."

"Maybe. But her daughter isn't." He pretended to shoot me with his index finger.

"What?" I almost jumped out of my seat.

"Relax, Katy. It was just talk."

"About Fabienne? What was she saying?"

"Oh, dumb things. How Fabby's so beautiful and how can I help but fall in love with her, blah, blah."

I stood up. "Are you kidding me?" I shouted.

He laughed out loud. "Hey, that's Sophie talking, not me." He stood up and took me in his arms. I was shaking all over. "Ooh," he said, grinning. "You *are* jealous. Payback." I pinched his arm. He laughed. "Come on, let's walk," he said. "I like how the sun looks on your hair."

We walked along the Seine, holding hands and angling our faces up to the warm, late afternoon sun until we reached the Rue des Âmes Perdues.

"Oh, shoot, I have to do something," I said, suddenly remembering why I was carrying a container of *coquille St. Jacques*.

When I was at Azrael's house—er, cave—I noticed that he had no refrigerator and no stove, except for the little brazier that heated the place. It didn't take a genius to figure out he didn't have much food, and that in order to get any, he'd have to go outside the tunnels and then walk a long way to get anything to eat. Of course, he'd said he didn't want to see me again, but so what. Food was more important than good manners.

"I can't go in the house just yet," I said. "I have an errand."

"What is it?"

"Er . . ." I wanted to tell Peter, but I'd promised Azrael I wouldn't say anything to anyone about him.

"I can go with you," he offered.

"No. That is—"

"Don't tell me you have secrets too?" Peter winced.

"No," I said. "Well, not exactly." I waved my container of scallops. "I just need to deliver some food."

"Can't it wait?" He looked stricken. "I've got to oversee a shipment of computers at the Gare du Nord at eight o'clock."

"I'll be back in half an hour," I promised. "Maybe less."

He sighed. "Okay," he said, his shoulders slumping in resignation. "I need a shower anyway."

"I'll make you dinner before you go," I said.

He walked away. I waved to his back.

CHAPTER • TWENTY

Fortunately, the exit Azrael showed me was nearby. I just had to zigzag through a few narrow streets to reach the ruins that led into the *carrières*. It wasn't a problem scrambling over a few fallen building blocks and finding my way to the building's former coal chute. I walked down six crumbling stone steps, then turned right to find a "door" just like the one I'd entered miles away when I'd first come with Joelle: a tall stone slab nearly covering a vine-covered opening that looked extremely unwelcoming. Then I slipped through the narrow portal into almost total darkness.

This time I had a more efficient pocket light to replace my defunct oinking pig. I kept the beam trained on the ground, though, because I didn't want Azrael to see me. He'd said he didn't want me hanging around, but I just couldn't let the old man go hungry. Not when I was going to one of the best cooking schools in the world.

"Azrael?" I called softly when I neared the glowing

candlelight of his living area. "I brought you some food. I won't stay."

I peeked inside. He wasn't there.

"Azrael?"

Interesting. Just where did you go when you lived in a cave? Out for a stroll among the bats? Or was he communing with the spirits of the headless dead people down the way?

I set the food container on the table near his cookstove and was walking out when I started to worry. What if the wound I'd inflicted on him had festered? What if he'd fallen someplace?

No, he was probably just going to the bathroom in one of his cavelets, I told myself. After all, he had a place where he kept lemons. Wouldn't he have a toilet somewhere?

I almost left again, but couldn't. If he was hurt, he didn't have anyone else. I'd wait for him.

I sat down in one of the beautiful chairs and pulled a candle closer to me. Then I took out Jean-Loup's story—or as much of it as I'd been able to put in order—and opened it to the next chapter. I'd stash it under my chef's coat when Azrael arrived.

1184

Veronique

Jean-Loup may never have seen Veronique again if it hadn't been for the accident, and only then because it left him close to death.

Jean-Loup had been melting some low-quality gold for use as dinnerware in the house of a provincial nobleman when the Pont au Change suffered one of its not-infrequent "adjustments." Perhaps the bridge had been struck by the oversized mast of a ship, or the stonework itself might have crumbled somewhere along its length. All the city's engineers agreed that the end-to-end buildings erected on the bridge would eventually topple the whole structure, spilling every goldsmith in Paris into the Seine, but it was the guild, not the engineers, who held the power on the Pont au Change. It had served as the center of the goldworking industry for a hundred years, and not one smith would leave it until all the others had.

The destruction was already beginning. It was not unusual for a house on the bridge to lose a door or a window. Occasionally a whole building would crumble into the river, taking with it a fortune in gold and silver. But more often—as was the case on the day of Jean-Loup's accident—there was nothing but a slight tremor that caused the old house with its ground-floor shop to sway.

The movement was small, even negligible, except that Jean-Loup was carrying an iron vessel filled to the brim with molten gold.

The first drops on his hand caused him to jerk his arms upward, pouring the rest of the gold onto his arms, chest, and neck. The pain was so excruciating that he could not even scream, but only gasp as he saw the skin on his arm sizzle.

Fortunately, his assistant Thibault had watched the whole scene and started running toward Jean-Loup as soon as those first fiery liquid drops were spilled. With one motion, the sturdy young man lifted his employer into his arms and headed out the door.

For Jean-Loup, the pain was almost more than he could

bear. He felt his mind shutting down even as he watched with eerie dispassion as the flesh fell off his arms like rotten meat, leaving the white bones beneath exposed.

He was given something to drink that sent him into a deep sleep for a time. But when he awoke, the agony of his burns returned. "Where am I?" he croaked, blinking as he looked around at the stone walls with their flickering candles. Each small flame seemed to melt into the others as the horrible pain blossomed into life again.

"Shh," a woman said gently. "You're in my house."

Her voice sounded familiar. He sought her face, although it proved to be too difficult for him to focus. After a time, however, she bent over him and he could smell the scent of lavender on her clothes. Then he eased his eyes open and looked into her perfect face.

"It's you," he said.

She covered his eyes with her long, slender hands. "Do not trouble yourself by talking," she said. "Just rest, Monsieur de Villeneuve."

"I'm dying."

"Not at all. You've been drugged, that's all. Poppies, to dull the pain." She gave him another drink.

"Poppies . . ." So that was why he felt so disconnected, almost as if he were caught between the land of the living and the realm of the dead.

His eyes filled with tears. He knew he was about to cross over into death, but that was not why he wept. He was not afraid of death. But he felt such desire for the woman who sat beside him that he almost could not bear her closeness to him.

He longed to hold her, to kiss her violet eyes and full lips, to touch her sweet skin, to breathe in her scent like perfume. But that was not to be, he knew. Instead, her face would be the last vision he would see in this life.

"What is it?" Veronique asked, so gently that he could hardly hear her. "Are you in pain?"

"I love you," he whispered.

He felt her stiffen, but he would not apologize for speaking the words that filled his heart. "I love you," he repeated, and tried to squeeze her hand before losing consciousness again.

Jean-Loup did not know how much time had passed before he awoke again, but he did feel better. Much better. With a sigh of relief, he realized he was not about to die.

Warm hands clasped his. Warm, with long fingers scented with lavender. "Thank you," he said, and the hands folded around his own. The poppy juice he'd been given was strong and he wanted to sleep again, but first he had to remain awake long enough to see Veronique once more.

"Please . . . ," he rasped, his throat parched. "I must—" His eyes opened, sticky and crusted. "Your hair," he said, unable to disguise his shock.

Veronique's beautiful dark hair had turned snow white.

She smiled sweetly. "Do not be troubled," she said. Then she slid silently onto the floor, unconscious.

Jean-Loup leaped out of bed. "Help!" he shouted, only tangentially aware that his right arm, once little more than bare bone, had filled out with flesh and the skin was nearly healed. "Someone, please come at once!"

A woman wearing a thick gauze veil around her head

rushed in as Jean-Loup was scooping Veronique into his arms.

"Put her down!" the woman, who Jean-Loup reasoned must have been a nun, shouted. Three other women followed behind her and one other, he would have sworn, simply materialized in their midst. Together they carried Veronique out of the room. Jean-Loup tried to follow, but the nun who had first answered his call forced him away from the doorway. "Now, sir," she said crisply, "you just stay in here. You still need your rest."

"But—"

"I am Sister Béatrice," she said authoritatively, "and I will see to it that the abbess is taken care of. So allow me to do my work, will you?"

Reluctantly, Jean-Loup agreed. Sister Béatrice helped him back into bed and left the room.

After a time, he examined his arm, marveling at its radically improved condition. *How long have I been in this place?* he wondered.

Long enough for Veronique's hair to turn white.

He looked at his hands. They were still a young man's hands. Except for one deep scar on his wrist, they looked just as they had before the accident, down to a smear of ink on the side of his thumb. And he was not stiff, as he should have been if he'd been bedridden for months. *Not so long, then.* But how could . . . her hair. . . . There were so many questions.

Quickly, he made his way to the door and walked into a busy corridor. A number of women were moving purposefully toward a room at the far end of the hall, where a bell was ringing. The women were dressed plainly, in woolen robes *with long, wide sleeves and gauze headdresses like Sister Béatrice's. There was a sense of urgency about them, as if they were being summoned.*

For prayer? Jean-Loup wondered. Was that what Sister Béatrice meant by her "work"? Staying close to the wall, he followed the women into the room, then hid behind a hanging drapery. To his surprise, the room was not a church sanctuary, but more like the living area in a noble's home, with rush mats on the floor and beautiful tapestries hanging over the stone walls. There were benches and stools set in groupings, and candles everywhere that lent a warm glow to the large, comfortable space.

*The most remarkable thing about the room, however, was not its furnishings, but the women who occupied it. A pair of tabby cats lying contentedly beneath a bench moved into the open, stretched, and then—amazingly—transformed into young women who joined the others, gathering into a circle around Veronique. The woman who had seemingly materialized out of nowhere in Jean-Loup's room suddenly vanished a few feet away from him. Then, in another moment she reappeared, saying that the doors were secure. As the circle tightened, another woman (*Are these nuns? *Jean-Loup asked himself) raised her arms, and from across the room a thick wand flew into her waiting fingers. Someone else languidly waved her hand in a circle over her head, and all the candles dimmed almost to guttering.*

Then Sister Béatrice spoke in a voice that was not exactly a voice, but more like an echo in Jean-Loup's mind: "Let us begin."

The women began to circle clockwise. As they moved, they sang:

We are the wave of the space between,
We are the flood that rushes to shore.
We sweep past all barriers set in our path,
Through corridors of time we pour.

Our Magick lends eternal proof
We give in return Healing and Truth.

Then they reversed the direction of their movement, singing the second half of what Jean-Loup knew must be a spell.

We circle and bind the hands of time;
Years swim in our embrace.
Our power spins in widdershins
To undo the riptide's pace.

Our Magick lends eternal proof
We receive in return Healing and Truth.

As they sang their strange song, Sister Béatrice's "voice"—which was more like a hum in the middle of Jean-Loup's forehead—sang its own low counterpoint: Heal. Heal, Veronique. Take our magic, and with it, take back your years.

Then, before Jean-Loup's eyes, Veronique's limp body twitched back to life. When she finally sat up, still in Sister Béatrice's arms, her hair had become dark again, except for one streak of pure white that ran down the side of her waist-length tresses like a silver ribbon.

"We cannot take back all the time you've lost," Sister Béatrice told her. "Having given so much of your life away, you must be more careful in the future, Lady Abbess. The next time, we may not be able to save your gift at all."

Veronique nodded solemnly, her eyes darkened to indigo with fatigue.

"What gift?" Jean-Loup asked, stepping out from behind the curtains where he had been hiding.

The women turned away from him. One of them fainted. The woman who had slipped in and out of sight disappeared again, although this time it took her ten full seconds to vanish.

Sister Béatrice fixed the young man with her sharp eyes. "What will he do to us with his knowledge?" she asked in her eerie non-voice, her lips never moving.

Veronique stared at him, her face anguished.

"I will say nothing," Jean-Loup stammered. "For in truth, I am more like you than you know."

Three months later, Jean-Loup and Veronique were married.

"I don't want you to heal anyone again," he said as he held his bride in his arms. They lay in the big bed he had built as a wedding gift for her. "Even me."

She examined his arms in the sunlight streaming through the window of his rooms above the shop. Not a single scar remained. "I'd say I did pretty well," she said, kissing his wrist.

The touch of her was almost overwhelming. He had loved her from the first moment he saw her, and now that she was his, he loved her even more than he had ever believed possible. It didn't matter a whit to him that Veronique had aged twenty years in one day.

She was the first person he had known since his time at the university that he didn't have to hide from. She regarded his talent for making gold as a gift, not a freakish curse. For that alone, Jean-Loup would have been grateful all the days of his life.

But there was more.

Veronique understood Jean-Loup so well because she, too, had been born with an inexplicable gift that, in its way, was as rare and remarkable as his own.

Veronique was immortal, or nearly so.

She had been born with the promise of living forever, but even as an infant she had felt compelled to use her unusual gift to help others. Her mother had enjoyed suckling her because of the feeling of well-being the child imparted simply by being near. From her earliest childhood—perhaps even before she became aware of what she was doing—she had been able to heal birds and small animals merely by touching them or blowing on their faces. And each time, she grew a little older. Once, when her younger brother had fallen out of a tree and the servants could not wake him, her ministrations had brought him back. The next day her mother remarked that Veronique had appeared to grow five inches overnight.

"How time flies!" she had exclaimed, laughing as her beautiful daughter was fitted for a longer gown.

But each time she saved a creature from death, she lost a small part of her immortality. With each breath given to heal another, she sacrificed a bit more of her life force.

"If you're not careful, you'll give away too much of your life," Jean-Loup chided.

"Better than having it taken from me," she said. Then

Veronique smiled and kissed him once more, and reassured Jean-Loup that she had no intention of dying anytime in the near future. Still, she would have no regrets, whatever happened. She had already lived longer than most dynasties. And her life, by any standard, had already proven to be extraordinary.

The French script that had been so hard for me to read at first was becoming a lot easier to understand, even though the lighting in Azrael's cave was creating a serious strain on my eyes. I looked up, then down, rolling my eyes and squeezing them shut until I stopped seeing phantom Gallic squiggles wherever I looked. Instead, to my surprise, I saw the big painting hanging on the cave wall, and recognized her from Azrael's book. She was Veronique! She had to be, with her beautiful violet eyes and the dramatic white streak in her long hair. I wondered if she or Jean-Loup had been Azrael's distant ancestors, or if he had simply painted her from imagination after reading about her.

Had Azrael himself written the fantasy of the alchemist and the immortal woman? There were so many things I wanted to ask him, but of course I couldn't say anything, at least not until I'd replaced the book I'd nearly destroyed.

"Who's here?" Azrael's quavering voice echoed from the passageway outside the cave.

Quickly I stashed the pages in the waistband of my jeans and pulled my shirt over them. I stood up, holding my chef's jacket in front of me so he wouldn't see the bulge. "It's me," I called out. "Katy."

He walked in looking disheveled and tired and carrying

two two-liter jugs of water, which he set down with a thump.

"There is water here in the *carrières*, but one must walk quite a distance to get it," he said. Then he stared at me, obviously uncomfortable with my presence.

"I brought you some dinner," I blurted, pointing to the scallops. *"Coquilles St. Jacques."*

"Very nice," he said patiently. "Thank you." He took a newspaper from the pocket of the sweater he wore. "But since I was not expecting you . . ."

"I know. I'm going." I edged toward the exit. "I just wanted to make sure you were all right. I mean—"

"Yes, yes. I understand. Again, many thanks." He plopped down on the same comfortable chair I'd been sitting in, and fanned himself briefly with the newspaper.

"I'll bring water next time," I said as I left.

He didn't answer. I think he was tired.

CHAPTER • TWENTY-ONE

I stripped off my chef's jacket and headed for my room, but on the way I nearly collided with Sophie de la Soubise.

"Goodness, you nearly crushed me," she said, giggling.

"I didn't touch you," I corrected as expressionlessly as possible.

"I suppose it's the way you Americans walk," she said. Then she performed a passable imitation of a gorilla before laughing delicately.

"Excuse me," I said, trying to squeeze past her.

"Oh, by the way, your friend Peter left."

My heart sank. I'd hoped I'd be back before he had to leave, but I supposed I'd spent too much time waiting for Azrael.

"Well, he's busy," I said, trying to sound indifferent. "With Jeremiah."

"But he wasn't with Jeremiah," Sophie said. "Now, who

was he with? Let's see." She tapped her perfectly manicured fingernail to her cheek, pretending that she was trying to remember something. "Ah, yes, of course. He left with Fabienne."

I tried to ignore the note of triumph in her voice. "She must have needed a ride somewhere," I said.

"*Mon Dieu*, but you're so *trusting*."

"Peter's a trustworthy person," I said, pushing the woman aside with my clunky American arms. "So is Fabienne."

I only wished I could have used my clunky American foot on her refined French *derrière*.

Sophie was transparent as ice—and almost as warm—but she'd still managed to shoot a little dart into my already fragile self-confidence. Peter and Fabienne? Together?

So Peter was gone. Again. With an impossibly beautiful girl. And this time, it was my fault. Now I knew how easy it was to stand someone up without meaning to. From now on, I'd cut Peter some slack when he had to cancel on me because of work.

I tried to wash away my disappointment and petty jealousy in the shower, but all I managed to accomplish was to turn myself red. *Oh, well,* I thought, trying to look on the bright side, *at least I can use the time to finish putting the pages of Azrael's story in order.*

It seemed I'd arrived at a new chapter. If only the pages had been numbered, I wouldn't have to read it at all, but as it was, I had no choice but to pay close attention to every word.

A.D. 813
Charlemagne's Wife

Veronique de Theuderic Avremarus was born in A.D. 794, 378 years before Jean-Loup turned the counterfeit coin into gold and began the process by which they would eventually meet. Her father was a Frankish chieftain whose liege lord was Charlemagne, the great leader who had accomplished within one lifetime the seemingly impossible challenge of uniting all the tribes of post-Roman Gaul into a single unified nation.

Charlemagne had been a remarkable man: clear-eyed, intelligent, powerful in both body and spirit, yet humorous and compassionate. He was seventy years old and the most important man in Europe when he took Veronique for his eleventh wife. That year was A.D. 811. She was seventeen.

Charlemagne gave Veronique many fine gifts during the remaining two years of his life, among them the gold and diamond necklace that announced to the world that nothing was too magnificent for the wife of the king of the Franks. There were also brooches, pins, cape-clasps, hair ornaments, ear-fobs, bracelets, torques, and rings.

Since the aged king had already sired eighteen children, Veronique was not pressured into bearing a child, as his earlier wives had been. His heir, the slovenly Prince Pippin, had already been named. So instead of being treated as a royal brood mare, Veronique was treasured as the king's companion in his old age. While his progeny went about the business of making war and converting the Lombards and Saxons to Christianity, the old king contentedly taught his young bride the stories of his youth, stories of his battles both on the field and within his widespread, discordant family.

"When I die, my beauty," he advised her near the end of his life, "do not allow my sons and grandsons and their wives to make use of you for their own benefit."

She was so young at the time that she didn't exactly know what the old king was telling her, but she found out soon enough. When his health began to fail, Charlemagne's eldest son, Pippin (whose posture was so poor that his father referred to him as "the hunchback"), summoned Veronique to a council meeting where a bunch of sweaty, belching warrior chiefs looked her over to decide whether or not she would make a suitable bride for a recalcitrant Saxon noble.

"Charlemagne's child-queen should be recognized as quite a prize, even to those barbarians," Pippin said. The others agreed.

"How dare you!" Veronique answered, her eyes blazing with fury. "Your father, not you, is king of the Franks. It is his wishes that must be followed, not yours. And it is not his wish to send me to the frozen land of the Saxons to live like a dog!"

Pippin shrugged in his usual lackadaisical manner. "What my father wishes is of no import any longer, as he will be dead within the week. If you are a prudent girl, you will pack your possessions quickly, because at the hour of Charlemagne's death"—with this he stuck his finger near Veronique's face—"you will be on your way to Saxony!"

As the men laughed at her evident dismay, she ran to her dying husband, who lay in a deathlike slumber. "Charlemagne," she whispered into his ear, "husband and friend, please hear me, I beg you." Then, blowing a soft stream of air across the old king's face, she willed him to consciousness.

The sensation Veronique had always experienced during her healings was physical, as if pinpricks of light were coming through her body into her hands, and then out through her slender fingers. Now, clasping Charlemagne's liver-spotted hands, she concentrated on sending the light within her into him, sensing her life force traveling from the center of her being into his, until at last the king's eyes opened as he gasped in surprise.

"Veronique!" he exclaimed. "By God, girl, how long was I asleep?"

"Four days," she said, almost weeping with relief.

He reached his hand up to touch her face. "Only four days? Yet in such a short time, you have grown to full womanhood."

"I have?" She looked into a mirror. Indeed, she had changed. Her face had lost its childish roundness, and her bosom had grown fuller. "I . . . I think I gave you some of my life," she confessed.

The king looked at her, uncomprehending, and then burst into hearty laughter. "If so, 'twas the greatest of gifts," he said.

When she explained what his son had planned for her after Charlemagne's death, the king called for his valet to dress him in his finest robes. Placing the royal crown upon his head, he walked to the chamber where Pippin and his cronies were still plotting, and burst through the doors like a bear surveying a herd of sheep.

"Make my wife the property of the Saxons, will you?" he roared.

Pippin was completely flummoxed by his father's unexpected appearance. "My king, I—"

"Be silent!" Charlemagne bellowed. "I am here to tell you, unworthy spawn, that you will never occupy the throne of

Gaul!" He turned on the others in the room. "As for the rest of you, I expect you to forswear any allegiance to this creature"—he cast a disgusted look at his son—"or else fight me here and now." He unsheathed his magnificent sword from its scabbard and held it aloft, as if he were about to charge into battle.

The assembled nobles looked from one to the other as the aged king stood prepared to fight them all.

"Subdue him!" Pippin shouted in desperation. "Don't you see, the old man's bluffing! He'll be in his grave by spring. You have your swords. Use them!"

"If you dare," Charlemagne said with quiet deadliness. He wore his favorite battle cloak, clean but still stained with the blood of his enemies. Beneath the crown that had been forged for him alone, his mane of white hair fell over his shoulders like a cloud. His large blue eyes burned fiercely in his florid face. The heavy sword remained poised over his head, held by a powerful arm that never trembled under its weight.

One by one the nobles, casting a wary eye toward Pippin, fell to their knees before Charlemagne. "My liege," they said, ignoring the would-be usurper. "My king."

His son tried to leave the room, but the old king stopped him with the tip of his sword at Pippin's throat. "Send in your brother Louis," he commanded.

Pippin scowled, but he knew that, firstborn son or not, the old man would not hesitate to run him through if he disobeyed him. "Certainly," he said smoothly. "May I ask why?"

"Tell him I'm going to change his name. To Pippin."

Pippin whirled around. "What?"

"I like the name. It should not be wasted on a cretin like you."

The young man sputtered. "But . . . but . . . what shall I call myself, then?"

The old man's eyes glinted. "Call yourself Dorcas, after the Saxon family I'll be sending you to," he said. "You'll marry a fine, strapping Teutonic maiden, and live out your life in the Saxon hinterlands, where I won't have to kill you."

"This is madness!" Pippin hissed.

"Sealing a treaty with the Saxons through marriage was your idea, and it was a good one. King Dorcas would rather have my son than my wife, anyway, even if that son arrives without title. I'll give you a nice chest of gold as a dowry."

"A *dowry*?" Pippin shouted, despite his father's threatening sword. "Are you saying I am to be banished to the Saxons like some *woman*?"

Charlemagne blinked in feigned surprise. "But wasn't that what you were planning to do with my wife?"

"Your *eleventh* wife, Father."

"My *only* wife, at the moment," Charlemagne said. "And my friend. But you wouldn't understand that."

Pippin groaned in disgust. The very idea of friendship with a woman was repulsive to him.

"That is why, to broaden your thinking, you will take the name of your Saxon wife, to perpetuate King Dorcas's line."

Tears of rage shone in Pippin's eyes. "I will never be subjected to such humiliation!" he spat through clenched teeth.

"Then go to a monastery," Charlemagne said. "Wherever you live is of no importance to me, so long as I never have to see your face again." He turned his back on the young man and crossed his arms.

As Pippin stomped out of the room muttering,

Charlemagne laughed the familiar booming laugh that had set his men at ease during the fiercest battles. Still on their knees, the former followers of his now-banished son tittered nervously, awaiting their fate.

"Oh, get up, you craven dogs," Charlemagne said. "Tonight we shall drink together, and you shall entertain no more idiot ideas if you want to keep those empty heads of yours."

To a man, they roared their approval, then bowed low to their king in relief and gratitude.

Charlemagne had won a decisive battle that night. Pippin was banished, and a new Pippin placed at the top of the list to inherit the kingdom. But as time went by, the king fell ill more and more often. And each time after he recovered, he saw that his young wife had aged beyond her years.

"By God, you've the look of someone nearer to thirty than twenty," he observed as he came out of his fifth bout with death.

"They were years I gave willingly," Veronique answered.

Before, he had treated her response as a joke, but this time he could not deny the proof of his own eyes. "Then it is true," he said. "You have given me your years to replace my own."

She looked away. She had known for some time that, although she did not understand how it happened, she had indeed been sending her life into him.

"They will call you a sorceress."

She smiled. "But you will protect me," she said.

"If I can." It was the first time she had ever heard him speak with even a hint of uncertainty. "But I cannot allow you to squander that gift on an old man who has already lived more than seventy-two winters."

She took his hand. "I've told you, I give it willingly," she said.

He smiled at her. "And it is with gratitude that I decline," the great king answered.

It was only a matter of weeks before he fell ill again. Dismissing his physicians, he called for Veronique, as he had for the past two years. The medical men, as well as many members of the court, whispered that the young queen was a witch. The new heir did not permit such accusations, but when the priests joined in the gossip, Charlemagne became truly worried for Veronique's safety.

"The jackals are circling," he said. "They say that you are keeping me alive through witchcraft."

Veronique pressed a cold cloth against his brow. "Just give yourself to me, sire. Allow me—"

"No." He withdrew his hand from hers. "Listen to me." His eyes glistened with fever. "If you remain here, my court and family will surely kill you," he said. "You must leave this place, Veronique. Now. Tonight."

"My king, I cannot—"

"Obey me!" He struggled to remain lucid. "Beloved, my time is short. Take the treasures I have given you and seek sanctuary in the abbey of Auvergne. I will provide a trustworthy escort."

Again she tried to object, but he silenced her. "Do not speak further of this," he said, gasping, hanging onto the last threads of his life. "And please, spare me the indignity of watching me wither."

Veronique could only look into the old king's face and weep.

"Go, my darling," Charlemagne commanded.

Those were his last words to her.

CHAPTER
•
TWENTY-TWO

For the past few pages, I'd been dimly aware of a sound crowding into my consciousness. I finally recognized it: a woman weeping.

Sobbing. And it was coming from Marie-Therèse's room.

I remembered what Peter had said about her having to leave the house on her birthday. *She probably knows,* I thought. It was a terrible thing to be kicked out of your home for no reason other than the fact that you got old. What kind of stupid rule was that, anyway?

I closed the book and went to her room. "Marie-Therèse?" I called, knocking on the door. "It's Katy. Can I come in?"

There was a brief scuffling before she appeared in a brocade dressing gown, a lace-edged handkerchief held to her nose. "Please," she said, gesturing for me to enter. Marie-Therèse still spoke English to me, even though no one else besides Peter did.

"Are you all right?" I asked.

"It's just a sniffle," she said, turning away from me. "Probably the weather . . ."

"Is it about your birthday?" I asked timidly.

She sank down onto her bed, her shoulders slumped and trembling. "After all this time . . . ," she sobbed. "They've voted me out, Katy. Like an old dog they are putting out on the street."

"Anyone who'd do that to a dog would be pretty repulsive," I said. "But to you. . . . It's unforgivable. I'll bet we could get a lawyer to—"

"No, no, no!" she exclaimed, alarmed. "We must never do such a thing."

"Why not?" I asked. "That's what lawyers are for."

"No," she repeated, shaking her head emphatically. "This was our agreement. If I contact the authorities, they will . . ." She threw up her hands.

"They will what?"

"Please," she whispered, looking at the door. "I have already said too much."

"But Marie—"

"I told you, I agreed to this!" She subdued her shaking hands into fists. Then, with a weary sigh, she sat down and buried her head in her arms. "We all do, before we ever come here." Her voice was ragged. "And I was far older than most when I agreed, so I cannot use my youth as an excuse. I just never thought this day would really come."

I sat down beside her and took one of her hands in my own. "What . . . exactly . . . is going to happen?" I asked as gently as I could.

She shrugged. "There will be a big party at which Sophie

and the other women will pretend to be saddened by my departure, after which I will be taken to a house in the country, where I shall live out my life in pampered luxury." She waved the thought away. "At least, that's what I was told when my so-called 'friends' decided that this birthday would be my last spent in this house." She walked over to her bureau and took out a brochure titled *The Poplars*.

"Is this it?" I asked, reading through it. She nodded. "Actually, this place doesn't sound bad," I said. "I mean, fireplaces in every room? Ongoing maid service? I could think of a lot worse places to live." My mind flashed back to my room in the Rue Cujas, with its falling ceiling and perennial stink. "A lot."

"I suppose," she said resignedly.

"Plus, you wouldn't have to live with *them*." I inclined my head toward the door and the Evil Queens who lived on the other side of it.

Marie-Therèse laughed halfheartedly.

"Do you know anyone at the Poplars?" I asked.

"Not anymore. There used to be three elderly women—we called them the three blind mice, because they were always misplacing things—who all left this house within a few weeks of one another. They were looking forward to it."

"See?" I said encouragingly. "That worked out."

"Not really. When I called to see about visiting them, I was told that visitors weren't permitted for three months. By that time, they were all dead." She shook her head.

I knew that a lot of old people died suddenly, but I didn't think that was the best thing to say to an eighty-year-old woman. "So you've never been to this place?" I asked instead, waving the pamphlet.

"No, but there's a map." She pointed to a page in the brochure. "It's in Vincennes, a suburb east of here." Suddenly she looked up at me with a glint of hope in her eyes. "Would you consider seeing it with me?"

"Sure," I said. "We could go this Saturday, if you're free."

She laughed. "Of course I'm free," she said. "I haven't been invited outside this house in years." She looked around the room. "I just hate to leave it."

"They say that change is good for the soul," I said stupidly. Actually, I had no idea what "they" said about anything. And as for change, I was starting to regret being here instead of back in Whitfield. If I'd stayed home, I might have gone to Japan with Gram and Aunt Agnes (and with Agnes's teleporting capabilities, the travel would have been free!). Or gotten a cool job in a movie theater or something, and hung out with my friends. Or just worked full-time at Hattie's Kitchen, the way I'd planned, where I'd have learned the same things I was learning at the Clef d'Or, except without the fancy names.

But I realized those thoughts were just me being scared of everything I didn't know, and that the same kinds of thoughts were probably going through Marie-Therèse's head right now. If there was one thing I'd learned from doing magic with adults like Gram and Agnes and Hattie, it was that nobody, no matter what their age, knew everything. And that everybody was scared of something.

"How long have you lived here?" I asked.

Her eyes darted around the room, as if she were afraid to answer the question. "A very long time," she said finally. "Perhaps too long. A change in my living circumstances might be good for me after all."

I nodded in agreement.

"Not that I can do anything about it, anyway."

"Sometimes that's a good thing," I said, remembering that I'd come to Whitfield kicking and screaming before finding that it was the one place on earth where I really belonged. "Sometimes what you think will be horrible turns out to be the best thing that ever happened."

"Perhaps you're right," she said, clasping my hands. "You are quite wise for your years, Katy." She smiled. "No wonder your young man loves you so."

I felt myself blushing as I stood up to leave. "Do you really think so? I mean about Peter."

"Peter?" She laughed. "I was talking about Belmondo, dear."

"What?"

"Such a nice young man. He's our landlord, you know."

"Er . . . yes, I think someone told me."

"The two of you make such a lovely pair."

It took me a minute to get over that. To tell the truth, I don't know if I really did get over it, but I left Marie-Therèse's room at that point and shot into my own like a bullet.

There was a note from Peter on the floor that I must have missed when I'd first come in. It said, *Sorry, had to go. Back by nine, I think. P.*

I took the towel off my head and shook out my wet hair. Then, clasping my bathrobe tightly around me, I got into bed with Azrael's manuscript and found chapter four.

Belmondo, I thought. That was ridiculous. How could Marie-Therèse even think such a thing? He wasn't interested in me. He couldn't be.

Absently, I folded Peter's note into a tiny triangle. *And even if he were—interested, that is—I wasn't. Not in Belmondo. Not at all.*

A.D. 1154
The Abbey

Veronique did as her husband had asked, and spent the next twenty years at the abbey at Auvergne, watching the other nuns and guests there grow old while she herself remained relatively unchanged. When her situation became too uncomfortable and her fellow residents too curious, she moved on to another convent, and another, for the next 341 years.

Occasionally during her travels, she would encounter some young girl or other who possessed a special gift as strange as her own, though different in its nature. The families of these girls were generally more than happy to be rid of their freakish daughters, and allowed them to go with the mysterious noblewoman on her way to some holy place or other. In time, though, her collection of acolytes had grown too large to pass unnoticed, and the older ones among them had been around Veronique long enough to know her secret.

"To everyone who sees us, we appear to be nuns," Veronique's friend Béatrice told her. "And so, as nuns, we must establish our own abbey."

Béatrice had been with Veronique for twenty-seven years. She had joined the strange band of supernaturally gifted women when she was a child of six, after her family had abandoned her in a forest to die from hunger or wolves. To Béatrice, Veronique was mother, queen, and goddess, and Veronique had come to trust her absolutely.

"I have been asking questions of people we've passed in our travels," she said. "Paris is nearby."

"Yes?"

"We should live there," Béatrice said baldly. "We need a permanent home, and Paris is a big enough city that we will not be scrutinized overmuch."

Veronique was nonplussed. "Live in Paris?" she asked, alarmed. "But the Church has a great stronghold there. If they find that we are not really nuns, the officials will seek to harm us."

"Not if they believe we are aligned with them," Béatrice said. "New abbeys and monasteries are springing up all the time. If we do not ask the archbishop for money, I do not believe we will be prevented from establishing ourselves as a new order. There is an old building just outside the city."

"But an abbey—"

"I shall cast a glamour around it so that we remain virtually unnoticed," Béatrice said with a wink. "We'll call it the Abbey of Lost Souls. We'll help the lost souls of the city, the poor and sick, and therefore will be of no interest to those in power. We'll be safe there, trust me."

Veronique thought about it. "I understand something of the ways of the nobility," she said. "A glamour may be a good defense, but I think a bribe might also be in order."

Bit by bit, she'd been selling off the treasure Charlemagne had given her, until not much was left. I can spare the gold torque, she thought, but not the necklace. That she would keep until there was nothing else.

That day came some thirty years later, when the "abbey" Veronique had bought was in such disrepair that it would soon be uninhabitable.

Through underground channels, it had become known among witches throughout Gaul—now called France—that there was one place where women of extraordinary abilities could live without fear of persecution for their differences. The Abbey of Lost Souls in Paris and its wise abbess had welcomed these odd women, most of whom were afraid to show their faces outside the building where they lived. As their number grew and the cost of food and other goods increased, money became a problem. First Veronique sold the abbey's land as the city sprang up around them, merging the building into the crowded mélange of shops and homes that made up the "new" Paris of the twelfth century.

The women did what they could to raise funds—wove shawls and blankets for sale at local fairs, provided nursing services for rich merchants—but their efforts were never enough. The "nuns" cared for the poor, and the poor could not pay. The women fed the hungry, sheltered the homeless, and, of course, continued to send "gifts" to the archbishop and any other high-ranking Church officials who might otherwise become overly curious about the unusual nature of the women in the abbey on the alleyway that had come to be called the Street of Lost Souls.

And so, on that day in March of 1184, Mother Veronique of the Abbaye des Âmes Perdues paid a visit to Jean-Loup de Villeneuve, master goldsmith and alchemist, and began a love affair that would last more than eight hundred years.

• • •

After they married, Jean-Loup built a house in the countryside west of the city. It was a beautiful place with lakes and orchards, livestock, and acres of rolling farmland. Jean-Loup named the estate "Toujours." Always.

On their first night in their new home, as he held Veronique in his arms, he knew he was a happy man. "I have a gift for you," he said.

"Oh, Jean!" She laughed as she curled herself more closely against him. "You have already given me so many treasures that I hardly know where to put them all."

"Just one more," he teased, producing a magnificent box of carved rosewood that he pressed into her hand. "Please accept it."

Inside was a pendant of a gold heart, so round it was nearly spherical, on which the words "Mon amour toujours"—my love forever—were carved in Jean-Loup's own elegant hand.

"My darling," Veronique sighed, her eyes bright with happy tears. "I would rather have your love than 'forever.'"

As it turned out, although she did not know it then, she would eventually get her wish.

In gratitude for restoring Veronique to health, Jean-Loup sent the abbey a chest full of gold every month. The money was sorely needed and the women were so thankful that they reciprocated the favor by instituting a ritual similar to the one Béatrice had invented when she cast the spell to bring back Veronique's lost youth. The ritual took place at every full moon, and Jean-Loup was invited to participate.

This new spell was less difficult than the complex magic

Béatrice had woven to give Veronique back the years she had sacrificed in order to heal Jean-Loup. In the full-moon ritual, the process of aging was slowed down for everyone involved. But it was not without sacrifice. For ten days prior to the full moon, all the women of the abbey had to cease using whatever magic they possessed in order to strengthen the spell.

"What it amounts to is that each of our individual talents is transformed," Béatrice explained to Jean-Loup. "The participants still grow older, but at a much slower rate than normal. You would not be asked to sacrifice any part of your own gift, of course, but you would benefit from the magic the rest of us contribute to the spell. In other words, if you continue to participate in our ritual, you may live almost as long as Veronique."

"I am grateful for the extra time I will have with her," Jean-Loup said. "More than I can say."

"But be vigilant," Béatrice said. "You must attend the ritual every month, or you will begin to age normally."

"I understand," he said.

"You see, we always have a choice to use our gifts to this end or not. The more magic we can put into the spell, the more effective it is. But not all of us can afford to give up our magic in order to lengthen our lives."

She was talking about herself. Her talents are a djinn who could discern and influence the thoughts of others, Béatrice found that her talents were constantly required to keep the abbey safe, not only from thieves and murderers, but also from greedy public officials and churchmen. It was through Béatrice's efforts that the abbey had remained virtually ignored in the *midst of what was becoming a major world capital.*

"So I cannot participate in the spell," she said.

"I'm sorry," Jean-Loup sympathized, but Béatrice only shrugged with Gallic indifference.

"One lifetime is enough for me," she said.

He did not understand her then. Nor would he have understood that in time, he would envy Sister Béatrice her short, purposeful life.

CHAPTER • TWENTY-THREE

La Rue des Âmes Perdues, I thought. Veronique and her ersatz nuns had settled in the same street where I lived. Was that just a coincidence? How would Azrael—or whoever had written the book—know about it?

Calm down, I told myself. Paris was a very old city. The street, with its peculiar name, had probably been around since the Middle Ages. For the first time in maybe a year, I wished I could communicate with my father the medievalist. He might know something about the street, or the "abbey" that the phony nuns—who'd really been witches—had established. I supposed I could call him—the post office had public phones that people could make long-distance calls from—but that would entail explaining more than I wanted to talk about. Or I could e-mail him from an Internet café, I supposed . . .

No, I decided I'd feel less uncomfortable being in the dark than I would talking with Dad.

I checked my watch. 8:45. Quickly, I unfolded Peter's note

saying he'd be back at nine and I wrote on the back of it: *Meet me in the kitchen!* Then I stuck the note in my door next to the knob, since he would probably come to my room looking for me.

I figured I'd make him something to eat. It might make up for my being so late after visiting Azrael. Plus, he'd missed the dinner I'd cooked for Sophie's dinner party.

In the kitchen I found some sausage, kale, onions, tomatoes, and garlic, plus some marinated artichoke hearts and black olives—all the ingredients I'd need for a terrific pasta dish. I cooked the sausage, made the sauce, added some kale, salt, and crushed red pepper, and put some cavatelli on to boil. Then I put together a green salad with the vinaigrette dressing I used to make at Hattie's and waited.

9:15. The pasta was ready.

9:20. I set the kitchen table.

9:30. The cavatelli was congealed and inedible. I threw it away and put a new pot of water on the stove.

9:40. The water boiled. I looked out the kitchen door into the courtyard to see if Peter had come back. He hadn't.

9:50. I put the rest of the cavatelli into the pot.

9:57. I drained the pasta and waited. The simmering sauce was turning brown. The salad greens were wilting.

10:01. The front door opened.

"Down here!" I shouted, nearly jumping with joy.

I was arranging everything on plates when I heard footsteps rushing down the stairs toward the kitchen.

"Hurry up!" I sang. "I made you some . . ."

Belmondo leaned his head into the doorway.

". . . dinner," I finished.

"What a nice surprise," he said, holding out a nosegay of violets and rosebuds. "These are for you. And these." He produced a box of perfect, small, bloodred strawberries that must have cost more than the flowers. In cooking school, strawberries like those were used only as garnishes on the most elaborate desserts.

I could only stand there blinking stupidly at him for a moment while all the things I could say shot through my head: *Actually, dude, this isn't for you. I started cooking this meal an hour ago for Peter, who was supposed to be back by now, although he's almost never here, so I guess I'll just throw it all away and hurt your feelings in the process.*

"Thank you," I said, taking the bouquet and sticking it into a glass of water. "Please sit down."

It was a wonderful dinner. Belmondo found some stubby candles to put on the white enamel kitchen table, then tuned the radio to a station that played scratchy recordings of Edith Piaf and Charles Aznavour. He opened a bottle of Chateauneuf du Pape, and explained the things that made it taste peppery. While we ate, the scent of flowers mingled with the aromas of the food and wine, and Belmondo must have told me a dozen times how much he loved my cooking.

"They teach you well at the Clef d'Or," he said.

I could picture Chef Durant wanting to hang himself at a comment like that. "This isn't one of the school's recipes," I said, almost laughing. "It's just something I threw together. We used to do a lot of that at Hattie's, where I used to work, so that we wouldn't waste food."

"It seems that this woman—Hattie?—is your real teacher."

I nodded. "I think you're right. I must have insulted her by coming here to study," I said. "Sometimes I wish I hadn't."

"No, no," he whispered, touching my face with the tips of his fingers. "Please don't say that. Because I am so happy that you are in Paris."

"I am too," I whispered, feeling myself blushing.

"You are nothing like the others," he said, tracing a heart on my hand with his finger.

"Really?"

He laughed. "And you know it perfectly well." He sat back in his chair and crossed his arms over his chest. "These silly women, they use all their magic for only one thing."

"What's that?"

He blew a puff of air out from between his lips. "Foolishness," he said. "A waste. But you . . ." His eyes narrowed into lazy slits. "You keep your power within you. You glow with magic."

We looked into each other's eyes for a long time. I could hear my breath going in and out and my heart thumping in my chest and my blood pounding in my ears, and all the while Belmondo was touching my cheek across the rustic wooden table while his beautiful face shimmered in the candlelight.

"But we've forgotten the strawberries," Belmondo said as he selected one from the box and held it next to my lips until I bit it off the stem. The flavor was so intense that I was afraid I might drool. "You eat beautifully," he said, his eyes locked into mine.

I picked up another strawberry and held it out, tentatively.

"Take off the stem," he said in a way that made my breath quicken. I did as he asked, although my hand was shaking slightly as I held it out across the table. He took my hand and brought it to his lips. Then, as the ripe berry disappeared, he covered the tips of two of my fingers with his mouth. I gave an involuntary gasp.

"*Katarine*," he said slowly, languorously, as the fingers of his free hand traced the outline of my lips. I felt something like a moan rise out of my throat.

"Now let me taste your magic," he said.

"What?"

"Just a bit. On your tongue."

I wasn't sure what he meant, but I felt my tongue moving between my teeth. Belmondo's lips pouted, as if he were going to kiss me from afar. I closed my eyes.

"Katy?" A jarring sound. I looked up.

"Oh, God," I said. It was Peter.

"What are you doing with him?"

"We were having dinner," Belmondo said, withdrawing his hand from my face. He picked up his wine glass and sipped from it.

Peter looked at my own glass. "Were you drinking?"

"Not really," I stammered. "I was just—"

"You do not have to answer to him," Belmondo said, smiling. "This is not your father."

"No, but you could be," Peter said, staring pointedly at Belmondo.

Belmondo cleared his throat. "Perhaps I ought to go," he said, sliding off his chair.

"Right," Peter said. "Before you get arrested."

"Peter!" I began, but Belmondo held up a hand and raised his chin. "Your friend is right, chèrie," he said. "It is not seemly that we should be together so late at night."

"But we didn't do anything!" I shrilled, although I knew that was only technically true. I hadn't physically done very much with Belmondo, but in my heart, I'd done everything.

Belmondo held his finger to his lips. Then he smiled and bowed slightly before leaving through the courtyard exit.

I was left with a lot of weird feelings, none of them good. When I was finally able to speak, what came out was a raspy explosion of anger, shame, and outrage. "I wasn't doing anything wrong," I repeated.

"You don't have to," Peter said. "That's up to *him*." He jutted his chin in the direction of the door.

"Well, if you'd come back in time, none of this would have happened."

"Getting the shipment through customs was more complicated than we'd thought," Peter said. "That doesn't change what was going on here."

"Don't be stupid."

"You can call me anything you want," Peter said. "But I'm not going to let anyone hurt you."

"He wasn't hurting me."

"He'd better not."

"Oh, stop it," I said. "Who's acting like Mom now?" I took the dirty dishes to the sink and ran hot water into the basin. I was too angry to use magic this time. Besides, I liked the feel of soap and water whenever I felt confused or guilty or ashamed or furious or, as was the case at this moment, all of the above.

"Anyway, you had Fabienne to keep you company," I said.

"What?"

His reaction was one of such pure surprise that I instantly

doubted what I'd thought had been fact. "Didn't you?"

"Fabienne? Why would I be with her while I'm working?"

"Oh. I mean . . . ," I blathered. "It's just that her mother . . . that is, Sophie . . ." Finally I shut up and devoted myself to dishwashing. Note to self: Never, NEVER believe Sophie de la Soubise. About anything.

Without another word between us, Peter collected the glasses and utensils off the table and scraped the garbage into the bin. We'd done this routine at Hattie's so many times that it was as automatic as breathing.

Then, while I was washing the dishes, he stuck his hands into the water and held mine. "I can't compete against someone like Belmondo," he said.

That made me feel terrible, but I knew I'd feel even worse if I just kissed him and acted like everything was fine. "I don't know what you're talking about," I said finally.

"I wasn't with Fabienne."

"I know."

He let go of my hand. Then, avoiding eye contact with each other, we went back to washing the dishes while the candles guttered and accordion music played in the background.

CHAPTER • TWENTY-FOUR

When I finally got back to my room, it was nearly two a.m., but after all the drama in the kitchen, I couldn't sleep. Fortunately, Azrael's manuscript was still on my bed, waiting for me.

A.D. 1207
The Doctor

Within the year, Veronique gave birth to a son, Drago, and the couple's happiness was complete.

The boy did not inherit his father's gift for alchemy, but he did excel as a scholar, enrolling at the University of Paris when he was only twelve years old and graduating at twenty-two as a doctor of medicine.

When one of the women from the abbey, a healer who went by the name of Sister Clément, sent them a message that Béatrice was dying, Drago asked if he could accompany his parents to see their old friend.

"Perhaps I'll be able to help," he offered.

Veronique and Jean-Loup doubted very much if anyone could do more for Sister Béatrice than Veronique, but as magical people themselves, they understood that anything was possible. It was for this reason that they never worried that their son had so far evinced no magical ability. It would come, they were sure. It was just a question of when this talent, whatever it was, would manifest.

"Very well," Veronique decided at last. "You may come. Béatrice may want a real physician."

But of course she did not. Nor did she accept Veronique's special ministrations. "Don't be ridiculous," Béatrice said, throwing back her head and chuckling. "Just how long do you think I want to live?"

It was then that Drago forced himself between the two women. "May I examine you?" he interrupted.

Veronique was shocked at the intrusion, but Béatrice waved away her objections. "As you are Veronique's son, I will submit," Sister Béatrice said. "So long as you don't take off my clothes." That was meant as a joke, since no physician would ever look at a female patient's naked body.

"Good. Just have a seat here," Drago said, positioning the old woman in front of him. "Relax, please, madame. Be calm . . ."

"Drago has a good manner about him," Veronique whispered to her husband. "His voice is so reassuring and pleasant that I nearly fell asleep myself. For a moment I actually thought—"

"What is he doing?" Jean-Loup shouted, pushing past her to his son, who was hovering over Béatrice like a lover. "Drago!"

The young man looked up with a dazed expression, his lips pursed as he inhaled deeply with a wet noise that was almost obscene. Beneath him, Sister Béatrice—or what was left of her—lay in a heap of rags and leathery skin, as desiccated as a frog that had been lying dead in the road for a summer.

"What have you done?" Jean-Loup whispered, aghast.

"She was about to die anyway," Drago answered innocently. "I've done her a favor."

Jean-Loup could only gape in horror at the sight.

"Everyone has a life force, Father." Drago leaned forward, eager to explain. "I've found that I can take that life force into myself, especially when my subjects are too weak to hold on to it themselves."

Jean-Loup regarded him with increasing alarm, but Drago, in his excitement, hardly seemed to notice.

"The result is a feeling unlike anything I've ever known, as if my blood were suddenly strengthened by starlight—"

"Get out," Jean-Loup said, choking down his disgust.

"But my findings will change the face of medicine! Just hear me out, Father. If you like, I think I can teach you—"

"Get out!" he shouted, raising his hand to strike. Drago skittered away, bewildered, as Veronique saw what had happened to her friend and screamed.

Sister Clément ran into the room, looking from Veronique to Béatrice, then making the sign of the cross. "What manner of evil has done this?" she whispered.

Drago fled the city. Some years later his parents learned that he had settled in a distant land to the east, where a fabulously wealthy nobleman, a count with a reputation for cruelty and a penchant for murder, had taken him in as his own son.

For Jean-Loup and Veronique, the joyous times of their lives were over.

It was epically late, I was beat, and I supposed there wasn't anything more I could accomplish—or mess up—in what was left of this seemingly interminable day, so I put on the T-shirt I slept in and spread the pages of Azrael's book in front of me on the bed, trying to figure out how I could put the thing together again.

Along the sides of the pages were tiny holes that looked as if they'd been painstakingly punctured by pins. Coming out of some of the holes were pieces of brittle thread. The binding had been sewn, I realized, and probably by hand, a very long time ago.

This was good news, because sewing—well, sewing a book, anyway—was something I could do. I divided the sections I'd already read into chapters, and sewed those pages together. I figured that when I was done, I'd sew the whole book together, and then glue the binding to the cover. It would be good as new.

It was almost dawn by the time I finished sewing the chapter about the abbey. My fingers looked like meaty pincushions, and most of the bindings were stippled with my blood, but nobody was going to see that after the book was glued together.

CHAPTER • TWENTY-FIVE

The next day after school I looked outside my bedroom window as I was changing out of my cooking clothes and saw Peter sitting on the back terrace with Fabienne. I threw on a pair of shorts and a T-shirt and ran down to meet them as fast as I could.

"Katy!" Fabby squealed as she leaped up from her chair to greet me, her arms gesturing wildly. "I did it!"

"Did what?" I looked to Peter for an explanation, but he just smiled and shook his head.

"I went to Japan!" she shrieked, then quickly covered her mouth. "I went to Japan!" she repeated in a whisper, jumping up and down. "I saw Agnes. And Gram."

I felt a little twinge of annoyance when she referred to my great-grandmother as "Gram"—that was my name for her, mine and no one else's—but I got over it. I just couldn't stay mad at Fabby. Despite her great beauty, she was nice. "I teleported there."

I was shocked. "You mean through astral projection?"

"That's what Gram called it, but Agnes told me that what I did—taking my body with me, and not just my spirit—is called teleportation."

"Er, great," I said. I hadn't known the difference. "How are they?"

"Fine," she said excitedly. "Gram has already learned enough Japanese to speak with the other guests at the resort. She even healed a lady with pneumonia. Oh, one thing." She handed me a slender book. "Your aunt wishes for you to have this."

Leafing through it, I recognized it: *A Compendium of Ritual Magic* by Rosamund B. Leakey, a collection of advanced spells that Aunt Agnes had given me two Christmases ago. It had been so far beyond my abilities at the time that I'd put it away in a drawer in Gram's house. I guessed Agnes must have thought I was ready for it now, although I couldn't imagine why. I never performed spells. All of the magical things I did had grown naturally out of my ability to move objects, a talent I'd been born with.

"Uh, okay," I said, tucking it into the back pocket of my jeans.

Then Fabby lowered her head and looked up at me shyly. "They invited me to Whitfield, Katy."

"Hey, cool," I said. And I meant it. If anyone deserved a chance at having a normal family—well, as normal as witch families get—it was Fabienne. "She and Agnes both say I have a true talent for astral travel," she added, brightening. "Of course, they are only being polite."

"Not true, Fabby," I reassured her. "I think you'd be happy

studying with Agnes." Actually, she'd be lucky. As far as the mechanics of astral projection—that is, teleporting—went, I couldn't think of a better teacher than my aunt.

"Perhaps," she said wistfully. "*Mais alors*, that cannot be."

"Why not?"

"Because I'm going to be initiated," Fabby said.

"Initiated?"

"Into the Enclave."

I looked to Peter, but he seemed to be studying his nails.

"Soon, at Lammas, the beginning of August," she went on.

"What happens then?" I asked.

"I don't know, exactly—the details of the initiation are a secret." She looked at Peter. "Do you?"

He shrugged and shook his head. *As if he'd know anything about that,* I thought.

"But I can't wait," Fabby said happily. "I'll be allowed to live here, instead of just visit, and I'll be able to vote on things. And of course, I'll take part in the full-moon ritual every month."

"There's a ritual?"

"Didn't Peter tell you?" Fabby looked confused. "There's one tonight. At midnight."

Reflexively, I looked up at the blue sky, where the white disk of a full moon shone dimly. Back in Whitfield, everyone knew the phases of the moon as well as we knew our own names, but I'd grown lackadaisical about observing magical traditions since I'd come to Paris.

Of course there'd be a full-moon ritual. All witches everywhere celebrated the full moon in some way: It was the time when power entered the human plane. Even during the medieval years of Azrael's story, the full moon had been a big deal.

"But why would Peter be part of the ritual?" I asked aloud, as if Peter weren't sitting right beside us.

"Because he's . . ." Fabby's head swiveled in his direction. "You're going to be initiated too, aren't you?"

Peter swallowed. "That's . . . that's . . ."

I turned to face him. Seriously. "That's what?" I demanded. In my head, I was inviting him to say *that's not true*.

"That's . . . supposed to be confidential," he said instead.

"Confidential?" I asked. "As in not telling me?"

He shrugged. "It's no big deal."

"But this *Enclave*, or whatever it is, needs you in their ritual?"

"No, they don't *need* me," he said irritably. "I'm just going to observe."

"Me too," Fabby said. "But everything will change after our initiation."

"What happens then?" I asked, hearing the hysteria in my voice.

"Hey, I just remembered something," Peter said, standing up. "There's, um, something I need to do."

"No, there isn't!" I shouted. "You're just uncomfortable talking to me about this thing."

"Maybe," he said. "I'll see you later."

I couldn't believe he was walking away from me.

"Oh, I'm so sorry," Fabienne said, looking bewildered. "Was I the cause of difficulty between you and Peter?"

"No," I said miserably. "We just don't seem to communicate that well anymore." She was going to try to say something to make the moment less awkward, but I waved away her concern. "Where is this ritual going to be held?" I asked.

"Downstairs. In the basement, I think. Would you like to attend? I could perhaps ask my mother—"

"No, it's okay," I said. I knew Sophie would never allow me into her secret meeting.

Which was not to say I wouldn't find out about it. The terrace where we were sitting afforded a clear view of the kitchen windows. Directly beneath the kitchen was the basement. I'd find a way.

"Have you ever had a boyfriend, Fabby?" I asked to cover up what I was really thinking.

"No," she said. "That is not permitted until after the initiation."

"Oh? So is this initiation thing like a Bat Mitzvah or something? Like it's when you become a woman?"

"I suppose. Once I am bound to this house—"

"Excuse me?" I sat up in my chair. I'd explore the basement later. "Did you say *bound to this house*?"

"Yes. Once I am part of the Enclave, I will only be permitted to become romantically involved with other initiates. There are many, including men, from all over Europe."

I could only blink in horror. "But what if you like someone outside of the Enclave?" I suggested. "I mean, maybe you'll run into someone at school—"

"I've told you, there will be no more school for me," she said, staring at her feet. "And I will meet no one outside of the Enclave."

"How do you know that?" I argued, remembering when my father caught me making out with Peter. As far as Dad was concerned, the two of us were never going to see each other again, but nothing he did could stop us. "You're young. Things happen."

"It is not permitted," she said.

So that was that, I thought. Maybe French girls just listened to their parents better than American kids did.

"That is why . . . ," she said uncertainly. "About studying with Agnes in Whitfield . . ."

"What, Fabby?"

"My mother has told me not to waste my talents on foolish pursuits."

"Foolish pursuits? Like teleportation?" Frankly, I couldn't think of anything *less* foolish than full-blown magic.

She looked around. "Yes, that is what Sophie meant, I'm sure," she whispered, "although I don't think she knows about my gift."

"What does she want you to learn instead?"

"Only things that will benefit the Enclave. I must do nothing selfish, and . . ." She looked at me as if she were embarrassed to disclose what Sophie had said. ". . . and I must always look beautiful."

"What?" I thought I hadn't heard right.

"I know." She buried her face in her hands. "I am ashamed to tell you. You, who possess so many talents."

"Well, always looking beautiful isn't one of them," I said. "Anyway, isn't that kind of selfish in itself? I mean, how is looking beautiful going to help the Enclave?"

"It will be our benefit, our gift in exchange for our magic."

"Are you kidding me?" I shouted. "You'd trade teleportation for long eyelashes?"

"But it's our tradition—"

Just then Sophie appeared in the doorway leading to the interior of the house. Her arms were folded over her chest, and her face had a distinct air of displeasure about it. "It's time for dinner, Fabienne," she said flatly. She jutted her chin in my direction. "That is, unless you would prefer for our kitchen girl to cook for you."

"Oh, Katy," Fabienne began, ashamed at her mother's bad manners. "I'm so sorry—"

"It's okay," I said. "Go on in."

Actually, not being included at dinner worked in my favor. There was a lot I could learn from this evening's ceremony, but I had to prepare for it.

My talk with Fabienne had only made things more confusing than they already were. For one thing, what had Fabby been talking about, exchanging magic for beauty? She already had more beauty than most people could even imagine. I figured I must not have understood what she was really saying—there was still a bit of a language barrier between us—but the ritual might help to clarify things.

And Peter! What was he doing with these people? It was a sad testament to how far our relationship had deteriorated that he wouldn't talk about it with me, but I couldn't solve that problem right now.

All I could do was snoop. Fortunately, that was something I was very good at.

First, I went into the kitchen and told Mathilde, the cook, that I'd wash the dishes and clean up for her. She was almost pathetically grateful. Apparently, the Enclave's short-term employee policy worked both ways: Sophie and her friends might not have wanted servants nosing around in their business, but neither did most of the city's domestic help want anything to do with the spoiled, rude women in the Abbey of Lost Souls. Consequently, those few employees who could bear to stay at the house longer than a day or two were hideously overworked.

After Mathilde left, I looked over my shoulder to see if anyone was watching (although I suspected that the women who lived with me would rather get root canals than visit the kitchen). Then I waved a wooden spoon to serve as a wand, and whispered the word "clean."

Instantly, a row of dirty dishes flew over the garbage bin to deposit their leftovers before submerging themselves into a sink full of soapy water. Pots arranged themselves into neat rows. Glasses hung suspended in the air like chandeliers, waiting for a turn in the suds.

I smiled smugly. Magic made everything better.

While the dishes were washing themselves, I sneaked down the back stairs into the basement.

Did I say basement? It was more like an underground city. At the base of the stairs was a large open area from which a number of passageways sprouted like roads around a central roundabout. *Or legs on a spider*, I thought.

The passageways all seemed to lead to rooms filled floor to ceiling with ancient artifacts—furniture under threadbare sheets gray with dust, gilded mirrors, books gone so moldy they were little more than wisps of smoke, rusted musical instruments, dozens of locked chests. . . . I wondered if there were other passages leading out of these into still more rooms, but I hadn't come to explore. If the Enclave was to conduct a ritual, it would have to be in a fairly large space without a lot of junk in the way.

I walked around until I found exactly that: a chamber chiseled out of rock, illuminated so brightly that I could see motes of dust in the air. Looking up, I saw a skylight going all the way to the roof.

A skylight, here? I wondered. And then I understood: It wasn't a skylight; it was a *moon* light. In the early evening sky above, I could make out the outline of a full moon, even though it was still light outside. This was the place of ritual.

Back upstairs, while the silverware was swooping into a basket ready to take to the dining room, I prodded the corners of the kitchen with a broom handle, looking for a hole.

It didn't take long. There were a number of cracks and mouse holes all along the baseboards of the old place. None of the ladies of the Enclave cared about the kitchen, and the staff were never around long enough to attempt any repairs. I found a broken place in the floor that opened into a far corner of the basement room. With a meat mallet, I forced it open wide enough for me to look through. Once the lights were extinguished, I was pretty certain I could watch the ritual from here without being seen. As a precautionary measure, I covered the hole with an old wooden bucket. Then I made myself a sandwich.

CHAPTER • TWENTY-SIX

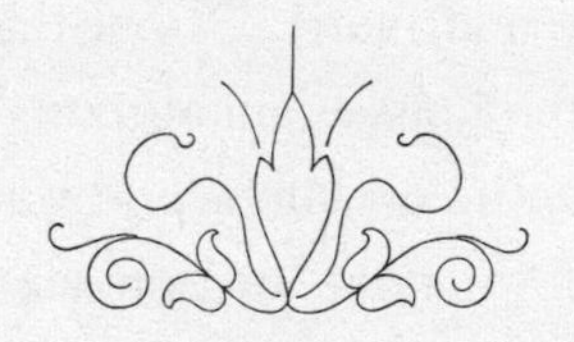

After the kitchen was cleaned up, I took my sandwich and Azrael's manuscript to wait in the library for the full-moon ritual to begin at midnight.

The library was my favorite room in the house, with its walls of polished wood and elegant, well-worn furniture, although it wasn't used much by the people who lived there. Unlike most of the house, which had been somewhat modernized during the 1920s, the library and the wing it was in were still not electrified and nowhere near any of the bathrooms. But I loved it for the same reasons the others avoided it. I loved its inconvenience, its ancient beauty, and its sense of nobility. It retained the characteristics of the great houses, the grand *hôtels* of Paris, almost none of which were used as private homes any longer. Because of the huge expense of keeping them warmed and lit and in decent condition, the vast majority of these palaces had been turned into museums or government offices long ago.

But the house on the Rue des Âmes Perdues was an exception. It was still livable. Since my arrival here, I'd discovered some of its secrets: The servants' entrance, for example, next to the kitchen on the first floor, was a lot easier to navigate than the zillion marble steps leading to the main doorway in the center of the courtyard. I'd bet that humble entrance had been used by the house's inhabitants from the very first. And the library, with its oil lamps and walk-in fireplace, was connected to the downstairs kitchen via a set of stairs just outside the door.

But the best thing about the library was that Sophie and her cronies never went there. It was a place for reading, for one thing. For another, there weren't any mirrors.

I spread out the pages of the book on the heavy oak table in the middle of the room, and settled in for another installment of the old man's story.

1349

Plague

The new abbess sent word to Jean-Loup in May, informing him of the death of Sister Clément.

Paris had become a city of the dead, its streets littered with so many swollen, discolored bodies that it was not possible to bury them before they putrefied. The Black Death was sweeping through Europe with a ferocity that could only be attributed to the Devil.

In the Abbey of Lost Souls, the women had sealed the room where Sister Clément, who had been their abbess for the past 149 years, had died three days earlier.

Jean-Loup offered to bury her, glad he had insisted that Veronique remain at Toujours while he answered the abbess's summons. Sister Clément's body was already beginning to decay. Retching, Jean-Loup carried the corpse to the courtyard and deposited it into a grave he had dug.

"Are you surprised that we can die?" the new abbess asked.

"No," Jean-Loup said. "Of course not."

"Some come to us believing we can make them immortal, but that is not true." She nodded toward the room where Sister Clément's plague-ridden body had lain. "It's just that if we can avoid death through pestilence, accident, or violence, our natural lives will be long."

"Yes, I know," Jean-Loup said, wondering why the woman was behaving as if he were a stranger to the longevity of Veronique's followers. "My wife founded this, er, order."

The abbess went on as if she hadn't heard him. "The problem, of course, is that sooner or later we will approach old age, despite our magic. And when we do, we fall prey to all the miseries that come with the end of life. More, since we linger longer than most."

Jean-Loup set his lips into a tight line. By "falling prey," was she referring to the dreadful act of his monstrous son nearly a century and a half before? Everyone in the abbey had heard the terrible story about Drago's violation of Sister Béatrice so many times that it had taken on the trappings of legend. "Drago will not return, if that is what you mean," he said tersely.

She shook her head. "Actually, he might have done us a service."

He did not understand her meaning, but he was tired from digging the grave and wanted to be back home with

Veronique. So he dropped the conversation, bade the young abbesss good-bye, and left for home.

By the time he arrived back at Toujours, he was already feverish.

Within two days the dread buboes, the swollen black lumps that were the sure sign of the Black Death, appeared in his armpits. "Stay away," he croaked as his wife tried to wipe his sweat-sheened face.

"Nonsense," Veronique said.

"Even you can die."

"But I won't. And neither will you." She smiled at him confidently, but even through his fevered vision Jean-Loup could see that she was worried.

He became delirious. Over the next few days he sank deeper into madness, shrieking and talking gibberish. Finally, he quieted as he fell slowly into a coma, separated from death by only a few shallow breaths.

"No, my love, no," Veronique whispered. She had not left his side since the first night of his illness, and had grown thin and haggard herself. At last she knew what she had to do. She was not able to cure him—that was not exactly her talent—but she could ward off his death. So now, when her beloved husband was so near to crossing over, she took his trembling hands in her own and willed her life force into Jean-Loup's ravaged body, all the while singing as if to a child:

> *My love, my love*
> *Walk through the door*
> *The voice that was calling*
> *Is calling once more*

Be well, my angel
Be strong, be whole
Your suffering has ended
Awaken your soul!

Her breath, sweet as lilacs, washed over him like a benediction.

But when her song was finished, Jean-Loup opened his eyes and saw the terrible toll that bringing him back from the brink of death had taken on his wife. "Oh, Veronique," he cried as a flood of hot tears coursed down his cheeks.

She sat in the chair beside him, her white hair fluttering gently with the breeze from the window. Straining, she raised her eyelids, and her violet eyes lit up her ravaged, ancient face.

"Take care of my sisters," she said. "Welcome others and give them sanctuary."

He nodded, unable to respond.

In her hand was the heart amulet Jean-Loup had given her so many years before. "Mon amour toujours," she said as her fingers opened.

"No!" he screamed. He had taken the last, the very last, of Veronique's life. Filled with inexpressible sorrow, he wept until the sun left the sky and the night wrapped around the two of them, as it had when they were first wed.

"Toujours," he whispered, and kissed her eyes closed.

The love of his life was gone forever.

I wiped the tears from my face. I didn't know if I was reading an allegory, or if Azrael had fallen into dementia, remembering a woman he had only read about as his wife Veronique, but it didn't really matter. It was a beautiful story. I wondered if Peter and I could have anything as good as the love those two had shared.

Love was hard. I was finding that out. There were so many distractions, pitfalls, temptations, mistakes. Seductions from sweet words, wild promises, ambition, hope, arrogance, impatience, greed.

Seductions. Yes.

Had we already taken those first steps in the wrong direction? A single misstep would be all that was necessary for Peter to abandon me for the golden future that awaited him, or for me to turn toward someone else for love . . .

No. I wouldn't think of that.

That wasn't going to happen.

CHAPTER • TWENTY-SEVEN

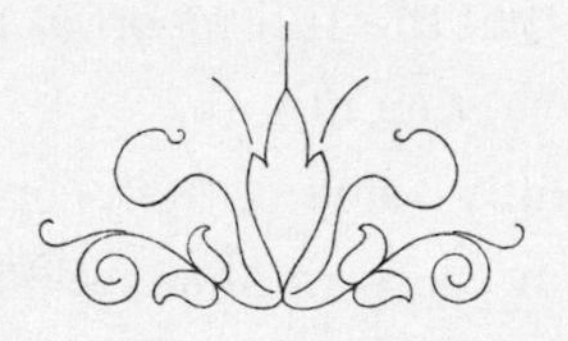

I stayed in the library until I heard the stirrings of the ritual participants. The door knocker banged constantly, so I knew the ritual included people who didn't live in the house. They all seemed to be gathering in the main parlor, where there was a lot of talking and laughter, but no music.

I checked the clock: five minutes to midnight. *They're ready to go down,* I thought. I expected everyone to come through the library and the kitchen below it en route to the basement, and I'd even planned a few choice remarks for Peter—the traitor—but no one showed up. The noise from the parlor diminished and then died into silence. *Another stairway, then.* There must be some sort of opening in the parlor that led directly to the ritual chamber in the basement.

Even better. No one would see me at all. I went down the rickety back stairs into the kitchen and uncovered the hole I'd staked out as my observation tower.

Crouched on my hands and knees, I watched as the stone

chamber filled up with what appeared to be half of Paris, all wearing gray hooded robes and carrying candles to light their way. *This is a real coven,* I thought as they assembled into rows packed tightly against one another in a circle around the central shaft of moonlight from the skylight I'd discovered earlier. I reasoned that the full moon at midnight must pass directly overhead every month.

I strained to identify some of the people I knew, but their hoods shrouded their faces in shadow. There were so many! From the rituals I'd attended in Whitfield, I understood that the more participants there were, the more magic would be created. That is, provided the participants had magic of their own to begin with. When witches get together—the groups are always in multiples of nine or thirteen—and use their combined powers for a common goal, the results can be mind-blowing.

Finally, one of the robed figures—the leader, I guessed, and a woman, judging from her graceful hands—stepped out of the circle and into the moon-drenched light at its center as all the candles in the chamber were extinguished. The smoke from them curled in the shaft of moonlight, where the leader raised her slender white arms as she spoke the opening words of the incantation:

We are the wave of the space between
We are the flood that rushes to shore . . .

I recognized her voice. It was Sophie.

She began to turn deosil—clockwise—and the entire assemblage turned with her like a gigantic wheel circling the stone-walled space.

We sweep past all barriers set in our path
Through corridors of time we pour

Then everyone chanted in unison:

Our Magick lends eternal proof
We receive in return Beauty and Youth.

I was having a moment of déjà vu. There was something about the chant that was familiar. This was the first time I'd watched this ritual, but I could have sworn I'd heard these words before.

And what was the point of the ritual? With so many participants, the magic produced had to be strong. Was this coven performing some sacred service, like keeping world peace? Did they protect Paris from alien invasions? Slow global warming? Prevent Earth from colliding with another planet?

If they were, then it was a little disconcerting that Sophie de la Soubise would be the leader of this group, but that seemed to be the case. Maybe Sophie had depths I hadn't noticed.

Then she stopped and slowly began to turn in the opposite direction. Once again, the others followed.

We circle and bind the hands of time;
Years swim in our embrace.
Our power spins in widdershins
To undo the riptide's pace.

Widdershins. A witch word. It meant counterclockwise, but was used only in rituals. But I'd heard it before, and recently.

Where had that been? Sophie chanted and the rest repeated:

Our Magick lends eternal proof
We receive in return Beauty and Youth.

Oh, of course! I knocked myself on the head as it finally came to me. Azrael's book! I hadn't heard this ritual; I'd *read* it, in the spell the *Abbaye* "nuns" had used to heal Veronique.

But how could that be? The events in the book I was reading took place centuries ago. Could he have been writing about *this* ritual, perhaps, and the ancestors of *these* people?

The group repeated the last lines. This time I paid close attention to the words.

Our Magick lends eternal proof
We receive in return Beauty and Youth.

Beauty and youth? I almost laughed out loud. It wasn't the same spell at all! What a travesty. Veronique and her followers had cast a spell for *healing and truth*, and in exchange they received long lives, which they'd spent in service to the poor. They would never have used their magic for something as shallow as . . .

I sucked in air. That was what Fabienne had meant when she'd said that, as a member of the Enclave, she "must do nothing selfish," while always looking beautiful. This coven, evidently an offshoot of the one begun by Veronique and her followers, had somehow transformed over the years from a sanctuary for extraordinary women into a pointless gathering led by a vain and shallow creature who cared about nothing but her own beauty. It was hard to believe that people born with the gift of magic would throw it away on something so trivial, but there it was: Each month these people pooled all the talents they'd been blessed with and sacrificed them simply to be attractive.

While I was ruminating about the purpose of the ritual, it ended. Suddenly everyone was talking again, shrugging out of their robes and heading toward the south end of the house, below the main parlor.

"You're kidding," I said out loud as, in the room below mine, Sophie tossed back the hood of her robe as if it were a dead animal perched on her head, and laughed gaily. Her hair, dotted with jewels, looked like spun gold in the moonlight where she stood. Once the robes were off, it was clear that everyone was dressed to the nines and ready to party once again.

I finally saw Fabienne, who had been standing right in my line of sight all along. As everyone was heading toward the stairwell, she turned to the tall figure beside her—it was Peter—and shrugged as if to say, *What was the big deal with that?*

Which was also what I was thinking. I mean, it was hard to believe all those people had been after nothing more magical than nice hair and acne-free skin. I'd have to read the paper tomorrow to see if a war had ended or a collision with another planet had been averted, but I somehow doubted that.

And Peter. What was the role Sophie had planned for him? To take over Jeremiah's job as Mr. Moneybags, funding the coven so that its members could go on living like pretty parasites? Was that really what Peter wanted to do with the rest of his life?

The room quieted down, and I looked back through my

spyhole to see what was going on. Sophie was waving her arms above her head, calling for attention. "I just wanted to say one more thing," she said, smiling. "Tonight marks the last full-moon ceremony for one of our longtime members, Marie-Therèse LePetit." She held out her arms, palms up, as if she expected Marie-Therèse to run into them. Some of the assembled guests applauded; the rest, deeming the announcement unimportant, buzzed with their own private conversations. "Marie-Therèse will be going on to greener pastures, and we're all going to miss her."

Did she really say *greener pastures*? As if anyone would miss the "put out to pasture" reference. I wanted to gag.

"So this evening, our refreshment hour will be in her honor!" Sophie went on ebulliently. "Make sure you say hello to her and wish her well!"

There was some more scattered applause. My heart ached for Marie-Therèse. That must have been so humiliating.

A moment later the moonlight shifted and the ritual chamber was cast into deep shadow. Sophie vanished into the crowd. Jeremiah led Peter and Fabienne away toward the general exodus, their candles relit and moving together through the darkness.

I was lying on the floor with my hands cupped around my eyes when someone spoke quietly behind me. "See anything interesting?"

I literally jumped to my feet, my heart pounding. It was Belmondo. He was smiling, leaning against the kitchen door frame. "What . . . what are you doing here?" I sputtered, my eyes darting from him to the hole in the wall where I'd watched the ritual.

"I came this way because there's always a traffic jam at the other stairwell," he said. "But I didn't expect to find such a pleasant surprise." He came up to me and put his arms around me. "*Mon Dieu*, I can feel the magic coming off you." He sniffed deeply, as if I were wearing some exotic perfume.

I squirmed away. "You're one of them," I whispered.

"The Enclave? No." He laughed easily. "I do not require their paltry tricks. But I am like an old family retainer, always present but usually invisible. I only observe, like your paramour, Peter."

"He's not—"

"Does he do this to you?" he asked, brushing my neck with his lips. Then, in a whisper, "Does he make you feel like this?" He kissed me behind my ear.

My breath caught. Suddenly it felt very warm. I could hear myself breathe. My knees threatened to give out.

"Make magic for me, my beauty," he whispered. Dark curls were stuck to his temples.

"What kind of magic?" I asked.

He wiped his forehead with his sleeve and laughed. "How about snow?" he suggested.

"Easy." With a nod of my head, the refrigerator door opened. It was a prehistoric model, probably from the sixties, and I knew from the dinner I'd cooked that the freezer compartment was definitely not frost-free. I shot out five fingers, and the two inches of frozen condensation on the coils peeled away and floated over to us, where we were showered with ice-cold flurries.

"Snow," I said triumphantly as Belmondo blinked away the fat flakes that had settled onto his dark eyelashes.

"You are a marvel," he said.

"I aim to please."

"And you do." He brushed snow out of my hair. "You please me very much."

I felt myself melting as fast as the snow on my skin. Too fast. Too dangerous. "Belmondo—"

He shook his head. "I know what you are about to say, Katarine. 'You must not love me, Belmondo. You must stay far away, for my lover will be jealous and beat me.'"

"I've told you, he's not my lover," I said. "And he doesn't beat me."

Belmondo smiled. "Of course not," he said gently. "Even an American boy would know how special you are."

I wouldn't exactly go that far, but I didn't say anything.

"So if you cannot give me love, perhaps you will accommodate me with the next best thing."

"Which is?"

"Supper," he said. "I cannot resist your cooking."

"*Mais certainment*," I answered, flattered.

The refrigerator door was already open from my trick with the snow, revealing a platter holding a ham. I sent it rocketing overhead, along with some lettuce, tomatoes, two hard-boiled eggs, a cold cooked potato, and a bunch of grapes. A half baguette floated from the bread box, and a bottle of wine came swinging out of the wine rack, uncorking itself as it flew toward us.

"It's raining food!" Belmondo said, covering his head in mock fright.

A gasp from the doorway nearly wrecked my concentration, and the ham came hurtling down. Belmondo caught it with an "*oof!*" while I snatched at falling eggs and lettuce leaves.

"Oh, I'm sorry," Fabienne said as a potato bonked me on the head and a tomato splattered on the floor next to me.

She leaped into the room in time to snag the grapes while they were still in a bunch.

"That's okay," I said. "We were just—"

I spotted Peter behind her, watching me from the shadows beyond the doorway. His face had no expression at all. In another second he moved on before I could say anything to him.

Behind him walked Marie-Therèse, looking pale and shaken. Her eyes seemed tortured, as if her own interior thoughts were blinding her to everything else. I don't think she even noticed me, or anyone else. I debated whether or not to say something to her, but I decided she'd probably had enough public shame heaped on her. I'd speak to her later, in private.

Pulling up the rear was Jeremiah, who paused only long enough to give Belmondo one of the most poisonous stares I'd ever seen.

"You don't belong here," he said. "Get out."

I was about to object, but Belmondo only bowed graciously, a slight smile playing at his lips.

With a gesture directed at Fabienne, Jeremiah walked away. Fabby gave me a "who knows" look as she followed him.

I was already worrying about what I would say to Peter tomorrow. "What was that about?" I asked, confused by Jeremiah's blatant rudeness.

Belmondo shook his head. "Silly old fool."

"But why did you . . . and the ritual . . . what did . . ." I couldn't pull all my thoughts together. The memory of Peter's face filled me with guilt and confusion.

"Don't worry about any of it," Belmondo said. "The old man matters little, the angry American boy even less. Tonight there is only you and me." He pulled me close again. "Just we two."

I breathed in his scent, spicy with a hint of cloves and anise. It would be easy—so easy—to listen to him, forget everything except what was happening in this moment.

But I couldn't do that. There were just too many questions, and not enough answers.

I hated to do it under the circumstances, with Belmondo touching me and talking to me so trustingly, but I knew that if I could only tap into his feelings, his essence, all my questions—at least the ones about him—might be answered. So I let the barriers down, allowed myself to relax, and opened up my mind to him.

Let me in, Belmondo.

I waited.

"Katy?"

That was weird, I thought, cocking my head and frowning.

"What is it?"

"Nothing," I said.

That was true. Nothing had happened. No thoughts, no feelings, nothing about Belmondo transmitted to me.

Nothing at all.

CHAPTER • TWENTY-EIGHT

After Belmondo left, I went upstairs to explain things to Peter, but I hesitated in front of his door. What would I say? That once again, I'd enjoyed a perfectly innocent evening with a man who clearly wanted more from me than friendship?

I knew that it hadn't been innocent, not in any real sense. Belmondo had touched me—again—and again, I had wanted him to. The truth was, it was becoming easier to be with Belmondo, while every day it was becoming more difficult to stay with Peter.

There was no light under Peter's door, so I backed away and walked to Marie-Therèse's room. It, too, was dark. That was just as well, I thought. She needed to be alone for a while. I'd see her tomorrow.

As I got into bed, I thought about my failed attempt to enter Belmondo's mind. Why hadn't I been able to read him? That was a talent I'd possessed all my life. I could even read *furniture*! But Belmondo . . . had he known? Did he block me? Or had I just been so giddy with his nearness that I'd lost my magic?

I closed my eyes. I knew I'd been asking for trouble just by being with him. Maybe losing my magic was the price I would have to pay for losing something else. My integrity, maybe. My loyalty to Peter. My innocence.

And maybe I'd lost that before now.

Last winter I had an encounter with the Darkness. That's a euphemism for something so terrible that it can't really be named or even adequately described: It's the distillation of pure human evil that lives among us all. Cowen can't recognize it, but witches can.

The Darkness moves into people through death. When someone infected with it dies, the evil in them jumps into whoever happens to be physically nearest to them. Of course, no one knows if he or she has been infected. Evil people never think they're evil. They just make excuses for the horrible things they do.

But sometimes the Darkness doesn't just peek out from behind human eyes. Sometimes it likes to show itself in its true form—massive and reptilian, a creature more like a snake than anything else, but a million times more vicious than anything nature could create.

That was what I met last winter.

I'm only alive now because of an extraordinary sacrifice someone made. That's another story, but the point is, I came close enough to the Darkness to feel like I'd be dirty forever. Even when it was all over and I was safe again and amazed that I was still in one piece, I knew that having been in the

Darkness's sights had somehow changed me. I'd been too close, gotten too familiar with death.

I'd never been anyone's idea of a typical all-American girl, but that experience made it so that I would always feel somehow apart from everyone I knew. Tainted. Damaged.

As late as it was, I knew I wasn't going to sleep anytime soon, so I picked up Azrael's book to distract me from my depressing thoughts. His story had become a sort of haven for me, a place where I could go to escape the questions about my own life that I wasn't able to answer.

Speak to me, Jean-Loup, I thought as I turned the page to the next chapter.

1453

The Apprentice

With Veronique's death, Jean-Loup lost his desire to live.

What do I care anymore? he thought as he rose each day from the bed that still carried the scent of the woman he loved. His life was empty and worthless to him. I should die, he thought. He wanted to, needed to be done with his suffering. But every time he thought about the peace that would come with death, he remembered his promise to Veronique as she lay dying. Care for my sisters, she had said. She had given the last of her life force to him, and all she'd wanted in exchange was his promise to protect the women of her abbey from the horrors of the outside world. With the gold he gave them, he brought them safety.

No, he could not grant himself the luxury of death. He owed it to Veronique to live.

But he did not have to live righteously. *I can do anything,* Jean-Loup realized, *be anything. I can dance for the Devil himself, if it suits me.*

And it did.

He became a pirate.

By the end of the Hundred Years War between England and France, Jean-Loup (now known only as *Loup,* the Wolf) had amassed a fortune by waylaying English merchant ships and their wealthy passengers as they were forced from their estates in France. Of course, he did not need or even want the money. It just felt better to steal it. Then again, there was a certain pleasure to be had in the danger involved in his new line of work. On any particular day, he might be killed.

And then his suffering would end.

He became famous as a swordsman. Legends sprang up around this man named Wolf, the pirate whom women in drawing rooms spoke about with soft voices and heaving bosoms, the captain whose crew would follow him into Hell.

As his men drove the terrified English nobles from their cabins, they assured the people whose possessions they were taking that at least their lives would be spared.

"The women and kiddies, anyway," the boatswain explained as he paraded them at sword point onto the deck. "Any man who wants can take his chances with the captain, though."

They all looked to Loup, who stood on deck holding his gold-hilted sword.

"It's the Wolf," one of the passengers murmured with relief. Loup did not kill innocent people who followed his orders. As *usual, they were deposited farther down the French coast, having been relieved of their treasures and weapons but with at least their travel and identity papers intact.*

One by one the male passengers, who nearly always declined to duel with Loup, slinked past him while their women looked on contemptuously. Occasionally a woman, despite the unpleasantness of her situation, flashed a lusty glance at the handsome pirate with the gold-hilted sword.

Loup was always courteous. He nodded graciously to the ladies, and only smiled at their cowardly husbands. In his entire career as a privateer on the high seas, he prevented only one person from leaving his ship. That was a ten-year-old cabin boy who had been trying to sneak off the deck unnoticed.

"You," Loup said, jabbing at the boy's leather jerkin with his sword. "Who are you?"

"I ain't nobody, sir," the boy said.

"Oh, stop it. You're not talking to an English lord. What's your name?"

The boy looked up through a mop of dirty hair. "Henry Shaw, sir."

"Shaw!" Loup roared with laughter. "Do you know what that means in your pitiful language?"

The boy shook his head.

"Wolf! It means wolf, the same as me! Perhaps you're one of my descendants!" He slapped the boy on the back. "What do you say to that, Henry Shaw?"

Henry swallowed. He had no idea what the mad pirate was talking about, but the man's fancy sword was still poking into his ribs, so his lifted his face and said in a clear, loud voice, "That'd be fine by me, guv."

"Good. I need a servant. The last one ended up getting thrown overboard."

That was the last venture in Loup's century-long spree as an outlaw. With young Henry Shaw at his heels, Loup returned to Toujours, although he'd never again referred to it by that name after Veronique died.

The place was in ruins. He had not visited it in decades, and the neglect was obvious. Aside from its sturdy Romanesque walls and part of a roof, there was little indication that human beings had ever lived there. All the furniture had been stolen long ago, as had nearly everything else that could possibly be carried. Rats and birds had made nests throughout the house. The fields and vineyards, once so carefully tended, now lay covered with weeds. The barn was no more than a pile of stones.

"Looks like you've got your work cut out for you," Loup told the boy as he emptied a bottle of rum into his mouth and then tossed it into a corner.

Impossible as the task seemed, young Henry managed to get the place into a livable, if primitive, condition before the first snows of winter.

Loup, meanwhile, uncovered a chest of magnificent leaded stained glass from one of his outlaw forays. "I never seen anything like this outside of church," young Henry said, picking up one of the sheets.

"Well, polish them up. And don't break anything, or I'll have your head."

The boy took a cloth to them, first wiping down the glass, then rubbing the lead pieces until they shone. "Blimey," he whispered. Even the colored glass panels in church didn't gleam like these. He went in search of his master, who had passed out from drunkenness, and shook him awake.

"Captain Loup! Come see this!"

"What is it, you little toad?" Loup roared as he reached for his goblet, which Henry had been instructed to keep filled at all times.

The boy had long since ceased to be afraid of the French pirate who had taken him from the cargo ship. Despite the Wolf's bluster and perennial drunkenness, Henry knew that his master was not a cruel man. Sometimes when the boy could not sleep at night, he heard Loup weeping. Henry never asked about these melancholy episodes—he respected Loup too much to embarrass him with his knowledge. He knew that Loup must have lost something more precious than life itself to mourn so deeply.

"Speak up, you bloody pig turd!"

"The leading around the glass, sir," Henry answered. "Look!" He held up the sheet of leaded glass.

"By Saint Peter's beard," Loup remarked as he touched the gleaming lead, which was not lead at all, but gold. "What'd you do?"

"Nuffink," Henry insisted. "Got beat once for coin clipping, but I didn't do nuffink then, either."

"Coin clipping?"

"One of the toffs on the ship said I was pinching gold off of his coins while I was cleaning his shoes, but I wasn't. All I was doing was shining his bleedin' buckle. I don't know how the gold got under me fingernails."

Loup looked up from the stained glass with its golden

border. "Gold was under your fingernails?" he asked, instantly sober.

The boy shrugged.

"Were you thinking about gold at the time?"

"How do I know what I was thinking?" Henry said irritably. "Thinking just happens. You don't plan it."

Loup nodded slowly. "Wait here," he said. In a few minutes he returned with a kitchen pot made of black iron. "I want you to think of gold," he said, placing the boy's hands on the sides of the pot.

"What?"

"I said think about making gold, you scurvy cur, or I'll feed your scraggly head to the rats!"

"All right, all right," Henry said. "Though you're a madser, and no mistake."

"Shut up and think. And hum."

"What's that you want?"

"I said hum, slimy worm! Make a noise."

"What kind of noise?" Henry asked.

Loup took off his boot and threw it at him. "A gold-making noise, idiot boy! Go on, go on." He flapped his hand at Henry. "And be serious about it, or I'll wring your scrawny neck. Don't think I won't."

The boy closed his eyes as he rubbed the pot. The area where his hands had come in contact with the metal changed from black to gold. "Can I stop thinking now?"

"No, damn you," Loup said.

The boy rubbed some more. And more. He rubbed the iron pot until his hands began to blister. "Loup—"

"Look."

When Henry opened his eyes, they bulged. "God and king," he breathed.

Loup laughed. "It took this long because you don't think well," he said. "But I'll teach you."

Henry hardly heard him. He was looking at the golden vessel between his hands.

"In case you have any ideas about running off, I should tell you that you're welcome to do so. But if you do, you probably won't live to your next birthday."

The boy knew Loup wasn't talking about what he himself would do to him, but about Henry's fate in the hands of the public. "Am . . . am I a sorcerer, then?" he whispered.

"That's what they'll say."

He looked closely at Loup. "And you?" he asked after a moment.

Loup took the lid to the pot and ran his hand over it. With one sweet caress, the lid transformed into gleaming gold. He grinned at Henry.

"So we're rich?" the boy asked.

"Is that what you want?"

Henry shrugged. "I'd rather stay with you," he said.

Loup nodded slowly. They were the kindest words he'd heard in a century. He didn't trust his voice. "Then keep your mouth shut," he said hoarsely. "And get back to work."

It had been that simple.

Loup and Henry did not live like rich men, but continued to farm the land that Loup owned. They employed only a cook who came in from the nearby village three days a week, and a few extra hands at harvest time.

In the evenings, the two of them read. Loup introduced Henry to mathematics and science and art—all the things that had once been his principal occupations in the days before he'd discovered the dubious gift of alchemy. He hadn't wanted to stop drinking, but Henry's avid interest in education forced Loup to keep his mind relentlessly clear. Finally, when Henry was twenty-one, Loup took him along to the Abbey of Lost Souls.

By this time Loup looked as if he were in his sixties. Although he'd arranged for a chest of gold to be sent to the abbey each month, he hadn't attended the ceremonies regularly. Consequently, he'd aged like a normal man during most of the years he'd spent raising Henry. Nevertheless, the abbess—a new one, with a controversial past—welcomed him warmly when he came to them with his ward.

"Ah, your son," she said, taking Henry's hand between her own. If she remembered Drago, she did not mention him.

Loup winced at the thought that his real son had lived in the thrall of evil, and had probably burned in Hell long ago.

Henry saw his reaction. "Not really," the young man answered.

But Loup clapped him on the back. "Close enough," he said. His voice was hoarse with emotion, and his deep affection was not lost on Henry.

The abbess held on to Henry's hand a little longer than was necessary. She was young, he noticed, and there was a sauciness in her eyes that was at odds with her nun's habit. Henry blushed under her direct gaze. "Ah . . . what is your gift, Lady Abbess?" he asked, trying to make conversation.

She pulled down the hood of her habit, revealing a cascade of blond hair. "My beauty," she said without any embarrassment at all.

"She is a siren," Loup explained on the long ride home. "She can bend men to her will. A useful gift during these dangerous times. I understand the archbishop is particularly fond of her," he added, laughing.

Henry blushed furiously, although night had fallen and his discomfort could not be seen.

"Hurry, Henry!" Loup called. "I need to get to bed."

But Henry did not keep up. He rode slowly, drinking in the light of the full moon and remembering the touch of the young abbess's hand in his own.

At the next full moon, to Henry's disappointment, he and Loup were met by a different abbess.

"My predecessor has gone out into the world," the woman explained. "Hers is not a gift that is easily discernible as witchcraft, so she will be safe until she returns."

"What's she doing?" Henry asked blatantly.

The abbess's response was just as blunt. "Finding a husband," she said. "She's looking for a title."

Loup shook his head. "Poor sod. Won't know what hit him."

Henry pretended to share the joke, but the waves of misery emanating from him were almost palpable.

He had never even learned her name.

From that day forward, Henry threw himself wholeheartedly into his work, which he decided was not farming, but commerce.

He invested in a number of enterprises, both in Paris and

London, and in merchant ships that traveled to the ends of the earth. Within ten years of his first foray into business, he had become one of the most successful traders in France. By 1658, more than 200 years after meeting Captain Loup, Henry had increased his master's wealth many times over, and had no plans to stop expanding his mercantile empire.

"I'd like to travel to the New World," he announced at dinner.

Loup raised his head from his soup. "Why?" he asked. "You don't need money, do you?"

"Of course not," Henry said.

"Then why bury yourself in business?"

"Because I need to work." Henry put down his spoon. "I'm actually rather good at what I do."

"Indeed," Loup said. "And so you'd like to test your skill in the English colonies across the sea?"

"Yes." Henry was nearly quivering with excitement now. "There's a ship filled with witches that's leaving from the English coast in a month's time."

"Filled with witches," Loup mused over a heel of bread. He was thinking of the rash of public burnings of which the Church had tacitly approved. "Will that be safe?"

Henry blinked. "Can you think of any safer vessel than one filled to capacity with beings possessing supernatural power?"

They both laughed. "That's fine, then," Loup said. "But keep your talent to yourself. Even witches can go mad at the smell of gold."

CHAPTER • TWENTY-NINE

I awoke in a welter of paper, with creases across my face and a pool of drool on my sleeve. Blinking against the sunlight, I gathered the loose pages of the book together. That is, I stretched out my fingers and the pages flew into them.

So maybe I haven't lost my magic after all, I thought, feeling a little more hopeful since my failure to read Belmondo. My joy was short-lived, though. As I came fully awake, I remembered the faces that had looked into the kitchen last night: Jeremiah's, so angry he looked practically radioactive; Peter's, blank and purposefully indifferent, as if he could no longer countenance anyone as sinful as I was; and Marie-Therèse's. Hers was the face that stood out most in my memory: Bloodless and preoccupied, it was the face of a woman who had more trouble in her life than she could handle.

I put Azrael's book away in my backpack and made my bed. There was nothing I could do about Jeremiah. Or Peter, either, unless I was willing to fall abjectly at his feet and beg him to forgive me for looking at another guy, which I wasn't. No matter how foolish I'd been behaving with Belmondo, I didn't need Peter to absolve me of my sins. But I could do something about Marie-Therèse, even if it was nothing more than listening. I knew what it was like to feel alone and unwanted. Sometimes just having someone around helped.

"Wait a second," I said out loud. I rummaged through the papers on my dresser for my meat-market calendar. It was Saturday! I'd promised Marie-Therèse that I'd go with her to look at the retirement home where she was being sent. That might perk up her spirits a little.

I got dressed and knocked on her door. She answered looking as put-together as ever in a pair of dark trousers and a silk blouse, with a string of pearls around her neck.

"Ready?" I asked.

"Oh, I don't think I feel up to traveling," she said with a vague wave of her hand.

"Hey, moving out of here isn't going to be the end of you," I said softly.

She sighed as she led me to a pair of exquisite gilt-edged chairs and gestured for me to sit down. "But it is. I wish I could explain it to you."

"So why can't you?" I asked, exasperated. "Do you think I'm cowen?" In the corner of the room, on a dainty vanity, was a small vase of flowers. Holding out my hand, I concentrated on the flowers until the vase flew across the room into my fingers.

Marie-Therèse looked surprised. "Goodness, what power you have!"

"Not really," I said. "Where I come from, I'm just sort of run of the mill."

"Ah," she said wistfully. "To have magic like yours . . . I think it must be very nice to use the gifts you are born with. Perhaps at one time I myself . . ."

She'd lapsed into silence. "Go on," I prompted.

"It's really nothing," she said, blushing, "but at one time I fancied I could talk with the dead."

"Oh?" I didn't want to be rude, but talking with the dead—in Whitfield, anyway—was pretty elementary. In fact, the Meadow, which was a kind of park in the middle of town, was filled with the spirits of witches who'd passed into what we call the Summer Country. To talk with them, all you had to do, basically, was go there.

"Of course, I can't do that any longer." She laughed. "None of us hold on to our magic very long. Perhaps when I am on the other side, the ability will come back to me." She looked puzzled. "At your home, do witches become stronger with age?"

"Yes," I said. I didn't want to seem arrogant, but magic was like a muscle. The more you used it, the stronger it became. They wouldn't know that here, of course, since witches weren't allowed to use their magic for anything except looking good.

She examined her hands. "Here, our magic is a sacrifice. We give away a little of it at every . . ." She caught herself, looking guilty.

"It's all right," I assured her. "I saw the ritual. And I know about the Enclave, and the initiation that's going to take place in August, at Lammas."

"Ah. Well, then," she said sadly. "That is when it begins. At Initiation."

"When what begins?"

Her eyes scanned the corners of the ceiling. "Oh, it's nothing, nothing . . ." At this point I was really getting annoyed at her dithering, but then she looked at me with such longing, such suffering, that it was almost painful for me to see her. "That is when we commit ourselves."

"To what?"

She bit her lip, as if she were deliberating whether to tell me or not. Finally she swallowed and then said thickly, "To being . . . youthful."

"Er, right," I said. Even though I knew that information already, the words sounded ridiculous. My great-grandmother would cluck like a hen at the thought of witches trading in their talents for something so idiotic.

"Our youth is a measure of our magic. We lose it with time, so it is understood that after a certain number of years, the magic will have waned to the extent that our participation in the Enclave will no longer be of benefit." She spoke with a quiet dignity that I knew hid an ocean of pain. "I'm afraid I have reached that age. If you attended the ritual last night, then you'll have heard Sophie's farewell speech to me," she said bitterly. "The coven has voted. On my birthday I must leave. That is the agreement I made when I came here, and that is what I am bound to honor."

"But what kind of crazy agreement is that?" I shrieked. "And who says you're 'no longer of benefit'? There are still a million things you can do!" I was really mad now, pacing around the room and shouting. "You can write your memoirs! You can take up quilting. Or photography. Or you could get a job. Shoot, you could learn to skydive if you wanted to! And you can certainly develop your magic again."

She laughed weakly.

"Maybe you don't believe me, but you should. These people have got you brainwashed." I pulled her to her feet. "Come on, Marie-Therèse. We're going to the Poplars."

"Now?"

"Right now." I went to her closet and pulled out a jacket for her to wear over her clothes. "Look, you don't need these creeps. All they're good for is posing." I looked at her levelly. "And scaring you. It's time you had a real life."

She looked down, her eyelashes fluttering with excitement. "Do you think so?" she asked. "Really?"

"You bet," I said.

It took two Metro transfers, three buses, and a taxi, but we finally got to the Poplars.

Marie-Therèse was right: The house was every bit as fabulous as the Abbaye des Âmes Perdues, with at least forty rooms on three floors, a palatial building right out of *The Three Musketeers*. It was starting to get dark outside, and as the taxi pulled up the curved driveway, we watched the lights inside the house go on, one room at a time, the chandeliers gleaming through the silk draperies.

"Looks pretty good to me," I said as I rang the doorbell. Marie-Therèse smiled, seeming to agree with me.

A butler in livery answered. "Good evening, Comtesse LePetit," he said with a slight bow, and opened the door for us.

Marie-Therèse was like a young girl, blushing and giggling. "He knew my name," she whispered as the butler led us into an immense sitting room filled with sixteenth-century antiques.

"You're a countess?" I asked, inadvertently whispering, afraid to disturb the studied elegance of the place.

She brushed the question away.

"The chateau has been recently refurbished, madame," the butler said. "We hope you are satisfied. Please let us know if you would like to have anything replaced or removed."

"No, it's . . . it's quite lovely," Marie-Therèse said.

"Perhaps Madame la Comtesse would enjoy a tour of the house?"

"Oh, yes," we both said, following him up the great curving stairway. At the top of the stairs, we passed a maid dressed in black and white, with a lace cap on her head. For some reason I couldn't understand, the young woman nearly gasped when she saw us.

"See that a tea tray is brought for the ladies in the sitting room," the butler snapped at her. The maid curtsied and averted her eyes.

"Is something wrong?" I asked.

The butler shook his head, a movement so slight it was almost invisible. "Rose is a new addition to our staff," he explained stiffly. "Please forgive her awkwardness." He shot her an evil glance. I supposed it was something personal between them, so I tried to forget about their brusque exchange and concentrated instead on the rooms.

They were beautiful and, like the sitting room, filled with perfectly preserved antiques. But something bothered me about them, something I couldn't easily explain. Marie-Therèse might have been a witch, but since the members of the Enclave didn't diversify their gifts, she would have almost no idea of what witches, and particularly object-empaths like me, could do. The vibrations in wood and metal lasted a long time, and furniture absorbed its owners' history well. If I paid attention, even the most ordinary end table or kitchen chair could tell me volumes about the people who had used them.

But what was weird about the pieces in the house Marie-Therèse and I were touring was that none of the pieces could tell me anything about who had lived there recently. There were traces of long-ago aristocrats worrying about the Revolution (including one old geezer who secretly dressed in his wife's clothes), and the indifferent touches of servants assigned to clean them, but I could find *nothing*—not one human marker—after, say, 1800. It was as if all the history of these things had been wiped away along with the dust.

"My, isn't this *lovely*!" Marie-Therèse exclaimed, delicately touching a porcelain vase that bore the psychic imprint of a family in mourning for a man who had recently been beheaded. I could almost see his blood on it.

"Um," I grunted, turning away.

We had our tea back in the sitting room. Marie-Therèse marveled at the tiny scones and petit-fours that the maid served us from a silver platter, but eating was the last thing I felt like doing. Something was wrong here. I just couldn't put my finger on what it was.

Then I saw the tray shaking, and I realized it was the maid. She was the same one the butler had spoken to on the stairway, and her hands were trembling. The cords on her neck were standing out too, as if she were doing everything in her power to keep from screaming. I tried to catch her eye, but she stared resolutely ahead.

"Excuse me," I said, touching her elbow. "Rose?"

We both gasped at the same time. The silver tray flew into the air, tossing pastries everywhere. Rose fell to her knees, murmuring apologies as she picked up the tiny cakes, just as the butler bustled in. His face was red. He looked as if he were about to burst with anger.

"It wasn't her fault," I blurted. "I startled her."

The man brought himself under control—at least momentarily—and managed a curt bow in my direction. "Very good, mademoiselle," he said, although the look he gave the maid could have burned through steel.

Marie-Therèse was looking bewildered. "Maybe we should go," I suggested, hauling her out of her seat.

"What . . . what was that about?" she whispered as I pushed her down the length of the driveway. "Could we not have called a taxi from inside the house?"

"I needed the air," I said, continuing to propel her forward. I wasn't about to tell Marie-Therèse, but when I'd touched the maid's arm, something like pure fear had shot out of her. Fear, and a single, screaming thought: *My God, don't make me watch another one die!*

CHAPTER • THIRTY

I really couldn't afford it, but in the interest of time, we took a taxi all the way back to the house on the Rue des Âmes Perdues.

"Thank you, dear," Marie-Therèse said. "You've done so much to set my mind at rest."

"Glad to help," I muttered, practically shoving the old lady back into her room. "Well . . ." I pretended to yawn. I still had things to do. "See you later."

"But Katy, can you explain why you insisted that we leave so—"

"Sorry," I said, stretching exaggeratedly. "Another time. Student's hours, you know."

She looked at her watch. "But it's barely seven o'clock."

"That late?" I said, yawning again. "Nighty night." I pushed her door shut.

Then I ran to Peter's room. I was still angry and confused about his participation in the Enclave—not to mention his holier-than-thou attitude afterward, but I could wait to discuss those things with him. At the moment, there was something more pressing on my mind.

I knocked on the door, hoping fervently that he was in. For a change, he was. "You have to help me," I said, plastering myself against the inside of his door.

"What'd you do?" He squinted at me suspiciously.

"I didn't do anything!" I hissed. "It's these people. I told you, something's wrong here."

Peter frowned. "What, exactly?"

I plopped myself onto his bed. "Remember when we were talking about the so-called country house where the old people go?"

He nodded.

"Well, they go, all right. But they don't come back."

"Huh?"

"None of the furniture's been used for hundreds of years. And when I touched the maid who brought us tea—"

"Wait a minute. You went there? To the old folks' home?"

"I had to see if it was a real place."

"And it was."

I nodded. "But when I touched the maid, she freaked out. And when I tuned in to her thoughts, all she could think about was that she didn't want to see anyone else die."

Peter looked at me expectantly.

"Well?" I shrilled. "What are we going to do?"

"What do you mean?"

"I *mean* we can't let Marie-Therèse go there!" I thought, *How dense could a person be?* "Didn't you say that Jeremiah asked you to move her out on her birthday? Well, don't!"

"Katy—"

"They *die* there, Peter!"

He blinked.

"Is something wrong with your eye?" I nearly shouted.

"No . . . no . . ." He rubbed his nose. "It's just that . . . well, it *is* a retirement home. I don't imagine too many of the residents leave there to go skiing in Vail."

I sat back, glaring at him. "I'm telling you, it was *weird* there, Peter."

"Okay. But a lot of places are weird. Whitfield isn't exactly normal either."

"But—"

He held up a hand so that I'd let him finish. "We are dealing with witches, after all. And it's not like the place was a haunted house or anything, if there were servants bringing you tea."

"The butler was weird too," I muttered.

He shrugged.

"Rude."

Peter rolled his eyes. "A rude French butler. How shocking. Better call the media."

"You're not being any help at all."

"I'm sorry, Katy. But I have to be up at five in the morning. Jeremiah needs me to—"

"Jeremiah!" I exclaimed. "Where is he?"

Peter looked stricken. "Actually, he's here," he said with a sigh. "He's with Sophie."

"Where?"

"In her room, I guess. But Katy—"

"Never mind," I said, leaping from his bed. "Forget I ever came here."

"I just wish you'd—"

I closed the door behind me. "—be reasonable," I heard him finish.

You be reasonable, I thought. *You and the Barbie witches you're so thick with.*

My next stop was at Sophie's bedroom door. This was going to be tricky, I knew. Sophie didn't like me, and if she was talking with Jeremiah, they were probably discussing something important. But what could be more important than someone's life? I squared my shoulders and prepared to knock.

And then I heard their conversation.

"How can I?" Jeremiah said, sounding exasperated.

"For God's sake, be quiet!" Sophie hissed. "Do you want everyone to hear you? Would you like to explain yourself to the stupid American girl?"

That made me take notice.

"All right," Jeremiah said. "But you ask for too much."

"Oh? And you think I do not deserve this thing I ask?"

"It's not that—"

"I, who gave you up so that another woman might have you?"

"She was my wife, Sophie."

"You were mine long before you married her!" Sophie spat.

"And I am yours still."

She made a sneering sound. "So? What good are you to me now? Look at you, an old man."

"Sophie, that's enough."

"And you want to see me become like you? Dried up, ugly, useless—"

"I don't think I want to see you at all, Sophie," he said with an air of deadly quiet. "Good night."

When I heard him walking toward the door, I jumped out of the way, sprinting as far down the hallway as I could get, but I don't think I fooled anyone. Jeremiah stood watching me for a moment as I peered over my shoulder, pretending to be absorbed in the wallpaper. Then he shook his head and hurried down the curved stairway.

At that point I dropped the pretense that I just happened to be in the corridor when he left Sophie's room. "Mr. Shaw," I called after him. "Please listen to me. It's about Marie-Therèse—"

He stopped and stared at me, looking very irritated. "What about her?" he snapped.

"Her birthday," I said, breathless from all my running. "You have to call it off."

"Call off her birthday?" he asked, looking genuinely confused.

"The celebration of it. The . . . you know," I whispered. I mimed abducting Marie-Therèse and carrying her away, but I don't think he caught on.

"You ought to speak with Peter," he said, preparing to bolt.

I put my hand on his arm. "I'm speaking to you, sir," I said. I was aware of how pushy I sounded, but I had to make him listen to me. "Mr. Shaw, I don't exactly know what's going on here, but it's not right to send an old lady away from the only home she knows, especially since that place—the Poplars—is so strange."

"Strange? In what way?"

I took a deep breath. "People die there," I said.

He frowned slightly, looking annoyed again. "I'm afraid I can't help you," he said, heading down the stairs.

Then an odd thing happened. He stopped suddenly, looked around, and then climbed back up again and met my eyes with his own. "I know you've been to see the old man," he said in a low voice.

For a moment I was flummoxed. I'd always thought of *him* as the old man.

"Azrael."

I gasped. *Oh, God,* I thought frantically. *How did he find out? Who had followed me?* A rush of panic flooded through my veins. *One day an enterprising young fellow will visit me and then kill me for my old clock. Oh, God, oh God oh—*

"Thank you," Jeremiah said. He touched my arm for a moment, and then retracted it. "Thank you for your kindness to him."

Thank you? He was thanking me?

"Er . . . what did you . . ."

But he was already down the stairs and out the door.

CHAPTER • THIRTY-ONE

If possible, things had become even more confusing. Peter hadn't been any help, and Jeremiah Shaw, who eerily seemed to have been spying on me, nevertheless wasn't about to change his mind about expelling Marie-Therèse from the house. I had to come up with something else to help my aging friend before she got sent to the Good-bye Corral as punishment for getting old.

After wracking my brain for a while, I decided there might be one other person I could talk to. I didn't think he could help me any more than the others, but maybe he'd be able to give me an idea or two.

"Azrael?" I called experimentally, hearing my voice echo eerily through the maze of tunnels.

He didn't answer me, but when I peeked into his candlelit alcove, he was shuffling toward the entrance.

"Yes?" he asked quietly. I couldn't tell if he was glad to see me or not.

"Can I . . ." I felt horrible, barging in on him after he'd made it perfectly clear—twice—that he wanted to be alone, but it was too late to turn tail and run. "I'm really sorry," I said, holding out a two-liter bottle of Perrier water and today's edition of *Paris Soir*. "I know you didn't want company, and you asked me not to bother you again, but I was just wondering—"

"Ah, I see it is my young friend Katy Ainsworth," he said, taking the bottle from my hands.

"You . . . you don't mind that I came here?" I asked.

"I did not say that."

"Oh." I hung my head.

"But since you are here, perhaps we might share a cup of tea."

I looked up. The old man was smiling. I smiled back.

"Besides, how could I turn away someone who brings me fizzy water?"

"I'm sorry I didn't bring any food today," I said. "It's Saturday."

"Quite all right. I won't starve without your culinary creations, delicious as they are."

"Really?" *Cervelles au beurre noir*, a.k.a. buttered brains of baby cows, was on the schedule for Monday's class. Chef Durant might like it, but personally, I'd boil my shoes and gobble them whole before I'd eat that.

"I take it you do not cook regularly *chez toi*?"

"No," I admitted. I didn't want to mention that even eating brains would be preferable to dining with those skanks. "There's a cook where I live."

"I know," he said.

"You do?"

He nodded his shaggy head. "I knew as soon as you mentioned the dreaded Joelle. The witches of the Rue des Âmes Perdues are a long-established coven."

I could only blink in response. "You know about them?" I whispered.

He laughed heartily. "My dear, everyone knows." He put the kettle on the charcoal brazier he used and took out two elegant china cups. "They're a silly coven. A bunch of vain chickens with hardly any magic."

His talk of magic and covens made me a little uncomfortable. A lot of people associated witches with evil or Satan or something, which simply wasn't true, although I'd discovered that once some people's minds were made up, the truth no longer mattered to them. I was hoping Azrael wasn't one of those people. "Er, by *magic*, do you mean—"

"I mean what you do," he said. "What you are."

I froze. "How do you know?" I squeaked.

He laughed. "My child, magic practically rolls off you. One needn't even see you perform to know that about you. I imagine Joelle is not the only one of your housemates who hates you."

He'd gotten that right. "I don't know if they hate me, exactly," I waffled.

"They are envious," he said with a chuckle. "Wildly, screechingly envious."

"Really?"

He nodded.

"I think they want Peter to join them," I said.

"The work-driven Peter."

"Yes," I said tightly.

"And will he?"

I slumped in my chair. "I don't know."

"Ah. Now I see. If Peter remains with you, he will not give his allegiance to them. That is why these women wish to force you to leave." He brought me a cup of steaming, fragrant jasmine tea and sat opposite me. "Perhaps you should give this young man more credit than you do. He can, after all, make up his own mind."

"Maybe," I said. "But there's a lot of pressure. It's not just the beautiful women hanging all over him—I'm pretty sure Peter wouldn't be swayed by them, if that was all there was—but there's a big position with Shaw Enterprises, too, not to mention . . ." I was going to say *he's being groomed to be the coven's resident alchemist,* but I caught myself in time. I cleared my throat. "Er, not to mention college. Peter's been all but promised an acceptance into the best university in America."

Azrael nodded. "Try having a little faith," he said.

I squirmed. There was also the matter of Belmondo, which I was also not about to bring up. I didn't even understand that myself. When I thought about what I was doing with him under Peter's nose, I felt ashamed. But good, too. Darkly, wickedly, daringly *good.*

"So is this why you came to see me?" the old man asked, startling me. I must have been lost in thoughts of my lust for Belmondo. "Because my experience with affairs of the heart may be somewhat rusty."

Get it together, I told myself. *Don't lose focus.* "No, I wanted to talk with you about something else," I said, sitting up straight. "There's a woman at the house, an older woman named Marie-Therèse. She's going to be kicked out because they have this stupid rule that you have to leave the house when you get old."

"Why not?"

"Why not?" I shouted. "Because it's cruel and idiotic. All they care about is their looks!"

"*Oui*," he said. "That is what they use their magic for."

So he knew about that, too. "So anyway, they're throwing her out like garbage."

"Now, now, Katy. Don't exaggerate."

I felt my pulse pounding. "No? Okay, then. How's this? They're going to *kill* her."

Azrael sighed and sat back in his chair. "Kill her?" he asked, not sounding particularly shocked. In fact, he sounded as if he were listening to a nut. A nut named Katy.

"Why are you acting like you don't know what I'm talking about?" I pleaded. "I went to the 'country house,'" I said, making caterpillars with my fingers. "No one lives there, Azrael. Nobody's lived there for hundreds of years. It's a shell, I tell you. Something happens to the people who get sent there, and it's not good!"

"All right, all right!" he said, laughing. "You Americans are so persistent."

"Persistent? We're talking about someone's *life*!"

He shrugged. "Life," he said. "What is life? A passing dream. The blink of an eye . . ."

"Oh, for crying out loud," I said.

"Well, what do you want me to do?" he snapped. "Kidnap the woman? Engage in fisticuffs with her captors? Frankly, you would be better suited to that sort of activity than I." He rubbed his neck. "I still bear the marks from our first encounter."

I winced. "I'm deeply, deeply sorry about that," I said, "but right now I really need for you to help me figure out what to do."

"But what concern is it of yours? This Marie-Therèse is an old woman. You, on the other hand, are young, with your whole life ahead of you. Surely her fate, whatever it may be, cannot be of much importance to you."

I looked up at him. "I can't believe you'd even say that," I said quietly. "She doesn't have anyone else, Azrael. It's me or the dung heap for her."

His watery old eyes looked at me steadily. "Are there really people like you still left in this world?"

"Lots," I said, thinking of Whitfield. "My great-grandmother would never speak to me again if I didn't help. That goes for just about everyone else I know too."

Azrael nodded sagely. "*Eh bien*," he said, slapping his hands on his knees. "Then we must come up with a plan."

"Yes!" I agreed.

"Ah, yes. I have it."

I leaned forward expectantly.

"We'll use magic."

I breathed a huge sigh of relief. "Whew. Great. Thank you. Er . . . what sort of magic do you do?"

He looked surprised. "*I?* No, no, no. You're the one who'll perform the magic."

"Me? *Me?* But . . . but aren't you a witch?"

"I believe we've only established that *you* are, Miss Ainsworth."

I swallowed. I'd been trapped. "I'm an object-empath," I said. "A telekinetic. I don't do spells."

"Then perhaps you ought to learn."

I stood up in a huff. "Why won't you help me?" I demanded, shouting so that my voice wouldn't break with emotion.

"Who said I could? Besides, no one ever learned anything by having things done for them."

I clenched my teeth together. "But there's so much at stake," I whimpered. "If I fail . . ."

"Don't fail," Azrael said.

I crossed my arms angrily in front of me. "Easy for you to say."

He smiled. "All right. A concession. If you need help, I shall help you," he said softly. "Does that satisfy you?"

So he was a witch after all. And he'd offered to help me if all else failed, which, frankly, was pretty likely. The chances of my succeeding at casting a spell that would protect Marie-Therèse from a coven of witches—even stupid ones—was, I knew, somewhere between zero and minus one. But I owed it to her to at least try.

"Okay," I said, less than enthusiastically. "I guess I'd better get to work, then." I took our teacups to the basin. As I washed them, a sinking feeling came over me. *Jeremiah.* I had to tell Azrael about him. "Er . . ."

"Oh, dear," he said. "What is it now, little *choux*?"

I set the cups out to dry and wiped my hands. "I don't know how to tell you this, but somebody knows about you."

He glared at me. "Who have you told?" he demanded.

"No one, I swear. But the other night Jeremiah—"

"Who?"

"Jeremiah Shaw. He's Peter's boss."

"He is one of the witches?"

"I guess. He was at their full-moon ceremony."

Azrael's wrinkled frown suddenly smoothed into an expression of understanding. "Go on," he said.

"He stays at the house sometimes. Whenever he wants to, pretty much. Anyway, I was trying to talk to him about Marie-Thérèse, and he basically ignored me, but then—"

"He asked about me?" Azrael whispered.

"Sort of. He said he knew I'd been visiting you."

The old man nodded.

"And then he thanked me."

He closed his eyes.

"Why would he do that?"

For a moment, I didn't think he'd heard me. But then he spread his hands, palms up, in front of him.

"I'm sorry," I said. "I've been careful. And I haven't said anything. I don't know how he knew."

"It's all right," the old man said hoarsely, and patted me on the head.

"I don't think he'll try to rob you or anything," I added.

"No." He smiled. His eyes were shining with tears. "Go cast your spell, little witch, and think on this no longer."

CHAPTER • THIRTY-TWO

I was pretty disheartened about learning a whole new branch of witchcraft that I didn't have any particular talent in, but supposed I was better off than I was before I'd consulted Azrael. After all, I'd asked him for an idea, and he'd given me one.

Even though I didn't think it would work.

Nevertheless, as soon as I got back to the house, I took out the book of spells Aunt Agnes had given me and leafed through the contents.

Weather, Summoning, Charms . . . I didn't think so. I didn't even know what charms were, except for things you hung on bracelets. The Dead? Really counterproductive, I'd say, under the circumstances. Protection was the next chapter. Protection?

Yes, okay, that could work.

But jeez, it was such a big deal! Incantations and calling in Elementals, creating a sacred circle made of salt, bowing to the Lords of Air. . . . How did the witches in *A Compendium of Ritual Magic* find the time to do all this pre-magic stuff, I wondered, as I moved the furniture in my room and set up the complicated spell. On TV, witches just had to know Latin and maybe wiggle their noses.

Actually, I'd never had to do much of anything to make magic. In Whitfield, we just worked on whatever talents we already had, so I'd only ever done magic with solid objects, and that was pretty easy. I'd never had to scour parking lots for weird rocks or "wander through the astral plane" in preparation for the Protection spell, as Rosamund B. Leakey suggested.

In fact, it was already after midnight when I finally got everything set up, so I skipped the wandering and cut right to the chase.

"Hear me, ye lesser and greater spirits!" I intoned, feeling really stupid. I could just imagine what Peter would say if he heard me. Or Hattie. God, I'd never hear the end of it.

"Thee I call from the far side of the Abyss. . . . Oh, crud." Suddenly I remembered: Marie-Therèse had to be there. It said so in the book.

All righty, then. Sighing and rubbing my sleepy eyes, I pounded on Marie-Therèse's door.

"What is it?" she asked, alarmed.

I didn't say anything until she opened up. "You have to come to my room," I said flatly.

"But why?" Her face was slathered in cold cream, and she squinted without her contacts.

"Because I'm doing a spell," I said, ragged with fatigue. I'd hardly slept at all the night before, and this activity had the earmarks of an all-nighter, too. "To protect you." I scratched my head. "Come on."

"Protect me from what?"

"Your birthday."

"But I feel much better about that," she whispered as I dragged her down the hall. "The house was nice."

"The house is a sham," I said.

"What? How do you know that?"

"Stand in the center of the circle," I commanded, pointing to the ring of salt. I didn't want to explain that I didn't know how I knew the Poplars was bad news. I just did, whether or not Peter or Jeremiah or Azrael or even Marie-Therèse herself believed me. I just knew. And if I had to perform this hocus-pocus in order to get rid of the horrible certainty about Marie-Therèse's future—or lack of it—then that's what I was going to do.

"Thee I call from the far side of the Abyss," I read dutifully from the spell book while Marie-Therèse shivered in her nightdress. "Spirits of fire!" I said louder, trying to put some gusto into it.

Flames erupted in a circle around the old lady, who gave a little shriek. I stomped the fire out with my sneakers. "Sorry about that," I said, resuming my spot as High Priestess of the circle. "Spirits of water, I do summon, stir, and—"

The exposed pipe in the corner suddenly sprang a leak, spraying water onto my bed. The first thing that came to mind was to quickly chew a piece of gum—I had a pack on my dresser—and stick it over the leak. "There," I said, wiping rusty water out of my eye as I squelched back into the circle. Marie-Therèse was shivering, her thin arms wrapped around herself.

"Earth?" I asked.

"No," Marie-Therèse said, her gaze deadly.

I looked out the window, where a light breeze was blowing. "I guess we don't want the spirits of wind, either."

"*Mon Dieu*, no."

I didn't know if the spell would work with only half the Elementals called, but it would have to do. As I proceeded, tossing salt around the wretched-looking Marie-Therèse and exhorting all the hobgoblins of the universe to form a protective coating around her, I tried to feign sincerity and authority. But in my heart, I knew that this playacting wasn't going to result in anything.

A witch can *feel* power. Even when we just flick five fingers, we can trace the course of power from somewhere inside us out through our hands. Throughout this whole elaborate ritual, I'd felt nothing except annoyance.

But I didn't want Marie-Therèse to know that. So I went through with it to the end, walking widdershins and dismissing all the spirits and whatever until the circle was empty (as if it had ever been filled).

"Are . . . are you finished?" Marie-Therèse asked uncertainly.

"Yep," I said, brimming with false confidence. "You're all set."

She looked around the room, which appeared to have been struck by the spirit of Chaos. "May I . . ." She gestured vaguely. ". . . help?"

"No, thanks," I said. "I'll just enjoy the vibes."

She nodded doubtfully. "Well, then, if you don't mind . . ."

"Please," I said heartily, opening the door for her.

When she was gone, I curled up in a chair, wet high tops and all, and fell asleep.

CHAPTER • THIRTY-THREE

I'd tried everything I could think of to ward off the so-called "celebration" in which Marie-Therèse would be carted off to the geriatric equivalent of the Roach Motel (They check in, but they don't check out!), to no avail. The following morning I tried to talk with her, but she wouldn't even consider fleeing with me to Germany or someplace else, and when I'd discreetly suggested a cozy little nest in the Paris sewers, she'd screamed in alarm.

Seriously, though, I could understand where she was coming from. She'd lived on the Rue des Âmes Perdues for more years than she was willing to tell me, and she wasn't about to run away now, so it looked like my only remaining option was to physically fight off whoever was going to try to haul her away. I just hoped Peter would be willing to help me when the time came. And then, of course, the two of us would have to run for our lives, but I figured we'd worry about that later.

I was busy stabbing my fingers with wicked-looking

curved needles—I'd bought some that were made especially for sewing leather—as I bound another section of Azrael's book when Fabienne bombed through the door to my room. "Katy!" she said breathlessly.

I stashed the book with the needle in it under my pillow, but I needn't have made the effort. Fabby was so excited, she couldn't have cared less if I'd been making voodoo dolls.

"This is about my mother," she whispered, her face earnest. "It is shocking."

I didn't think I'd be shocked at anything Sophie de la Soubise would do, but since Fabienne was her daughter, I kept my opinions to myself.

"I have seen her only three times in my life, so I am hardly acquainted with her. I know almost nothing about her."

"Okay," I prodded. "So she's not Mom of the Year. Did she, like, *do* something to you? Because—"

"Shh. Just listen to me, Katy." Her fingers were digging into mine, and her voice was trembling with intensity. "Remember when you said something is odd about the people who live here? *Alors*, you were right!" She blinked several times and swallowed, as if she were afraid to tell me.

"Well?" I asked. "What is it?"

She took a deep breath. "Perhaps you will not believe me, but they . . . that is, the people here . . ."

"What about them?" I pressed.

"They are *old*," she whispered.

"Old?" I frowned. Fabby was fifteen. To her, high school seniors were old.

"I overheard Sophie and Joelle talking about Edouard Manet." She looked up at me. "You know this painter, Manet?"

"I do," I said. "Do you?"

"I know only that he was one of the famous painters of La Belle Epoch, at the end of the nineteenth century," Fabienne said. "That was why I paid attention. I was walking through the dining room when I heard them. It sounded interesting, so I hid behind the cabinet that contains the Fabergé eggs and listened to their conversation."

"So, what'd they say?"

Fabby's eyes were bright in her pale face. "Sophie said that she had posed for him, and then Joelle said that she had too, and then she showed Sophie a book. This book." She reached behind her to take a slim volume out of the waistband of her skirt and handed it to me. "They left it on one of the coffee tables. I picked it up after they left the room."

I turned the book over in my hands. It was bound in gray linen with the name *Edouard Manet* printed on the cover. Its publication date was April 1911. "A first edition," I said. "This must be valuable."

Inside was some biographical text, but most of the pages just showed black-and-white reproductions of Manet's work, with explanatory captions beneath them. I flipped through the pages. "All his most famous works," I said. There was nothing I hadn't seen before in art class.

"That one," Fabby said, placing her hand on a page.

"This?" It was Manet's most well-known painting. It was of a nude woman lying on a divan. I read the caption out loud. "*Olympia, 1863*. A nude portrayed in a style reminiscent of Titian's *Venus of Urbina*, 1538, and also of Francisco Goya's—"

"Look at her face," Fabienne said.

I did, and burst out laughing. "Oh, my God!" I shrieked. "She looks just like Joelle!"

Fabienne wasn't laughing. "It *is* Joelle," she said. "She is nearly two hundred years old."

"Two . . . Don't be ridiculous, Fabby. It's just a passing resemblance."

"No. There are other books. In the library. Sophie mentioned them, and I looked them up. Her picture is in them too. And they are far, far older than this."

I rolled my eyes. "Sounds like all those trips to Japanese hot springs are burning out your brain cells. Sophie's your *mother*, Fabby. She can't be older than forty, and that would be a stretch." Not to mention the general dearth of Parisians—or even yogurt-swilling Russians—over the age of one hundred.

"But I can prove this! Come with me."

Reluctantly, I trudged behind her into the library, which was empty as usual. Fabby lit an oil lamp. Then she took a book from the case and opened it to a portrait of a woman wearing the elaborate clothing of the late eighteenth century and a Marie Antoinette–style wig as high as Marge Simpson's. Beneath the picture was the caption, *Portrait of Mme Sophie de la Soubise, c. 1785.*

"What?" I gasped. I flipped the book over and checked out the title: *Slipping the Noose: French Aristocrats Who Survived the Revolution.*

"It can't be," I said. The woman in the painting looked a little younger than Sophie, perhaps, but the resemblance was unmistakable. I began reading the text. "This says that . . ."

Madame de la Soubise was reputed to be the mistress of King Louis the Sixteenth as well as a number of other noblemen.

I closed the book. I didn't think Fabby had read it, or she would have freaked out by what it said about her mother. "This woman must be an ancestor or something. That's got to be it, Fabby. A relative."

"No, it is not a relative." She took down another book and opened it to a page on which was another portrait, painted by Jean Louis David in 1815, of someone who also looked exactly like Sophie.

"Eighteen Fifteen?" I asked.

"Thirty years after the other painting," Fabienne said. "But it is the same woman, no?"

"Thirty years," I whispered. The two portraits looked nearly identical. And the living Sophie de la Soubise looked just like both of them.

On the facing page was a painting by Adelaide Labille-Guiard, *Comtesse Marie-Therèse LePetit d'Orleans, 1788*. In it, the same Marie-Therèse I saw every day was sitting in a garden with a book in her hand. It could have been no one else.

"A lot of our housemates are in these books," Fabienne said.

"Then . . ." I flipped through the pages, pausing briefly at faces I recognized. Things were beginning to make sense, but they were still hard to believe. "But how . . . how do they do it?"

"Through the full-moon rituals," Fabienne said pointedly. "I just figured it out. All their magic must be used to keep them young. It says so in the words of the ritual."

"I know," I said. "I listened to it. But I thought it meant that they wanted to *look* young. That is, *younger*. Not that they'd actually stop aging entirely."

"But they don't stop aging," Fabby said. "Don't you see?" She compared the paintings again. "They get old like everyone else. But it takes longer."

"Hundreds of years longer?" I asked, incredulous.

Fabby shrugged. "Why not?"

Marie-Therèse's eightieth birthday, I thought. If Fabienne was right, then eighty wasn't anywhere near the real number. "So how old are they when they have to leave?" I asked.

Fabby shrugged. "I suppose it depends on when they begin the rituals."

"In the painting, Marie-Therèse looks almost as old as she is now."

"Yes, I saw. She must have come to the Enclave late in her life."

"So her time has run out, while Sophie . . ."

". . . is still young." Fabby crossed her arms over her chest.

"Well, relatively."

We sat in silence for a moment while I digested what I'd just learned. The ritual I'd witnessed, which seemed to be so similar to the one I'd read about in Azrael's book, had, in fact, been the *same* ritual, except that the words "healing and truth" had been changed somewhere along the line to "beauty and youth."

And it was no coincidence that the Abbaye des Âmes Perdues and the house I lived in were on the same street. It was the same street, and the same house, and I possessed an account of it from its earliest days.

So much made sense to me now. The ritual had changed, and I'd bet I knew when that happened. The author of Azrael's book hadn't named the siren "abbess" whose talent had been to entice men, but I had a pretty good idea who she was.

That was why Sophie had led the ritual the other night.

"So we're not talking about a bunch of silly women who just like to look good," I said. "The Enclave is about achieving nearly eternal life, with the youth to go with it."

Fabby nodded. "It seems too good to be true."

"Maybe it is," I said. "You know, at some point, your magic runs out."

"That takes a long time."

"For you, maybe. Not for Marie-Therèse. Hers runs out tonight."

"What do you mean?"

"Her so-called birthday party. It's when she gets kicked out of the house."

"Oh, no," she said, putting her hand over her mouth. "Is there nothing we can do to stop it?"

"I'm trying to come up with something, but so far I haven't had a lot of luck."

"Perhaps if we stay near her tonight, the two of us, we can help. Plus Peter, of course."

I lowered my head. "I'm not sure we can count on Peter," I said.

Peter had once been my rock, the way I'd been his. But since we got here, in this place, all our values seemed to have been turned upside down. I was doing things with Belmondo that I wouldn't even have been able to think of back in Whitfield, and Peter . . . Well, Sophie had seemed pretty sure that he was never going to come back to America. Or to me.

"Peter's going to join the Enclave, isn't he." It wasn't really a question.

"I don't know," Fabienne said gently. "Peter's gift is different from ours. The coven must keep an alchemist. It is the most important position here. After Jeremiah is gone, Peter will be entrusted with our care."

"You mean he'll keep you in designer clothes and jewelry."

"I suppose," Fabby said quietly. "So you see, he will not have to sacrifice his talent . . . if he joins."

Not like you, I thought. What was in store for her was even worse than the scenario for Marie-Therèse. Not being good at anything was bad enough. But being good at something you weren't allowed to do was beyond depressing. How many witches with tremendous potential had been forced over the years into being living dolls for their whole lives? How many great healers, musicians, scientists, teachers, visionaries, artists, mathematicians, and philosophers had women like Sophie destroyed by keeping their children ignorant and focused on the most trivial aspects of human life, until the day when they were taken away to the Poplars to die, alone and unfulfilled?

It made me sick to think about it.

"What about you?" I asked. "Doesn't your gift mean anything to you?"

"Of course it does," she said, "but this life is what I was born for—" Suddenly she inhaled sharply, her sensitive features quivering like a deer's. "I think I hear people," she whispered. "The witches would not want us to know their secret. Not before the Initiation."

We both sprinted back to the shelves. "Hurry," she said, snatching the last book out of my hands and replacing it quickly.

I followed her out of the library. "Fabby . . ."

She looked at me with big, frightened eyes.

"I know it's tempting, but . . . if you join the Enclave, you'll not only have to give up your talent, but you'll be here forever, following their rules. Like literally *forever*," I said quietly. "Are you sure you want that?"

Her eyes welled. I don't know if Fabienne would have—or could have—answered me then, but our conversation was cut short when Sophie and Joelle met us at the bottom of the stairs.

"What are you doing with her?" Sophie snapped at her daughter. She indicated me with a toss of her head.

"Probably learning how to act like an American teenager," Joelle said before turning her malevolent gaze on Fabby. "Is that it, darling? Is the cook teaching you how to chase after grown men?"

"Excuse us," I said, moving past them up the stairs.

"Oh, must you go? We were hoping you'd tell us all about how you forced Belmondo into spending an evening with you."

"Oh, *Mother*!" Fabienne said. She tried to take my hand, but I shooed her up the stairs. She ran into her room and slammed the door behind her.

"Yes, why not?" Sophie joined in, ignoring her daughter's exit. "I imagine you'll tell all your little friends about your tawdry exploits. Americans are so poor at keeping secrets."

"You're so right," I said as brightly as I could. "In fact, I'll tell you a secret right now. I didn't spend an evening with Belmondo." I smiled sweetly. "It was three."

Joelle backed up a step.

"Three evenings," I said, just to make sure she got the point.

For a moment Joelle's eyes blazed at me furiously while I clenched my jaw and tried to hold my ground. Finally, Sophie took Joelle's arm and led her away, forcing a laugh.

"Oh, by the way," she said, barely raising her voice as she turned to address me, "Pierre is adjusting very well to our life here. I imagine he'll be staying after you leave."

Joelle laughed for real this time.

I ran upstairs and opened the door to my room with trembling hands. *Pierre.* They'd even changed Peter's name to make him one of their own.

CHAPTER • THIRTY-FOUR

Don't think. Sew.

Marie-Therèse's last hurrah, the immortal witches, Fabby's future, Azrael, Belmondo, Peter . . . just about everything in my life, including my totally waning enthusiasm for French cooking, was turning to dreck, and there didn't seem to be anything I could do to change anything. Marie-Therèse's birthday party would begin in a few hours, and the rest of her life was going to depend on how I handled things there. The problem was, I didn't have any idea what I was going to do to prevent her from going to the Poplars.

So I sewed the book together and hoped that if I could just relax, maybe an idea would come to me.

It was strangely comforting to move the needle in and out of the ancient binding. I wanted to get the job done, but at the same time I didn't want Jean-Loup's story to end. I wondered if it was possible that his apprentice, Henry Shaw, might be the same Henry Shaw I'd heard about in Whitfield. If so, that would make Peter one of his descendants. How weird would that be?

Peter had always been ashamed of his connection with that Henry Shaw, who had been a dishonorable tycoon who'd turned in his own wife to the authorities when he'd found out she was a witch. To protect her, my own ancestor, Serenity Ainsworth, together with a West African shaman named Ola'ea Olokun, had cast a spell over part of Whitfield that would render it invisible. That was why so many witches lived there today: Those early witches had lived with no outside influences at all for generations, until Massachusetts was safe for our kind again . . . no thanks to Henry, who'd disappeared when the witch hunters couldn't find anyone to persecute.

No one knows what happened to him. Fifty years later, a relative of his showed up and revamped the businesses Henry had started, but the Shaws never regained favor with the witch community. I guess people who've been accused of being demons can be slow to forgive.

But I was getting too caught up in the book. Shaw was a common name, and coincidences happen.

These days, they seemed to happen all the time.

1568

Henry

So Henry Shaw, now 215 years of age, embarked on a new chapter of his life in what would come to be called Whitfield, Massachusetts, where he established one of the first import-export firms in North America.

Shaw Enterprises brought great wealth to Henry—so

much that in time he nearly forgot that he had the ability to make gold. He certainly didn't need it; he wanted for nothing. Unfortunately, his personal life was not nearly as successful as his business ventures.

Henry was lonely. Try as he might, he could not erase the memory of the beautiful young woman from the abbey from his mind. He had known from the moment she'd touched him with her long siren's fingers that she was dangerous for him—too beautiful, too carnal, too intoxicating—and yet he had longed for her with an ache in his heart.

And then, just as he was finally able to admit to himself that he wanted this woman regardless of what damage she might inflict upon him in the future, she was gone. Just like that. What had her replacement said? Oh, yes, that she had left to find a husband and a title. A terrible woman, surely, a grasping, mercenary vixen.

And yet, his thoughts revolved constantly around her, her golden hair and sparkling, mischievous eyes, and the way her hand had touched his, as if offering a promise of things to come. . . .

But only for the right man, he knew. A duke, perhaps, or a foreign prince. A woman like that would never give herself to one such as Henry, an orphan raised as a pirate's apprentice, a farmer with a farmer's rude manners and callused workman's hands.

She—whose name Henry did not even know—was the main reason he had crossed the ocean. He had meant to begin a new life in the new land, forgetting the strange, unending life associated with the Abbey of Lost Souls.

He grew older. The years Henry spent away from the

abbey and its youth spell showed in his face and body. He'd lost much of his hair, and was already beginning to walk with a slight stoop. Soon my legs will become too old to move, he thought, although his body was still far from old. But he knew he could not spend the rest of his life—his short life—dreaming about a woman who would never be his.

He had to marry.

For his wife, he chose the plain-faced but efficient Zenobia Ainsworth, who had been on the ship with him. Zenobia and her twin sister, Zethinia, had been children during the sea voyage to America, but over the years they had grown into intelligent, respectable women.

Zenobia possessed more magic than her sister—so much magic, in fact, that she had dazzled even the normally unflappable Henry. Her gift was esoteric but domestic: She specialized in knot magic. Into her quilts, rugs, sweaters, and children's clothes were woven spells of protection, of love, of creativity and contentment and passion. Pregnant women vied to possess the shawls Zenobia crafted that brought peace into their hearts. Men wore gloves that ensured their success in the hunt.

Henry wanted to tell his wife about his own gift as an alchemist, if only to assure her that she was marrying among her own kind, but he never forgot Jean-Loup's warning to him: Even witches can go mad at the smell of gold. He knew Zenobia's head would not be turned at the prospect of unlimited riches, but he could not be certain that she would not mention it to anyone else, particularly since she had a twin with whom she shared almost everything.

And so he said nothing about his talent. It didn't seem to matter, anyway. Zenobia provided a good home for him even though she believed he was cowen. Perhaps she even loved him.

And in his way, he loved her, too. He locked away his memories of the beautiful abbess in the recesses of his heart, and went on with his life.

Until the witch hunters came. In Salem, these Puritans heard about the woman who infused spells into her woolens. Nearly everyone in Whitfield possessed something that Zenobia had woven or sewn, and her name had spread to outlying communities. A bunting she made for the Fowlers' baby had cured it of whooping cough, they whispered. Her towels made the skin feel smoother. Feet never got cold in socks sewn by Zenobia.

Through his many business connections, Henry had learned that the fanatics from Salem had placed Zenobia in their crosshairs and were on their way to Whitfield, hoping for the kind of bloodbath that had shaken their own settlement to its foundations. Knowing that he would be the first to defend his wife, the witch hunters had already sent out spies to watch Zenobia's husband.

Henry had been close to panic. Zenobia had bore him two children whom he knew might also be in danger if the witch hunters had their way.

Then something happened that was to change the course of Henry's life. An African shaman who had settled in Whitfield provided him with a plan to save his wife and every other witch in town.

"I am Ola'ea Olokun," she said, introducing herself. "Your mother-in-law and I would like to enlist your help.

She went on to explain that she and Serenity Ainsworth had nearly perfected a spell that would transform a tract of land known as the Meadow into a place where witches could put themselves out of the reach of the hunters. "We will transport our people to another plane of existence until the Puritans offer no more danger to them."

"How long will that be?" Henry asked. In his experience, nothing took longer to dissipate than hatred and fear.

"A generation or two," she answered. "Maybe three."

"Three generations?" He swallowed. He would die in Whitfield, then, or in whatever version of Whitfield his wife would be inhabiting if the shaman's plan came to pass. He would never return to the land of his birth or partake again of the magic that had extended his life for hundreds of years.

"Only witches would be able to enter this alternate plane," Ola'ea pressed.

It took Henry a moment to fully understand what the woman was saying, which was that everyone in Whitfield believed Henry Shaw to be cowen. He had kept his alchemy a secret even from his wife.

"But—"

"Listen to me," Ola'ea hissed. "The magic that will save your family is not yet ready. And even when it is perfected, the spell will be a lengthy process because only one person at a time may enter the portal we will have created. During this time—perhaps a week or two—someone must prevent the witch hunters from coming here." She looked deeply into his eyes with her own steady gaze. "Do you understand?"

Henry was silent for a moment as the full implications of her words sank in. "What happens after the spell is complete?"

he asked. "After the witches have all left this plane?"

"The Meadow will be sealed as soon as the last witch has entered," Ola'ea said. "To the outside world, it will be as if the people who once lived here had simply disappeared."

"And no one else will be able to enter?"

"No one," Ola'ea said pointedly. She did not have to add, *including you.*

"Who else knows about your plan?"

"No one," she repeated.

That was for the best, he understood. If a whisper of this magic were to reach the Puritans' ears, the whole town and everyone in it would be burned to cinders.

"I understand," he said.

The first thing he did, which shocked everyone, was to repudiate his wife and children, putting them out of their home and then announcing to the world—and to Whitfield's tightly knit community of witches—that he had learned of the accusations against Zenobia, and would have nothing to do with anyone, even his own wife, who may have dabbled in magic.

This served two purposes. One was to throw the posse from Salem off the track by making them believe that Henry Shaw was of a mind with the Puritans. The other was to alert the Whitfield witches to the extreme danger they faced, in case any of them might consider refusing to participate in Ola'ea's plan. They *must* leave, he knew. They must do it quickly and without exception, if they were to save their own lives.

After he established himself to the Puritans as a righteous hater of witches, Henry led the Salem zealots on a merry chase through the American colonies until they gave up looking for Zenobia and consequently, with the disappearance of all the other witches in Whitfield, anyone else who might be suspected of possessing talent or knowledge beyond the ordinary.

It had been an exhilarating ride, but after it was over and Henry walked through the ghost town of what had once been magical Whitfield, he was nearly overcome with sadness.

"There is a ship leaving within the hour," someone said behind him.

He turned around in alarm. No one had been near him a minute ago, but now Ola'ea stood before him, large as life.

"So you can leave after all?" he asked hopefully.

The shaman laughed. "I can," she said. "No one else."

"And I can't get in."

"Do you want to?" She cocked her head. "Really?"

"My wife . . . ," he faltered. "My children . . ."

"If you care for them, you will want them to remain in the place of safety where they now live."

"But of course. It's just—"

"And if you were with them, would you not resent having to grow old and die, knowing that another avenue was available to you?"

Henry sucked in air. "You know about that?"

Ola'ea made a cryptic gesture. No one knew how the woman came about her knowledge, and it was useless to try to find out. "This will be but a small part of your life," she said. "The long, rich life that is waiting for you across the sea."

His face was pained. "But my family will forever know me as a villain."

"I will tell Zenobia. No one else matters."

"The townspeople—"

"Let them talk." Ola'ea shrugged. "If they knew the truth—that you'll still be making gold a century after they're all dead and buried—they'd hate you twice as much." She grinned broadly, her beautiful white teeth gleaming against her dark skin.

"You know about the gold, too?"

Ola'ea laughed at that, a deep, hearty sound that welled up from the very depths of her shaman's heart. "I know everything," she said.

Henry believed her. There was nothing more to say. He couldn't explain his circumstances to his family even if he tried. "Thank you," he said simply.

Her eyes twinkled. "I'd say you had a ship to catch, wouldn't you?"

CHAPTER • THIRTY-FIVE

OMG.

It *was* the same Henry Shaw. The same guy who returned to Whitfield fifty years after his disappearance, claiming to be his own descendant.

What name had he used, I wondered, my eyes sliding toward the door.

I'd have to tell Peter. He needed to know that his ancestor, the founder of his family, hadn't been nearly as awful as everyone in Whitfield believed.

I heard the big grandfather clock downstairs chime eight o'clock, so I put away the book and got dressed for Marie-Therèse's party.

I still hadn't come up with a plan to save her. So I guessed that unless a sudden brainstorm came my way, I'd have to depend on sheer muscle and moxie if it came down to a fight with whoever was planning to abduct the old lady.

I did a few pushups in preparation for battle and went

downstairs. Fabienne was already mingling, dressed in something that looked like cotton candy.

"Are you okay?" I asked out of the side of my mouth. "With your mom, I mean."

"*Oui*," she answered in that way French women have of sucking in air while speaking.

"Um . . ." I didn't know whether to broach the subject or not. "Have you decided what you're going to do? About staying here?"

"I don't know," she answered, and I knew from her voice that it was something she'd been thinking about a lot. "Right now I am only concerned for Marie-Therèse."

"Yeah," I said. "Me too." To put it mildly.

"Unfortunately, I think you and I are the only ones who *are* concerned."

"I'll bet you're right," I said. I looked over my shoulder to see if I could spot the thugs who would try to strong-arm Marie-Therèse into the old folks' home. "I'm not even sure of Peter anymore."

"Peter will always stay by your side, don't worry," Fabienne said. "But I do not believe it will happen the way you think."

"Oh?"

She leaned in closer toward me. "There will not be a fight. I believe that Jeremiah Shaw will simply come and escort Marie-Therèse out."

"Good," I whispered. "I can take the old man down."

I circled, keeping my eyes peeled for Jeremiah.

Who, incidentally, never showed up.

I waited, yawning and bored, until after one in the morning, but there was no sign of the old man. Marie-Therèse, on the other hand, was thrilled with all the (fake) attention she was getting, and even wanted to know where Jeremiah was! When she came out with that, I poked her in the ribs.

"No news is good news," I muttered.

"Now, Katy," she said good-humoredly. "You see? All our worries were for nothing."

No, they weren't. "Maybe my spell worked," I offered, but Marie-Therèse only cleared her throat and moved quickly to another group.

And then he arrived.

Not Jeremiah.

Belmondo.

Oh, God, I prayed, *don't let me lose my concentration now.* I could feel him, the crackling energy that exuded from him in waves. I just stood there, transfixed, as Belmondo entered the room. Women immediately gathered around him like moths around a flame. When I thought I saw him glance my way for a moment, I actually gasped before realizing that I'd forgotten to breathe.

"Marie-Therèse," he purred, extricating himself from the gaggle of women surrounding him to approach my friend. He hugged her and kissed her on both cheeks, murmuring in rapid French. I saw a faint blush rise in the old woman's face as she accepted his compliments with a smile.

I tried to slink away before I did something stupid—fainting came to mind—but as I was leaving, Belmondo slipped his hand into mine.

It was like falling into a dream. Belmondo's aura surrounded me in a cloud of sandalwood and dark roses. It wasn't scent, exactly, but more like pheromones or something—an inexplicable force that drew me toward him with a longing I couldn't explain.

"Are you being good, Katarine?" he asked.

"Er . . . yes, fine," I said. *Oh, clever, Katy.* The queen of the witty riposte.

"It's late for you."

"I was keeping Marie-Therèse company."

He took my elbow. "Marie-Therèse doesn't have school in the morning," he said. "Besides, the party's in her honor. She won't be left to languish like a wallflower without you." He winked at the old woman. "Am I right?"

"Absolutely," Marie-Therèse said, her eyes twinkling. She turned toward me. "He's right, dear. You really ought to be in bed."

What? They were both talking to me—*about* me—as if I were a child.

"Now don't be grumpy," Belmondo said with an indulgent smile. "Think of it as beauty sleep."

Bristling, I stepped away from him, but he pulled me near to him. "Whatever you're worrying about, stop," he whispered in my ear. "Everything is all right. I promise."

I trembled. *How did he know?*

"You will be fine tomorrow."

"What?"

"At school," he said. "It must be difficult to study in a house like this, with so much noise."

Study? "Oh . . . oh, yes. I mean no." I swallowed. "That is, I'm great." My cheeks felt like they were on fire. He was talking about cooking school.

Just then, Joelle snaked between us and hooked her arm around Belmondo's. She whispered in his ear and then giggled. He whispered back, and she gave me a sideways look that said, *He's mine now, turkey.*

Then Belmondo looked up, laughing, his white teeth gleaming, and kissed Joelle on her neck. It was a small kiss, barely a peck, but it was the most sensual thing I'd ever seen. Or imagined. With that one kiss, my heart broke into a thousand pieces.

"We should be going," he said. Joelle squeezed his arm and breathed in sharply, her nostrils flaring as she threw me another "poor you" look.

Do you know how old she is? I wanted to shout. But it wasn't my place to ruin their evening, just because they'd ruined mine.

I pretended to wave at someone across the room. "I've got to go too," I said, my heart feeling as if a dagger were sticking out of it.

"To bed," Belmondo reminded me. "Marie-Therèse, darling—"

"I'll see to it that Katy gets her rest," she said.

I watched him walk to the door with Joelle simpering beside him, showing him off like a trophy as the other women watched her the same way I did, with jealous, angry eyes. Then the two of them went outside into the night, and all the air in the room seemed to go with them.

"You know you're making a fool out of yourself," Peter said behind me. I jumped when I recognized his voice. *Was it so obvious?*

I turned around. "When did you get here?"

"A while ago. You seemed to be looking for someone." He jerked his head toward the door where Belmondo had just exited. "Him?"

"No," I said. "I was looking for Jeremiah, if you must know. I was afraid he'd take Marie-Therèse."

"I doubt that. He's in London."

"Oh." *Great,* I thought, my stomach churning. *A perfect evening.* "Really?"

Peter grunted. "And it looks like your new boyfriend's found somebody else to feed strawberries to."

"I don't know who you're talking about," I said, as if I weren't writhing with shame inside.

"Let me tell you something, Katy," Peter said. "He's playing you. You're nothing but a toy to him."

"Why don't you shut up?" I shrieked. *"Pierre!"*

"Keep your voice down," Peter said. Two spots of red colored his cheeks.

"Why should I? You just think I'm childish and stupid, anyway. Besides, you're never here—"

"That song is getting old, Katy," he said evenly. "Things haven't gone wrong with us because of my work schedule, and you know it."

"Oh, go boss someone else around," I said. He grabbed my shoulders. I shook him off. "Get away from me!" I shouted. Some people turned to stare at us.

"Fine," Peter said with deadly quiet. "If that's what you want, fine." Then he walked away, his fists clenched.

I tried to blink away my tears, but my whole face was threatening to fall apart, so I ran upstairs into my room, where I threw myself on my bed and sobbed into my pillow.

A few minutes later someone was knocking on my door. "Katy?" Marie-Therèse called from the hallway. She kept knocking until I got up and opened the door.

"You left so quickly," she said. "Are you all right?"

"I'm okay," I said, averting my face so she wouldn't see my swollen eyes. "I'm glad nothing happened to you tonight," I added.

"Yes. All that worry, for nothing!" She laughed. "When I am ready, I shall go to the Poplars under my own steam."

"Right," I said flatly. I didn't want to think about that just then.

"Well, get a good night's rest, dear. I hope the party isn't too loud for you."

"No problem," I said dully.

I kept my eyes closed as she kissed me briefly on both cheeks. "I do appreciate all you've done," she said. "Oh, dear. Are you sure you're well?"

I started to cry again. I couldn't help it.

"Ah," she said. "You're overwrought."

"Tired," I said.

"Then I'll go. Everything will look brighter after you've slept." She smiled and closed the door quietly behind her.

I doubted if anything would look brighter ever again. Belmondo had gone off with Joelle, Peter had walked away from me—*again*—and instead of protecting Marie-Therèse, I'd acted like a bawling baby in front of her.

She'd been right about one thing: Our worries had been for nothing.

Everything I'd done in this city had been for nothing.

CHAPTER • THIRTY-SIX

The next day I went to see Azrael after school. "*Fricadelles de veau mentonnaise*," I said, holding out my latest offering, veal patties with tuna and anchovies. We'd made the calf brains, too, but I'd deposited them in the garbage before I left.

"Delightful," Azrael said without looking up from the newspaper I'd brought him.

I wiped my sweaty face with a tissue. "I ran the whole way," I confessed.

"Oh?" He turned a page and snapped the paper. "Then you must either have been dodging a pursuer or anxious to ask me some difficult and embarrassing question," he said.

"Well . . ."

He sighed. "Go ahead."

"Okay. Remember when I told you about that guy Belmondo?" I asked baldly.

"Of course," the old man said.

"I think he's in love with Joelle."

He didn't respond.

"She left with him the other night. After the party."

Azrael peered over the newspaper. "And?" he asked.

I shrugged.

"Is this news you're telling me?"

I shrugged again, embarrassed by my misery.

With some reluctance, he folded the newspaper and set it on the table in front of him. "What are you trying to say, Katy?"

I shrugged again.

"Stop that!" he snapped. "You're beginning to look like a marionette." My eyes filled. Azrael's rolled ceilingward. "Would you like some tea?" he asked more gently.

I shook my head. "I'm sorry," I said. "It's just that . . . Oh, I feel so *stupid*."

I told him about the party, how nothing had happened, and that Jeremiah Shaw hadn't even shown up.

"Oh? And you're unhappy about this?"

"I just don't understand it. At the house in Vincennes—"

"Yes, yes, the agitated maid, the mysterious butler." He waved his hand in a circle, urging me to speed up my recap of events.

"I was just *sure* that something was going to happen to Marie-Therèse."

"Would you have been happier if something *had* happened? If she'd been spirited away by assassins? Or perhaps murdered beside the banquette of hors d'oeuvres?"

"No, but—"

"It could be that your spell worked after all," he offered.

"I thought about that," I said. "But . . ." I had to be honest.

"It couldn't have been that. The spell was lame. At least the way I did it."

"You don't know that," Azrael said. "Why, it may have been a perfect—"

"I set fire to the floor, and then a leaky pipe squirted water in Marie-Therèse's face," I said.

Azrael blinked a few times. Then he turned away. I could tell he was trying not to laugh.

"Go ahead. I know it was stupid." I sighed resignedly.

"And this concerns Belmondo?"

"Huh? Oh. No, I guess not. But he was there."

"With the evil Joelle." He rubbed his hands together like a silent movie villain.

I had to laugh in spite of myself. "Why did he pick her, of all people?" I said, mostly to myself.

Azrael cleared his throat. I looked up. "Perhaps the debonair Monsieur Belmondo is not the sterling character you take him to be."

"What do you mean?"

He spread his hands. "Katy, you are a very young girl. Ah." He put one hand over his mouth. "Forgive me. I can see by your expression that you do not agree with me on the subject of your youth. However, I hope you can appreciate that, from my vantage point, you are far from . . . shall we say *meretricious*?"

I didn't know what that meant, but I was pretty sure I didn't like it. Still, I let it go.

"What I mean is that if Belmondo had escorted you from the party instead of Mademoiselle Joelle, he would have been behaving badly indeed. Also illegally."

"That's what Peter said."

"Peter, the undemonstrative paramour?"

"My boyfriend," I said. "Ex-boyfriend."

Azrael tutted. "Surely you are not discarding him because of one remark—a truthful remark, I may add—uttered at a party."

"It's more than that," I confessed. I took a deep breath. This was going to be hard. "Someone told me something about the Enclave," I said. "It's going to sound very weird."

"Is it about their trivial use of magic to maintain their youth and beauty?"

"More than that." I swallowed. "They're old, Azrael," I whispered.

"You say that as if age were a disease."

"I mean *really* old. Older than you can imagine." I told him about the book Fabby had found, and the conversation between Sophie and Joelle that she'd overheard. "The book had a portrait of Sophie in it, and it was really her. It said she was the mistress of King Louis the Sixteenth."

He chuckled. "I rather doubt that," he said.

"I did too, at first—"

"Louis had little time for women."

"What?"

"He was too busy playing with his toy soldiers, from what I've read—"

Suddenly he lurched forward, his face purple.

"Azrael!" I screamed, grabbing him before he fell.

"Please," he gasped. "It's nothing. Nothing."

"It's *not* nothing," I said. "We've got to get you to a hospital."

"Nonsense. Just a spate of indigestion," he said, pulling himself to his feet. "I feel better already."

He really didn't look as if he felt better, but there wasn't much I could do, short of dragging him through the underground passageways to the street above. "Are you sure?" I asked uncertainly.

"Do stop worrying," he said, and smiled. "Now, if you don't mind, I have some things to attend to."

"Oh," I said. I couldn't imagine what he had to do that was so pressing, but I guessed he wanted me to leave. "Maybe I ought to stay with you until—"

"No," he said flatly. "I told you, I feel better." He gave me a hard stare.

"Okay, I'll go."

"Katy?" he said before I reached the doorway. I lifted my chin in answer. "Don't look too closely at those aristocrats. They have secrets that are too ancient and dreadful to explore."

"I guess," I said.

"And stay away from Belmondo."

I coughed. "Why?"

"He can't give you what Peter can."

"Peter," I spat as I walked away. As if Peter could—or would want to—give me anything.

But halfway down the corridor, I stopped. There was a sound coming from Azrael's cave. A dry, whooshing sound, like the noise a snake would make as it slithered along the walls of the tunnel.

"Az—"

"Go!" the old man shouted, his voice echoing through the passageway like a dream.

CHAPTER • THIRTY-SEVEN

The evening was quiet, for a change. Marie-Therèse was in her room, resting. Fabienne had pretended to be in bed with a stomachache, but was really teleporting to Hakone, Japan. She'd invited me to come along, but I still wasn't finished repairing Azrael's book. Besides, I wasn't sure I wanted to be a passenger with a novice teleporter. Who knew where I might end up?

And Peter was gone. I didn't know what he was doing. Working, I guessed, although he might be going out with one of the coven women, for all I knew. With a sigh, I took the book and my sewing things out of my backpack and settled into a pile of pillows on my bed. I was sad and confused enough as things were, without the bizarre coincidences that kept cropping up in Azrael's manuscript. But reading it was turning out to be like watching a car accident: Jean-Loup's long-ago world—and its inexplicable connection to what was currently going on at the house where I lived—was horrifying, yet I couldn't look away.

1688
Blood Kin

While Henry Shaw was making his way back to France, Jean-Loup lived quietly at Toujours. Jean-Loup's neighbors sometimes brought him vegetables or milk out of pity, because the lonely man had no children to care for him.

He was pottering in his garden when he sensed, rather than heard, a presence behind him. Turning around, he saw a young man dressed in odd, foreign-looking clothes and shoes that were completely unsuitable for standing in a muddy field.

"Yes?" Jean-Loup began, but any further words dried up in his throat.

The stranger's dark hair was accented by a thick streak of white in exactly the same place as Veronique's. "I don't suppose you remember me," he said softly.

"I don't . . . but . . ." Jean-Loup swallowed. He suddenly felt as if the air in the field had grown still. Still as death.

"I see you've done well, Father."

A strangled sound escaped from Jean-Loup's lips. "Drago."

"Surely you're not still angry with me."

"That was . . ." The old man's voice trembled. "That was nearly five hundred years ago."

Drago smiled. "There are many ways to live beyond one's years," he said. "Yours is not the only magic."

"Magic?" Jean-Loup repeated vaguely. For the past two centuries, the only gold he had made had been for the casket delivered to the Abbaye des Âmes Perdues each month.

He no longer railed against the life that meant so little to him. Through the centuries he had resigned himself to his nothing of an existence, aging slowly but inexorably, forever alone.

"Actually, I came because I heard about an immortal man in France who kept a harem of witches."

"I am not immortal," Jean-Loup said, nearly overcome with an urge to be away from the intense aura of evil surrounding Drago.

"Oh? That's not what I—"

Suddenly there came the sound of panicking horses and shouting men from the road nearby. Almost relieved, Jean-Loup ran immediately toward the commotion, with Drago following behind.

A robbery was in progress. A merchant's carriage lay on its side, its horses straining and choking on their twisted reins as a man—no doubt one of the bandits who'd toppled the carriage in the first place—struggled to free the animals.

A richly dressed corpse was draped across the window of the carriage, while another well-dressed man fought, unsuccessfully, with a second highwayman. Jean-Loup arrived in time to see the hapless fellow run through with a sword. Blood spurted out of his mouth as he stared, immobile, in surprise.

"Hurry up with those horses," the man with the sword growled. "Either get them free or kill them."

"I'm trying!" the other bandit shouted. "It's just . . . oh, merde alors.*" He spotted Jean-Loup and Drago. "We've got company, damn it."*

Nervously, Drago unsheathed his sword. "Do you know how to use that?" Jean-Loup whispered. Drago didn't answer, so the old man snatched it away from him.

A lot of time had passed since his privateering days, but as soon as the sword was in his hand, the old man's skill returned. He ran the blade through the bandit with the horses first. Then, with a single stroke, he cut through the animals' strangling reins, and the horses fled. He stepped away to clear a path for them, only to see the second bandit lunging at Drago, a dagger held high.

Jean-Loup ran toward them, but his years had slowed him down. Just as he neared the two struggling men, the bandit's dagger jabbed deep into Drago's gut.

It happened fast. The thief fell back as Jean-Loup's sword entered his neck and came out again, making hot, sucking noises as it exited the man's windpipe. Then, pushing the filthy body aside, the old man knelt beside his son, who was blinking in bewilderment as his hand came away from the wound in his abdomen coated with his own blood. A second later, he crumpled to his knees.

The world seemed to have grown suddenly silent. Even the horses galloping down the road made no sound. In his mind, Jean-Loup heard only the faint murmur of an infant nestled in Veronique's arms.

"We shall name him Drago," Veronique had said, blowing on the baby's forehead. *"And like the dragon for which he is named, he shall be full of magic."*

"Father," Drago groaned, breaking the silence and the terrible sweet memory, "bring me my attacker."

Jean-Loup looked over at the highwayman to whom he had delivered a mortal blow. The man's legs were twitching, and blood gushed from his mouth. "He will be dead soon enough," he said softly as he placed his coat beneath his son's head.

In a fury, Drago threw the coat at his father. "I said bring him to me!" he shouted, bloody spittle spraying from his lips. "Bring him now!"

Jean-Loup obeyed. The highwayman was still alive, but did not possess even the strength to resist when Jean-Loup dragged the robber over to his dying son. "I'm afraid it won't do any good to—"

"Give him to me!" Drago bellowed, clutching at the outlaw and pulling him close beside him.

"Son, what are you doing?" Jean-Loup whispered, but Drago had no time to answer. With shaking fingers he forced the bandit's mouth open and put his own lips near enough to catch the rush of fetid breath that exuded from the man's mouth along with a clacking death rattle. It reeked of blood and rotten teeth, and Jean-Loup winced in distaste, but Drago was trembling with excitement as he sucked in the man's final breath. Then he sighed, cast the body aside, and lay dazed and blinking into the sun.

"Drago?" Jean-Loup probed. "Son?" Tentatively, he parted Drago's bloody waistcoat to look at the wound.

There was no wound. Beneath the blood-soaked clothes, Drago's skin was perfectly intact.

Astonished, Jean-Loup felt his son's neck for a pulse. Drago slapped him away, then sat up, laughing.

Jean-Loup felt as if the wind had been knocked out of him. Drago's wound had been mortal, but not even a scratch remained. He sat back on the muddy ground, remembering the sight of his son bending over Sister Béatrice those many years ago, sucking out her life with his greedy lips. Drago had the same satisfied look on his face now as he wiped his mouth on his sleeve, his eyes fixed defiantly on Jean-Loup's. Beside him lay the dead highwayman, facedown in the mud.

Jean-Loup turned the body over with his boot. The man's face was as dry and withered as a corpse that had lain in the sun for a thousand years. Jean-Loup did not know how long he *remained there, staring at the dead man as if he were stuck in a dream. But when he came to his senses, Drago had moved farther down the road to the highwayman's partner, who still lay where the old man had felled him. He was leaning over the man, the muscles in his back working.*

"Drago, don't," Jean-Loup said, choking, trying not to vomit. "Please . . ." He swallowed. "Drago, listen to—"

The words dried up in his throat as Drago turned his head to face him. The second man's face was as unrecognizably dessicated as the first's had been. And Drago's lips were smeared with blood.

The sight was more than Jean-Loup could bear. "No," he rasped unsteadily. "No . . ."

"Don't judge me, Father," Drago said, his tongue questing obscenely for the blood around his lips. "I did not choose this gift. It is from my mother."

Jean-Loup staggered. "Your mother!" Even the words seemed like a sacrilege.

"Her gift was to give life through her breath. Mine is to take it through the same means."

Jean-Loup could only gape in terror.

"I told you there were many ways to extend life," Drago said softly.

"Your life," Jean-Loup said.

The two men stared at each other for a long moment. Finally Drago spoke. "Yes, my life," he said. "It's why I've come. The women in your coven—I've heard they number in the hundreds—"

Looking back at the dried-up thing that had once been a living man, Jean-Loup began to understand what his son was asking of him. "My God, no. You don't mean to—"

"Why should they live forever, long past the time when they're of any use?" Drago argued. "I can unburden those crones of their overextended lives."

"Unburden!" Jean-Loup snapped. "You want to kill them!"

"So that I may live, yes. How is that so different from what you do?"

"I don't suck the life out of anyone!" the old man shouted.

"No. You take advantage of their magic until they are too old to give any more, and then you allow them to lie in their own filth, praying for a death that will not come."

In truth, Jean-Loup did not know what happened to the women once they grew too old to participate in the abbey's day-to-day affairs. He had noticed, however, that the full-moon rituals had become much more populous, with a number of motionless, insensate individuals propped up on chairs in the far shadows of the stone chamber. "But why do you want these old women?" he asked.

"Would you prefer that I murder the young ones?"

Jean-Loup sputtered. "No!"

"I thought not," Drago said. "To tell the truth, I'm intrigued by the fact that they're witches," he said. "Magic satisfies me best. Oh, cowen will keep me alive"—he indicated the two dead men on the road—"but witches feed my magic more fully. Even if they're hags." He smiled. Jean-Loup thought his son resembled a hyena, dining on offal.

The old man backed away. "No," he said. "What you suggest cannot be."

"I'm afraid you can't stop me," Drago said softly. "If you try, I'll kill them all."

"What? You can't—"

"But I can. And I'll enjoy it, I promise you."

Jean-Loup thought of his promise to Veronique. *Take care of my sisters.* He couldn't allow them all to be massacred. And yet he couldn't agree to his son's horrid proposal.

"One other thing," Drago said. "I've heard that you have a companion."

Henry. "He's not here," Jean-Loup said quickly. "He's gone to the American colonies."

"Good. See that he doesn't come back."

"I . . . I can't do that. I don't know how to get word to him. For all I know, he may already have left to return home."

Drago shrugged. "Ah, well. Then come he must. But if you enlist his help against me, I'll kill him, too."

"Oh, God," the old man moaned. "My God, my God . . ."

"Tell your former ward that your son has returned, and that you neither require his attentions nor desire his company."

"My son," Jean-Loup said bitterly.

"Yes. The son you sent away and never missed for five hundred long years." Drago's lips curved, but his eyes remained blisteringly cold. "How does that sit with you, Father?"

Jean-Loup backed away. "I have no son," he said woodenly. "I have no son." He turned and stumbled through the field. "I have no son!" he shouted, his throat hoarse with tears.

He ran back to his house and scrambled inside, locking the door behind him and leaning his back against it while he sobbed and shook with fear. "I have no son," he whimpered.

In the distance, he could hear Drago laughing.

• • •

After his time in America, Henry came back to Paris and Jean-Loup, who was the closest thing to a father he had ever known. To his dismay, he found the old man shaking and fearful and filled with stories of vampires and other ghouls.

"Bandits on the road," Jean-Loup babbled. "His mouth was covered with blood. Take your last breath from you."

"Captain Loup," Henry pleaded, using his childhood name for his former guardian. "Please—"

"Not my fault. Couldn't stop him." Jean-Loup clutched Henry's shirt and hung on with his aged fingers like a drowning man. "Go," he whispered wildly in Henry's ear. "Go now, and don't come back."

What had happened? Henry hadn't been gone very long, less than thirty years. A heartbeat, in the context of Jean-Loup's and Henry's lives.

"I tell you, *go!*" Jean-Loup insisted, looking over his shoulder. "My son has come back, do you understand?" he whispered hoarsely. "Drago."

Henry could only shake his head. The old man had never before spoken of a son.

"He will kill you. He will kill all the women. He will kill you all."

"Shh—" It was pathetic, Henry thought. Somehow, during his absence, the old man had gone mad. "Have you been to the abbey?" Henry asked, hoping to steer Jean-Loup's mind away from thoughts of murder and death. "You've gone to the rituals?"

"Yes, yes. But it is not the same. Not since . . ." Jean-Loup cringed, hunching his shoulders and peering behind him. "You must provide the sisters with gold," he said, close to Henry's ear. "I am not permitted. You must take care of them. Promise me, for Veronique's sake."

"Jean-Loup—"

The old man grasped the lapels of Henry's coat. "I vowed to provide for them, but I cannot. Please help me."

"Of course I'll help," Henry said, alarmed.

"Promise!"

After a long, stunned silence, Henry nodded. "I promise," he said at last.

Perhaps it was time for him to move his former master into the abbey, Henry thought. If Jean-Loup no longer wished for Henry to stay with him, he would be better off among the so-called "nuns" than he would alone on the farm. They would certainly not turn the old man away. After all the gold he had given them, they owed their benefactor at least a bed in which to live out the rest of his life, however long that may be.

"Tonight is a full moon," Henry said gently. "We can go to the Rue des Âmes Perdues together. I'll speak with the abbess—"

"That won't be necessary," interrupted another voice. Jean-Loup gave a little cry as a young man stepped out of the shadows.

Henry blinked; he hadn't seen anyone before. It was as if the man had simply materialized.

"I'll see that my father attends the ritual," Drago said pleasantly. "In the meantime, I believe he's asked you to leave."

Puzzled, Henry looked at Jean-Loup. The old man was weeping openly. "Yes, go," he said, and wiped his sleeve across his nose. "Please go. Don't come back."

CHAPTER
•
THIRTY-EIGHT

I hadn't expected Jean-Loup's life to take such an unhappy turn. Suddenly I didn't feel like reading anymore.

I decided to take a walk. That was one thing about Paris: Wherever you went, there was something interesting to see. I had a vague idea about heading toward the Eiffel Tower, but I didn't really care if I made it all the way or not. Maybe I'd buy an ice cream, I thought as I bounded down the stairs and through the courtyard onto the street. Or a marshmallow cone.

I didn't get very far, though. A crowd was gathered at the alley behind the Rue Déschamps, the street next to mine. The lights of a police car were flashing.

"Did you see her?" a man grumbled to a woman as they walked past me.

"It looked as if she had no blood," the woman hissed. "A mummy—"

"Don't talk foolishness, Francine," the man said, and

pressed his hand against her back, pushing her out of the crowd.

I took her place. "What's—" I gasped. On the ground in the alley lay what looked like a log, gray and dry and withered and hard.

Except that it had arms and legs.

"You," the policeman said, pointing at me with his stick. "Go. This is no place for you."

I couldn't move. It wasn't that the thing was so gross, really—it wasn't any worse than mummies I'd seen in museums, and to tell the truth, it barely looked human. It was just that there was something weirdly *familiar* about it.

The body was naked except for one green earring tangled in its hair. It looked so out of place under the circumstances. I bent down to touch it to see if I could read anything, but the police officer pushed me away with some force. "What do you think you're doing?" he shouted.

I cleared my throat, wondering if I should tell him that I'm an object empath and could probably learn something about the dead woman from her earring. But then, that might lead to someone coming to the house on the Rue des Âmes Perdues and possibly finding out about the activities that went on there. So I just backed away.

"Somebody get that girl away from here," the cop said. A burly man complied, grabbing me by the shoulders and steering me, fighting and squirming, into the street.

"Go home," the man said. "Try not to think about it."

Right, I thought. *I'll just blot the image of a naked mummy in an alley clean out of my mind.* I sighed. I no longer felt like a marshmallow cone. Or a walk, either.

I went back to the house. Peter was sitting on the stairs of the servant's entrance when I arrived. I was nervous about seeing him after the debacle at Marie-Therèse's birthday party, but he'd been my friend for a long time. It was hard to forget that.

His head was resting on his hands. "Hi," I said. "What's up with you?"

He looked at me with sad eyes. "Have I lost you?" he asked.

I hadn't been expecting that. "I don't know what—"

"Yes, you do. Belmondo," he said, as if it were the name of a rodent.

"Oh." My stomach clenched. *Not again,* I thought. "I didn't think you cared what I did," I said. "Or with whom."

"Stop being a drama queen, Katy."

"Hey, I didn't bring this up. Besides, I hardly even see you anymore. Between your work and these people . . ." I gestured toward the house.

"Yeah. Well, about them . . . Katy, I think something weird's going on."

I rolled my eyes. "Do you think?"

"For one thing, they're all older than they look."

"Tell me something I don't know."

"You know? And you still want to go out with *him*?"

I felt my heart sink. "Belmondo's not one of them," I said.

"Really? Is that what he told you?"

I didn't answer.

"Because he'd never lie to you, would he?"

I thought about Belmondo kissing Joelle on her neck. "I don't want to talk about it," I said.

Peter sighed. "All right," he said. "That's your business, I guess." He stood up. "Jeremiah wants me to be a part of this. The Enclave."

"I pretty much figured that out," I said.

He looked around and lowered his voice. "He wants me to take over the company."

"What, Shaw Enterprises? Are you kidding?"

"Well, not right away. The company's CEO runs the actual businesses under the Shaw banner from New York. For the time being, Jeremiah only needs me to . . . do things with the Enclave."

"Such as what?"

He sighed. "You know what I do, Katy," he said quietly.

I lowered my head. Yes, I knew what he did. I'd known since his party last spring. Peter made gold. Just like Jean-Loup de Villeneuve. And Henry Shaw. And Jeremiah. Peter was just the newest link in the chain, the latest Sugar Daddy that Sophie and her cronies lived off.

"So that would be your whole job?" I asked. "Keeping these ladies in designer shoes?"

"Of course not. In time I'd take over all the things Jeremiah does. Oversee the shipping and imports. Coordinate the Shaw offices in Europe. A lot of things."

"Is he going to retire?"

"He wants to, yes."

"I'll bet he's not planning to live at the Poplars," I said acidly.

"Look, you're dead wrong about that place—"

Suddenly there was a shriek from inside the house. Peter and I both stood up, and were nearly run over by a herd of women who ran out, their high heels clacking, leaving us in a cloud of dust and expensive perfume.

"What was that?" Peter asked. "A fire?"

"A phone call," a man said from the doorway. I recognized him from Belmondo's club. Also from the day Joelle led me into the sewer and left me there. As I recalled, the man's name was Jacques. He was—or at least had been—Joelle's boyfriend. "Apparently, there's a body on the Rue Déschamps," he said, rubbing his arms as he headed for the street.

"A body?" Peter asked.

"Not much of one," I said. "It's all dried out."

"You've been there?"

I nodded. "It's a mummy. But she's wearing earrings. Well, one earring."

Peter frowned. "But how long could a *mummy* have been lying in the middle of the city?"

"I guess someone moved it there," I said. "I might have been able to find out if I could have handled her jewelry, but the police kicked me out before I could get close enough."

"Too bad," Peter said, distracted.

"So go ahead. It's only a murder. You were talking about your plans to become an international mogul."

He gave me an angry look. "Don't, Katy," he said. "I'm not like these people."

The hell you're not, I thought. *You're ready to throw away everything you are to be one of them.* But instead I said, "You're luckier than they are. You won't lose your gift with time."

Fabienne had said Peter's gift wasn't like the magic the

other witches possessed—that he wouldn't need to sacrifice a small part of it every month in exchange for the benefits of the full-moon ritual. Of course, that made sense. The coven wouldn't want to lessen his ability to make gold. He'd get a free ride on the longevity train, just as Jeremiah and the alchemists before him had.

"It's not like I'd be stuck here forever. In time, I'll be taking over the American branches too. I'd just have to come back here once a month, like Jeremiah."

"Great," I said without much enthusiasm. So he really was going over. "Sounds like what you've always hoped for. Money, power, and a *soupçon* of eternal life, all in one fell swoop. What more could you want?"

He turned away. "I should have known I couldn't talk to you about it."

That felt like a slap. There had been a time when Peter and I could talk to each other about anything. I was going to apologize for my sarcasm, but Sophie and Annabelle appeared, with Jacques trotting behind them. They were talking excitedly as they crossed the street.

"So deliciously *creepy*," Sophie was saying. "Like something in a horror film. Oh, hello, Pierre." She gave him her most dazzling smile. "Have you heard? There's a—"

"Yes. Katy told me."

Almost reluctantly, she shifted her gaze toward me. "Hello there," she said, as if she'd forgotten my name. "Did you have a nice day cooking?"

"Yes, thank you," I said tightly.

"I wish Joelle could have seen it," Sophie was saying as she headed toward the front steps. "She loves freakish things."

Jacques's face collapsed at the mention of Joelle's name.

"Oh, don't be so theatrical, Jacques," Sophie said. "You were Joelle's boy of the moment, and your moment has passed. Get over it."

Jacques just shook his head. "What a beast you are," he said as she walked away.

Joelle. The name stirred something inside me. I didn't know what, but I'd learned to trust my instincts. I sprinted up behind Sophie and grabbed her arm. "Where is Joelle?" I asked.

Glaring, she snatched her elbow away from me. "How should I know?"

"Didn't she come home?"

Sophie exchanged a look with Annabelle. "No, dear," she said with exaggerated gentleness. "I'm afraid our bad boy Belmondo has kept her out all night." She put her hand over her mouth in a parody of shock. "No doubt, such things don't go on in your world," she said.

"A lot of things that happen here don't go on in my world," I answered.

"Then I suppose you'll be eager to get back," she said, smiling oh so sweetly as she pushed me out of her way.

Peter was looking up at me from his spot on the steps, his eyes narrowed as I trudged back. "Still thinking about Belmondo?" he snapped.

"Quit it, Peter," I said. "It's not him, it's Joelle. Do you remember the earrings she had on?"

He looked blank. "She was wearing earrings?"

"Forget it," I said.

CHAPTER • THIRTY-NINE

The party—I supposed it could be called the "Discovery of the Corpse" party—began almost immediately, with everyone toasting whatever came into their heads and going on about the body in the alley. Not everyone in the house had gone to explore the Rue Déschamps. Those who hadn't had obviously used their time well, ordering snacks and filling ice buckets.

Jacques, apparently somewhat recovered from his broken heart, leaned against the fireplace with a glass of champagne in his hand, laughing heartily at a story someone was telling. Sophie was holding forth in her own little area, describing the ghoulish mummy in grisly detail.

"Excuse me," I said, interrupting her story.

She looked up at me angrily. "What do you want *now*?"

"Her earrings," I waffled. "That is, the earrings on the mummy—"

"The mummy's earrings?" she shrieked. "Is that what

you were looking at? Were you planning to steal them?"

"Sounds like a movie title," someone said. "*The Mummy's Earrings*."

"I just wondered if they looked familiar to you."

"Familiar?" Sophie repeated.

"Were they Joelle's?"

Sophie sighed. "Joelle again! Look, she's with Belmondo, all right? If it makes you feel any better, Joelle often doesn't come home after a date. Sometimes she's gone for weeks. It's just the way she is."

"And you didn't recognize the earrings?"

"No," she said pointedly. "I didn't."

"All right." I nodded and backed out of her circle. "Sorry to have bothered you."

"Idiot girl," Sophie muttered.

I headed up the stairs to my room and lay on my bed. Peter hadn't wanted to go into the house. I felt bad about how far our relationship had unraveled. If we were closer, I might be able to talk him out of joining the Witches that Time Forgot. But I didn't think he'd listen to me anymore.

He was being seduced. By the future. By what might be.

And maybe I was too.

Maybe we both ought to turn and run while we still could. If only the prizes being offered weren't so tempting. If only it weren't already too late.

I opened Azrael's book again. The binding was almost finished, but I thought some of the pages might be missing. The story took up nearly a hundred years later, during the worst years of the French Revolution.

1793
The Angel of Death

Open revolt had broken out. The monarchy had been deposed and the royal family imprisoned. Self-appointed leaders vied for power over the citizens, who were still hungry even after the nobility's blood had run red in the streets. To make matters even worse, it became known that, before his execution, the king had hired Hessian mercenaries to fight his own subjects in order to quell the uprising, so that no one, anywhere, of any persuasion or station, was safe.

In the midst of this horror walked a handful of women, according to Sophie de la Soubise's account of the day as she would relate it to Henry Shaw years later. Among the women was Countess Marie-Therèse LePetit, who walked purposefully beside Sophie through the dangerous streets, their opulent gowns concealed beneath plain cloaks taken from their servants.

"But what is this place you're taking me to?" the countess asked. She was very agitated. The hem of her skirt was heavy with the jewels that had been sewn into it. They were all she could salvage from her home, which had been ransacked and taken over by revolutionary "leaders," men who stank of sweat, with dirt under their fingernails. The only thing she had to be grateful for was that her husband had died before he'd had to see the world as it had become.

"It is an abbey," Sophie said. "I was once its abbess."

Marie-Therèse gasped. "Surely not!"

Sophie laughed. "Indeed, madame. There are more strange things in life than any of us can understand. But this place is a true sanctuary, and we'll be safe there."

"Hey!" called a gutter cleaner who had never seen any aristocrats until he had watched them lose their heads under the guillotine's blade. "You're a fine one, aren't you?" He pulled Sophie's hood off her head. "Hair like spun gold."

Sophie slapped the man's hand away. "Stop," she whispered, skewering him with her gaze as if he were a butterfly pinned to a board. The man froze, rooted to the spot where he stood, as the women rushed away. "Hurry," she urged the woman with her. "He'll remember everything in a few minutes. If he talks, they'll kill us all."

"Unless we can produce a miracle, they'll kill us anyway," Marie-Therèse said as they approached the doors of the Abbey of Lost Souls.

But they did produce a miracle. Working together under the abbess's direction, they used their combined magic—for once—in the service of something other than the preservation of their own youth. They produced a glamour that shielded the abbey from notice. "The building is not really invisible," the abbess explained. "Just uninteresting to those who see it. It is a magic that one of our first abbesses, Sister Béatrice, used to perform."

Sophie laughed. "This is the first time I've been pleased to be thought of as uninteresting," she said.

And so the women had waited out the worst months of the Reign of Terror. At Sophie's insistence, others with psychic abilities were also permitted to take refuge in the abbey and were thus spared the acquaintance of the "National Razor," as the ever-present guillotine had become known.

Within a year the abbey became crowded, not only with the new people seeking sanctuary, but also because of the aged *among them who were so infirm that they were unable to move from their beds.*

"I don't know what we're going to do," the abbess confided to Sophie, who had known her since childhood. She was new to her office, having taken over after the former abbess, a duchess, had the misfortune to venture outside, where she was set upon by thieves who cut her throat for her woolen cloak. "We're running out of space."

Sophie shrugged. "So get rid of them," she said.

The abbess was taken aback at her friend's lack of compassion for the old nuns. "But they've been here for centuries," she said.

"Exactly. It's time for them to move on. Call for Jean-Loup de Villeneuve," Sophie said. "He'll know what to do." She looked at her nails. "We need more money, anyway."

Henry went alone to the ritual, as he had for more than a hundred years. Unlike the austere enclosure he had entered the first time Jean-Loup had brought him, the abbey now looked like a royal palace. The once-bare walls had been covered with lacquer and gold leaf. Thick carpets cushioned their footfalls. The rooms were filled with beautiful furniture and paintings taken from the homes of the new residents, rescued before the mobs broke in to steal them. In a corner, a woman played a harpsichord while people milled about dressed in their finest fashions. Even the "abbess"—who had never been a real abbess, or even a nun, of course—looked as if she belonged at a party in Versailles.

"Welcome," she said, curtsying to him.

"Has Jean-Loup de Villeneuve arrived?"

"Not yet. But as you know, he never misses our gatherings. Perhaps you'd like to . . ."

He heard nothing more. His gaze had fallen upon a woman standing some distance away, a painted fan fluttering in front of her face. A woman he had dreamed about since before he'd left for America more than a century before.

He left the abbess abruptly, his heart thundering, and went over to the woman with the fan. "My lady," he said, bending to kiss her hand. "Henry Shaw."

"Sophie de la Soubise," she said, an amused expression playing on her lips. "I think I remember you. You were just a boy."

Henry blushed deeply. He hadn't considered how his own appearance had changed. He had not attended the life-extending rituals during the decades he'd lived in America, and consequently looked a great deal older than he had when he'd first met the exquisite Sophie. Now he resembled a man of fifty, while she still possessed the dewy face of a twenty-year-old.

For all the long years between their first meeting and this, he had thought only about his own attraction to her. He had never dreamed that she would find him acceptable. "Forgive me," he said, preparing to retreat in shame. "I've been too forward."

"Nonsense, Henry, darling," she purred, taking his arm. "Let me show you around."

As they strolled through the opulent rooms of the abbey, Henry was nearly overcome with a sense of well-being he had never before known. Oh, he had certainly been content during his years in Massachusetts, and if he had been a man with a normal lifespan, that contentment would have been enough.

But his lifespan was not normal. It had been more than a hundred years since he had left Zenobia and their children, *and already his life in America was beginning to seem more like a dream than a memory.*

He had returned to the colonies many times for the sake of his businesses. He had used different names through the years, pretending to be his own descendants. He had walked through the graveyard in Whitfield's Meadow, where the African shaman's spell had separated him forever from his mortal family, and had visited the graves of his wife and children, who had all grown old before meeting their ends. He had seen their children, and their children's children, as strangers who passed him on the street without a glance of recognition. But it no longer pained him to be parted from them.

And nothing, nothing he had ever experienced in those days had filled him with the perfect joy he now felt as he walked beside Sophie de la Soubise, enveloped by the warmth of her touch, intoxicated by the fragrance that surrounded her. With every step, he could almost hear music.

"We've done so much to make this ghastly building a worthy home for our poor exiled ladies," Sophie said. Even her breath was enticing. "Did you know that Marie-Therèse LePetit is here? Who would have thought that the countess could be a witch?"

Henry barely heard her. Just being near Sophie caused his blood to beat in his ears.

"Perhaps you'd like to see my quarters, Henry," she offered.

He accepted without a moment's hesitation.

As they sauntered slowly through the crowd, Sophie caught the attention of the current abbess. "Bring in our friend," she said.

The abbess nodded. *How lovely it must be to be a siren,* she thought.

While the participants gathered for the ritual in the bottom level of the abbey, Jean-Loup was looking at a much less pleasant scene. In a room that had not been touched by the incoming aristocrats, a chamber of bare stone and straw beds illuminated only by the candle carried by the abbess, lay the old women of the abbey.

The abbess had opened the door in silence. Being new, she was not aware that Jean-Loup had visited this room before.

The first time he had come, he had woodenly repeated Drago's argument to the woman who had then been in charge: "These ladies are too infirm to leave their beds," he had explained, "yet they will not die for decades to come."

The abbess of the time had nodded her head in agreement. "That is the price we must pay for our long lives," she had said. "When we grow so old that we yearn for death, death taunts us by moving too slowly."

Even though he detested his son's plan to kill off the old ones, he could see its merits. After so much time, was life really so desirable? He thought of his own long life. Of all the centuries he had lived, he wondered, how many happy moments had he known?

Only the briefest candle's flicker, he thought, picturing Veronique's face.

"Death would be a blessing for them," the abbess said.

"Yes." He closed his eyes. "A blessing."

That had been long ago. Now no one even gave a thought to what happened to the crones in the special room.

"They shouldn't be here," Jean-Loup said, offended by the constant neglect these women obviously suffered. Some of them had been lying in this place for fifty years or more. It was clear that they were never bathed and rarely fed. "This room is little more than a prison," he pronounced bitterly.

"But Monsieur de Villeneuve—"

"It is my money that funds this establishment!" he roared. His echo reverberated off the damp stone walls, but none of the room's occupants stirred. "See that they are moved to a decent dwelling, with windows and comfortable beds."

"Yes, monsieur," the abbess said, chastened. "It will be done."

"Now leave me," Jean-Loup said quietly.

Without another word, she departed with her candle, and the darkness of the room settled around him like a soft blanket. In the silence, a faint hiss and a now-familiar sloughing sound, the sound of a snake moving over dry stone, signaled that he was not alone.

"Do you think it matters to these creatures whether their beds are soft or not?" Drago whispered as he emerged from the darkness. He chuckled softly. "Ah, well, you've eased your own conscience. That was the point of your little tirade, wasn't it?"

"It will get you away from me," Jean-Loup said. "At least I will not have to watch you feeding."

Drago's smile vanished. "Then enjoy the sight while you can," he said as he closed the door that separated this room from the rest of the abbey.

For a moment, Drago stood immobile in the dark room with only the feeble breathing of the invalids to break the profound silence. He had instantly forgotten about Jean-Loup, *who pressed his back against the stone wall, trying to think of something, anything, other than the horror that was about to take place in front of him.*

Without making a sound, Drago moved toward one of the aged nuns and knelt beside her, quietly mouthing the words of the lullaby that his mother used to sing to him:

My love, my love
Walk through the door
The voice that was calling
Is calling once more

"It works both ways," he told Jean-Loup, who turned away. "Entering or leaving life . . . it's all the same. Frightening but beautiful." He sighed reverently. "And always, without exception, exciting."

His lips came close to the old woman's, and he pressed against her chest with his hand. A rib cracked—so fragile—then, with a slight moan, she succumbed to him as he breathed in the last of her life force.

The woman never awakened. She only relaxed into her pillow with a look of what might have been interpreted as sublime peace on her face. Then, in another moment, the unnecessary flesh collapsed in on itself.

Drago took a deep breath. "So easy," he whispered. The woman had been very, very old. Jean-Loup could almost hear the aroused thrum-thrum of Drago's heartbeat while he imagined something dark and smooth moving behind the young man's eyelids.

The second woman also died uneventfully, but the third

struggled to open her eyes in surprise. "Who are you?" she rasped, clutching at Drago's clothes.

He took her hand into his own. "I am the Angel of Death," he said softly. He bent over the woman and she cried out, a small mewling sound that was soon drowned out by Drago's own rapid breathing. From the corners of the room, a dark vapor began to coalesce, winding itself slowly around him and the crone he had been given to feed on.

He sang the song to her, Veronique's song, while he held her in place, careful to avoid her panicked gaze.

> *Be well, my angel*
> *Be strong, be whole*

She pummeled his chest and tried to scratch his eyes, but with each struggle Drago appeared to grow stronger, surer, as the dark vapor in the room coiled around him, reinforcing his rightness, his purpose.

> *Your suffering has ended*
> *Awaken your soul!*

"Ah, yes," he whispered as the woman's eyes glazed over in terror and her last breath found its way into her killer's mouth. "This is a sacred rite," Drago said, savoring the deliciousness of her life as it passed into him. "The blessing that I give to you. The harvest that you give to me."

Feeling sick, Jean-Loup closed his eyes. He never wanted to open them again.

CHAPTER • FORTY

"Yuck," I whispered, wanting to spit the bad taste out of my mouth. Drago was too creepy for words. When he . . . I swallowed hard. *Was Drago still around?* I wondered as a frisson of fear crawled up my spine. Was Henry? Had Henry been Drago's last meal?

Whoa, I told myself. I was reading a history of the coven, not a description of its current affairs.

Still, it had made me nervous, especially the part about moving the aged members of the abbey into a separate home where they could be killed in private. Had that been the original function of the Poplars? Was that why none of the objects in that place told me anything about its past? Or why no one who had gone there was ever seen again?

Too many questions, I thought as I got out of bed and pulled on a pair of shorts and a T-shirt. I needed to talk seriously with Marie-Therèse. She'd changed her mind about the

Poplars and was all for going there these days, but I still had a bad feeling about the place.

"Marie-Therèse?" I called softly outside her bedroom door.

Downstairs, the volume of conversation increased along with the consumption of alcohol. "Joelle? Who's Joelle?" Jacques slurred.

Sophie's high, tinkling laugh came in response. "But sir, was she wearing *earrings*?" she asked in a thick American accent that was supposed to sound like me.

"I wouldn't care if she was wearing Saran Wrap, the cow," Jacques said.

I knocked. "It's me, Katy." The door gave way, as if it hadn't been closed tightly.

"Marie, are you here?" I whispered as I inched my way into the darkness inside. There was no answer. I almost turned around and left. I didn't want to scare her if she was asleep or something. "Marie—"

Then I felt it, the absence of human life, and I knew. I switched on the light.

The room was empty. Everything was gone—the bed, the antique dressing table, even the pictures on her wall.

"No," I whispered, hearing my voice quaver.

"Some guys in a truck came by about an hour ago."

I whirled around. Peter was standing in the doorway behind me.

"Where is she?" I shrilled.

"I don't know. They wouldn't talk to me."

"The movers? But I thought *you* were the one who was

supposed to move her out. Did you refuse to do it?"

"No. I thought you were being paranoid when you asked me to refuse. But I guess Jeremiah just took me out of the equation."

"Why would he do that?"

"Hmm. Let me see." Peter struck a pose like he was thinking hard. "Could it be that when you assaulted him on the stairs demanding that he cancel the old lady's birthday, he had second thoughts about my loyalty?"

That was interesting. And probably right. It was Peter's association with me that had changed Jeremiah's mind. "Hey, I'm sorry if I messed things up for you," I said. "But the real question isn't whether or not these people can trust you. It's the other way around."

"Are you giving me advice?" He bristled. "Because—"

"I'm not," I said, exasperated. "Do whatever you've got to do. But why didn't you tell me, at least? I was in my room."

"What could you have done, Katy?"

"I don't know. Something." I threw him a dark look as I turned to leave the room. "I have to do something."

It was a long journey to the house in Vincennes, most of it by bus. For a while I just stared out the window as the scenery changed from city to country, but my mind kept going back to Marie-Therèse.

Don't let your imagination run away with you, I told myself. She might not even be at the Poplars, although I couldn't imagine anywhere else she might have been taken. But even if my worst fears were true, there wasn't anything I could do until I got there.

To calm my nerves, I took the remaining pages of Azrael's manuscript out of my bag. Reading it would at least pass the time until I could either make sure Marie-Therèse was all right or get her out of that place.

Toujours

Jean-Loup arrived late for the ritual, and left the abbey in search of his carriage as soon as it was over. He didn't worry about Drago; the evil whelp would have no difficulty finding his own way back to the farm. Jean-Loup was never certain whether or not Drago was even in the house with him. He moved like smoke, silent and invisible, unless he wanted something. Then he would appear with a terrifying presence, making it clear that he was the new master of the house.

In the courtyard of the abbey, Henry slipped his arm in Jean-Loup's just as the old man was about to fall on the uneven stones of the pavement. "You shouldn't have come alone," he said. "I could have brought you."

"How pleasant that would have been." Since Henry's return, Jean-Loup had made a point of keeping a certain distance between them. He knew that if he ever asked for help against Drago, Henry would do everything he could, including dying in the old man's service. And he would die, Jean-Loup was sure of that. Against Drago, neither of them would stand a chance.

"You've delivered the gold?"

"Every month, Captain Loup," Henry said. "You don't have to worry about that anymore."

"Good, good," the old man answered. "I appreciate that."

He patted Henry's hand. "And you. Are you doing well?"

"Wonderfully well," Henry said, fairly bursting with happiness. He looked up at one of the windows of the abbey, where Sophie smiled and waved to him, her diamonds sparkling in the torchlight.

Jean-Loup sighed.

"Are you all right?" Henry asked as he helped the old man into his carriage.

"Yes, quite." He knocked for the driver to go, then tipped his hat to Henry. There was no point in warning him that by allowing himself to be entranced by Sophie de la Soubise, Henry was playing with fire. How could he, when he himself had such an intimate familiarity with Hell? Jean-Loup knew well that he and Henry Shaw had both already been burned beyond redemption.

When he came in sight of his house, Jean-Loup saw that a carriage he did not recognize was outside, the horses still bridled and stomping with hunger. There were a number of other horses tethered to the post as well.

Visitors? He had not had a visitor since Henry's homecoming a hundred years ago. With a sinking feeling of foreboding, he walked through the open front door. A half-dozen men in makeshift uniforms rose and faced him.

"Are you Jean-Loup de Villeneuve?" one of the soldiers asked in guttural French.

"Yes," he answered, looking from one Revolutionary soldier to another.

"We are confiscating this house in the name of the people of France."

Jean-Loup was taken aback. What reason would they have to come here, to this tumbledown farmhouse in the middle of the countryside? There was nothing for them. . . .

But of course there was. He realized what the "soldiers"—who were as far removed from trained military men as the women in the Abbey of Lost Souls were from religious nuns—had come for. One of them hefted a bag of gold in his hand. Another placed his foot on top of a chest that Jean-Loup knew was filled with treasures, including the necklace that Charlemagne had given Veronique. "Where'd you get this?"

"My savings," Jean-Loup said, although he knew that whatever he told them would not matter. He was done for.

The soldier whose foot was resting on the chest sneered. "Then you are guilty of hoarding gold that the Revolution needs," he said. The others laughed. He scratched his belly. "What is it he was hoarding, boys?" he asked. "Not this." He gave the treasure chest a little kick. "This is for our expenses."

"I think he was hoarding this," another man said, pulling Veronique's gold heart pendant from his pocket. He squinted at the inscription. "Mon amour toujours," he read. "Very sweet."

Jean-Loup lunged at him. It was the perfect opportunity for the soldiers to beat him with whatever came to hand. Once he was on the ground, they kicked him until he was unconscious.

CHAPTER • FORTY-ONE

By the time I got to the Poplars, it was nearly dark. I didn't know how I'd get in, but for once I was lucky: One of the servants was out in the back courtyard gathering firewood, and the kitchen door to the house was open. Moving as quickly and carefully as I could, I dashed inside and made it up the stairs without running into anyone.

Here were the bedrooms that Marie-Therèse and I never got to see during our visit. And I was willing to bet they were all empty. I flung open the first door I came to. It was dark inside, and I snapped on the light.

To my horror, I saw a frail, ancient woman lying in the bed. Shocked at my entrance, she whimpered and tried to shield her eyes with her hand.

"Oh, excuse me, I'm sorry," I said, flipping off the light. I was closing the door when the woman spoke.

"Katy?" she croaked.

I stopped dead where I stood, unsure if I'd heard anything at all.

"Katy?" she repeated.

Suddenly air whooshed into my lungs, and I realized that I'd forgotten to breathe for some time. "Who . . ." *Oh, no. Oh, God, no.* "Marie-Therèse?" I whispered.

"Take me . . ." She tried to sit up. I ran to her side to help her, and turned on the lamp by her bed. ". . . out of here," she rasped.

She was almost unrecognizable. It was as if she had aged forty years literally overnight. Yesterday, Marie-Therèse hadn't appeared to be anywhere near eighty years old, but now she seemed too aged to even be alive. Her head, once covered with a beautiful coiffure of white hair, was now nearly bald except for a few stringy strands that lay across her pink scalp. Her once-beautiful face was now a map of wrinkles and brown spots. Her hands were like claws, their bones stark beneath her papery skin. And she was so thin! She looked as if she'd lost fifty pounds or more. But how could that be? It had been only one day since I'd seen her.

It couldn't be Marie-Therèse, I decided. I must not have heard her right. "Ma'am, I'm sorry I disturbed you," I said, reaching for the bedside light.

She grabbed my hand. "Don't leave me!" she hissed.

With her touch, I felt every experience that Marie-Therèse and I had shared—our first trip to this place, my botched magic spell, her birthday party. The memories weren't clear. They sparked in and out of one another like dreams. Like a mind crossing into senility.

So old. What had happened?

"Who did this?" I asked. There wasn't enough time to ask politely. "Jeremiah?"

"Jere . . ." She looked up at me with haunted eyes.

"How did he do this to you?"

"No," she said, her voice raspy. "Not Jeremiah. The . . ." She blinked once, slowly. ". . . the young one."

I stumbled, nearly falling on top of the old woman. "The young one?" I repeated stupidly as I felt my stomach drop. "You mean Peter?"

Marie-Therèse's eyes were closed.

"Was it Peter?" I shouted as I put my arms around her and lifted her out of the bed.

She was so light, as if she had no blood left in her.

"Answer me!"

Just then the door opened, and the maid I'd tried to talk to on our last visit stood staring, aghast. For a moment she didn't move as she took in the sight of me screaming at an unconscious old woman in my arms. Then she recognized me, and turned abruptly to leave.

"No, don't go, don't go," I hushed. Gently, I lay Marie-Therèse back onto the bed and rushed over to the maid. "Your name's Rose, isn't it?" I spoke quickly, careful not to touch her. She'd panicked the last time I'd done that. She'd also been thinking that she *didn't want to watch anyone else die*. Those words had been shooting through the pores in her body.

"Help me get her out of here," I said quietly. "No one's going to blame you, I swear. But we have to talk."

Rose's eyes filled with tears. "It's too late," she whispered. "None of them lasts more than a day or two."

Fear was drying out my mouth. "Are there many . . . like her?"

She shook her head. "Not now." She spoke as if she was in a daze. "They're all gone." She nodded toward Marie-Therèse. "She'll be gone soon too, that one."

Suddenly she jerked her head toward the door. "Miss, you'd better—"

The butler stood in the doorway. With a glance, he sent Rose out of the room. "Take it," he said.

I didn't know what he was talking about. "Take what?"

"Take her last breath. The Master has saved her for you."

I closed my eyes. *This couldn't be happening.* What I'd been reading about wasn't real. It was a *story*! You couldn't really take a person's last breath, as if it were some kind of good-luck charm.

How many people knew about Azrael's book, anyway?

"Quickly, mademoiselle. She is expiring."

I went over to Marie-Therèse and put my arms around her. She seemed so frail, as if she were a sculpture made of dry leaves. So helpless. So doomed.

"Yes, that's it." The horrid butler moved close to me on his silent, predatory feet. His eyes were wide with anticipation. His thick lips touched and parted, like a fish feeding. "You will enjoy it, mademoiselle. The Master has provided a very special treat. Just position your head . . ."

Then his big clammy hand touched the back of my head and pushed it toward Marie-Therèse's face. In that instant I felt all the cowardice and venality that coursed through the man's veins. He was a heinous excuse for a human being, a toady for forces too evil to imagine.

"Get away from me!" I shouted, ducking out of his grasp.

"But—" For a moment he seemed bewildered that I could possibly turn down such an enticing offer. But in another moment his expression turned hard with anger. "Very well," he said as he bent over my friend. "Her life's end will not be wasted." It was perfectly clear what he was about to do.

I threw five fingers out at the bedside lamp. It levitated instantly, then followed my direction to smash into the side of the man's head. "You filthy pig," I said.

He lunged toward me. I sent a porcelain figurine crashing into the middle of his forehead.

He reeled backward. "I'll notify the Enclave of your visit," he said, trying to muster his butler's dignity while a red goose egg grew between his eyes. "Someone will be coming for you shortly. Someone you won't be able to hurt so easily."

"Ooh, I'm scared," I said, thwacking him with Marie-Therèse's shoes.

"I'm afraid the authorities will have to be contacted as well. Whatever you've done to this patient . . ."

"Get out of here," I said as I moved back beside my friend. Marie-Therèse looked like a waif, lying in the middle of the white sheet. Her eyes were clouded. And open, fixed. She was dead.

I felt the air rush out of my lungs. I hadn't been able to save her after all. My vision wavered with tears as I closed her papery eyelids.

"Don't think for a minute that you're going to get away with this," the butler panted from across the room. His eyes darted back and forth, trying to anticipate what I was going to send his way next. "I'll . . . I'll . . ."

"You do that." I flicked five fingers at him, and a huge mahogany table crushed him against the wall as I walked out.

CHAPTER • FORTY-TWO

There wasn't much left of Azrael's manuscript to read, only a few more pages. But I knew now that it wasn't just a story. Somehow, in some way I didn't yet quite understand, the ancient tale of Jean-Loup de Villeneuve affected me in a very personal way.

What I did understand was that the aura surrounding the house called the Poplars was coming from the Darkness. The Darkness, my old friend. It had almost killed me once; now it loved me as its own.

The Master has saved her for you . . . a very special treat . . .

The Master.

Yes, I knew who that was. What it was. And I guessed it remembered me, too.

I sorted out the pages, but it took me a while to be able to concentrate. It wasn't what the butler had said that preyed on my mind. He'd been trying to scare me, but I'd already seen too much to fall for that line about sending the police after me. He knew as well as I did that the Enclave had killed Marie-Therèse. It had happened just as I'd feared it would, only on a different day.

"It was the young one," Marie-Therèse had said.

What I hadn't known was that her killer had been Peter.

Going Home

Jean-Loup awoke near dawn. His left eye was swollen shut, and his hair was stuck to the floor where he had lain in a pool of his own coagulating blood. With a groan, he pushed himself into a sitting position. His sides and back were already mottled with bruises, and he felt a constant nausea in his belly from the beating he'd endured.

He stumbled out of his house. His carriage and horses had been stolen. His treasures were gone too, all of them: Charlemagne's necklace, the pot that Henry Shaw had turned to gold, the golden heart he'd made long ago for a black-haired woman with violet eyes.

Mon amour toujours. My love forever.

Nothing was forever. That was God's ultimate revenge for cheating death, the lesson learned by all who lived too long: There was no such thing as forever.

"Veronique!" he cried, falling to his knees in the dry earth.

He wanted to stay there until the life left his body, but death is cruel and slow. It brought insects and filth and the stink of rotting flesh. It brought Drago and his kind, eager and hungry.

"No," he said aloud. "No, I will not wait for him to gobble me up like ripe fruit."

And so Jean-Loup began to walk, not toward anything in particular, but away. Away from the house that had been stripped of everything that had made it a home. Away from the horrid perversion his life had become.

By the time the sun came up, the house was out of sight. Nine hours later he arrived back in Paris. Where else, he thought as he watched a Revolutionary guard smash a woman's face with the butt of his musket. All roads led here, to the center of the apocalypse.

Then he heard loud gunfire, close enough that Jean-Loup could smell the cordite. A group of five or six young men were running down the street, with a cadre of soldiers some distance behind. One of the men fell in front of him, his head exploding like a melon.

Jean-Loup looked about in confusion and fear. He knew the soldiers wouldn't care if they shot him by mistake. Turning swiftly, he followed the young men who were being pursued into an old building and down the stairs into the earthen basement, where they disappeared.

The old man searched frantically for them, but when he heard the soldiers thundering down the stairs, he had to run anywhere he could. Perhaps he could find a corner littered with debris somewhere that the guards might overlook, he thought, scrambling into the darkness.

But he never reached the corner. There was no corner. The basement of the building was part of the complex underground configuration of tunnels that had honeycombed the limestone beneath the city since the time of the Romans.

Some of the tunnels were well used, even by respectable citizens. There were occasional torches, and even signs on some walls indicating which streets were above. Once or twice Jean-Loup thought he saw the young men he had followed from the street, but they were much faster than he was, and he lost them, although he continued to hear the shouts of the guards. He knew they would not trouble themselves to question him about whether or not he was associated with the others. After this long and tiring chase, the soldiers would make a game out of snuffing out his life as painfully as possible.

So he ran willy-nilly into the darkest and most narrow tunnels he encountered, into the catacombs, where King Louis had decreed that the bodies in the city's fetid cemeteries be transferred; and past them into the horrific, stinking pits where multitudes of headless corpses recently killed lay putrefying. At one point he screamed as he tripped over one of the bodies and felt its slimy flesh under his hands, but he kept running. Running, and then walking in stages steadily down, farther, farther, until the air grew still and cold and he could no longer hear the orders issued by the guards.

Why didn't I let them kill me? he asked himself.

He had long ago tired of living. But soon he realized the futility of even asking the question. It no longer made any difference whether he lived or died. He just kept walking.

There were more than a thousand miles of underground tunnels beneath the city. Jean-Loup felt as if he had walked every one of those miles. In some places the slow dripping of water in the passageways formed forests of stalactites; in others, he discovered underground lakes filled with pristine water still as glass. And still he walked. He walked until he found the end of the world, a small cavern where he could hear nothing, see nothing. Think nothing. Remember nothing.

It was where he wanted to stay.

And he would have, if he hadn't been so hungry. After a long time—he had no idea how long—he began to walk again. Eventually the pathway began to slope slightly upward, climbing higher, until the ground grew damp and he could hear the sound of rushing water.

Three days after he'd left Toujours, Jean-Loup found his way out of the underground maze to emerge from a sewer grate near the ruins of an ancient stone building. From there, he managed to stagger, starving, to the Abbey of Lost Souls, where a housemaid who mistook him for a beggar directed him to the kitchen.

The cook was a kindly woman who took pity on the old man. "Here's a basin," she said, pouring water into a bowl. "Clean yourself up while I fix you a plate."

He thanked her, grateful to wash the grime off his hands and face. After he had eaten, he watched through the high window as a carriage came round the curved courtyard and a well-dressed man stepped out.

"Henry," Jean-Loup said, surprised. He headed for the door, but the cook stopped him.

"Now, how would you even know a toff like Henry Shaw?" she teased.

"I . . . I must speak with him," the old man muttered. "Toujours . . . the Revolutionaries . . ."

"Never mind them. Those what live here'll have my head

if they know I've been giving food away to strangers." She waved a wooden spoon at him. "So you keep quiet about this, or I'll turn you in to the militia myself, got that?"

On the other side of the window, Henry was kissing Sophie de la Soubise on both cheeks in greeting.

"The siren," he said.

"Is that what they're calling her these days?" the cook said with a raucous laugh. She slapped Jean-Loup on his back. "Oh, it's a new world, Gramps, make no mistake." She dried some spoons with a rag. "Nothing's the way it used to be."

Outside, Henry and Sophie entered the carriage and drove away. In the street beyond, a small boy screamed as he was dragged into the prison wagon along with his parents. Farther away, a row of prostitutes flirted with a group of self-appointed soldiers in dirty uniforms. Muskets sounded in the distance while intermittently, when the wind was right, the sound of the guillotine's falling blade sliced through the air with its silvery song.

"No," he repeated numbly. "Nothing is the same."

He left the abbey with a loaf of bread, a piece of cheese, a sack of candles, and some flint—items he'd purchased from the cook for a handful of gold nuggets he'd made from lead pie weights while she wasn't looking.

Then he walked back to the abandoned building where he had emerged from the tunnel.

"I remember this," he said in wonder, running his hand along the crumbling stone wall. It was the building where, six hundred years before, he had caught a zinc dénier that had changed his life forever.

"Such a small thing," he whispered as he lifted the sewer

grate and lowered himself once again into the darkness and peace of the distant past.

Jean-Loup had finally found his place in the world.

Azrael.

I supposed I'd known for some time, without admitting it, who Jean-Loup was. *What a strange and terrible life*, I thought as I closed the last page with a heavy heart. I remembered what he had said, that there was no such thing as forever. Was that true?

Was there nothing that wouldn't be corroded or destroyed by time, even our own souls?

CHAPTER • FORTY-THREE

I sneaked into the abbey's kitchen. I couldn't risk going back to my room because I was pretty sure the life-sucking butler at the house in Vincennes had made good on his promise to call the witches of the Enclave, so Sophie and her friends would probably have a surprise welcome waiting for me if they found me. Fortunately, it was unlikely they'd venture into the kitchen for any reason, so I felt fairly safe while I worked on sewing the last pages of the book.

It was after ten when I finally finished. Then I bound the pine with some glue I found in one of the pantry drawers. When I was done, the book looked as good as new, or at least as new as it looked when I'd first wrecked it. I stuck it in my backpack and let myself back out.

I had to see Azrael, even if it meant waking him up. I needed an explanation about the events in the book I'd read. Even if parts of his account were fictitious, Azrael knew a lot about the Enclave, and it was important that I learned what he knew. The similarities between his story and my reality were just too close. And Joelle still hadn't come home.

"Azrael?" I called into the darkness. In the distance, I saw the light from one dim candle. Maybe he was still awake. "Are you there?"

"Yes," came the grizzled old voice. He sounded confused, and for a moment I thought he'd been sleeping after all. But when I walked in, I saw that the old man had taken down the painting of Veronique from the wall and was standing in front of it with a palette of paints and a brush. He was painting the white streak in her hair.

Obviously absorbed in his work, he blinked at me for a moment as if he didn't recognize me.

"Hi," I said softly. "I apologize about the time."

Finally he smiled. "What? No chicken livers in aspic? No frog legs in browned butter?"

I laughed. "I don't think I'm cut out for *haute cuisine*," I said. It was true. I'd spent all the money I'd saved up for college to come here and cook food I wouldn't even eat. But that was just one of many mistakes I'd made in the past couple of months, and probably the smallest of the lot. "I like what you've done to the painting," I said, changing the subject.

"You were my inspiration."

"Me? What did I do?"

"You stole my book," he said, quite conversationally.

My mouth went dry. "I . . . I'm really sorry about that," I stammered. "That is, I didn't really steal it. In fact, it's right here." I ran over to my bag and took out the book. "You see, I dropped it, and . . . and . . ."

"Are you sorry to have read it?" He added a few more brushstrokes to the painting.

I swallowed. "It's always better to know the truth," I said carefully. "That's why I came tonight."

He sighed, a wheezing, whistling sound. "What do you wish to ask me?" He seemed so *rickety*, as if he were held together with chewing gum.

"Are you all right?"

"Of course." He waved me away irritably. "Was that your question?"

"No." I laid the book down carefully. Then I took a deep breath and tried to keep my voice steady. "Marie-Therèse died," I said. "She'd been drained of whatever life she'd had left. And that skeevy butler . . ." I shuddered. "He tried to get me to take her last breath." I looked up at him. "Like in your book."

"And did you?" he asked. "Take her last breath?"

"Are you kidding? I slammed him with a table."

"Ah," he said with a chuckle. "Good for you, Katy Ainsworth."

I put my head in my hands. "I don't even know where to begin," I said. "Peter's going to be initiated into the coven."

"Peter . . ." He looked as if he were trying to place the name. "Ah, yes. He has decided to join that herd of idiots?"

"They're not just idiots, Azrael," I said. "They're the ones who killed Marie-Therèse. There's something evil at the core of them. I can feel it. That's how this coven is different from the one in your book. And Peter's right in the thick of it."

"Can you stop it?"

"What, the Initiation? I wish I could."

"But Peter's participation, perhaps?"

I sighed. "I don't think he'll listen to me anymore," I said. "Jeremiah's promised him a free ride to the presidency of Shaw Enterprises. His future's made. All he has to do is sell his soul. And I think he's already done that."

"A familiar theme," Azrael said. "Someone dangles a trinket in front of our eyes, and suddenly we are hypnotized. We walk toward evil willingly, without a thought, our eyes fixed only on the shiny object."

"Is that what happened to Henry?" I asked.

He smiled. "Surely you've guessed who Henry has become."

"Jeremiah?" I asked.

He nodded. "It's a relatively new name. The first time I'd heard it was when you said that he'd asked about me." His lips pressed together. "He was a good friend. I miss him."

"But he's still here, in Paris. Don't you ever see him?"

"No," Azrael said sadly. "We have not spoken for many years."

"I guess he was lured by Sophie. She was his shiny object."

"There are many sorts of temptations, little one. No one is immune to all of them."

"What about you?" I swallowed.

"Me?" He looked amused. "I'm afraid I'm a bit old for most seductions. A slice of cream pie, perhaps, or a night's sleep without having to walk to the bathroom may be the limit of my forbidden desires. Henry—Jeremiah—now supports the coven, you know."

"Yes. He's grooming Peter."

"Ah. Your young man is an alchemist, then."

"That's why they want him in the coven. Those witches need their gold." I crooked my head, curious about something. "Do you still go to the rituals?"

"To perpetuate my endless life? Alas, yes." He closed his eyes and sighed. "It is not my idea to attend. I am made to hobble around like a penitent begging for another day in this cave. I occasionally see Henry at these events. I see his face and remember the boy he was, before . . ." He winced.

"Before Drago," I finished.

"Yes," he said bitterly.

"At least your son hasn't . . ." I cleared my throat.

"Hasn't killed me?" he rasped. The old man's eyes narrowed. "My son, like Henry, no longer bothers much with me," he said.

"But he does bother with some people," I went on doggedly. I had to. It was the reason I'd come here in the middle of the night. "Is Drago still here? Or has he taught someone else to . . . to . . ." I felt such disgust that I couldn't even form the words. "Azrael, Marie-Therèse was *drained.* Nearly dessicated, and all but dead. And there was a mummy on the street—"

"*What?*" The old man leaned heavily against the arm of a chair.

"I don't think it's a coincidence." Then, with a sudden sob, all my worst fears came pouring out of me. "When I found Marie-Therèse, she said that Peter had left her in that condition. *Peter!*" I wiped my eyes with my sleeve. "He wasn't a killer when he got here. Someone had to show him. And now . . ." I was shaking all over, and crying so hard that I was choking on my tears.

"Shh." Azrael put his arms around me and held me until I could bring my grief under control. "Do not think on this, child. There are things in this world that are not meant for the pure of heart to see."

Pure of heart. How wrong he was. "I'm not pure of heart," I said miserably.

"So you believe."

"Do you know what the Darkness is?"

"I've heard of it." He looked away, disinterested.

"Well, I do know. I've seen the Darkness. I understand it. I've felt it in myself."

"But that is what makes you pure," he said. "Purity does not mean sterility. Or perfection. It just means walking toward the light, one step at a time. That is how we defeat evil, whatever form it takes."

I felt myself trembling. "I think It wants me," I said. "The butler at the Poplars said that the Master had saved Marie-Therèse's last breath for me." I took a deep breath. "I think the Master is the Darkness."

"And . . ." The old man's smile quickly changed into an expression of pain.

"Azrael?"

He stumbled forward.

"Oh, God," I said, catching him in my arms. "Come sit down." I eased him into a chair, wishing with all my heart that I had a cell phone. He'd collapsed before. I couldn't ignore it this time. "I'm going to go for help," I said. "Now, I know you don't like hospitals, but—"

"Quiet." He put his hand over mine. "No, little cook. Again, it is not time."

"How do you know?" I asked, trying to keep the note of hysteria out of my voice.

He was panting. "Because . . . I have always known . . . that I will choose . . . the hour of my death," he said between breaths. "Be still."

I sank down beside him. If he didn't want medical help, there wasn't much I could do unless I went against his wishes and exposed his hideaway to the authorities. I didn't think he'd want that, no matter how dire his situation.

My Gram says old people think differently about death than young people. I never knew exactly what that meant, but while I sat with Azrael, I was beginning to see that he didn't view dying as something terrible and weird.

"Is it hard to be old?" I asked quietly.

He smiled. "Not as hard as it is to be young," he said.

We sat together in silence, there on the floor, for a long time. Finally I spoke. I said what had been on my mind since I'd read the last words of his book. "There's no such thing as forever."

He patted my hand. "One day you'll be glad of that," he said. "Now leave me. I need rest."

"But Peter . . . the Enclave . . ."

He snorted. "Losing is always painful, but you cannot win every battle," he said. "The Enclave has been doing what it does for a very long time. You will never reform it. Those people are too corrupt to listen."

Although there were a lot of things about the Abbey of Lost Souls that were more frightening and terrible than their treatment of their children, at that moment I couldn't help but think about Fabienne. Her gift of astral projection, a gift much greater than mine, was never going to be developed because her mother wouldn't allow it. But then, Fabby didn't object to her sacrifice as much as I did. As wrong as it seemed to me, the Enclave was her world.

"Believe me, Katy. It is too late for any of them."

I nodded, digging my fingernails into my palms.

"But not for you," Azrael said softly. "For you, perhaps there is such a thing as forever."

He inclined his head. His eyes were shining with unshed tears.

CHAPTER • FORTY-FOUR

It was after midnight now, but naturally, Sophie and her gang were still up. There was no doubt in my mind that the butler from the Poplars had called and filled them in on the details of our altercation, so this time I walked into the house prepared—no, *eager*—to confront whoever was assigned to punish me for finding out their ugly little secret. My telekinetic talent might not hold a candle to Peter's gift for making gold, but it was still pretty useful in a fight. It's hard to argue with a flying frying pan.

But no one in the house said anything. They just kept chatting and acting like they didn't see me come in. *Okay*, I thought. *Being ignored is fine with me.* But if any of them started anything, I was going to finish it.

Before I went to my own room, I stopped to say good-bye to Fabby, but she wasn't in. Neither was Peter. Well, that was nothing new. It took me less than ten minutes to gather up all my things—two chef's jackets, my knife kit, one suitcase filled with clothes, and a paper bag with handles that held books and letters and whatever small things I'd picked up. My passport and other ID, plus my plane ticket home and the small amount of cash I had, were all in my backpack.

As I was lugging everything downstairs, Sophie called out, "Going somewhere, darling?"

"Yeah," I said. "Anywhere you're not."

She laughed. Strange about that laughter: What I'd once thought of as tinkling and feminine now sounded like a crude, ugly bray. I was going to force her out of my thoughts as soon as I left this house, and never allow her to enter them again. It was too bad that I'd missed Fabienne, though. She couldn't help who her mother was. I just hoped she'd be able to find some sort of happiness in what promised to be a very long and boring life.

"Ta-ta," Sophie sang as I closed the heavy front door behind me.

Good, I thought. I was out of there, at least. The problem now was where I was going to go next. I sat on the steps and checked my watch. 1:45. My old digs were out, unless I could impose on Hernan the drag queen to put me up for the night. That was two Metro transfers away, though, and I was already exhausted. I supposed I could stay in a hotel, at least until I decided what to do. Although that would eat up a lot of my money, it seemed like the best idea, given how late it was and the fact that I had school in the morning.

"Can I help?"

I looked up. "Belmondo?" No one seemed to be with him. "What are you doing here?"

He shook his head slowly. "Someone from the house called me. She said you might be in trouble."

"Who was it?"

"Doesn't matter," he said.

"And she asked you to help me?" I asked incredulously.

He smiled. "No. She just found it amusing."

"That figures," I said. "Well, I'm out of there now."

"So I see." He took my suitcase. "Where to? My car's just around the corner."

I swallowed. "Um . . ." I looked around as we walked. "Do you know of any cheap hotels around here?"

"I can do better than that," he said. "Get in."

"Er . . ."

"Yes?" Belmondo asked, leaning toward me.

"Can I ask you about Joelle?" I blurted.

"Joelle?"

"She's disappeared."

"Really? I thought she was in Vienna."

"Vienna? When did she go to Vienna?"

"After the party. I took her to the airport."

The airport? "You mean . . ."

He laughed. "Did you think that Joelle and I were going out?" His face took on a pained expression. "Definitely not my taste."

"Oh," I said. He gestured toward the Jaguar's open door. "I don't really know where I want to go," I said.

"I do. I'm taking you to my apartment."

That was what I was afraid of. "No," I said, my disappointment evident in my voice. I was just so tired and freaked out. I didn't want to fight off a guy, even one as good-looking as Belmondo. "A hotel would be better."

"Relax," he said. "I won't be there."

"Huh?"

He shooed me into the car and stashed my suitcase in the backseat. "I have to spend three weeks in London with my band. I'll be driving there tonight. My bags are already in the trunk." He started the engine, and the car took off like a rocket.

"Then why did you come to the Rue des Âmes Perdues?" I asked as we zipped through the crowded streets.

He shrugged. "I just wanted to help." He looked over at me. "I thought you might not want to stay in the house."

"You were right," I said. Then, in a small voice: "Belmondo?"

He laughed. "Yes?" he squeaked, imitating me.

I cleared my throat. "Um . . . how old are you?"

He was smiling, but his brows knit together. "Twenty-five. Why?"

"So you're saying you don't know what they do? The Enclave?"

He shrugged. "They have parties. I know that." He laughed. "I guess everyone within a two-kilometer radius knows that."

So maybe he was telling the truth when he said he wasn't one of them, I thought. Relief washed over me like a wave. He was twenty-five.

Sitting next to him, I could sense his warmth, the electric vibrancy of his energy. *Stop it,* I told myself. But it was so hard to stay away from him. I wanted so much to touch him, as if that would erase all my questions and fears and make me feel safe again.

We walk toward evil willingly, Azrael had said. But this wasn't evil, was it? Just an attraction.

Don't walk. Don't.

We drove in silence for a while. Finally he said, "I'm sorry about Marie-Therèse." When he saw my surprised face, he added, "Apparently, the butler at the Vincennes house said that she'd died."

"Something else the witches found amusing?" I asked bitterly.

He didn't answer. I looked out the window.

"She was old," he said after a long silence.

"That wasn't why she died." I sighed. "She was killed."

"*What?*" The car swerved wildly. "What are you talking about?"

I looked at my hands in my lap. "It was Peter," I said, feeling the words turn to sand inside my mouth.

"Peter?" His voice was almost a whisper.

"Please don't go to the police," I begged. Already I was feeling as if I'd betrayed Peter even by speaking his name.

"Of course not," Belmondo said. He pulled the car off the road. "But *murder* . . ." His voice trailed off.

"Before she died, I asked Marie-Therèse if Jeremiah Shaw had done something to make her so sick and old-looking, and she said no, that it was 'the young one' who'd done that." I looked up at him, wishing desperately that he could say something, anything, that would make it not be true. "The life was drained out of her."

"Oh, Katy," he said. I knew that Belmondo wanted to make me feel better, but he just didn't know how.

I brushed my hand across my eyes. "I'm fine, really," I said. "I mean, you can go on driving."

"Why? We're here." He gestured toward the handsome

limestone building beside us on the fashionable Rue Foubourg St. Honoré. He popped the trunk and got out. "Do you want to go in?"

Suddenly I was terribly confused. There was a long and awkward moment between us, but he finally said, "You don't have to worry," as though he were reading my mind. "I won't let anything happen to you."

"I thought you said you weren't even going to be here," I said.

He smiled as he came over to my side of the car and opened the door for me. "There won't be any danger from me," he said. "And I have some influence with the Enclave, in case they're planning some kind of dirty trick."

"So if someone kills me . . ."

"They won't."

We stood facing each other on the sidewalk. "Or you'll break their heads?" I asked.

He laughed. "Worse than that. I'll kick them out. I'm the landlord, remember? My family has owned that building for three hundred years, and what I say goes!" He shook a fist. I tried to smile. "Now, do you want to come up or not?"

"I . . . I don't know," I said miserably. It was a terrible decision either way. I really didn't want to wander the streets, but I wasn't an idiot, either. I knew that by going into Belmondo's apartment, I was making myself vulnerable in too many ways. Even if he wasn't a card-carrying member of the Enclave, he was still a handsome, charming man who could easily make a fool of me. And I was already so heartsick and tired that I just didn't want any more problems.

He took my bags out of the trunk. "Okay, I'll make it easier for you," he said, handing me a set of keys. "These are for you. There's a deadbolt inside the door. Use it. Even I won't be able to come in then. Fair enough?"

I blinked. It seemed safe. At least for one night, or however long it would take me to find another place to live.

"Come on." Gently, he took my arm and led me into the building, where he spoke to the doorman before carrying my bags to the elevator. "I can take these up for you," he offered.

"That's okay." I picked them up myself, but as I headed into the elevator, the shopping bag that held most of my small possessions ripped open and everything spilled onto the pink marble floor. When I got on my knees and started to pick things up, I nearly collided with Belmondo, who was doing the same thing.

"Let me help you," he whispered, his face inches from mine.

I felt my heart beating inside my chest and my arms tingling with goose bumps. A part of me wanted to collapse inside his arms. I could almost feel his breath, so close were our faces. Almost involuntarily, I closed my eyes. *Yes,* I thought, *yes, yes . . .*

His hand enveloped mine. "Get up, Katy," he whispered.

I blinked. He was standing over me, trying to pull me to my feet. "Oh, sure," I said, mortified.

My ears burned during the interminably long elevator ride to Belmondo's apartment on the twelfth floor. *Had he known?* I wondered as I tried to avoid looking at him. Had he sensed what I'd been feeling about him, that mixture of desire and fear and guilt that had confused me so badly that I hadn't even known if I was sane or not?

When the elevator doors opened, I realized I'd been holding my breath for the entire ride up.

"It's right over here," Belmondo said, turning down the corridor. "Use your key."

Almost in a daze, I put the key he'd given me into the lock and turned it. The door opened onto a gorgeous room where one wall was made of glass, giving the impression of being suspended in space somewhere above the city of Paris.

"It's beautiful," I whispered as I walked over to the enormous window, but Belmondo didn't hear me. He stayed outside the front door.

"I'm not coming in," he said. When I looked over, he gave me a shy shrug. "I want you to feel safe," he added.

I walked over to him. "It's not that I don't trust you," I said.

"I know. I'm the one who doesn't trust me around you." He grinned, but his eyes were sad.

I should have thanked him then and closed the door. And that was what I was going to do, I swear. After all, I really didn't know anything about Belmondo. All I was sure of was that Gram would be so disappointed in me if I lost my head over someone just because he turned me on.

So I had no excuse for what happened next. When he turned to leave, I—*I*, with no encouragement from him—reached out for his sleeve and pulled him back toward me. Then I pressed against him so closely that I heard him utter a little strangled sound in his throat as he closed his eyes as if he were in pain. And then I kissed him full on his mouth until my blood thrummed through my body like deep music.

And all I could think of was *wrong, wrong. This is so wrong.*

He pulled away first. "Katy—" His voice was ragged.

"I'm sorry," I breathed. "I didn't mean—"

"I know," he said. "That's why I need to leave you now." He touched my cheek with his fingers. *"Au revoir, ma belle Katarine,"* he whispered. Then: "You don't know how long I have waited for you, only to let you go."

And then he walked away.

"Belmondo." Only my mouth formed the name. There was no sound.

Inside, I rested my head against the cool glass of the huge window. *What have I done?* I asked myself. I'd *kissed* him. Even if he wasn't a member of the ageless coven, he would have been too old for me. I'd known that from the beginning. Belmondo wasn't someone I could introduce to my family, or tell my secrets to. He was someone I'd always have to lie about, sneak out to be with, worry about, distrust.

When our lips touched, I'd felt a rush of heady pleasure mixed with bald fear. That wasn't what love was supposed to feel like, was it? At least I had never felt like that with Peter, as if I were doing something dirty that I was ashamed of. That I wanted to do again.

We walk toward evil willingly.

Maybe I'd done that. In Whitfield, the witches believed the Darkness was a real, tangible thing, an entity with consciousness and intelligence that made its way into people through their weakness and corruption. I'd had enough experience with the Darkness that I wouldn't have been surprised if it walked into my room and asked for a cup of coffee. In fact, I was pretty sure I'd already been singled out as the Darkness's new best girl.

Why else would I have kissed a man—a grown man—about whom I knew next to nothing?

But had that really been *evil*? It was a kiss, that was all. And his lips had been so soft . . .

I touched my mouth, remembering. Had Peter ever kissed me like that?

Did that even matter? Peter wasn't the same boy who'd kissed me in Whitfield. This Peter, the one in Paris, had left me for a coven of corrupt witches. This Peter would remain young forever while I grew old and died.

It was the young one, Marie-Therèse had said.

This Peter had killed my friend for the privilege of eternal youth.

I heard a low wail escape from me as a shudder of horror threatened to tear me apart.

How much sweeter it was to think of Belmondo. His name for me—*Katarine*—sounded in his mouth the way honey tastes.

Remember that, I told myself. Remember his lips as they spoke your name. *Katarine. Katarine.*

CHAPTER • FORTY-FIVE

The chiming clock in Belmondo's apartment had struck two some time before, but there was no way I'd be able to sleep. Not with the memory of that sweet, forbidden kiss that kept coming back to me in waves of shame and longing.

I took a shower. I walked around the apartment, admiring the artwork on Belmondo's walls. I listened to the radio. I stared out the panoramic window. I tried to watch television, but I couldn't concentrate on the stupid show that was on, and since there were four remotes, I couldn't figure out how to change the channel.

On the cut glass coffee table, beside the remotes, was a slim black leather booklet. At first I'd thought that it was a *TV Guide*—which wouldn't do me any good, since I didn't know how to do anything with the television except turn it on and off—but then it occurred to me that it might be a user's manual. I hate reading instructions, even in English, but I was beginning to obsess about watching TV. So I picked up the booklet, hoping for some nonverbal international symbols that would tell me how to use the remotes.

But it wasn't a manual. It didn't have anything to do with the television. It was exactly what it looked like, a book. Another spiky-lettered, handwritten book.

I groaned. Did everyone in Paris keep diaries? On the other hand, if it was a diary, it would be *Belmondo's* diary. And he hadn't hidden it, so he really couldn't complain if I read it, could he?

I wondered if he mentioned me in it. With my breath coming fast and my fingers twitching, I tried to make out the pages. Like the writing in Azrael's book, this script was florid and old-fashioned, obviously written with a fountain pen. As my gaze settled on the words, I thought again of our kiss, of the sweet warmth of his lips on mine.

1831

The Last Chapter

I stand naked in front of the mirror. My body is thrilling to watch: the muscular thighs, the taut belly, the strong arms. I pull on trousers made of moleskin, soft against my flesh. I pick up my shirt, white linen, and circle it like a cape around me so that its brightness catches the light from the lamp before I tame the expanse of cloth with buttons. I add a lace jabot and a black silk scarf, knotted precisely. Then a waistcoat to show my slim physique to best advantage, and a jacket of black Scottish wool with a huge collar and cutaway lapels and swallowtail—to mimic walking into the wind, I suppose, since those innovations serve no practical purpose.

Thus prepared, I don my tall hat and leave the old man's dungeon, heading for the lights of the Palais Royale. I have a party to go to.

What was he talking about? Holding my place with my finger, I turned the small leather-bound book front to back, looking for a title, a copyright, anything, but there was nothing but the handwritten text. It *was* a diary, then, but it seemed to have started in the middle of things. And it couldn't be Belmondo's, because the clothes he described were all wrong.

Unless . . . unless he lied to me.

Peter had said Belmondo was lying when he'd told me he wasn't part of the coven.

But then, Peter himself had been lying. And he'd been lying about more than just his membership with the witches at the Abbey of Lost Souls.

So was Belmondo one of the near-immortals of the ancient coven of Paris? Had Peter sold his soul to the Darkness?

Did anyone tell the truth anymore?

Feeling as if my heart had been replaced by an anvil heavy as the weight of the world, I found my place in the book and continued reading.

During the past three decades, so much has happened: For one thing, Maximilien Robespierre, the Revolution's master executioner, was himself guillotined, to loud cheers. For another, Napoleon, that self-proclaimed champion of the people, abandoned all thought of anything resembling the Republic he was supposed to have represented and instead crowned himself not just king, but Emperor of France. After he was deposed and sent into exile, the nephew of the executed King Louis the Sixteenth (this one called himself Louis the Eighteenth) took the throne for a few years, until the silk workers staged a revolt and the crown passed to his brother Charles the Tenth, who in turn was booted out of the palace and fled, like his brother, to England. At present, our monarch is named Louis-Philippe, who also considers himself a "man of the people" despite the fact that his father lost his head in the wholesale slaughter of the nobility.

You'd think at least he would have learned a lesson about the unreliability of power, non?

And so here we are in the palace, while outside the peasants are fomenting another rebellion. Eighteen years from now, this king will also be taking a midnight ride to England, leaving the throne of France to his ten-year-old grandson. "Better him than me" will be Louis-Philippe's epitaph.

Only one thing is certain: Nothing will ever change. How many lives were taken in service to an ideal of liberty, equality, and brotherhood? Thirty years after the first heads rolled off the executioner's platform, are the poor any cleaner? Are the rich any kinder? Is anyone better off?

Of course not. It was all for nothing. Pain, misery, suffering, despair, war . . . they are always for nothing.

The night is dark, and as I walk, I fill my lungs with it.

• • •

The brazen opulence of the court of King Louis-Philippe is laughable. These aristos who, thirty years ago, were hiding in public toilets while armed revolutionaries marched their families to the guillotine are now dancing again as if the horror of those times had never happened.

I am one of them now, incidentally. In the confusion following the Reign of Terror, it was easy and commonplace for nobodies with money to buy titles. I am, I will admit, truly Nobody, but I have a title now, the fifteenth Duc du Capet.

It was easy enough to come by: My ancestors shared the name. It was my father who foolishly forsook it in favor of the life of a tradesman and farmer. Jean-Loup de Villeneuve never appreciated the heady pleasure that power brings. Having possessed the greatest magic possible—the ability to create gold—he chose instead to dine on thin soup and live in a tunnel like a sewer rat.

But that has changed. I am the duke now. I have the power. In my blood stirs magic greater than poor Villeneuve could ever imagine.

The occasion I am attending is a ball, and I am looking for a woman. A particular woman, a young witch who has learned that she can remain young and beautiful forever if she will decline marriage to the fop her father has chosen for her and join the Abbey of Lost Souls.

The young woman's name, I believe, is Helène, or Helena—something falsely Grecian. She is not a very talented witch. I think I was told that she starts fires, which means she could easily be replaced by a hot coal or a piece of flint, but no matter. If her freakishness were to be discovered by the outside world, she would surely be persecuted, as her kind has always been, unless she were clever enough to hide it. But these girls are rarely clever.

I have come to rescue her. It is a humanitarian service I render, one of several. I have brought a great number of these poor girls to a place of safety, where their extrasensory abilities will be appreciated, if only by their mirrors, since the witches at the abbey use their gifts solely to maintain their beauty and youth. One might say they literally live for fashion, the dears. And despite their wasted lives, they live nearly in perpetuity. Or they think they will. I have made a point of seeing to it that they do not overstay their welcome in this overpopulated world.

Still, they love me for my help to them. To be truthful, they would love any man with a well-cut frock coat and connections to the theater.

Ah, there she is. My God, her dress is covered with pink bows! There are bows along the gigantic hooped hem of her skirt, around her hips, on her shoulders, and decorating her bodice. Bows are even in her hair, which is coiled into tubes that resemble sausages dangling from her head.

Yes, without my intervention, this one would surely go to the gallows.

She is flirting with me, too young to realize how boring she is. She'll be right at home in the abbey.

We dance. She is nimble and lithe, and smiles prettily at me behind her fan. I suppose she imagines that she has some sort of power over me. Amusing.

"We are near the door," I whisper into her ear, and she blushes so deeply that you'd think I'd just made an indecent proposal to her. Beneath her perfume, I sense a faint odor of fear. The lovely if bovine Helène probably has never defied her parents before this. No doubt she feels as if she's betraying her family.

I wonder why the gift of magic is so often given to the undeserving.

"Come with me," I say, forcing her to look into my eyes. "Now."

She swallows. She wants me. She allows me to lead her through the doorway into the corridor, past the footmen and into the night.

"My coat!" she exclaims, but I wave away her objection.

"We can't go back."

"But . . ." She looks back at the festive lights of the palace. I push her forward.

At the entrance to the abbey, I speak with the officious harridan who believes she is in charge of the place. She tries to take the girl inside, but I prevent her.

"What do you have for me?" I ask. The woman's eyes do not meet my gaze. I take her arm, roughly. "You said someone was dying."

"She . . . she recovered." The woman tries to pull away from me. "Please, Monsieur le Duc, for the sake of the girl . . ."

I shove the "abbess" away from me, and she falls to the floor. With the same motion, I clasp Helène's arm and drag her away from the abbey's door.

"Monsieur—" she begins, but I force her around the corner of the building. Before she can become frightened, I press her against the stone wall of the abbey and kiss her full on her lips.

At first her eyes are open. She is like a deer in the moonlight, trying to decide whether or not to run. But I touch the tip of her tongue with my own, and she emits a little gasp. It is only a moment, but that is all it takes to make her abandon her natural caution. She kisses me back with wanton passion, her eyes closed now, her breath coming fast. She thrusts her breasts at me; she explores my mouth with her own. She touches my face as if I were an honorable lover. Such pretense!

"My wicked darling," I murmur, and she smiles through swollen lips. Boldly she pulls my head toward hers, and that is when I do it.

I press her wrists against the wall as I begin to pull her life out of her through her willing, loving mouth.

As the breath rushes out of her, she begins to struggle. The dainty wrists push feebly against my hands. Her eyes fly open. She wants to speak, but cannot. The pink ribbons in her hair tremble and quiver like petals in the wind. Then she makes a sound like a rabbit caught in a trap, a rasping cry that wants desperately to grow into a scream but fails because with every second, the life is rushing out of her. Into me. I feel myself expanding as she falls nearer to death.

It is always delicious, even with cowen, but with witches the feeling is particularly satisfying. It makes no difference if they are young and beautiful or ancient, with hobbled feet and rotten teeth, although the more magic they possess, the better the harvest. At the last, when I take that magic, the sensation is magnificent.

Tears spring to Helène's eyes. Poor creature, I would comfort her if I could. I would tell her that the pain will soon end, that it would be better for her not to spend her final moments in a frenzy of terror, but I doubt if anything I said would make much difference at this point.

This is the moment when all the masks come off, both the disguise of the demure and obedient daughter and the silly pretense of the sensuous, worldly woman. All that's left is her naked, animal fear as she expels her last breath.

My masks are gone as well. As her soul flies into my mouth and her body crumbles to ash before me, I feel my leathern wings stir. I grow enormous, filling the sky. Passersby look up, uneasy, ignorant, their arms instinctively wrapped around themselves as if trying to hold on to their own souls, and in the lightless night they see my face and shiver, and hurry on, denying to themselves that they'd seen anything at all.

They always deny what they know to be true, because as anyone who has seen me clearly in those last few precious moments of their lives would attest, the sight is too terrible to remember.

And I . . .

I am simply here.

With you, Katy, now and always.

Forever.

CHAPTER • FORTY-SIX

With a shiver, I jumped up and threw the book on the floor as if it were on fire.

How did he—it, that is, IT—know my name?

My name!

I felt myself shaking. How? How? But a part of me already knew the answer to that question.

How could It not *know me?*

That chapter had been written by the Darkness itself, and even though I'd never met Drago, I was well acquainted with the Entity that possessed him. I had seen It in Its true form. And much as I'd tried to tell myself that it wasn't true, *that that was then, this was now*, as much as I'd wanted to believe Azrael when he'd said my soul was pure, I knew it was just a matter of time before the snake I'd fought in the Meadow would find me again.

Because the Darkness is patient. It waits. It knows. And It never forgets.

It hadn't forgotten me.

I stumbled into the kitchen, trying to think, and poured myself a glass of water. But my hands were shaking so hard that the liquid sloshed over the side of the glass. I was looking for a paper towel to clean up the mess when the phone rang, scaring me out of my wits. Forgetting that it wasn't my home, I automatically lunged to pick up the receiver, but before I could hit the "talk" button, I slipped on the spilled water on the floor.

I skidded across the kitchen on the heels of my sneakers until I ran into a tall chrome garbage can, at which point I fell over backward, letting go of the phone in my hand. Still ringing insistently, it went flying along the marble countertop, finally crashing into a glass jar filled with coffee that exploded into a thousand pieces while its contents spewed over everything like a black cloud.

The phone was still ringing. "Oh, shut up!" I shrieked. Wiping coffee grounds off my face with my sleeve, I resigned myself to a massive cleanup.

Great, I thought. Just what I wanted to do at three in the morning after having the snot scared out of me.

And the phone kept on ringing.

I must have misread the last line of the book, I reasoned while I tore off some paper towels. That was the only explanation that made sense. I mean, sure, I'd been spooked by the Darkness in the past, but that didn't mean It had decided to include me in Its memoirs. I was just punchy with fatigue and still reeling from the events of my day.

"Shut up!" I screamed at the still-ringing phone.

I swept the shards of glass into a dustpan as the phone

finally fell silent. "Thank God," I mumbled. Quiet at last.

And then I saw it, facedown in the corner under a pile of spilled coffee grounds: a green earring.

I squinted at it for a moment. What was it doing there, tossed in a corner of the kitchen like a discarded gum wrapper? I reached for it, but the moment I touched it, I nearly slammed against the wall, so powerful were its vibrations.

A woman, knowing she was going to die. In a desperate move to reveal her killer, she throws the earring into the corner as her life is leached out of her. She gasps as she slides down the wall toward the floor, where this monster will finish feeding on her. But before she closes her eyes for the last time, she catches a glimpse of herself in the shiny metal of the toaster.

So old, *she thinks.* He has taken my youth. *She marvels, horrified, at the wrinkled, aged creature she has become. One emerald earring dangles against her wizened neck. Her once-beautiful features transform into ropy strands that resemble an abandoned hornet's nest. And she thinks, at the last:* My face! What has he done to my face?

Joelle's face, I realized numbly. The murdered woman in my vision had been Joelle. I remembered the earring on the body on the Rue Déschamps. The one in my hand was its match.

The body in the alley had been hers.

While the sounds of Joelle's final agony reverberated through my mind, the phone made a clicking sound as the message light flashed and I heard Belmondo's voice being recorded.

"Katy," he said in that teasing, smiling way he had that made my insides turn to jelly. "I know you're still awake."

My breath came in a swift whoosh as I reached for the phone. Belmondo! Belmondo would know what to do. He always knew.

But something was wrong, I could feel it. My hand seemed to stop of its own volition before it reached the receiver.

Joelle's face, reflected in the toaster as she sinks to her knees. So old, so old . . .

"Katy?"

And behind her lifeless face is the reflection of the monster who killed her, his lips still tasting Joelle's last breath, curved now into a charming smile, his eyes full of seduction and promise, the author of the last chapter . . .

"*Katarine,*" he whispered.

Belmondo.

The earring dropped out of my hand.

CHAPTER • FORTY-SEVEN

"I imagine you've read my essay by now," the voice in the phone message said. "So you know who I am. Or was, rather. That was before I met you, Katy."

Drago, I thought, suddenly understanding more than I wanted to know. *Drago and Belmondo are the same person.*

"I really don't think you ought to be alone. Perhaps I should come by." My heart stopped. "To protect you."

I scrambled to my feet.

"For the record, you misunderstood my visit to Marie-Therèse," he went on in his smooth, caring voice. "She was glad to see me."

"Oh, God," I moaned. "God, no."

"I'll be there soon, my darling," he said before the phone clicked into silence again.

My legs rubbery with fear, I stumbled into the bedroom, where I'd put my things away and threw everything that fit into my suitcase, all the while chattering to myself to keep from screaming:

There's no place like home, there's no place like home, oh please let me get home, please, please . . .

I swallowed down the nausea that was rising in my throat as I closed the suitcase and swung it off the bed while slipping into my shoes.

Peter hadn't killed Marie-Therèse. The "young one" had been Belmondo. It had been Belmondo all along.

There's no place like home, there's—

Two feet before I reached the front door, the bell rang.

The song dried up and came out a pathetic whimper. Quickly, I glanced toward the window. Twelve stories to the street. Jumping was not an option.

The bell rang again. I closed my eyes and thought hard. In light of my recent reassessment of Belmondo, I doubted that he'd been telling the truth when he said I had the only key to the apartment, so ringing the doorbell was probably just a formality. Still, I could use that. I could start screaming as soon as I opened the door. At this time of night, someone would notice, and maybe call the police.

It wasn't much of a plan, but—I looked back at the window—it was all I could come up with at the moment. Taking a deep breath and hoping fervently that it wasn't my last, I opened the door and prepared for my swan song.

"Katy."

I choked on my own spittle. "Peter," I said, ridiculously relieved.

We stood facing each other for what seemed like an awfully long time. When we finally spoke, it was at the same time.

"Can I come in?" he asked.

"He killed Marie-Therèse," I said.

"Huh?"

"Never mind," I said. I threw my arms around him. The suitcase thumped on his back. I felt a flood of pain and fear flow out of him into me. But over everything was love. Peter's love for me.

"I never should have doubted you," I said.

"About what?" he asked as I rested my face against his chest. "Hey." He pulled away from me, then pointed to my suitcase. "Are you going somewhere?"

"Yes," I whispered, shoving him backward. "And you're going with me. Hurry."

We ran for the stairs—I didn't trust the elevator—and hustled down the twelve stories to the ground floor. The doorman nodded as Peter and I streaked past.

"I . . . have . . . a car," Peter panted as we hit the street.

"Where?"

"Here." He threw my suitcase into the backseat of a Peugeot.

"Hurry, Peter," I urged. "Please."

To his credit, Peter never questioned why I was so frantic to get out of there, and so bossy about it. He just got in and burned rubber.

"Where to?" he asked when we got on the highway.

"Anywhere." I looked out the back. It didn't look like anyone was following us. "The airport," I amended.

"What?" He looked over at me. "You're leaving the country? Now?"

"I have to. We both have to, Peter, believe me."

"But I can't just—"

"Look out!" He'd been so engrossed in our conversation

that he'd drifted into the next lane. The car beside us blared its horn, and Peter yanked the wheel of the Peugeot.

"Wait a second." He pulled off at a rest area and stopped by an overlook. "You need to tell me what's going on, Katy," he said.

I hung my head. "Belmondo," I said. It was hard for me even to say his name.

"What'd he do?" Two red dots appeared on Peter's cheeks. "Tell me, did he—"

"He killed Joelle," I said. "I found her earring."

"What?" I don't think he'd been thinking along those lines at all. "Then the mummy on the street . . ."

I nodded. "He killed her in his apartment. He killed Marie-Therèse, too. And I think I was going to be next." My voice cracked. "When the doorbell rang, I thought it was him. But it was you." I pressed my lips together trying not to cry with happiness.

"When I got back to the house, Sophie said you'd been there to get your things." He looked down at his hands, avoiding my eyes. "And that Bel—*he* was going to look after you." I guessed Peter didn't want to say his name either. "I figured you were done with me."

"Then why did you come?" I asked.

He looked into my eyes. "If you're breaking up with me, I want to hear it from your own mouth," he said.

I felt so ashamed. I hadn't been nearly as loyal. "I'm so sorry," I whispered, not daring to look at him. "For everything. I've been acting like a skank."

Peter swallowed. "Me too," he said. Gently he touched my hair. "I got greedy. They were offering so much . . ."

"I know."

"So maybe I deserved to lose you to a handsome creep."

"You didn't lose me," I whispered.

He took my hand. "Good," he said, "because I can't." His hands were shaking. "That's what I needed to tell you. I can live without Harvard and Shaw Enterprises and just about everything else." His voice cracked. "But I can't live without you."

"Oh, Peter." It was all I could think of to say.

"We'll make it through this." He'd said it before, but now I believed him.

"We will," I said.

As he drove, I tried to memorize Peter's profile: the sensitive nose, the soft gray eyes, the honey-colored hair that blew gently in the wind from his open window.

How did I get so lucky? I wondered. The best friend anyone could have was on my side. Always.

We passed under a sign for Orly Airport. "Do you really want to leave Paris?" Peter asked.

"Totally."

"Even cooking school?"

I rolled my eyes. "It can't hold a candle to Hattie's."

"Okay, then. I'll go with you." He veered off the nearest exit ramp and got back on the highway going the other direction.

"Hey, what are you doing? We were headed for the airport."

"I have to go back to the house first."

"You're kidding," I said incredulously. "Belmondo's *after* me, Peter."

"It'll just take a minute. Jeremiah gave me a check. It was

part of the package he was offering. I'll have to give it back to him before I go."

"Couldn't you mail it?"

"Relax, Katy. Belmondo isn't going to look for you there. He just took you away from that place."

"Well . . ." He might be right. Belmondo knew that I would never count on the witches at the abbey to protect me against him or anything else. "So he won't think I've gone back to the house because I'd be crazy to?"

"Something like that," Peter said. "Anyway, I'll need my passport."

"Okay," I said dubiously.

As we entered the city again, Peter turned down the car's air conditioning, which made things really quiet. "So how'd you find out about Belmondo?" he asked quietly. "You seemed to really be into him."

I sighed. "It's a long story," I said.

"I've got time."

He was asking me about stuff I didn't want to think about anymore, but Peter deserved an answer. "Okay," I said. "It started with a book I found. An autobiography, sort of. He was an alchemist, like you."

I told him about Jean-Loup's story and all the coincidences I'd found that linked it to the house on the Rue des Âmes Perdues. "There's even a link to Whitfield, because Henry Shaw—"

"Who?"

"Your ancestor," I said. "He was an alchemist too, but he wasn't the creep that everyone in Whitfield thinks he was. He didn't turn his wife and children over to the witch hunters.

He protected them, even though it meant never seeing his family again. You're probably one of his descendants. That's how you came by your gift."

"Oh," Peter said. "That's interesting."

"Not nearly as interesting as the fact that Henry's still around. He goes by another name these days."

Peter blinked. "Not—"

I nodded. "Jeremiah. He's been part of this coven since the fourteen hundreds. And it was founded a long time before that. In the Middle Ages they started doing the spell that keeps them young, but they didn't begin trading all their magic for long life until Sophie took over. Which is how I first got interested in what they were doing."

I was talking fast now, eager to share everything that had been on my mind. I explained Marie-Therèse's fear of her birthday and being sent away, and Fabienne's discovery of the old paintings of Sophie and Joelle. "These witches live a long time, but not forever. That was why Marie-Therèse was so scared. She thought she was going to be sent to a retirement home to live out the rest of her life, but that was only half-true. She was taken to the Poplars—against her will, probably—but she lasted only a few hours before Drago sucked the life out of her." I didn't explain that he'd left enough life in Marie-Therèse for me to feast on her last breath. That was just too revolting. "It's how he killed Joelle, too."

"Drago?" Peter asked. "I thought you said Belmondo killed Joelle."

"He did. Belmondo and Drago are the same . . . thing."

"Then he's part of the coven too?"

That was a question I really couldn't answer. "I don't know

what he is, exactly," I said, feeling a chill crawling up my spine. "And I don't want to find out."

We drove in silence for a while. Finally Peter said, "I'm sorry about your friend."

"Me too," I said.

"But I'm kind of glad that you found out about Jeremiah. He's been pretty good to me."

I looked over at him, alarmed. "You're not tempted to stay because of what I've told you, are you?"

"No. The opposite. I can't sign on for all the baggage around this place, Harvard or no."

"You don't need Shaw Enterprises to get to Harvard," I said.

"Maybe not. But I'll miss Jeremiah all the same."

"He might still let you work for the company," I suggested.

He shrugged. "I'll ask him about it when I return the check he gave me." We were approaching the house. Peter gestured toward it with his chin. "You don't have to go inside," he said.

"That's okay." Peter was probably right about my being safe here. Belmondo would be looking for me at his apartment, where he could kill me quickly and privately, not in a house filled with people. That was what my mind told me. But the cold sensation inching up the back of my neck was warning me about a different outcome.

That's just fear, I told myself. *Childish, unreasonable boogeyman fear. Nothing more.*

"I'd like to see Fabienne, anyway," I said, trying to dispel the feeling that was making the hair on the back of my arms stand on end.

In truth, I felt bad about having left without seeing Fabby.

When Azrael said it was too late for any of the witches in the Enclave, he hadn't meant her. She wasn't an initiate. And unlike the others, she had a great talent for real witchcraft. There was still a chance I might talk her into coming to Whitfield with me.

We pulled up to the back entrance of the abbey. Peter turned off the car, then squeezed my hand. "Don't worry. If anything happens, I'll take care of you."

If you can, I thought. I loved Peter, but I sensed the Darkness coalescing around me like a cloud. It knew me, where to find me, how to hurt me. And I knew what It could do. I'd watched too many people die when It came near.

"I'll be fine," I said, trying to make myself believe it.

CHAPTER • FORTY-EIGHT

All the lights were on in the Abbey of Lost Souls, even though it was well after three a.m. Loud music spilled into the street.

"Party time," Peter said as we entered the courtyard and walked up through the kitchen. "What a surprise."

It was a lot louder inside. By the time we reached the living room, the music was too loud to talk over. Peter gestured upstairs to Jeremiah's room, although I couldn't imagine how the old man would be able to sleep through the din.

I pointed toward the library. It was always the quietest room in the house. Peter nodded, meaning that he would meet me there. As I walked toward it, I passed Sophie, who was draped over some guy who looked like a male model, but she ignored me.

Good. I wasn't going to miss any of these people. Except Fabienne. She was probably asleep by now, but I couldn't just walk out on her without a word. If she wanted to leave, this might be her last chance. I turned and went back the way I'd come, through the living room and up the stairs to her room.

She didn't answer my knock, but her door wasn't locked, so I walked in. She was asleep. I knelt beside her bed. "Fabienne," I whispered, shaking her gently.

"What?" she asked groggily. "What is it, Katy?"

"I need to tell you something. About Belmondo."

"Belmondo?" She sat up, rubbing her eyes. "What about him?"

I hesitated. "He's not the good guy you think he is." I sat on the bed beside her and took both her hands in mine. "He's dangerous. He killed Marie-Therèse, Fabby. He killed Joelle."

"Oh, *Dieu*—"

"And I think he's coming after me. That's why I have to leave."

"What? You're leaving? Now?" Her thin arms were trembling. "But where . . . where are you going?"

"Back to Whitfield. With Peter. You can come with us too, if you want, but there's no time to think about it. You've got to decide now."

"Now?" She smacked her lips sleepily as she scanned the room.

"I know. I'm sorry."

"But the Initiation—"

"Yes. If you leave this place, you'll be giving up your place in the Enclave. In Whitfield, your life won't be any longer than anyone else's."

She frowned. "But my other talents?"

"Those will be developed beyond your wildest dreams, if

Aunt Agnes has anything to do with it," I said. "But you'll mostly be a normal person, with a normal life span. You have to understand that." There was a long silence. "It's a hard choice."

She took one deep breath, then threw off her covers. "Not really," she said. "I've been thinking about this for a long time." She grabbed my shoulders and hugged me. "This is going to be the greatest adventure of my life."

"There isn't time to pack much," I said. "I'm meeting Peter in the library as soon as he talks to Jeremiah."

Fabby looked around, put on a T-shirt, jeans, a hoodie, and a pair of sneakers. Then she took a small photograph out of a dresser drawer and stuck that in her pocket. "Guess that's it," she said.

She followed me downstairs to the library. Sophie never noticed either of us.

"Peter will be here in a minute," I said, lighting the oil lamps in the room. They illuminated the glass-fronted bookcases that lined three walls and shed a soft light on the well-worn furniture. In the future, I thought, when Paris and the Abbey of Lost Souls have become no more than a memory, this is the place I will remember most fondly.

Fabby looked over the books. "Some of these are so *old*," she noticed. "Some aren't even printed. This one . . ." She fell silent as she put the book back on the shelf. "Katy," she whispered, gazing toward the doorway.

Belmondo was standing there. He was looking at me.

Don't panic, I told myself. Fabienne looked uncertainly from Belmondo to me.

"You ran away from me," he said. His eyes were filled with sadness.

"I left the keys to your apartment with the doorman," I said.

"Is that all you have to say to me?" He walked over to me purposefully and put both hands on my shoulders. "After all I've done for you?"

"Get away from me." I brushed his hands away.

"I see," he said coldly. "This is apparently how Americans show gratitude."

"I found Joelle's earring." I forced myself to look into his eyes. "I know what you did to her."

He frowned, puzzled, his anger gone, replaced by a kind of hurt innocence. "But that was for you," he said. "I did it out of love for you."

I took a step backward. "What are you talking about?" I couldn't believe my ears.

"Joelle was your enemy. She led you into the sewers and left you there. Why, if it hadn't been for that old fool—"

"What have you done with him?" I demanded.

"With Azrael? What do you care?" Then he smiled, beautifully, hopefully. "But of course you care. Your heart is as strong as your magic." He wound his fingers around my arm. "How could I not love you?"

His grip was so tight that I was afraid the bones would snap. I wanted to say something to make him stop, but all my vocal cords could manage was a whimper.

"Leave her alone!" Fabienne shouted, smashing Belmondo across his back with a book. Without even glancing at her, he grabbed her with his other hand and threw her across the room. She crashed against one of the oil lamps.

Then, with a scream, she saw that her shirt was on fire.

"Fabby!" I croaked, but Belmondo wouldn't let me move. Instead, he grabbed me around my neck. "Let me taste your magic again," he whispered, bringing my face close to his. "You know you already belong to me."

He lifted me off the ground. I couldn't breathe. I could feel my heart beating in my throat as I lowered my eyes in shame. I had done this. I had given in to a madman, and now his madness was directed at me.

As I was losing consciousness, I saw something out of the corner of my eye. Someone was rushing into the room to help Fabienne. I tried to focus, but everything was going dark.

Belmondo started to inhale, his mouth moving closer to mine, his lips looking as if they were about to kiss me. I remembered my first kiss with him. It had felt as if all the magic in the world were flooding into me.

It didn't feel that way now. In fact, what he was doing seemed like the farthest thing from kissing. I could almost see the stream of air—of life—he was pulling out of me. I felt myself growing weaker as he held me even more tightly, his eyes half-closed in pleasure.

He blinked once, slowly, and his mouth curved into a slow smile. "Darling, you are *delicious*!" he whispered.

"And you're a dirtbag," Peter said, pulling off his belt and looping it around Belmondo's neck with a slap. "Get away from her!" he spat as he yanked Belmondo backward. Suddenly released, I fell to the floor as Belmondo struggled with the makeshift noose.

For a moment I couldn't move. My mind was swimming as I wavered between consciousness and oblivion, but I tried to will myself awake so I could help Peter.

He'd taken Belmondo by surprise, but it didn't take long for the man to overpower the boy. Belmondo snatched the belt out of Peter's hand and slashed it across Peter's face like a whip. A huge red welt was beginning to form on Peter's cheek, and his eye was swelling as he came after Belmondo.

"Just how stupid are you?" Belmondo taunted as he threw Peter into one of the remaining bookcases. Broken glass flew everywhere.

"Peter," I said groggily, crawling over to him.

Fabienne stopped me, pulling me upright. I saw that my hands were bleeding. Pieces of glass were sticking out of my palms. Fabby looked just as bad. She had cuts all over her hands and face, and her shirt, streaked with char marks, was half burned off her body.

"We need . . . help," I managed. I saw Fabby's eyes flicker toward the doorway, where some of the party guests had gathered. I held out my hand to them, but to my amazement, they went on drinking and laughing. Some of them were taking bets on who was going to win the fight. I lurched out of Fabienne's grip, but before I could get to Peter, Belmondo kicked him in the stomach.

Then he pointed to me. "I'll come back for you later," he said, then strode out of the room.

"Peter!" I whispered, throwing myself on him. He pushed me aside and, crunching through the broken glass, staggered out the doorway after Belmondo. "Don't go!" I tried to shout, but my throat was so raw and damaged that all that came out was a croak. "You can't beat him, don't you understand? He's the Darkness! The . . ."

“Come on,” Fabby said. She tried to put her arms around me, but I wriggled out of her grasp.

“I have to stop him,” I rasped. Then I saw that the bottoms of the heavy draperies were on fire, probably from the broken oil lamp. “Put that out,” I said, pushing Fabby toward the flames. “Hurry, before . . .”

I wasn’t thinking straight. Before what? I no longer knew. All I was aware of was that Peter had gone after someone who could—and would—kill him without a second thought.

CHAPTER • FORTY-NINE

I staggered down the hallway to the kitchen, which led to the courtyard outside. It was empty. A part of me wanted to stay there, leaning against the cool stone of the building while the river air washed over me. But then I heard Peter shouting over the tinny sounds of the music. His voice was coming from the basement.

I made my way to the door, which was ajar, and tumbled down the first few steps before pulling myself erect.

Think, I told myself. *Don't give up.* Whatever Belmondo had taken from me when he'd been stealing my breath had left me disconnected, feeling as if I'd just awakened from a deep sleep. But I couldn't afford to stumble around, not down here in the dark. More than anything, I wanted to call out to Peter to make sure he was all right, but I couldn't risk being caught by Belmondo. Not if I was going to be of any use at all.

Some distance away, I spotted a shaft of light and trotted toward it. It turned out to be the skylight at the center of the room for the full-moon ritual I'd spied on from the kitchen. I sighed with relief as I got my bearings, grateful that at least part of my brain was still operational.

In the dim illumination of the skylight, I was able to see a candle in an old-fashioned pewter holder and some matches. I lit it and moved to the far side of the shaft of light, listening.

It was nearly impossible to hear anything besides the music and laughter from the party upstairs. Still, I knew that Belmondo and Peter had to be here somewhere. The house—and therefore the basement—was big, but not so big that two six-foot-tall males could disappear in it.

I began to walk in a circle around the light from the skylight, looking for some sign. In the direction opposite the way I'd come was a set of stone steps. I recognized them as the secret passageway leading upstairs. But I didn't think Belmondo would want to be back at the party. I was sure that he was planning something else, and he was leading Peter straight to it.

Then, a short distance from the steps, I saw something: a passageway made of earth and arched stones. *Yes,* I thought. *This is the place.* I didn't know how I could be so sure, but every instinct in my body told me they'd gone in there.

I followed as fast as I could, my way lit only by the flickering light of my candle, down what seemed like an endless corridor inclining steadily down, down, until my ears popped, and down still farther, sloping steeply then, so steeply that I could scarcely stay upright. I sheltered the fragile candle flame with my hand. If I were to fall then, I knew, I would be blind as well as lost.

When the pathway became so steep that my feet were

skidding out from under me, I sat down and scooted along the slick mud veneer on my backside until I reached . . .

Bones. With a swift intake of breath, I stopped and cast the candle's light around me. Bones were everywhere, small bones and fragments at first, scattered like litter at a garbage dump. But farther ahead I could see that they were more plentiful and larger. Some even lay in the configuration of bodies. Headless ones.

I stood up slowly and walked, hearing the crunch of bones beneath my feet, until at last I saw a pile of skulls grinning up at me.

I knew where I was then. I'd fallen into this repository of ancient bones before, on the day I'd met Azrael. . . .

Azrael! He said that he'd "hobbled into" the ritual chamber, which meant there must be some kind of passageway between the Abbaye des Âmes Perdues and Azrael's cave. That had to be where Belmondo was headed, with Peter following behind him like a lamb going to slaughter. Frantically, I tried to remember which direction I'd gone that day to reach the place. I spun this way and that, trying to get a fix on where I was. Had the skulls been on my right or my left? Coming or going? I couldn't remember. Overhead, the arched ceiling branched into three directions. Three paths now, instead of one.

Swallowing hard, I tried to remember, but it was pointless. I would have to choose one passageway and hope for the best. Taking a deep breath, I took the middle path and loped along, very conscious of the fact that I'd lost time and might lose a lot more if I'd picked the wrong path.

The candle was getting low. I covered the flame with my

hand to protect it from the air, which was swirling now as the passageway widened. Was that a good sign? The ground had leveled out, but there was more debris in my path now. Still, I couldn't slow down. I knew from the final chapter of Azrael's book that Belmondo was more than human, and that Azrael and Peter together were no match for him.

I was running at a fairly steady pace now, hearing my breath and wishing I could stop but not daring to, when I tripped over a rock and fell sprawling on the ground. I saw the candle fly out of the holder, its wick glowing for an instant as it tumbled end over end through the air, and then fell into the darkness.

I could see nothing. Uselessly, I swept the ground with my hands, but the candle was nowhere within reach. *And even if I found it,* I thought, *what good would it do me without a match to light it again?*

I'd smashed my knee against something when I'd fallen, and when I touched it now, my hand came away wet with blood. My face and elbows had suffered a good scraping too, not to mention my neck, which was so bruised from Belmondo's stranglehold that I couldn't even breathe without pain.

I tossed the candleholder aside and, for a moment, lay my head on the ground in despair.

Then I saw something. It was so faint that at first I believed it was my imagination, but as I continued to stare at it, I knew what it was: a light. A glowing, flickering light from an oil lamp.

I'd found my way to Azrael's cave.

CHAPTER • FIFTY

Let me be in time. Let me not be too late.

The first thing I saw when I reached the cave was Peter's face, and I screamed when I saw it. He was ashen, and worse. His features were pinched and pulled forward as if his skin were made of rubber. His eyes bulged out. A strangled sound gurgled from his mouth. His arms dangled helplessly at his sides, his bony hands trembling.

And above him stood Belmondo, powerful and cold as a reptile, gripping Peter's throat and sucking the life out of him.

Peter's eyes flashed toward me for an instant, and I knew he was trying to tell me to leave.

Not today, I thought as I cast around the room for a weapon. There wasn't much time to be choosy, so I concentrated on the first thing I saw with any weight: Azrael's teakettle. With my mind, I lifted it off the cookstove and sent it flying into Belmondo's head with as much force as I could conjure.

It struck with a sharp thump and a splash of water as the

lid popped off. Belmondo gaped and reeled backward, still gripping Peter's neck. Even though a thought was taking shape in the corner of my mind—*Where is Azrael?*—I knew I couldn't allow myself to be distracted. Not if I was going to have a ghost of a chance against this beast.

Beast. Yes. Now I understood why I'd felt nothing when I'd tried to read Belmondo. It was because he wasn't human. And now, at last, I recognized him. Whatever he was calling himself these days, he—It—was someone I knew rather well. Well enough to be scared witless.

"Ah. Katarine, my sweet," he said, "I was hoping you'd come." He touched the blood trickling from his forehead, tasted it. "Your bodies are so fragile. I really don't know how you manage to keep them as long as you do."

I kept my eyes on him, but my mind was glued to a bin where Azrael stored his kitchen knives. They were levitating now, finding direction.

Belmondo shook Peter like a terrier would play with a rat. "As much as I love you, my beauty, I'm frankly insulted that you would consider choosing this . . . this *boy* over me," he said. Then, with an expression of utmost disdain, he spat in Peter's face.

Moving objects with my mind is something I've been able to do since I was a child, but never had I been so grateful to have that ability as at that moment when I blinked and set those knives sailing across the room.

They would all have struck Belmondo in his chest if he hadn't seen them coming. But he did. With a lazy tilt of his head, he dropped Peter and raised his hands to catch the blades, one, two, three, four. He moved out of the way of the others, even though they were traveling only a fraction of a second behind the first group.

"Very good," he said admiringly. "My, you are a talented little thing, aren't you? And you taste like . . . *candy*." He licked his lips.

"Slimeball," I muttered as I threw my energy at every item in the room with any weight. Books, furniture, dishes, artwork—everything swirled around in a low arc as if the room were caught in a tornado that was picking up speed by the second.

"Run, Peter!" I screamed, feeling my throat burn with the effort. "Get out now!"

Looking dazed, Peter picked himself up off the floor, blinking in bewilderment.

My magic was wavering. The objects I'd raised in my cone of power were beginning to fall away. "Hurry, Peter," I said. "Before it's too late."

"Yes, go."

It was Azrael, shuffling into the light. He was covered with bruises. He staggered as he walked and held one hand against a bloody spot on his forehead, as if he had only recently become conscious.

"He beat you," I said as I started to move toward him, but he waved me away with a feeble gesture.

"Please," he said, his face contorted in pain and panic as the last of my flying objects hit the floor. "Leave now, little one. Run as fast and as far as you can—"

"I told you not to show yourself!" Belmondo bellowed, pulling himself erect.

"Drago, I beg you. Let her go. She has done you no harm."

"Let her go?" Belmondo laughed. "Are you mad? How long do you think I've waited for someone with as much magic in her as she has? She is perfect, this one. Perfect." He looked at me and winked.

"Yes, and so you must not kill her, Drago." Azrael spoke quickly but calmly, as if he were talking to a child holding an assault rifle. "You must let her go, son, and her friend, too. You must—"

Belmondo swatted him away. The old man fell against the bookcase, hitting his head. A burst of red blood spread over his temple.

"Azrael," I cried, running to him. He was squinting and blinking against the blood that was pouring into his eyes. I did my best to clean it off with a tissue I had in my pocket.

"Oh, my poor dear," Azrael wheezed. "I should never have allowed you to come back."

"I thought you were afraid of robbers," I said. "But it was *him*, wasn't it? All along you knew what he wanted."

"I'm so ashamed," he said. "Forgive me for my cowardice."

"The regret of the helpless." Belmondo shook his head in disgust.

That was when I noticed Peter disappearing behind the big cherrywood bookcase that stood near Belmondo. Azrael must have spotted him too, I realized; he'd been talking to me in order to distract Belmondo.

A second later the bookcase came crashing down. Belmondo didn't even flinch. Without so much as a look behind him, he shot out one arm to block the bookcase as it fell. Then, beneath a rain of books, he threw it, as if it weighed nothing, in the other direction. Peter tried to move out of its way, but it was moving too fast. The heavy bookcase glanced off his back, knocking the breath out of him before it smashed against the far wall.

I scrambled to get up. “Leave him,” Belmondo ordered. “Unless you want me to kill him now.”

I stopped in my tracks.

He retrieved a book that had fallen on his shoulder and tossed it aside with a sigh. “You’re becoming an annoyance, Peter,” he said.

This time when Peter got up, he was limping and blood was trickling from his nose. “Don’t,” I pleaded. “For God’s sake, don’t fight him!”

The only one who stood a chance against Belmondo was me, even though my magic had been steadily waning since my frenzied entrance into the cave. Nevertheless, I managed to assemble the broken pieces of the wooden bookcase into what I hoped would become a fusillade of flying stakes.

But the magic was working slowly, and Belmondo saw what I was doing. “I wouldn’t try it, Katy,” he said, “unless you’d like to see young Peter here skewered with a few dozen of those.”

The stakes fell. But Peter kept moving toward Belmondo, this time with a kitchen knife in his hand.

“Oh, no,” I moaned. I knew Peter. He was slow to fight, but once he started, nothing would stop him.

Peter swiped at him with the knife.

“So you want to cut me?” Belmondo taunted.

“Get away from my girl,” Peter said.

Belmondo grinned. “That isn’t going to happen.” He smacked his lips. “I’ve got plans for her.”

Peter lunged at him, but with a single, effortless motion, Belmondo snatched the knife out of his hand and drew it swiftly across Peter's chest.

I screamed as a thin line of blood appeared through the slit in his shirt and cascaded down in a sheet of red. Peter stared in disbelief at the wound.

"Didn't you think I'd at least defend myself?" Belmondo asked as he sliced into Peter's arm, and then his leg. He pierced the webbing between Peter's fingers. He cut a gash in his cheek. Through it all, Peter never made a sound.

"Stop it!" I shouted at last, slamming into Belmondo with all my weight. I tried to yank the knife out of his hand, but he was too strong for me. "Just go!" I shouted, but Peter kept coming, his steps leaden and slow, his face bathed in his own blood.

"Do as she says," Belmondo said, casting aside the knife. He scooped his arm around my waist. "I'll spare your life if you leave now." He cast a glance at me. "For Katy."

Peter stumbled forward and fell to his knees.

"This is a one-time-only offer, Peter," Belmondo reminded him.

"Do it," I whimpered. "Please go."

But Peter just kept coming, crawling on all fours. I should have known that he would never leave without me, even to save his own life.

So there was only one thing I could do.

Concentrating with every molecule of magic left in my mind, I *pushed* Peter. He flew backward as if struck by an invisible beach ball going a hundred miles an hour, sending him hurtling through the cave's opening. Then I summoned all the broken pieces of wood from the wrecked bookcase to fill the opening so that Peter wouldn't be able to get back inside. They stacked themselves like a pile of kindling for a great bonfire. I tossed in two of Azrael's chairs for good measure.

When I was fairly certain Peter was out of the way, I sank back, exhausted. "Now you'll only have to fight me," I panted. That was pure bravado. My magic was nearly spent, but now that I knew Peter had a chance of staying alive, I didn't mind what was surely going to happen next.

The Darkness always won. But I wasn't going to give in easily. I would fight the way Peter did, until I couldn't take another breath.

"Don't waste your magic," Belmondo whispered, holding me even more tightly. "Save it for me."

I struggled to stay focused. *Knives*, I thought, forcing all the blades that had fallen to the floor, including the blood-spattered one that Belmondo had used on Peter, to stir. As I willed them, they levitated off the stone floor slowly, uncertainly.

"It won't work," Belmondo said, twisting my hair around his fingers. "Your magic's gone." He forced my neck back. "You should have listened to me, before you diminished yourself."

I scratched his face. He inhaled sharply as four red welts appeared beneath his eye, and I felt a shift in his attitude. When Belmondo turned to face me, the movement was like a snake's, sudden and total, as if his head could swivel completely around if he'd wished it. Then he fixed me with an ice-cold stare that had nothing to do with any human emotion.

His grip tightened around me. Talons seemed to take

the place of his fingers, enormous talons that formed a cage around me. I say that things *seemed* to change because, even as it was happening, I wasn't sure whether the transformation I was seeing was really occurring or was just something his hypnotic, inhuman eyes were causing me to imagine.

As I watched, transfixed by his glowing, slitted eyes, I felt the floor recede as he grew larger, and larger still, his clothing taking on the scaly sheen of a snake as leather wings sprang from his back and slowly opened, nearly filling Azrael's cave.

I forced myself to turn away from him, willing my arms to hit him again, but they felt as if they were submerged in molasses.

"Don't fight me," he whispered in my ear. "I want you whole."

I watched as my slow-motion hands struck his face, as my feet kicked, as a distorted scream poured out of my throat like a scarf being pulled from a magician's hat.

How foolish you are, he said. Or I thought he did. I wasn't sure if I was hearing him or my own thoughts. Because deep inside, I was afraid that the Darkness already possessed me. That fighting It was fruitless. That nothing I did could make any difference to me or anyone else.

That there was no such thing as forever.

Suddenly I heard a loud noise coming from beyond the barricade I'd erected over the cavern opening. In an instant I was back near the ground while Belmondo, once again looking like himself and not the reptilian monster I'd imagined, stared at the doorway as Peter burst through.

My heart sank. Even though blood was pouring from his mouth and hands, Peter had come back for more punishment.

Belmondo dropped me then. His eyes snapping, he strode toward my friend—*my foolish, reckless love!*—prepared to finish him. And Peter stood there, teetering on his wounded legs, his jaw set, ready to die.

I ran over to stand next to him, ready to fight alongside him to the end. But to my surprise, Azrael stepped between us and the madman who was planning to kill us both.

"My son, this must stop," the old man said quietly. The cut on his head had congealed, but he still looked battered and pitiful as he begged Belmondo to allow Peter and me to live.

"Get out of my way," Belmondo said.

Azrael reached out with his open arms. "No, you must listen. Hold my hands, Drago. Please." Belmondo made an impatient gesture, but allowed the old man to grip his hands. "Now be still, my child," Azrael said. "Be still."

For a moment the two of them stood facing each other, their hands clasped between them. "Yes," Azrael said somberly. "Yes, like this."

"Like this?" Belmondo repeated gleefully. Azrael gasped. Belmondo's hands had turned into claws—the claws I remembered from what I'd believed to be some sort of dream—and their five-inch-long talons had impaled Azrael's palms. "Is this what you meant?"

Blood was dripping from the old man's wounded hands. "Yes," he said, speaking with the same calm, clear voice despite the pain he must have been suffering. "We shall remain like this. Together."

Belmondo rolled his eyes in disdain. "Hardly," he said. "Senile fool." He tried to shake off the old man, but Azrael refused to let go.

"Get away," Belmondo spat, but his voice no longer conveyed the confidence it once had. As he tried to pull away, his shoulders twitched. His eyes opened wide. The talons retracted. "Let me go!" he demanded, sounding frightened.

But the old man only stood there, holding his son's hands with his own.

Peter glanced over at me. He hadn't noticed Belmondo's elegant white cuffs. They were taking on an unearthly golden sheen that spread upward, crackling like fire as it moved steadily up his arms.

"What . . . what are you doing?" Belmondo demanded, twisting violently, his belly heaving while his limbs, heavy as the metal they were becoming, remained rooted to the spot where he stood.

"What I must," the alchemist said. He was creating gold.

"No. No, don't do this," Belmondo urged as the sound of flesh becoming metal grew louder. "You won't be able to live with yourself."

"I don't plan to," Azrael said.

Belmondo's golden fingers were splayed, curved as if he were about to strangle someone. But they would never move again.

"Help me!" Belmondo screamed. He tried to turn toward me, but his neck was stiffening with the metal that was engorging it. "My darling, please!" His voice sounded strangled as his throat slowly turned to gold. "Please," he whimpered, all pretense of control gone. "Help me . . ."

The crackling continued as inch by inch Belmondo's living flesh was replaced by gold. His eyes darted wildly toward Azrael as he screamed at last, high and terrified: "Father!"

Tears coursed down Azrael's face as he watched his son die, but he never let go.

He had honed this magic for a thousand years. It would not be reversed.

Soon, whatever other words Belmondo might have spoken were lost, reduced to a harsh rattle before the profound silence. The expanse of gold creeping up his chest seized his heart and stopped it. His brain fell into frenzied activity which showed only in his wildly rolling eyes, the last part of his body to succumb, the eyes of a steer at the moment of slaughter.

And then nothing. The man was gone. The monster was gone. Only a golden statue remained, its expression almost innocent in its surprise, its lips still forming the last word Belmondo had spoken: *Father.*

Finally, Azrael released his son's hands.

I covered my face. During the long life of Jean-Loup de Villeneuve, the only thing he had ever needed his great gift for was to kill his own child.

In the dim light of the cave's few remaining lit candles, I saw something like a wisp of smoke leave Belmondo's golden mouth and float lazily into Azrael's.

"His last breath," I said.

"No," Peter said, grabbing my arm. "It's the Darkness, finding a new home." He shoved me toward the cave opening. "Hurry," he said.

"Yes, hurry," Azrael rasped behind us. "Soon I will not be able to stop this thing inside me."

"Azrael," I cried.

"Go!" he shouted, and his voice was like the roar of the sea.

CHAPTER • FIFTY-ONE

As soon as we reached the tunnel, we heard screams coming from far away.

"The house," Peter said.

Together we ran along the underground passageway to the basement of the Abbey of Lost Souls, where the rank odor of smoke hung like a pall.

"The place is on fire," Peter said, bolting up the stairs. I followed, remembering the smashed oil lamp in the library. At the time I'd thought it could be contained, but evidently I'd been wrong.

The house was in flames. People were running everywhere, clutching precious treasures or slapping frantically at pieces of furniture in an attempt to keep them from being destroyed. Some simply ran around in aimless panic, screaming or vomiting, despite the open front door.

"Get out!" Peter called, trying to throw the residents out bodily. But none of them seemed to want to leave. They just scurried around like squirrels, picking up picture books, china, paintings, jewelry, clothing. One of the women he tried to rescue was Annabelle, Sophie's friend. She was bending over a glass étagère, picking over a collection of Fabergé eggs.

"For God's sake," Peter shouted, forcing the woman toward the exit. "Get outside! Save yourself!"

"But my things," she wailed. "What shall we do without our beautiful things?"

He stooped to pick her up. She screamed as the priceless jeweled eggs fell from her arms.

I also tried to get the witches to evacuate the place, with equally disappointing results. Two women were trying vainly to move a harpsichord down a flight of stairs. Another was shrieking wildly, a pile of satin shoes clutched to her chest.

"I can't believe it," Peter said. "What's wrong with these—"

"Oh, God," I whispered.

The woman in Peter's arms had shriveled almost to ash. He dropped her—or rather, *it*, a desiccated, long-dead body with the texture of a wasp's nest—with a groan of revulsion.

"Are they all . . ." He didn't finish the sentence. I followed his gaze to the secret portal joining the main parlor to the ritual chamber below.

Azrael was standing there, his yellow eyes glowing, as around him flames leaped up like fiery ghosts. One by one he pointed to the witches of the Enclave, who, as if obeying his command, shriveled slowly into dust, just as if Drago had sucked the breath out of them.

"Did you believe this day would never come?" the

Darkness thundered. "You, who have done nothing to warrant your privileged, worthless lives?"

A woman screamed, then fell silent as her life streamed out of her and into Azrael's open mouth.

At that moment I spotted Fabienne tugging on her mother's arm. Sophie was standing in front of a mirror, studying her face with morbid fascination.

The Darkness had spotted her. Now Sophie's trembling hands ran along the deep creases and sunken flesh of her face as if she hoped they could stop the terrible damage to her once-perfect features. As I watched, one of her eyes drooped suddenly and then fell out of its socket. She screamed in horror.

"Hurry, please," Fabby begged, her own voice rising in panic. "The place is on *fire*, Mother. Please, I don't want to burn!"

"What do I care if you burn?" Sophie shrieked, her lips cracking as she spoke so that blood coursed down her chin. She tugged at her hair, which fell out in clumps that stuck out between her bony fingers. "Look at me!" she screamed, holding out her hair for her daughter to see. "Look what's been done to me!"

"Mother—"

"It doesn't matter to you, though, does it! You'll still be beautiful, while I—"

At that point, Peter grabbed Fabienne and threw her over his shoulder. "Talk later," he said.

Fabby stretched out her arms toward Sophie. "Mother!" Tears ran down her face.

But Sophie had already forgotten her. Instead, she fixed her mad eyes on me. "You!" she spat. Her voice was calm now, dripping with disdain. "Everything was fine until you came along."

In the back of the room, a beam fell with a deafening crash. Flames shot through the arched doorway toward us. "Come outside, Sophie," I urged, extending my hand toward her.

She lunged forward and slapped my face. Her hand felt like dry bones. Then, with another brief, bitter glance in the mirror, she backed away from me, away from the exit.

"Sophie—" Whatever I was going to say was lost as the windows all imploded. I flattened myself on the floor as a whoosh of broken glass went flying through the room at the speed of a tornado. Ahead, I watched in horror as the razor-sharp glass shards shot into Sophie with so much force that her body twitched and bucked with their impact. Still, she never turned away. Her single remaining eye, staring now from the ruined face that had once been so beautiful, held no expression whatever. It was as if she knew—or believed—that without that beauty, she no longer existed. Like a wraith, she glided to the floor. With one final spasm, she lay still, her terrible staring eye open as her flesh grayed and sank into itself.

"Oh, Azrael," I whispered. "Look what you've become."

He was near me now, standing on a low step as if he were an orchestra conductor directing the music that obeyed the unspoken commands of his hands. Behind him was a wall of flames.

I wanted to ask him to stop, to beg him to spare the lives

of these helpless women, but the kindly old man I had known was no longer inside that body. He was purely the Darkness now, his flesh merely a container for the evil within. And more than that, I'd seen him—It—too many times to hope for anything resembling compassion.

The yellow eyes glowered at me. I expected It to point at me next, to signal that my turn to die had come. But oddly, what I felt wasn't fear. I'd lived with the fear of meeting the Darkness again for so long that it was beginning to take over my life. Well, here It was. Again. It had been in Belmondo, and now It was in Azrael. And maybe this was going to be the day when my worst fear would come true and It would be in me.

But I was tired of running from It. That was what I felt. Not fear, but *impatience*. I'd had enough. If the Darkness was so determined to have my life, then okay, we'd have a showdown right here, in the flames that led to Hell.

"Am I next?" I asked. I stood up amid the rubble that had once been the palatial Abbaye des Âmes Perdues. "Because I don't care what you do to me. I'm sick of running from you. If you want me so badly, then here I am." I spread my arms. "You hear me, good buddy? Take your best shot."

The ancient face clouded. Nearby, another beam crashed to the floor, sending up a fizzing display of sparks. The heat of the fire around me was suffocating.

The creature who had been Azrael struggled to speak. His mouth opened and closed. His hands stretched open, then curled into fists. Finally It managed to utter one tortured sentence:

"Life . . . is . . . precious," he croaked, each word a monumental effort, "if you . . . make . . . it . . . so."

That was Azrael speaking. He had somehow managed to fight his way through the Darkness that had taken over his body to give me his message.

I sank to my knees. "I see you," I whispered.

His eyes met mine. They were not yellow. They were not glowing. They were my friend Azrael's eyes, and they were filled with the heartache of a hundred lifetimes. Then he nodded once, in benediction, and walked backward into the flames.

The old man's hair caught fire. He was destroying his body because he would rather be dead than a carrier of the Darkness. I understood. Some things are worth dying for.

He never spoke another word until his skin blistered and charred, and he staggered to stand upright.

"Oh, Azrael," I said with a sigh, but he didn't hear me. He was listening to some other music, beholding some other face beyond mine. His eyes lit up at the sight. I twisted around to see who it was, but there was no one.

"Veronique," he whispered, and I knew.

Some things were forever.

Then he moved farther back into the flames.

I fell down and crawled like a crab over a lot of bodies and broken objects. I cut my hand on something, but I was aware of that only because I saw the blood; I didn't feel anything. A blanket of smoke was descending over me, covering me with numbness and forgetting.

It doesn't hurt, I thought, remembering Azrael. Maybe he hadn't hurt either. Had he sent the Darkness into me? I'd been the closest person to him. I should have been the chosen one. But I didn't feel it. I didn't feel anything.

Well, there was at least that. Feelings were a crapshoot. Too many bad ones. But Peter . . . I didn't want to die without seeing him, without telling him how much I loved him.

Peter . . .

It was the last thing I remember thinking before giving in to the nothingness.

I felt something pulling at me.

"What," I said stupidly, not knowing what it was I was asking. The word came out in a sandpapery rasp. My tongue felt like some gigantic thing that was too big to fit in my mouth. I opened my eyes with an effort. They were crusted closed, and I realized I must have been unconscious. The room seemed to be moving now, what I could see of it through the thick smoke that swirled around like a whirlpool.

I tried to lift my head. All I could see were flames and fallen timber. All I could smell was the acrid stench of burning bones.

Oh, my God, I thought, *am I in Hell?* Had I become the Darkness at last?

Then I saw a face come into focus above me. Peter's face. Or at least his jaw and above it, his nose, crusted with blood. That was all I could see of him. He was sweating. There were black streaks on his skin. He was carrying something disgusting-looking. A body covered with blood and soot.

Oh, yeah. It's me, I realized. Peter was carrying me out of Hell. "Hey, thanks," I said. Or thought I did. I wasn't sure I could speak anymore.

I began to cough, so deeply that it sounded like a bullhorn, so long that I started to choke.

"Just hold on," Peter said. He was coughing himself, but he pressed me tighter against him. I nestled my head against his chest, where I heard his heart beating. And with each beat, I could hear what he was thinking.

I will never . . . let you go . . . I will never . . . let you go . . .

"I know," I said, just as we burst out the door into the clean outdoor air. Peter placed me gently on the grass, out of harm's way.

A fire truck pulled up nearby, its blaring siren winding down in a low wail as the firefighters unwound the big hose.

I sat up, and Peter threw his arms around me. I coughed some more. I wanted to tell him how much I loved him, but I couldn't talk very well. So I touched him instead. It was just a brush across the top of his mangled hand, but I knew he understood everything because of the way he looked at me. At that moment I knew absolutely that even though I was bloody and dirty and my hair was probably burned off, he still thought I was the most beautiful thing in the world. In that instant I understood what Azrael had meant with his dying words:

Life is precious, if you make it so.

It really wasn't about how long you lived. It was about how much love you could squeeze into the time you had. That was the real meaning of forever.

Azrael had been with Veronique for only a fraction of his

unnaturally long life, yet his love for her was strong enough to defeat even the Darkness. In the end he had called her name, and though I hadn't been able to see her, I believe her spirit came to take him to the Summer Country, where they would always be together.

I kissed Peter. "Forever," I said.

He understood. "Forever."

EPILOGUE

When I was finally able to stand up after picking out the glass shards that had shot into my skin when the windows burst, I saw Fabienne. She was kneeling on the ground with her face buried in her hands. There wasn't much I could say, I knew, to make her feel better, so I just sat down beside her.

She raised her tear-stained face. "They're all gone," she said. "All of them."

Fabienne, Peter, and I were the only ones who'd made it out of the house. Her mother was gone. The man she'd thought of as her uncle was dead. The place that was the only home she'd known was a smoldering ruin.

Peter came over and hunkered down beside us.

"Did you find Jeremiah?" I asked.

"He wasn't in."

I sat up. "So what happened to him?"

Peter shook his head and blew air out of his nose. "I don't know."

"Is he still alive?"

Peter shrugged.

"Well, did he just disappear, or—"

"For goodness' sake, I told you, I don't know!"

"All right," I said with a sniff. "I was just asking."

He sighed. "Are we fighting again?"

"Is that bad?"

He smiled. "No." He rubbed a handkerchief across my face. "It's normal." Gently, he put his arm on Fabienne's shoulder. "The main thing we have to do right now is find our way home," he said softly. "Are you up for that, Fabby?"

"It would probably be best if we didn't stick around to talk to the police," I added.

Peter shushed me, gesturing with his eyes toward Fabienne, who was facing a lot of loss at the moment.

But she was stronger than she looked. "Katy's right," she said. "We should leave now, before anyone questions us."

That was for sure. Once we started to explain anything about the Abbey of Lost Souls, we'd be opening a can of worms that might never get closed again.

"Okay." Peter stood up. "I've got a car waiting—"

"No car," Fabienne said. "Come with me."

Peter and I exchanged worried glances, but we followed as Fabby walked toward the river, where it was a lot quieter.

She wiped her eyes as she turned back to look at the charred ruins of the abbey, shimmering in waves of heat and spray from the fire hoses. From the pocket of her hoodie she took out the photograph she'd taken from her room. It was an old sepia-tinted picture of Jeremiah Shaw, wearing a tuxedo.

There was a woman on his arm, a flapper from the Twenties, judging from her spangled dress. Sophie.

"I didn't even get to say good-bye," she said.

We rarely do, I thought. We'd all had to leave so many people, or had been left by them. But the greatest losses were the ones who might have loved us but couldn't. I would never know my mother, who'd died before I could imprint her face on my memory. Peter, too, had missed out by being orphaned at six. His great-uncle Jeremiah had come into his life too late to have given him a real sense of family.

And Fabby . . . well, her mom hadn't been very good to her, but maybe that's what made her death so painful for Fabienne. There was nothing left for her but a lot of "might have beens."

Maybe, in time, Sophie might have come around to realizing that her daughter was a greater gift to her than being a siren, and that the bond between them had been more powerful than a spell to keep them beautiful. But there hadn't been enough time for that.

Funny thing: No matter how much time we have, it never seems to be enough. I guess we are all lost souls, in a way, with only this moment to live.

"There's just one thing," I confessed reluctantly.

Peter looked annoyed. "We've got to get out of here, Katy."

"Yeah, well, you might not want to take me along after I tell you."

He blew hair out of his eyes. "Go ahead," he said. "What'd you do now?"

"Well, I—er . . ."

"Yes?" His hands were on his hips.

"I might be infected with the Darkness," I said.

Peter threw up his hands and turned his back to me. "Great," he muttered.

"But this doesn't seem possible," Fabienne said, frowning. "You do not seem to be evil."

"I don't feel evil either. But I was the closest person to Azrael when he . . ." Thinking of him made me choke up. "When he died. That's how it spreads, through death."

"Are you sure he died?" Fabby asked. "At that moment when you were close to him? Did you see him—"

I held up my hand to stop her. The memory of my friend walking willingly into the fire was more than I could bear.

"I'm sorry," she said. "I only thought . . . that maybe . . . he waited . . ." Her voice faded away. She was squinting at something in the sky. "Katy . . ."

"He did wait," Peter said, pointing toward the house.

Above the smoldering wreckage of the ancient abbey, in the rolling clouds of soot and black smoke, an image was appearing. As I peered more closely, I could begin to make it out: a face, ferocious and depraved, covered in scales, with yellow slitted eyes that glowed through the black clouds like jewels.

"The Darkness." There It was again. *It.* Feeling nauseous, I staggered backward, but Peter caught me.

"It went up in smoke because there was no one close enough to infect when the old man died," he said. "He must have stayed alive until he knew you were safe from him."

My eyes welled with tears. Azrael had done that for me, stayed alive for me, even though his burned body had been in agony. How hard that must have been for him, I thought. How badly he must have suffered during those last minutes of life.

Thank you, I said silently. *Thank you for giving those minutes to me.*

Fabby squeezed my hand. Then she placed my other hand in Peter's. "Hang on tight," she said. "We're leaving now."

"Where are we going?" Peter asked, puzzled.

"Whitfield." She looked at me and smiled. "You're—*we're*—going home."

Then, with a sensation that was sort of like how it feels when a flashbulb goes off in your face, the whole world instantly whited out while Peter, Fabienne, and I hung suspended in space with nothing to hang on to except one another. It felt like going down a roller coaster at top speed, with no gravity and no time.

For a moment I almost panicked, but then I told myself that Peter was holding my hand. I knew he would never let me go even if his arm were cut off, so I could stop worrying. Besides, Fabby was smiling like she'd done this a hundred times before. Her hair was blowing all around her. She looked like a mermaid or something, swirling in magic. *Her* magic.

Gosh, she's pretty, I thought. But Peter was looking only at me.

The nut.